Ed Savage And The Decimated Savage Demise

ED SAVAGE AND THE DECIMATED SAVAGE DEMISE

THE SAVAGE SAGA:

A HOLLYWOOD HORROR SOAP OPERA

VOLUME II

Bryan Roberts

Ed Savage And The Decimated Savage Demise

THE SAVAGE SAGA:

A HOLLYWOOD HORROR SOAP OPERA

VOLUME II

Bryan Roberts

AUTHOR'S NOTE

Ed Savage and the Decimated Savage Demise: The Savage Saga; A Hollywood Horror Soap Opera, Volume 2 is a work of fiction. All names, characters, businesses, plot, events, incidents, and places—Port Roberts, Black Ridge Falls, Vreeland Hills Sanatorium and the *Manchester* submarine—are either the products of the author's imagination or used in a fictitious manner. The southern arm of the Greenland Trench nearing the United States is also complete fiction. Any resemblance to actual persons, living or dead, or actual events is purely coincidental.

Some events happen in real places or are about real things—New York; West Point Military Academy; Catskill Mountains, New York; Rye Lake, New York; Staten Island, New York; Concepción, Chile, South America; Greenland, NASA's Operation IceBridge; Naval Station Norfolk; the *Andrea Doria;* and the story of the Dutchman, Dutch Shultz—and in writing my fiction, I used these places and events and changed them to best tell my story. And if you're a graduate of West Point, please forgive me for spinning my tale.

Contact: Savage Roberts Publishing at www.SavageRobertsPublishing.com.

A special thanks to my brilliant developmental editor Amy Lignor, who took the time to explain the areas I need constant brushing up in—a heartfelt thank-you for teaching me and allowing this writer to thrive. And to Matthew and Stephanie for my second and third rounds of proofreading edits—I can't thank you enough.

And a giant shout-out to my illustrator, Dave Seeley—an amazing illustrator who pulled the images from my mind to my book cover—I am truly grateful, and I would highly recommend him to anyone needing his services. The level of skill he possesses blew me away when I saw my book cover come to life. I can't stress how pleased I am with the final result. He took my thoughts and came up with something I didn't see coming, and that is talent in a nutshell. As a writer I tend to overthink every sentence and action my characters say and do—now imagine trying to create an image with all that in your head, and you can really drive an illustrator straight up a wall. So a big thank-you to Dave Seeley for making Ed Savage everything I'd wanted.

I created this story by starting with the horrific fun from my first novel and dialed it up tossing it all into a blender to splatter on a clean white wall.

Thank you to all.

—Bryan Roberts

ED SAVAGE AND THE
DECIMATED SAVAGE DEMISE

THE SAVAGE SAGA:
A HOLLYWOOD HORROR SOAP OPERA
VOLUME II

Bryan Roberts

PS: Dear Reader, enjoy the many storylines I've laid out for you in this book. A special thank-you to my test reader, Jane Foshay, and here's what she thought while reading my book: "How the hell is he going to tie all this together?" Then she held up her hands to a point and said, "The story keeps getting wider and wider," and then she brought them down in a wide triangle and laughed as she bought her hands back together to a point, making a diamond shape. "I didn't see how you could do it—but you did!"

Thank you, Jane.

While I'll admit she had me scared until she brought her hands back together, the storylines are with purpose, and I can't wait to get into volume 3.

—Bryan Roberts

I can still remember my dad telling me stories of how I was when I was a kid. "You tell him no, and that's the first thing he's going to do," he'd say.

So this book is for anyone who's been told no.

I can look back at the times I was told no as I wrote my first book: that I wasn't ready to release it and that I needed to buy other books from people to make my writing better, that I couldn't tell my story this way, that I had too many components or moving parts combined within my storytelling, that it just wasn't done.

Judging by the awesome book review earning four out of five skulls in *Scream Magazine* that my first novel, *Ed Savage and the Savage Murders Trilogy*, received and the wonderful comment from *Scream Magazine*'s Kieran Fisher—"The Savage Trilogy is a genre mashing treat that provides plenty of excitement throughout. The story is fast-paced and constantly unpredictable, made all the better with its satirical elements pertaining to scandalous celebrities"—I was right to forge ahead and believe in myself.

Take pride in your strong will and survive, and before you know it, you'll be looking back at your accomplishments and adding more to them.

Cheers!

Bryan Roberts

For the full book review, see my website: www.SavageRoberts Publishing.com.

————

As promised, *Ed Savage and the Decimated Savage Demise* picks right up right where my first novel, *Ed Savage and the Savage Murders Trilogy*, ended. Enjoy!

—Bryan Roberts

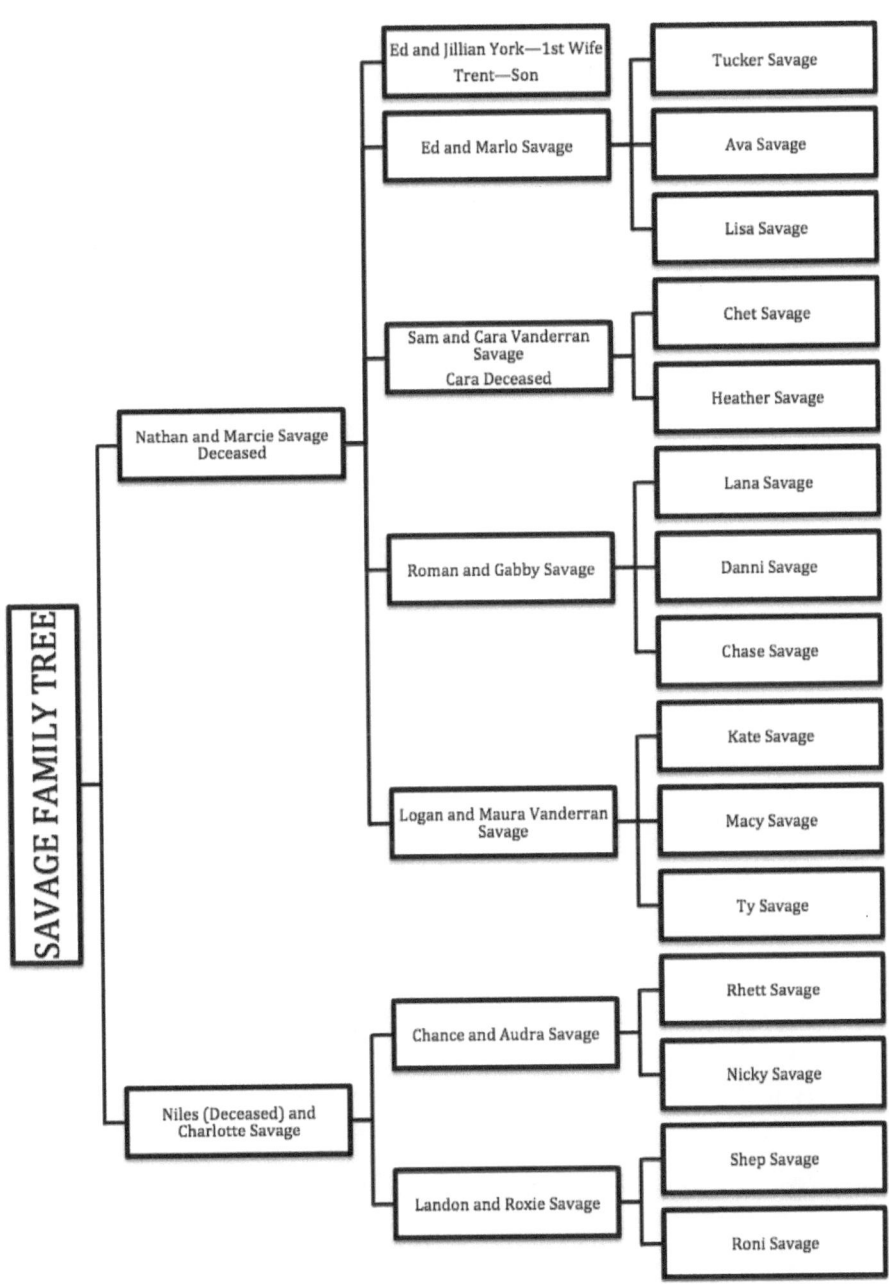

SAVAGE FAMILY TREE

Nathan and Marcie Savage (Deceased)
- **Ed and Jillian York—1st Wife** Trent—Son
- **Ed and Marlo Savage**
  - Tucker Savage
  - Ava Savage
  - Lisa Savage
- **Sam and Cara Vanderran Savage** Cara Deceased
  - Chet Savage
  - Heather Savage
- **Roman and Gabby Savage**
  - Lana Savage
  - Danni Savage
  - Chase Savage
- **Logan and Maura Vanderran Savage**
  - Kate Savage
  - Macy Savage
  - Ty Savage

Niles (Deceased) and Charlotte Savage
- **Chance and Audra Savage**
  - Rhett Savage
  - Nicky Savage
- **Landon and Roxie Savage**
  - Shep Savage
  - Roni Savage

The Savage Family Tree

CHAPTER 1

E d Savage finally had piece of mind after investigating the sanatorium Patty Galloway would be spending the rest of her life in. Locked away from society, he felt that now he and his family could all move on with their lives. But what he didn't realize was how short lived those thoughts would be.

Before the first brick of Vreeland Hills Sanatorium was laid, trouble had already started on the land chosen for the monstrous site. The land originally owned by the Von Staller family was swindled away by the Vreelands after a marriage between the families—or so the Von Stallers claimed. When Greta Von Staller married Dr. Cornelius Vreeland in the nineteenth century, the Von Stallers happily gave a large land endowment, and a huge home was built—and after Greta gave birth to her first son, she became reclusive in the grand manor. When her death came mysteriously after the birth of their second child, another boy the following year, the Von Staller family wanted answers. Cornelius, however, wanted nothing to do with them and kept them away from his home—and his children. And when the news came that Cornelius remarried a woman named Cassandra Le Fey within weeks of Greta's death, the Von Stallers wanted their many acres of land surrounding the home back, and the fighting began.

When it was discovered Cassandra had been pregnant when she married Cornelius, whispered conversations of debauchery were spoken by the local townsfolk, *including* the Von Stallers, and that was also when the hauntings started in the grand, illustrious home, according to the house staff. Sightings of the late Greta Von Staller were reported, and many of the staff quit. Cassandra, however, seemed to like the rumors and had a fascination with the occult, experimenting with séances and turning to black magic to compel the spirits to manifest before her presence.

Wanting a vacation before the baby was born, Cornelius took his family to Salem, Massachusetts, to visit Cassandra's family, and while gone a fire had been mysteriously set, destroying the opulent home. The town gossip continued with speculation that it was the ghost of Greta Von Staller herself that started the blaze as revenge to her cheating husband.

Bitter words between the families escalated over the land, and now with their daughter Greta in the Von Staller family crypt and the home burned to the ground, they wanted *all* the land back, including the lot the huge home had been built on. The Von Stallers tried suing the Vreelands to no avail. Since the home was destroyed, and the Vreeland boys were *never* allowed to see that side of the family, a feud broke out between the families, and that was just the beginning.

But with the century winding down and Cornelius building a newer and much larger mansion on the edge of their expansive property lines, tuberculosis was starting to appear in the United States, and Dr. Cornelius Vreeland wanted to build a grand hospital on the grounds of *his* estate. During construction, several attempts to vandalize the building by the Von Stallers seeking revenge plagued the hospital, and once it was completed and celebrated in the news, the Von Staller family couldn't dare cause trouble for the Vreelands, since *they* were doing so much *good* for the community, and when it was announced in the paper a second tower would be built, *anyone* causing the Vreelands headaches was shunned.

At the grand opening in the early 1900s, Vreeland Hills Sanatorium celebrated with the richest families in the area; bankers and politicians backed Dr. Cornelius Vreeland, along with several insurance executives, and not long after that first tower was built did the hauntings start up again. Strange accidents would occur during construction of the second tower, and when a pair of skyways was added to make it easier to transfer patients instead of going to the basements, where the two buildings were originally connected, the scaffolding collapsed from the weight, causing a cave-in on the workers in the basement, who were buried alive, dying when a retaining wall had come down, covering them with over forty feet of earth. To say the hospital had a taste for blood was an understatement, considering what was planned for the damned who no one cared about and who would be trapped inside its walls.

On top of the massive twin building's sixth floors were a pair of matching smaller floors centered over the entrances, where it was originally thought to have an outdoor rooftop area for patients that were too infectious to be allowed on the ground-floor recreation areas. An elevator was the main way to access the smaller seventh-floor room's; however, a private stairway for employees from the sixth floor led up to the roof near the emergency fire stairs at the back of building to access the seventh-floor. When the East Tower was first completed, preparations began to make it as safe as possible, and tall fences were added around the outdoor rooftop. With it working out so well after they opened the East Tower, they planned on doing the same with the West Tower—that was until Cassandra had taken over the West Tower's seventh floor room as her own. She loved the glass skylights in the roof, allowing her to spend countless evenings there under the many small square windowpanes to see the moonlight, where she'd try to contact the dead. And after she hired an artist to paint the raven gargoyles around the ceiling's skylight, she began conducting middle-of-the-night séances, and it wasn't long before human sacrifices were performed up on that floor.

One night while Cornelius was working late, he looked up from his East Tower office window and saw the lights on in the seventh floor's West Tower. Thinking Cassandra had gone to their home on the far end of their property, he made his way to the top of the West Tower to see what was going on, and when he opened the door, he was shocked.

A large carpet had been rolled out across the floor, and centered under the skylights was a beautiful chaise longue made of silk. There he saw his beautiful wife, Cassandra, in a heated moment of naked passion under a man and moaning in delight. Rage ignited within him, and he rushed to the man and grabbed him, pulling her secret lover from on top of her and pushing him into the table she'd have her séances at. Shocked by his wife's betrayal; his anger nearly blinded him as his blood filled his face red hot. Watching the old table shatter to pieces as the naked man hit the floor, Cornelius realized her lover was a Von Staller and grabbed a chair and smashed it over the man as he tried to stand, breaking off one of the heavy wooden legs. Picking up the club-like leg of the chair, he beat the man, hearing his cheating wife scream behind him as he continued bashing the man's skull until the blood and the brains were being splattered from the man who had been intimate with his wife.

Finally seeing what he'd done, he turned to Cassandra and advanced. He grabbed her and choked her until she couldn't breathe; he then let her go and slapped her across the face so hard she fell against the windows, cracking the glass behind her and falling to the floor. During this heightened state of furious anger, he saw her: the manifestation of his first wife, Greta Von Staller, appeared within the cracked glass above the woman he'd murdered her for. Her smug contempt blazed from the cold look on her face, and then she smiled.

Madness met his mind over Cassandra's screaming and begging for forgiveness, covering her naked body with the sheer curtains in shame. That was when Dr. Cornelius Vreeland grabbed her, pulling her to him as he lifted her up and threw her through the cracked glass, shattering it amid the smirking face of his first wife, hearing the sheer curtains rip from the rod, and sending her to her death on the stone entryway below in a death scream.

CHAPTER 2

E d Savage heard the footsteps behind them in the darkened building and turned as the sound of gunfire filled the air. He felt the blast of the gun hit him squarely in the chest, knocking him backward against the medical supplies, and he pushed Zolie Vanderran down and away from himself for cover. He heard Zolie's scream, and the sound of smashing medical equipment pierced his ears as they both hit the floor. Zolie's cries for help faded in his mind as he slipped into his own darkness.

Zolie hit the side of her head on the edge of a counter and could feel more blood coming down from her temple. She could hear the killer at the entrance to the medical facility's laboratory and crawled into the darkness to get as far away as she could. The lab was big for the old, crumbling hospital, but from the moonlight, she could just make out an exit door in the far back wall.

When the man found Ed Savage lying on the ground, he laughed. Ed was motionless on the floor, and the man raised his gun just as Zolie stumbled against a cart, pushing it and breaking the glass vials on its top as she ran for the door. The man looked to her at once and aimed his gun, firing, missing her by a fraction of an inch.

Zolie screamed as she slammed her body into the door; when it opened, she took off down a back hallway. The storm outside was not letting up. The rain had stopped, but the wind was fierce, and she could hear the wind and the branches of the unkempt landscape scratch against the small square windowpanes, like claws of a monster digging at them…trying to get her.

"Damn it!" the man with the gun yelled. He followed in pursuit, stumbling over the fallen debris and slamming into a counter and pausing for a moment as he swooned. Blood dripped from his wound onto the countertop. He looked down at it and wiped it away, knocking over more lab equipment as he continued the chase.

Zolie heard him; she got to the stairs and ran down the three flights as fast as she could. Getting to the main level, she pushed open the emergency doors and ran out into the wind, staying close to the building for cover. She could see her car parked near the garden, and in the distance was Ed's Range Rover. Seeing and feeling that freedom was finally within reach, she used all her remaining strength to run as fast as she could to hide.

As she got to her car, the sound of several rounds of gunfire filled the night, and she screamed when the glass shattered from her Rolls-Royce. She tripped on the curb to the garden and fell to the ground, rolling down the small embankment to join Ed in the strange darkness, fleeing the terror and death, her memory flashing to the beautiful evening of that first dinner at her home after the madness at Black Ridge had finally ended.

Or so it had seemed.

CHAPTER 3

Days earlier

Ed Savage had put off the damn interview for as long as possible; worse, now it was several interviews piled up in front of him. The days with his family at Zolie's compound had been incredible. The family had pulled together, and the support for everyone was united, with the exception of Sam, Zolie, and Maura. The loss of Cara Vanderran Savage was huge, and it hit them the hardest, especially Sam. Sam's loss was affecting him deeply, and even though his daughter, Heather, and son, Chet, were mourning their mother too, they themselves were more worried about their father, Sam.

When Ed Savage's son Tuc and Tuc's cousin Chet got to the house, it was Chet's sister, Heather, who broke down and moved carefully into her older brother's arms. Chet was just as hurt and could feel his childish ways flooding back and wanted to cry along with his sister over the loss of their mother; however, when he looked to his father, he could see the emptiness in him and decided to stay strong. Sam smiled at seeing his son safe and finally at home, but the distance emerging from their widowed father was evident, like a flooding swamp filled with unseen things that could grab you and pull you down into its murky depths, keeping you there forever.

Sam had been asked to interview with Ed, and at first he had accepted. But as the days passed, when the madness had finally ended, a new insanity surrounded him. His wife, partner, and lover was gone, and he slipped further away, passing on the day's soirée in hell with cameras.

The interview had originally been scheduled for an evening-edition entertainment gossip show, but as the press mounted and the salacious headlines filled the tabloids across America, Ed's agent, Rachel Shepherd, booked earlier programs, all clamoring to get Ed Savage's side of the story. Ed was to go to a local TV station in Port Roberts at noon, but Rachel texted him an earlier newspaper interview. Then, after dinner, he was flying to New York for the night to be ready for the next day's lineup of interviews.

The nude shaving cream commercial he'd done all those years ago got resurrected and the company wanted him for an updated advertisement. This time, however, they wanted a more provocative shoot for their skin care advertisement and he was paired with a beautiful fashion model—and between his great shave—and the waxing of her legs—he had signed on the line to have her wax his hairy chest. The shot was fun—and painful, and he swore he'd never do it again afterward, much to Marlo's agreement.

To say Ed had a busy schedule was an understatement, considering what was about to transpire throughout the coming days. Everything was about to change yet again, and he had no clue what was coming.

With the day finally present, Ed Savage left Zolie's estate and drove to work on a beautiful, sunny day. The time with all his family was exactly what every Savage needed after the hell they'd experienced since that damned trip to the mountains. Having his brothers, Sam, Roman, and Logan, at his side had been helpful in dealing with the madness that he couldn't share with the children, let alone Marlo. She seemed to be coming back to him, and he knew he had to tell her about sleeping with Aisha Thomas, a conversation he most certainly did not want to have.

Driving on this clear, cool day, Ed smiled and was happy his son Tucker was home from the navy. Tuc and Chet were like two peas in a pod. It reminded him of when he and Sam were younger, back in the days when everything seemed simpler. Ed was glad Tuc and Chet were close, and the conversations he and Tuc had earlier about his firstborn son with Jillian had been hard.

Everyone was aware of the ugly headlines splashed across the papers and the nasty grocery-store rags at checkout counters everywhere. And Ed remembered his son telling him he had been absolutely blindsided when he read about it online coming home, but he was fine with it once it sank in and even looked forward to meeting his half brother. Ed loved his son more than anything and also knew the man his son Tucker Savage was growing up to be. He also knew he wasn't fine with getting blindsided about a personal family matter online and playing it cool like it didn't bother him. Maybe it was all those damn rules inbred in all the Savage men since birth, all the internally hidden emotions passed down from tyrant to bastard grandfather to dad and now to son. Ed was now seeing the pent-up frustration coming from his own child.

No—*this* was going to be different. He would make sure of it. He thought about all of this as he drove into town, to Savage Tower, where he had a meeting with his first wife, Jillian York Savage Bigelow. Just invoking that woman's name caused the sun to hide behind a cloud, and Ed was laughing to himself when he saw two young women coming toward him on motorcycles and waving their arms. Slowing and waving his arm out the window in return, he brought the Range Rover to a stop after recognizing his nieces Lana and Kate.

Roman's daughter Lana Savage was first to arrive, on her brand-new red Indian Springfield motorcycle.

"Hey there, Uncle Ed, what do you think of our new toys?" Lana said, wearing her mile-wide smile just as Kate pulled up beside her on her matching black one.

"So this is what your dads were scheming about. God, I wish I was still at the house so I could see the looks on Gabby's and Maura's faces when you two pull up on those," Ed said, admiring the bikes.

Kate pulled off her helmet, letting her long hair free to fall over her shoulder, and placed her helmet on her thigh. "Ah, come on back to the house, Uncle Ed. We can get the other bikes, and all of us can go for a ride."

"Yeah, Uncle Logan said they were stopping at the office and then coming home after we left them at the dealership," Lana said.

"Roman and Logan are going in? I missed them this morning, and now I know why." Ed offered a warm smile. "I'm headed in myself, and I need to talk with them. I'll call them now, and if we can get away early, a bike ride sounds great."

"Perfect—see you later then," Lana said as Kate was putting her helmet back on.

"Bye, girls." Ed waved, and the two of them watched him pull away.

"Come on. I'll race you," Kate said, revving her engine.

Lana laughed. "You're on."

As the two drove away from Ed, they could see him in their mirrors; they raced back to the house, and the noise from their engines caused Ed to look back in his own rearview mirror and smile. As hard as everything had been, the healing process was beginning. Maybe meeting with Jillian wouldn't be as bad as he thought, and the sun appeared from behind the cloud as if answering his question. Looking forward to coming home early, he felt the breeze from the open window as he drove onto the main road to the freeway. He took one last look at the girls in the mirror as they faded in the distance when he reached for his car phone on the touchscreen, and it started to ring.

Lana arrived at the gate to Zolie's mere seconds before Kate when she realized she had to manually enter the code because they didn't have a gate-opener remote with them. "Ha-ha, loser," Lana teased her cousin as she entered the code.

"Loser? I *let* you win," Kate teased back as the gates began to open.

Together they rode side by side up the long driveway to the garage, where Chet and Tuc were working on their Harley-Davidson bikes, polishing them to a high shine near the yard. The guys looked up at the same time as the girls pulled up next to them.

"Indian motorcycles?" Chet asked with a smirk. "What's the matter—Harleys too much of a man's machine for you to handle?"

Lana got off her bike and fumbled in her high-heeled boots to get the kickstand down. Her anguish was audible as she finally got the heavy bike situated and took off her helmet, freeing her own long hair. She set her helmet on the seat and ran her fingers through her hair while holding her other hand up at the big bike. "Don't fall again," she said in the girliest voice she could muster. Turning to her cousin Chet, she moved in for the kill.

"A *man's* machine? What's that part called?" she said, pointing to the engine of his bike. As her cousin turned his head, she quickly grabbed Chet's hand that was holding the polishing cloth, elbowed him in the gut, and threw him over her shoulder into the yard in a basic maneuver every West Point cadet knew well.

Tuc and Kate burst out laughing; they watched Lana move on top of him and push his chest into the ground to try to pin his arm behind him as they wrestled on the grass. At first Chet thought she was kidding, but he turned his head to see what she'd been pointing at as she grabbed him and caught him off guard. He could easily have pinned her to the ground, a fact they both knew, but he played along, letting her get the upper hand and the upper position too.

"Say it!" Lana demanded as she rolled him over.

"Oh boy, here we go," Kate said with a light laugh.

"Come on, Chet. She's gotcha." Tuc laughed along.

Lana grabbed Chet's chin and squeezed his face, turning his cheeks red.

"Mercy," Chet said, almost laughing. "Mercy."

Lana let up on him, and Chet went for the tickle zone on her sides. Laughing and rolling over, the two cousins enjoyed the fun until Tuc pulled him off her.

Catching her breath, Lana sat up. "Come on—let's go for a ride."

"Where to?" Chet asked as he brushed the grass from his pants.

"The Cliff House?" Lana suggested.

"Yes," Kate said as Lana got up, and the four moved to their bikes.

The Cliff House was an old restaurant that had closed down after a car had lost control on the road and driven right into it. The accident had happened last year, and the owners of the building had let the insurance lapse. It was a sad day all around when the car was also found to be uninsured. With the building boarded up, and the lawsuits filed, the restaurant had served its last meal. On the upside, the location was beautiful, situated up high on a bluff near the ocean. It wasn't as far as the Vander Place Hotel, and they used to go there with their families when it was open. After it closed its doors, it became known as a haven for teenagers to enjoy some alone time.

The four older cousins were close, just like their younger siblings, who always hung out together. They didn't have much time left together before the girls had to report back to West Point, and they were making the best of the time they had left.

As Tuc let the others pull ahead of him, a trait he'd picked up from his dad to keep an eye on the family, he thought about his father and the half brother he knew he would be eventually meeting. Growing up the oldest of all his cousins, with Chet almost a year behind him, he'd always taken on the role of leader when dealing with everyone. Now that was going to change—that and the fact he'd always had his cousins around him, a blessing he cherished. He wondered how it must have been to grow up alone all those years and then to suddenly find out you have this whole other family.

Add to that all the insanity his family had just gone through— along with all the money inherited and the stories he had heard about Jillian—and Tuc Savage had a lot on his mind. He'd seen his dad when he left for the office earlier and knew he had meetings to get to. All these thoughts bounced in his brain as he rode behind the others, and he knew he would be bringing this up once they all got to the Cliff House. Yes, whether the others knew it or not, the next generation of Savages had a meeting of their own to convene.

"I love you too," Ed said disconnecting the phone from his wife, Marlo; the conversation they had earlier over his son with Jillian at first hadn't gone over too well. But with all the tragedy of the recent events in the mountains, she had called to tell him she loved him and that no matter what, they'd be able to work things out. Ed smiled, looking at the open road, and thought the worst was behind them as he punched in the number for the office.

CHAPTER 4

I f Nettlewood Psychiatric Hospital scared Marlo as a child, the sanatorium Patty Galloway was being taken to would surely create a
full-on nightmare. Vreeland Hills Sanatorium had a past, one of
the only lunatic asylums still running in the country. Built in the
1900s to serve as a hospital for those suffering from tuberculosis,
the facility offered the newest accommodations and touted the best
minds in the country at the time. The hospital quickly filled, and
the Vreeland family money grew. Everything was going well, according to Dr. Cornelius Vreeland, head of the Vreeland legacy at the
time, until the underhanded stories started going around town. It
had been when Cornelius announced his second wife, Cassandra,
had died after contacting tuberculosis that the chatter around town
died down. But that didn't change the fact that the death count was
immeasurable, and that was the least of the things the Vreelands
were hiding. As the years passed and more patients were admitted,
Cornelius's three sons had grown into men, and each one studied to
become a doctor. After Cornelius died, he left the hospital equally
to his three sons, yet Corbin, who was Cassandra's son took charge—
and as the horrifying stories died down, the atrocities inside continued, only more secretively. Then came the third generation of sons,
and by the time Cornelius's grandson Victor Vreeland became the
head of the sanatorium, more stories of doctors and nurses performing satanic rituals on unwilling patients locked deep in the basements of the building were whispered about in the dead of night,

and Victor Vreeland had grown into the likeness of his grandfather, Dr. Cornelius Vreeland. After having three sons of his own, he not only felt pleased he was following his family's legacy, but was determined to keep up his grandfather's studies, and the nightmares continued within the walls of the hospital.

After tuberculosis had been eradicated, the hospital had become a place for societies helpless. Disgraced families sent their less fortunate ones there, turning their backs on the poorly downtrodden discards they wished to keep secret for all time. And when the money was growing short, the Vreelands remodeled parts of the buildings into more of a jail to hold the criminally insane. Horrible stories came out regarding sadistic experimental surgeries performed on the fresh batches of betrayed souls, as well as reports on the mysterious deaths that ended up plaguing the hospital. It had nearly been shut down during an investigation but was eventually cleared of all wrongdoing. After that, the Vreeland family shifted their focus to bringing the prestige back to the hospital, remodeling the fifth floor of the East Tower to accommodate the wealthy, and soon after, it was business as usual—and the best part was they were able to continue providing their own horrific version of health care within the hospital walls because they still had the poor and the criminally insane to experiment on. That was until the family disbanded many years ago, leaving the hospital to the State of New York in a lease that was nearing its end—it was also a pivotal time for one particular Vreeland doctor, whose abused life had driven him to the edge. It came as no surprise to anyone that the building was haunted, and some thought the hauntings came from one of the Vreeland lunatics that worked there.

The ominous building had six main floors reaching from end to end and originally had three wings coming off it. The two outer ones were slanted slightly forward to the front, like the wings of a bird of prey; the middle one jutted back behind the main building, half the distance of the wings, to mirror the hungry bird's tail. Turrets were perched at its ends like prison guard towers, and centered high over the entrance, the imposing tower rose to the smaller seventh floor like a murderous widow's walk to watch over the damned, protected by menacing gargoyles. Originally the seventh floor had been a recreation room for the patients; fences rose around the perimeter of the roof to keep them from jumping off the building in the outside areas. But over time the fences had been torn down, and the recreation area had been turned into a file-storage room. The tuberculosis outbreak had been a cash blessing to the Vreelands at a time they couldn't keep up with the constant demand for rooms, so they constructed a mirror-image building across a circled driveway, making it look like a giant hand that was reaching out to grab you and keep you there forever. For many poor souls, that's exactly what happened.

In later years a glass atrium entrance was built over the main doors of the two monstrous buildings, looming over the entryway.

The only skyway still viable was the one on the third floor, because the one on the sixth floor, exactly where the buildings were closest, had been heavily damaged in a lightning storm, making it impossible to cross, and it was sealed at both ends for safety reasons.

The towers had giant gargoyle ravens looking down from above, and the staff as well as the locals gave the place the nickname "Raven House," an ode to the raving mad who dwelled inside its walls.

The rabbit hole Patty had slipped down was deep. From everything that had happened, she felt betrayed by everyone, including her sister, Stevie Galloway. Her mind was on fire with the realization that her mentor, Marcus Bowers, was dead—and a liar. In the days after her surgery, the pain had subsided, making it easier for her to watch the news from her hospital bed. Then came the surprise that Marcus had gotten her to sign over her general store and café and gas station to him, along with her cabin, during her heightened state of gullibility. She was ashamed and felt like a fool, and that made her angrier than she had ever been.

Stevie had a lawyer looking into the mess that Patty had gotten herself and everyone else into, and there was a moment when she thought she was going to get everything back for Patty, until the new owners showed up to claim the cabin, store, café, and gas station, starting more legal problems.

Poor, predictable Patty felt like there was nothing she could do, and she wanted to burn it down—burn it all down and everyone with it. With her wild antics, the staff sedated her. The more she fought, the more they gave her, but she didn't care anymore. The anger inside was growing. She was going to make them all pay.

When the day came to release her from the hospital to her confinement at Vreeland Hills Sanatorium, the hospital staff was glad to see her leave. The drive there was long, and the medics in the ambulance couldn't wait to be rid of her—not to mention they absolutely despised having to go anywhere near the frightening Raven House.

Patty was tied to her transport and kept muttering strange words in Latin, overcome from the drugs in her delirium: "*Incendes...incendes...incendes...*" She kept repeating the words, screaming at them as if in a mad tirade.

When one of the medics tried to sedate her further to stop her mumbling, she screamed and tried biting at him from the confines of her gurney, scaring the heebie-jeebies out of them. The medics were both glad when they finally pulled up to the daunting hospital.

When they arrived, she was thrashing about until they opened the ambulance doors. She suddenly stopped moving, her eyes widened, and she appeared to be listening to something no one else could hear.

"You're home, honey," came the voice.

The calming woman's tone in her head was as familiar as her reflection, and Patty shut right up at the greeting. Patty stopped her madness for a moment and listened.

"Everything is finally going to be all right."

As they wheeled her through the doors, Dr. Stanley Sinardi welcomed them. He made it a point to greet *this* new patient upon arrival. He had heard all about Patty Galloway and couldn't wait to meet his latest patient.

It would be hard to not know anything about her. With the news of the Savage family's nightmare playing out in the press, along with the headlines of the huge inheritance the family received, everyone was talking about it, and Dr. Stanley Sinardi hated it. It was bad enough seeing it on the TV, but when he spotted one of the copies of Ed Savage's centerfold in *Cosmopolitan* next to a computer behind the reception counter a nurse had left behind, he picked it up and threw it in the trash just as the doors opened and Patty was wheeled toward him. Vreeland Hills Sanatorium was the perfect place to lock her away for more reasons than anyone could have thought.

Surprisingly, her broken back suffered from Roman and Logan knocking her down was not as bad as it could have been. After a hemilaminectomy with microdiscectomy to her lower back, she would be up in no time. Only Patty wasn't going anywhere for a long time—if, in fact, she was ever to be released at all.

As they wheeled her in, Dr. Sinardi smiled. He picked up the new chart with the room number E606-F/Galloway written on the edge of the binder and made his way to them, placing the chart down on her gurney. With a big smile, he looked right into his patient's eyes.

"Don't trust him," the voice said in her ears, and Patty's reaction was instant. She hissed at the man in the white coat as he placed his hand on her forehead, and she tried to bite him. Dr. Sinardi pulled his hand back and smiled wider. While keeping Patty's focus, he nodded at the nurse, who injected her IV with his special mixture of fentanyl and Versed. Then, for an added layer of discomfort, he pulled another syringe from his pocket that he called "the ketamine dart," a drug with PCP that brought about hallucinations, and injected it into her shoulder.

"Glad to be dropping this one off," the lead transporting medic reported, handing the clipboard to the good doctor to sign off on.

"I'm glad you are too," Dr. Sinardi said. He signed the papers and handed back the clipboard, all the while watching Patty snarl and fight the medication from her place on the gurney.

Watching her, they waited for the quick-affecting drug mixture to do its job, and when Patty's eyes glazed over, they untied and transported her from the gurney. Placing her onto a hospital bed, they once again secured her with restraints. Once completed, the two men who brought her left in a hurry, and Dr. Sinardi ordered Patty to be taken to her room in the East Tower. The staff wheeled her bed into the elevator, and Dr. Sinardi pressed the third-floor button, which was where the lab and the skyway built between the buildings were at. He then pressed the fourth floor to go to his office.

On the fourth floor, he made his way down the long lonely hallway to his office and closed the door behind him. On the wall behind the door was a poster of the TV show he used to be part of; it had been his "ticket to the stars" that had crashed and burned. There on the poster he stood, dressed in black; the name of the show, *Phantom Finders*, was above him in bold, and standing slightly behind him was Ed Savage.

CHAPTER 5

Charlotte Savage was scared. The strange noises she heard outside the hotel were like a beast's guttural death cry. She had called for help and now saw the terrace doors in their office suite open, leading to the bluff next to the Vander Place Hotel. The wind had picked up, and the curtains were blowing toward her, like twin ghosts welcoming her to the darkness of her nightmare.

"Charlotte!"

She heard her name called out from the bluff in a terrifying shriek. She ran out on the terrace and took the side steps down to the path that led to the stairs to the skeet-shooting area. Rushing up the stairs with the wind blowing her dress, she saw him in the distance near the Mystic Theater. He was waving his arms in a desperate cry for help—and there were others.

Niles Savage was terrified; the voices of the dead teenagers were haunting him. Mia Delgado's broken arm hung at an impossible angle; bent in the middle of her humerus, it hung down and swayed with her movement, splattering blood in all directions. Her face was broken from the rock that'd come in violent contact with her skull, and her pretty hair was matted down with blood and dirt. Niles tried to get away from her, but his steps were heavy, like he was wearing cement shoes caught in the tangled tall grass. Noah's stabbed body rose from the ground in front of him; the slits in his skin and torn shirt dripped blood. His cervical spine protruded from his neck with his head hanging to the side; he was gargling on broken bits of bone lodged in his throat when he joined Mia in her focused attack.

Niles screamed like a girl at the sight and turned right into Jake—his blown-away face with one eye was there—and then Nash appeared; glass from the RV's window jutted from his face, dripping blood. Niles Savage felt the lingering stench of death over power him like putrid cologne, and he pushed through Nash and Jake when Mia's and Noah's hands grabbed him from behind. Together the four victims of his long ago victims pulled him down into the tall grass of the bluff.

He struggled and crawled away from their rotting hands. Just as he was about to get to his feet, the woman's arms reached out from the ground beneath him and clawed at his flesh. She grabbed his shirt collar with one hand; with her other, she dug at his face and tore his skin with her jungle-red nails as she climbed from the earth. Blood dripped from his face where her nails scratched him, as Cara Vanderran's corpse dug its way straight from the bowels of hell to take him. She was screaming, and the stench from her voice made him barf. As he choked on his own vomit, panic swept him deeper into the nightmare when he heard his brother *laughing* at him.

Nearby, Nathan Savage was sitting on a rock, dressed in his favorite suit, which he'd worn way too many times to the office. "Help me!" Niles pleaded to his brother. That was the moment he watched his own brother's head turn into that of Satan himself. In a terror-stricken state, he turned away from the beast just as he felt the unfortunate teenaged-clawed hands on him again, tearing at his legs, and Cara—pulling him down to hell, where he belonged.

It was at that horrific moment that Charlotte dropped the cold, wet bath towel over his head to wake him from his frantic night's sleep. In his irrational retelling of his nightmare, he caught his reflection in his bedroom mirror that night, and he watched it change into that of Satan himself—just like his brother's had.

Seeing that in her sleep, Charlotte woke from her nightmare, finding herself still sitting on the transatlantic red-eye flight from Miami to London, England. She was in first class, and the cabin was dark. The dream Niles Savage had had prior to driving up to Black

Ridge Falls had been a warning, she thought. And that night, in the hours that passed after he'd awoken from the dream, Charlotte Savage not only listened to him retell his nightmare but also learned the ugly truth her husband, Niles Savage, had been keeping from her and the even deadlier secret he had been keeping from his brother, Nathan.

CHAPTER 6

harlotte Savage sighed with happiness when she saw her sons, Chance and Landon Savage, waiting for her beyond the airport security checkpoint. After the hours spent on the plane, it felt like forever since she had spoken with them, let alone seen them.

The cruise her sons and their families had been on had been a gift from both her and their father, Niles Savage. It was a thank-you cruise for all the hard work they had put in getting the Vander Place Hotel ready to open.

She knew they'd wanted to come home early when Niles had first alerted them of the murderous night in the mountains—although being at sea at the time, it was impossible to leave at once, and it was planned that way by Niles, who had purposely waited to make the call to keep them as far away as he could for their safety.

When the news, with Ed being in the headlines, hit the gossip entertainment shows, the ship, the HMS *Queen Anne II*, the biggest ship at the time, built by Menard International Cruise Lines, had just left Saint Thomas, and the family hadn't heard of it until Niles contacted them. They felt trapped at sea, and while they could have disembarked on the last small island before the long voyage to London, a fact Niles didn't think of, he had also reassured them that they couldn't make it home in time for the funerals anyway. After learning what little their father told them, they tried their best to keep their kids away from computers and television news, wanting them to enjoy their time on the ship before learning the ugly truth of what had happened back home.

Secretly, both Chance and Landon discussed the horrible news with their wives, Audra and Roxie, and they had decided to fly home once their ship arrived in port in Southampton, England. That was until they got the message from their mother telling them of the divorce and that she had left Port Roberts and gone to their Miami home. But when Niles was murdered, she panicked. The next call they received worried them. She was frightened; the fear rang out in her voice on the overseas call. She begged them not to leave London until she got there and told them that she'd learned the truth of what Niles had done in Black Ridge all those years ago that had set this revenge against the family in motion. And when they thought the nightmare was over, it wasn't, and the murderous night at the hotel commenced. She was scared out of her mind for her sons and their families, and she demanded they stay put until she arrived.

She was exhausted and worn out from the flight, and just seeing her strong sons, now grown into handsome men, filled her spirit with love, and she smiled brightly. It was their presence that made the long flight worthwhile.

Waiting for their mother, they had seen the news and knew their father was dead, but what they didn't know was why. They were distraught and didn't know what to think. But after hearing of what had happened at the Vander Place Hotel, they were glad they'd stayed away.

"She looks tired," Landon said to Chance.

"After what's gone on at home, it's a wonder she's even here," Chance replied.

Just as Charlotte passed the security line, she fell into her sons' arms for a long-awaited hug. Chance reached for her bag. "Let me take that, Mother."

Charlotte handed off her bag and leaned into Landon's arms. Chance also reached around his mother and held her close.

"I love you, boys," Charlotte said as she squeezed tight to the two most important men in her life.

Pulling away, Landon looked to his frail, petite mom. "Are you all right?"

"Now that I'm here with you, I'm fine, but get me to the car. I want to see the children," she said, hanging on their arms.

"This way, Mom," Chance said as they walked toward the baggage-claim area. Together they got her belongings. In their thoughts, however, they were both anxious to know what she'd found out that their father had done. They couldn't wait to get to the limousine to talk privately.

Once they were settled and on their way to the hotel, the conversation turned intense. Their teenage kids had seen the news when they disembarked, and when they checked into the hotel, they wanted to go home right away. They all wanted to get going, but with Charlotte on her way and in her frightened state, they had no choice but to wait. And when Charlotte told them in detail what their father had done to that family's car so long ago—that moment that'd begun this nightmare—they were shocked and hesitant to go home themselves.

Before the tragic accident in the limousine on the way to Black Ridge Falls to pick up his battered family, Niles had had a moment with Charlotte. They had spoken about the company. He told her that finally, with his brother dead, he'd be ruling Savage Construction, and things were going to change. Charlotte, however, saw things differently and knew Niles's brother, Nathan Savage, was nothing but an ass and figured Niles was dreaming again. The Armagnac flowed that evening, and the dream that had taken Niles later in the middle of the night was an absolute horror.

She told the boys she had gone to bed, and when Niles joined her later, he was sloppy drunk. He woke her by stumbling into bed, and she got up and went to her private bedroom for the evening, locking the door behind her.

The yelling that woke her an hour later terrified her. He was screaming for his life, and she got up and ran to her husband. Opening the bedroom door, she saw him on the floor. Wrapped in the blankets and bedspread, he had rolled to the wall curtains and was thrashing about. She turned on the light and ran to him. Shaking him to wake up, he had struck her in his delusion, and she fell back. Regaining her focus, she got up and went to the bathroom, soaked a bath towel in cold water, and came back to him. As she attempted to wring out the water over his head, she felt the sting from her face where he had struck her and slammed the wet towel down over his face. Squeezing the water from it and soaking him—he woke in a frightened rage. Choking on the water he'd inhaled, he suddenly came to the realization that his wife was there, and with the fright of his dream dissipating, he calmed. And that was when the scary part had started.

Niles began to cry. Not only had he confessed his sins, revealing that he'd started this hellish series of events that continued to befall the family, telling her the whole story of dropping that rock from the overpass that killed that mother and father and the severe accident that followed, but he also confessed a secret he'd been keeping from his brother.

His brother wasn't the only one who had been with Rose Galloway, and the real reason why he'd dropped the large rock over the railing that day was because he thought *he* was the father of her baby, yet he had let his brother think it was all *his* fault.

If that wasn't enough, he told her the dream she'd saved him from was at the hotel property. The dead teenagers had come for him, and Cara had finished him off, but before she was able to pull him into the earth, he not only saw his brother as the devil himself, but later he saw that face on his own as well.

After telling her sons in the limousine that ugly story that their father had started in motion back near a town called Black Ridge Falls—what brought on the mountain murders, the Vanderran dining yacht disaster, and the insane night at the hotel that followed—she had them at a loss over what to do next. There was also the fact that their kids not only went to school with the deceased teens but had been friends with them too—was something they would need to discuss with them. Chance's son Rhett played football with Nash and Jake, along with Landon's son Shep (short for Shepherd), and their girls Nicky and Roni (Veronica) both knew Mia and Lucy, and they hung out with Ava and Heather. No, this was information they needed to digest before being stuck on a plane for an eight-hour flight without privacy.

Learning the sensationalized news of what had happened, the family now knew firsthand the severity of the truth and decided to take the ship back to New York. With the time at sea, alone from the world, it seemed like a good and safe place for the family to come together and explain to their kids what had happened and to prepare them for what was occurring and what to expect before arriving back home. With the decision made, Chance Savage booked an additional stateroom for their mother on board the *Queen Anne II*, and the family felt a bit of relief boarding the largest cruise ship in the world for their safe seven-night voyage home to New York.

Or so they thought.

CHAPTER 7

With the bikes parked at the closed Cliff House restaurant, the older Savage cousins had taken a walk on the bluff near the ocean. The breeze was calm, and they all had the feeling of being safe in a place they had been to so many times in their youth. The girls were heading back to West Point in the morning, and, to be honest, they wished they had more time with the family. They were all worried about Chet's dad, their uncle Sam, and didn't want to leave him.

"How's your dad this morning?" Kate asked Chet.

"I'm sure he's sleeping it off. At least I hope he is."

"So you didn't see him?"

"No, I thought to drop by, but Uncle Ed said they got him in bed last night, and he passed right out," Chet said, looking lost in thought. "God, I hate all of this!"

"Remember when we made him his favorite dessert? That blueberry pie that tasted pretty awful," Lana said.

"Oh my God, how did we ever mix up the salt and sugar measurements? That thing was nasty!" Kate laughed.

"You were just kids then," Chet said.

"You weren't that much older, and if I remember, you were there *helping* too!" Lana said.

"Yeah, and Tuc kept eating the blueberries," Kate reminded them.

As the three laughed and continued their walk, they realized Tuc was trailing behind them, deep in thought. "Hey, Tuc, why so quiet?" Lana said, looking back to her cousin.

"Huh?" Tuc suddenly brought his focus back to the group. "Sorry, I'm worried about my dad too. He's all excited to be meeting his son with Jillian, but with everything that's happened and what he went through with Lisa, I don't want him getting hurt."

"Why would he get hurt?" Lana asked.

"Maybe I'm on overload with everything that's happened. I don't know. But what I do know is we've always had each other growing up. This guy I don't know anything about—he's a stranger, and now he's my half brother. What's it going to be like for him?"

"Dude, you're overthinking this shit," Chet said.

"No, I'm not, Chet. The other night I overheard my dad on the phone with that woman Ellie Collins hooked him up with to help figure things out."

"Aisha Thomas—I talked with her at Savage Tower," Kate said.

"Yeah, Aisha was the name my dad said. Anyway, I didn't hear everything, but he mentioned something about his kid, and I figured she knew Jillian or something. He also said he was nervous, I think, about meeting this guy. And I heard him say he was a little scared."

"Well, wouldn't you be?" Lana said.

"That's exactly what I thought until my dad saw me in the next room and realized I could hear him. After he hung up, we had a talk." Tuc shook his head. "He told me what he was really worried about was me, Ava, and Lisa getting to know our new half brother. He said he was fine with it and excited as hell. He just turned on a dime with what he'd just told Aisha."

"He's a Savage; our dads always do that," Kate said.

"Come on—you know that," Lana agreed.

"Yeah, I get it. I agree with you on all that, but you didn't see him. Something seemed off. And normally it wouldn't bother me; it's just that I heard his side of it *before* he knew I was there."

"So why was he talking to this Aisha chick about all this instead of talking with your mom?" Chet asked.

"I don't know," Tuc said, thinking of that for the second time and remembering mentioning it to his mother. Now he was thinking maybe he shouldn't have brought it up in the first place.

"Talk with him when he gets home. I'm sure it's all in your head," Chet said.

"Hey, I've got an idea; let's head into town and pick up a blueberry pie for your dad, Chet," Kate suggested. "At least one from the bakery will taste perfect."

"Good idea. Come on, let's go get it," Lana said.

"Blueberry pie," Tuc said with a half smile. "Better than the mind trip I'm on right now. Let's go."

As they went and got on their bikes, Tuc couldn't help but wonder why his dad had been talking with Aisha Thomas about all this stuff to begin with.

CHAPTER 8

At Savage Tower, Ed Savage buzzed his secretary and asked if she had heard from Jillian. It was well past the time she had said she would be there to meet with him, and the waiting was adding to his frustration of wanting to meet his son. When his secretary told him she hadn't heard from her, he told her to send her right in when she finally arrived.

Getting up from his desk, Ed limped over to the window and looked out at the city. His gaze zeroed in on Parnell F. Bancroft's office tower, where Bigelow's construction company was finally replacing the blown-out window from Parnell's demise. Seeing the temporary boarded window being removed was like a slap in the face, knowing the job had gone to his rival Bigelow. The unsolved murder was still in the headlines, and Ed had talked with his brothers about the sneaking suspicion he had that their father, Nathan Savage, was behind it. He picked up a phone on a table near the window and buzzed his secretary.

"Paula, where is Nathan's secretary, Sally Anne, working now?"

"Sally Anne moved to accounting."

"Can you have her report to my office—now?"

"Yes, sir."

Ed hung up the phone as his office door was opening. Expecting to see Jillian, he was surprised when Tallulah Tuesday appeared instead.

"Tallulah? What are you doing here?"

"Ed, something's come up, and we need to talk."

"I told you I wasn't—"

She cut him off before he could finish what she knew he was trying to say. "Ed! The structural integrity has been compromised!"

Ed looked away from her for a moment in thought—he was stunned. The code Tallulah just mentioned was about the missing submarine *Manchester*, which was a case he had worked endlessly on, following leads that had never turned up any hard evidence, never coming close to finding the missing—or stolen—submarine when he'd worked at Agency One.

The story had been huge back in the decade after WWII ended. The submarine was due back to port at the Naval Station Norfolk, and when it didn't show up as scheduled and disappeared from radar, a search team was sent out to its last known location. There, only a few of the crew members' bodies were found still in their life jackets, partially eaten by sharks amid a giant oil slick.

The FBI and the CIA, not to mention the navy, had all been on high alert at the time, due to the very clear and present danger of the payloads on the submarine at the time it had vanished. Eight top-of-the-line torpedoes loaded with warheads of different payloads were indeed on that sub, and if it were to fall into enemy hands so close to US soil, it would have been an unprecedented disaster. Another submarine was called, yet nothing had ever been found on the ocean floor.

Since the murders of the crew and the missing *Manchester* in 1955, reports of the torpedoes coming up for sale during the Cold War had always triggered a red alert within all the agencies, and Ed had looked into many during his days with Agency One. He recalled the many times he'd thought he had been getting close to finding out what had really happened to the *Manchester*, only to be disappointed over and over.

Tallulah closed the door and leaned against it. "It's confirmed. And it's close to home."

Ed saw the grave look on her face and nodded as she moved closer to him.

"We've picked up on a black-market sale of post-WWII torpedoes here in the States."

"What?" Ed said in disbelief. "Where?"

"Eastern Seaboard. Seems there was a third vessel involved in the sinking of the *Andrea Doria* all those years ago."

"Wait a minute. The *Andrea Doria* sank near Nantucket after colliding with the *Stockholm* in 1956. There wasn't a third ship."

"Ed, that millionaire that disappeared in a dive to the *Andrea Doria* last year started a legal battle among his heirs like you've never seen."

Ed gave her a funny look, given that with the death of Niles Savage and his 15 percent of Savage stock probably going to his two sons, Chance and Landon Savage, the phone conversations and scandalous stories of *his* own family's inheritance issues were all over the place—a subject they both knew dearly.

"Forgive me." Tallulah cleared her throat. "Anyway, the recovery and salvage company they hired had been digging around the *Andrea Doria* site, and they found the casings of two of the warheads from the *Manchester* underneath the *Andrea Doria*!"

"Casings?"

"Ed, the casings were *empty*, and the serial numbers are a match!"

"Are you telling me the *Manchester* wreck is below the *Andrea Doria*?"

"It doesn't appear to be the sub but a smaller boat, Ed. It's murky down there, and most everything has rusted and deteriorated to time, but the housing casings were made of a top-secret military mixture of glass and aluminum, and the serial numbers were etched in gold. There's no mistake: the casings came from the *Manchester*."

"And this led to…"

"Wait, there's more. Upon further investigation, they unearthed two more of the casings from down there—intact."

"You're telling me the navy has uncovered *live* postwar torpedoes off the shore of Nantucket, and they're acting like it's business as usual?"

"That's exactly what I'm saying! Eight total went missing that day in fifty-five. Two have been found—and they're hot. That leaves six still out there, Ed!"

"So the search is ongoing?"

"Yes, so maybe more will be found, but the sale we believe is tied to a terrorist group that's eyeing the Eastern Seaboard. All agents are being pulled to this one assignment."

Ed's mind flashed to Agent Winston Weston Thrasher III and the rift that'd started between them so long ago when working this exact case. But considering Thrasher had helped in saving Marlo during the shootout, Ed thought things were changing for the better. "Is Thrasher in on this one?" he asked.

"*All* agents," she repeated.

The knock at his office door startled them, and Ed moved to the door and opened it. Tallulah moved to the window and got a bird's-eye view of the window being installed in Parnell F. Bancroft's office tower.

"Sally Anne, please come in." Ed held the door open with his invitation, closing it behind her.

"Mr. Savage, I was on my way downstairs when I heard you needed to see me. What can I do for you?" she said, clutching her purse and noticing the impeccably dressed woman at the window.

"Sally Anne, I want you to think back to when Dad's last will and testament came to the office. Tell me everything you remember."

Sally Anne thought for a moment and then started to speak but stopped when she looked to the woman still standing with her back to them.

Ed followed her gaze. "It's all right, Sally Anne. She works for me."

Tallulah smiled to herself, knowing Ed was coming back to Agency One, and turned and faced the frail woman, offering her a smile.

"Mr. Savage, I did exactly what your father asked me to do."

"Good, I'm glad you did. But we're trying to figure out a few missing things, and anything you can give us will be a big help," Ed said, adding a comforting smile to his request.

"It wasn't so much, really. I simply made a copy before giving it to Mr. Sam Savage and mailed it like your father instructed," she said.

Tallulah wanted to grab the little wisp of a woman and strangle the information out of her, but she bit her tongue and dug in her heels, letting Ed coax it out from her.

"Where did you mail it? Exactly," Ed said point blank.

"The post office box he told me to send it to," she replied, looking at her new boss. "Here, I may still have the address in my phone." As she started to dig in her bag, Ed reached out and touched her arm to lead her over to his desk, where she could place it down comfortably and search for her phone. He looked over at Tallulah, and both of them could read each other's minds just as Sally Anne found what she was looking for.

"Here it is," she said, showing him the picture she had taken with her phone. "I took a photo of the instructions your father gave me and took the documents to the mailroom to be sent. Sorry—I forgot to delete it."

Ed took her phone and read the note and address written in his father's handwriting. He nodded. "Don't be sorry, Sally Anne; you did great. Was there anything else my father asked you to take care of?"

She shook her head. "That was it, Mr. Savage."

"And the original document my father signed is where?" Ed asked.

"It's filed with the original will, sir."

Ed sent the photo to his cell phone and then pulled out his phone and waited for it to arrive. Once he had it, he deleted the woman's copy, as well as the message sent from her phone to his.

"Well, thank you for stopping by. If you think of anything else, please come to my office at once." Ed handed back her phone and escorted her from his office.

Closing the door, he tapped a message to Tallulah's phone. "Sending you a copy," he said, noticing he had messages on his phone as he limped back to his desk.

"You'll have a full report and an exact address that goes along with that mailbox within the hour," she promised, as his phone buzzed in his office.

"Yes, Paula," Ed said after putting down his cell.

"Mr. Savage, Rachel Shepard is on line one."

"Oh God, that other interview—I forgot! Thanks, Paula."

Quickly, Ed punched the button. "Rachel! Good morning."

"Ed, I've been calling your cell, but it's going straight to voice mail. Can you still make the interview?" Her voice was more than a bit hurried.

Ed picked up his phone and saw it was on mute. He immediately unmuted it and placed it back on his desk. "Yes, I'll be there. I'm leaving now."

"Great, I'll let them know."

Ed hung up his desk phone and looked to Tallulah.

She nodded. "Go take care of your interview, and meet me at our local office when you're done. I'll have everything you'll need, and we can brief you on the rest of the case once you arrive."

The door to Ed's office opened, and Jillian York Savage Bigelow made her grand entrance in a dress that was hands-down gorgeous. The two women eyed each other, and Jillian could see that she'd walked in on something.

"Ed, I'm so sorry. Paula told me to come right in."

Ed's mind was going in too many directions at once.

"Hi, I'm Jillian Bigelow." Jillian extended her hand to Tallulah.

"Of course you are," Tallulah said in a dry voice, moving past her to the door. "Ed." She nodded to him and left the office.

"Who's that bitch?" Jillian asked as she threw her fur-collared coat on one of the chairs across from Ed's desk and made herself comfortable in the other.

Ed was instantly reminded of the article "Bastard Son Wins Daddy Lottery," and he grabbed his phone, keys, and cane—he wasn't going to explain Tallulah Tuesday. The knee injury was healing, and he could move around a bit without the cane, but for longer periods of time, he still needed it. "Jillian, I'm sorry, but something's come up, and I'm late for an interview I completely forgot about," he said as he moved around his desk toward her.

"You don't give a damn about your son, do you?" She eyed him the same way she had all those years ago after she had emerged from her bubble bath to find that handsome, hurt man holding that damning evidence of her adulterous affair. The fighting had commenced that very day; it felt like only yesterday when the memories flooded back in a flash.

"Jillian, you know that's not true. Now, let me call you later, and we'll still meet today. Please," Ed said with the love of his lost son coming through him.

Jillian looked her ex-husband in the eyes and wished she'd never left him. "I'm sorry, Ed. I've been a nervous wreck about coming here to see you. Yes, call me later, and we'll meet," she agreed, getting up from the chair and grabbing her coat.

"Thank you, Jillian," Ed said as they moved toward the door. He paused a moment and looked into her eyes.

She imagined this was the moment, the moment he would tell her he had missed her and wanted her back—the moment she seemed to pray for a lot lately. She looked at the man she'd thrown away with a look of a wounded child asking for forgiveness—wishing she'd never cheated on Ed Savage all those years ago and hating the woman she'd been back then.

"His name?" Ed asked. "What did you name my son?"

Jillian could see the hurt in Ed's eyes and the love of a father wanting nothing more than what was his own flesh and blood. She looked down and took a breath, realizing her hopes of a reunion may be vanishing. "Theodore York, Theodore Trenten York, well... Savage," she said, looking to the man, Edward Theodore Savage, whom she'd named their son after.

Ed smiled, and his heart sank over too many years of loss. "Teddy. Ted Savage."

"He likes his abbreviated middle name, Trent; he goes by that," she said.

"Trent Savage." His heart filled with love, and a broad smile came across his face.

Feeling like her scheme was back on the upswing, Jillian slipped and offered more information. "He's got an exhibition of his work. He's showing in town this week at Gallery 26 on Twenty-Sixth Street by the park," she said, remembering the good times with Ed.

He's here? Ed thought. *He's here, and this is the first I'm hearing it?* His mind was cluttered, and he needed time to think. He suppressed his shock of learning his son was so close to him and took his ex-wife's hands in his. He stared into her eyes. "I'll call you as soon as I can."

Jillian smiled as he opened the door; a glimmer of hope filled her heart, and they both left his office just as Roman and Logan were coming toward them. Both brothers were surprised to see her, and they exchanged a confused look when they set eyes on her.

"Well, well, it's been a long time," Jillian said, studying them and seeing the hunk Logan had become. "Logan, you've changed more than I imagined, and for the better, may I add," she said with an almost hungry smile.

"Jillian, this is a surprise," Logan said.

"Yes, it is," Roman added. "Ed, we got your message."

"About the motorcycles, right?" Ed immediately answered back.

Since they were to talk about Sam and his behavior last night, the brothers shot a look between them and quickly agreed to stay silent, knowing Ed wanted to keep this from Jillian.

"Motorcycles?" Jillian asked.

"Lana and Kate got new motorcycles," Roman said.

"Jillian, thank you for understanding, and I'll call you later," Ed said. "Guys, I have an interview I'm late for. I'll call you from the car on the way there."

"Sounds good," Logan said, standing next to Roman and watching Ed escort Jillian to the elevators.

Just as the brothers watched the elevator doors close, the other car arrived, and Nathan's secretary, Sally Anne, stepped out. She saw Roman and Logan as she hurried toward Ed's office.

"Hello, gentlemen. So good to see you."

"Hello, Sally Anne," Logan said.

Roman nodded with a smile.

"I remembered something." Sally Anne's voice held an air of excitement. "I was here a few minutes ago talking with your brother, and I need to see him."

"You just missed him. Something we can help you with?" Roman asked.

Sally Anne looked nervous. "I'm not sure—I'll just leave him a message," she said, moving to Paula's desk to reach for a notepad.

Logan looked at Roman, but his brother was already reaching out to the woman.

"Sally Anne, it's all right; you can tell us."

Paula looked at Sally Anne, and the Savage brothers saw the worried look on their late father's secretary's face.

"Here, come on inside for a moment," Logan said, opening Ed's office door.

With the door shut, away from the prying eyes of the office gossip pool, Sally Anne breathed a sigh of relief.

"Sally Anne, don't worry. We knew Ed was going to ask you about our dad's final instructions regarding the will. That's what this is about, right?" Logan said.

"Yes, sir," Sally Anne said, feeling the ease returning back to her. "Your father had me make a copy of his will and send it to a PO box. I gave that information to your brother, and he asked me if there was anything else. I didn't remember until I got to my car downstairs. There was that mean woman in your father's office that day."

Roman and Logan looked to each other and tried to recall who that could be.

"Mean woman?" Roman asked.

"Asian—I wasn't sure from where. When I thought she was Chinese, she put me in my place and reprimanded me, telling me she was from the Philippines. Come to think of it, your father laughed when she scolded me," Sally Anne said, remembering more from that strange day.

"Can you remember her name?" Roman asked.

Sally Anne thought for a moment, and her reaction told the brothers she had remembered. "Mingyu...something. Let me look into this, and maybe I can dig up her last name."

Mingyu, Logan thought. *Where have I heard that name before?*

CHAPTER 9

The insider-trading scandal was huge, and several big-name people got caught with their hands in the proverbial cookie jar. Even the self-proclaimed brainchild of *Tycoon Wives*, Randall Bishop, was involved. Although it was his business partner, Bentley Fencer, who had first pitched the reality show idea, it was Randall who nearly lost everything. But he was no stranger to hot water.

At the time, all those years ago, it was the current *Tycoon Wives* queen bee, Marilyn Caspian Hart's, soon to be ex-husband, Anthony Caspian, an executive at Global Film and Television who had been in the center of the storm—controlling which films were released and when. Back then a new overhyped Hollywood blockbuster was due to be released. However, the studio knew it was a bomb, and although plagued with problems, the movie trailer looked promising—too bad the trailer showed the best parts of the entire movie.

When Randall Bishop was tipped off regarding the impending disaster, he immediately sold his stock; at the same time, he had lost his shirt in a bad real-estate deal, and when the prosecutor bought his story of needing cash after the real-estate disaster, he was off the hook—well, almost.

Anthony Caspian had taped all his phone calls and kept the recording of him telling Randall Bishop of the hit the studio would be taking once the film was released—and that recording was well hidden. The only reason it had never come to light was because Anthony's wife, Marilyn Caspian, had just starred on the first season of *Tycoon Wives*, and she loved it. And everyone knew better than to cross Marilyn Caspian, now Hart.

Randall was in a jam. The blackmail was hanging over his head like the cartoon anvil that was always hitting some hopeless sap on the head. With Anthony Caspian now behind bars, Randall was stuck with this demanding woman on his hit show. The problem was, the fans loved her, and no matter what happened on the show, she always came out on top. But all that was in the past, until this newest wave of hot water came boiling his way.

In his office on the upper floor of the high-rise, Randall Bishop was putting the finishing touches on Marlo Savage's contract as the movers were replacing the sofa in his large executive office. He lifted his coffee mug and downed the last of it as he gazed at his newest moneymaker. Covering his desk were several newspaper articles on Ed Savage's bizarre happenings, the money, and the Vanderran sisters.

The pressure he was feeling from the executives above was mounting, and this time he was actually worried. The last time he'd gotten in too deep at the company, his partner, Bentley, had come to the rescue and bailed him out. Bentley was a producer at the network that owned stock in the company, and when the two of them became friends, they'd pioneered the *Tycoon Wives* reality show, which became an instant hit. Bentley later coanchored a tell-all with Barbara Walters, not realizing at the time that he had a talent for the format. In later years he'd started his own specials, taking the anchoring responsibilities on as a solo career.

But when Randall banked on the wrong cast additions to last season's epic disaster, the ratings tanked, and the backlash was instant. The women brought on the show were at first a welcome sight, but their true colors emerged as they systematically plotted the takedown of the queen bee, Marilyn Hart. Then there was that *other* matter of sleeping with one of the chief executive officer's daughters on a drunken night out when the sex had gotten too rough. And when her father saw the bruises on her neckline, she told him everything.

Yes, Randall Bishop, from the outside, seemed above it all. Everything he touched turned to gold—except for the black-and-blue bruises of the rough sex he enjoyed, choking his passive partners when he was at his moment. But he wasn't the darling of the network his many fans thought him to be. With the numbers sliding for weeks on his number-one show, it was the report that Cara Vanderran Savage—with her best-selling author sister, Zolie Vanderran, and her connection to Ed Savage—had signed on with *Tycoon Wives* that the numbers immediately jumped. And with her death, the show shot to the top with speculation of who was to be signed on to replace her, and Zolie Vanderran's name was at the top of the list on all the entertainment gossip shows.

Yes, he was in trouble yet again, and this time his dear friend Bentley even distanced himself, afraid Randall's bad luck might rub off on him. Feeling alone and vowing to never go back to being an assistant, he hatched a plan—an ugly plan at that!

Putting the contract down, he turned in his chair and looked out at the skyline. The warm sunlight and blue skies made the city look beautiful as the movers took the wrappings off the new sofa in his office. And as other workers lifted the old one to take it away, their loud, clumsy shuffling interrupted his thoughts. Getting up, he went to the bar not far from his desk and poured himself another cup of coffee, watching the remaining movers place the new sofa where it belonged.

Outside his office door, Marilyn Hart stepped off the elevator just as the casting couch was being replaced. She waited patiently for the men to move the "thing that must never be touched" and entered Randall's office completely unexpectedly.

"How could you?" Marilyn said as she slammed the door behind her.

Randall's back was to her, and he nearly spilled his coffee. As he turned around quickly, his face registered the total surprise he felt. "Well, this seems familiar," Randall mocked, seeing her in his office.

"Don't play your scripted games with me!" Marilyn snapped back. "How dare you offer that Savage bitch a contract without talking with me first?"

"Care for a drink?" Randall offered with a smile.

"Bourbon—neat, and make it a double." Marilyn laughed, clearly not caring that it was well before noon. "I guess now I won't have to worry about Zolie, with Cara being dead, but really, Randall, that was dirty, even for you."

"You aren't telling me Andrew's still holding a torch for Zolie Vanderran, are you? It's been years!" Randall said, pouring her favorite brand.

"That woman tore his heart out on her way to one of her other ex-husbands!" Marilyn said, practically ripping the bourbon from his hands. "No, those two will never cross paths as long as I have anything to say about it." She looked away from Randall.

After a moment, Marilyn turned toward his desk, and Randall smiled. Touching her elbow, he led her to his new casting couch. "Darling, that's some pretty damaging shade you're throwing in here. We film in reality; how do you know I don't have cameras in here?" he said smugly.

Marilyn laughed. "Two reasons, darling," she mocked in return. "First, I would personally destroy you. And the beauty of that is I wouldn't have to do a thing; the fans would. Second, what with your revolving door of casting-couch sluts, you really would be a fool if you did. What with the rumors and all." Marilyn gave him a knowing glare and caressed her own throat as she pulled away from him. "Thank you, but no thank you," she said as she took a seat in one of the chairs across from his desk.

Randall wondered if she knew of Anthony's blackmail and hid his hatred behind his TV smile as he leaned against his massive desk. He put down his coffee and leaned back, folding his arms. "Marilyn, you're early. The Cinema Shake-Up doesn't shoot for days. What are you doing here?"

"I'm serious about that Vanderran woman," Marilyn said, placing her bag on the edge of Randall's desk and taking a healthy drink from her glass.

Randall gazed in the direction of her bag and eyed the paperwork on his desk with Marlo Savage's name on it, along with the newspaper articles. "Something tells me I'll be needing to write a few things down," he said as he leaned back and reached for a yellow legal pad, strategically knocking the papers on top of it over Marlo's contract. As he stretched for the tablet, his jacket lifted a bit, and Marilyn got an eyeful of Randall's smarmy commando preference. Being impressive, the bulge was hard to miss, and for a moment Marilyn was flabbergasted. She raised her eyebrows and looked away with a gasp.

"Oh, stop," she said, getting up and going back to the bar to add ice to her drink. She topped it off with more bourbon and turned to see Randall looking down where he'd caught her gaze, and he pulled his jacket back down as he gripped the pad and pen in his hand.

Not wanting to anger his highest-paid and most-popular Tycoon Wife with the largest following of any of his reality TV stars, he placated her. "Marilyn, what can I say? I didn't run it by you because I really didn't think it was an issue."

Marilyn was a smart businesswoman and ran in the highest echelon of celebrity circles. Perhaps it was the stardom she enjoyed that made her so vain or the fact her ex-husband, Anthony Caspian, was a man no one would go up against—considering the snitch that had exposed him was later found dead—but for some reason she didn't see through his bullshit lies.

"Now, what can I do for *you*, Marilyn? I'll write it down now and sign it for you. What will it be?" he asked with the sincerity of a dogcatcher.

"No Vanderrans," she said, returning to her chair and putting down her drink. "For the record, I never had a problem with Maura. Cara, rest her soul, well…let's just say she's one less bitch to deal with, just like that Zolie Vanderran."

Randall wrote across his legal pad, *No Vanderrans will be offered a contract to replace Cara on Tycoon Wives.* He then signed his name below it and went over to his copier and made a quick copy, knowing both Maura and Zolie had already turned him down cold, and handed Marilyn the original.

"Happy?"

"Like this means anything," Marilyn said as she eyed him carefully and folded the paper while reaching for her bag.

Randall noticed part of the Marlo Savage contract was still visible, and he tossed the legal pad on his desk to cover it completely when Marilyn picked up her bag.

"That was easy," Randall said proudly, escorting Marilyn from his office.

"Thank you." Marilyn air kissed him on both sides of his face. "I've got business here the next few days, and I've checked into my room at the Plaza earlier than we'd planned. Have my car pick me up there, and I'll see you at the shake-up," Marilyn said just as the elevator doors opened and a secretary exited the car.

Randall held the doors open as she boarded. "Oh, Marilyn, I am sorry about this last season; I didn't see it coming."

"You didn't see it coming?" She laughed dryly.

"One more thing. How about a favor?"

Marilyn looked at him with suspicion.

"We added one more interview this week."

Marilyn glared at him, waiting for the other shoe to drop.

"*Tabitha's Tea Talk* had a last-minute cancelation, and they asked for Tonya. Now, I know Tabitha Tealey isn't one of your favorites, but we can surprise them with you last minute they won't be able to back out. What do you say? You want it? Or shall we send Tonya?" Randall said, knowing the answer before she told him.

Marilyn recoiled at the thought. That unscrupulous and unfiltered man-stealing whore she'd caught trying to get with her husband gabbing with that vapid velociraptor hostess-in-heels was nothing but a recipe for disaster. The last time Marilyn Hart had been on *Tabitha's Tea Talk*, Tabitha had launched right into Andrew Hart's ex-wife, Zolie Vanderran, a topic that was off-limits. Tabitha was a shark with a villainous grin and would do anything for ratings. She hated interviewing actors, wishing she was the one in the guest chair, and these reality stars that were getting bigger careers were an insult. She loathed them all, especially as she languished, stuck in her particular career. Tabitha was a player, and Marilyn gave her credit for it, but the line had been crossed, and the feud was on. Her part-time cohost, Carly Tilton, on the other hand, was as gracious as could be. The attractive woman with another evening-edition show had helped steer the conversation in another direction—a move Marilyn would never forget.

"Not one word to Tonya. I'll cover it," Marilyn said, pushing the elevator button.

Randall Bishop smiled. "I'll call you with the time before the shake-up."

Letting go of the elevator doors, watching them close, he then went back into his office and closed the doors behind him. Going to his desk, he moved the yellow legal pad and picked up the newly drafted contract to Marlo Savage and laughed to himself when he noticed the article about the murdered Cara Vanderran Savage and picked it up. With his job temporarily saved by the pretty much guaranteed cast addition of Marlo Savage and the ratings boost from Cara's death, Randall realized murder was money, and money and ratings would curtail any harshness from the executives above, bruises or not.

The plan forming in his head seemed simple enough, but the choice had to be perfect. Tearing a page from the Savage headlines his brow furrowed; he looked at the closed doors of his office, and a devious look emerged on his face as the thoughts raced in his mischievous mind. If Marilyn knew he had paid those two disastrous wives extra money to make her life hell on the show so she would quit—she would've killed him. That had been the only way out for him since he couldn't get rid of her.

Or so he had thought at the time.

CHAPTER 10

The loss was heavy.

Everyone had sensed it at dinner last night; it showed up in the loss of appetite, the incomplete sentences—and the drinking. Sam Savage was teetering on the edge over the loss of his wife, Cara Vanderran, yet he was keeping up the charade of normalcy that'd been instilled in every Savage man growing up under their father's rules. Conversation had been carefully thought out in Sam's presence because the rumbling of the imminent volcanic eruption inside the poor man was apparent.

When Sam did engage in conversation, his voice had the dry rasp that came with too much alcohol, whether scotch or his favorite Crown Royal XR whisky, a voice both Ava and Heather remembered from that morning in Nash's RV on that ill-fated trip to Black Ridge Falls. And when it looked like Sam had had enough of the evening and wanted to return to his guesthouse, Ed motioned to both Roman and Logan, and they helped their brother get safely back—passing the pool they feared he might stumble into.

Later, on her way to her room in the guesthouse, Heather met Logan outside and was told her father was out like a light, and they'd been able to get him to down a few aspirin before he passed out. She peeked in his room to see him snoring soundly as Ed tossed Sam's shirt he had been wearing onto a chair next to the bed.

The next morning, finishing her awkward bath and still attempting to move normally with the cast wrapping her broken tibia, Heather Savage looked in her father's bedroom and eyed the empty space. It alarmed her that she had not heard him leave earlier. Moving to the main room of the guesthouse, she called up the stairs to the art studio on the second floor. Hearing the emptiness answer her back, she picked up her purse and looked for her phone. Remembering she had left it in the main house, she tossed her bag on the counter, grabbed her crutches, and made her way to get it.

As she entered from the pool terrace, Marlo was making tea in the kitchen and offered her some.

"No thanks. By the way, have you seen my dad?" Heather asked.

"Not since last night. But I turned in early, skipping dinner. Everything all right?"

Eyeing her cell phone on the sofa in the sitting area adjacent to the large kitchen, sitting beside her aunt's novel *Vander Place*, which she'd been reading, she turned back to Marlo. "I think so. Dad was having a hard time last night after dinner. I just want to check on him."

"God love that man," Marlo said.

The teapot started to steam, and Marlo went back to her task of making tea, while Heather picked up her phone to make a call.

Heather listened to her father's cell phone go straight to voice mail, and she hung up. She then entered her home number. Listening to the rings, she imagined the empty house once filled with her mother's love, when the answering machine clicked on; she heard her mother's calm British voice fill her ears, and her heart sank. Hanging up the phone, she called a neighbor, who answered right away.

"Hello."

"Hey there, Mrs. Keller. It's Heather from next door."

"Oh, Heather, how are you? How's the family?"

"I'm fine, thank you. We're doing the best we can. I was wondering if you would do me a favor."

"Sure, what do you need?"

"Can you look in our driveway and tell me if any cars are over there?"

"Yeah, hang on."

Heather heard the sound of the phone being placed down and waited a few moments.

"Honey, your father's truck is in the driveway. Is everything all right?"

"Yeah, thank you. I was wondering if he got there yet because he isn't answering his phone," she said, lying on the spot to avoid explaining. "He probably left his phone in the truck and is out back. Thanks again, Mrs. Keller."

Heather hung up and stared down at her novel on the sofa when the sound of another cell phone started to ring behind her. She turned to see Marlo reaching for her phone.

"Sam doing okay?" Marlo asked, picking up her phone.

Not really knowing, Heather gestured and left the kitchen area to find Zolie and Maura.

Marlo watched her go and looked at her phone; she recognized the Manhattan number immediately. Wanting privacy, she answered her phone and stepped outside to stroll to the pool house.

"Hello."

"Marlo Savage. Randall Bishop—*Tycoon Wives*. How's my new Tycoon star?" His voice, filled with confidence, caused her to smile.

Marlo looked back over her shoulder as she continued to the pool house. "Mr. Bishop," Marlo said with excitement, "I'm fine. Thank you for asking."

"You sound great."

"I feel great. These last few days of rest with my boy home have been the best ever," she said as she sat down at the table near the pool.

"I'm glad he's home with you." Randall continued, "Marlo, I wanted to finish talking to you about joining the show. I've got the initial contract drawn up and am going to get this to you today. I was wondering if you had decided on anything yet."

"Mr. Bishop, I—"

"Randall, please," he said, cutting her off.

Marlo smiled. "Randall, thank you. No, I haven't decided any-thing since we last spoke. But like I told you, I'll need some time to go over all this once I get it. And as much as you know I want to do the show, I'll have to have my lawyers take a look at it before I can tell you anything."

"Not a problem, Mrs. Savage," Randall said, appeasing his newest passion. "But I do want to remind you of our shooting schedule. It's all outlined in the package I'll be sending you today."

"I remember," Marlo said as she sat back in the comfortable pool chair. "You'll have an answer long before that," she added.

"Good going. Take care, and we'll hear from you soon."

"Yes, you will," Marlo said and hung up her phone. Placing it on the table, she breathed in the fresh air as a breeze blew some of the fall leaves from the trees into the pool in front of her. She looked at the beautiful landscaping and the pool house; she then got up, picked up her phone, and headed back to the house for her tea.

Inside, Heather heard her aunt Zolie on the phone in her office and saw Maura in there as well, looking at her notes for her newest novel.

"I should be able to leave for London in about ten days." Zolie paused. "Yes, love you too, Tom, and give my babies kisses." Zolie said and hung up the phone. "It's been too long without my dogs," she added glancing to her sister.

"I bet." Maura said, seeing the worried look on her Heather's face. "Heather, what is it?

Heather looked from Zolie to Maura and shook her head. "I'm not sure. I just talked to my neighbor, and my dad's at our house."

"The house!" Maura said with concern, looking over at her sister.

"What did they say?" Zolie asked, waking her computer with the mouse.

"I just asked if there were any cars in the driveway, and she said she saw Dad's truck," Heather said, just as Ava came into the room.

"Oh no," Maura sighed.

"The guys got him to bed last night, and I saw him there. I thought he was safe, and I didn't hear him leave," Heather said, sounding a little scared for her father.

"Let's go get him," Ava said, moving closer to the others.

"No," Maura said, getting up with Zolie, "we'll handle this."

Zolie picked up the landline in front of her and punched in a number. "Benjamin, have my car brought around." She paused. "On second thought, bring the convertible instead." She waited, before adding, "Thank you." She looked at the others in the room. "The fresh air might do him some good coming home."

"What's going on with your dad?" Ava asked, feeling the dread in the room.

"Dad left some time after they put him to bed last night," Heather replied.

"That's exactly why it's best we take care of this, honey," Maura said. "Trust me on this."

"But this has been building; even Chet mentioned something yesterday about Dad not being all there."

"We've all been noticing that too. But now that all the irrational insanity has, thank God, finally come to an end, he now has time to grieve," Zolie said. "Heather, if he's as bad as you seem to imply, it might embarrass him if you see him like that."

Heather nodded, watching Zolie open a closet in her office and grab a long coat, put it on, and pick up her bag from a nearby table. Maura disappeared to a room off the entryway and returned moments later with her own coat and bag over her arm, and the women moved to the front door of the mansion. When they walked outside, Zolie's white Rolls-Royce Dawn convertible was waiting for them with the top down. Benjamin, their majordomo, was opening the door, and the chauffeur exited the car with a clean polishing towel; he wiped the fingerprints from the door handle and moved to the other side of the vehicle to open the door for Maura.

"Benji, have Sam's guesthouse aired out, and I want fresh bedding—and a fresh pot of coffee—waiting when we get home." She paused as she was getting in the car. "Maybe a pitcher of my Bloody Mary mix might be needed; have one made one up, and I'll call when we're on our way," Zolie instructed.

"Yes, madam." Benji gave a polite nod as the chauffeur closed Maura's door and moved around the car to Zolie.

"I've got this, thanks," Zolie said as she got behind the wheel.

Heather and Ava stood at the grand doorway and watched the car pull away down the long driveway.

Coming from the pool house, Marlo reentered the kitchen and placed her cell phone on the counter. Grabbing her tea, she took a sip and added some honey to it. She leaned against the counter and took in a deep breath, and a smile appeared on her face as she looked at the flowers through the windows of the grand kitchen. *Yes, she thought, a new career with a TV show of my own is just what I need.*

CHAPTER 11

andy Storm had been told she was being discharged from the hospital the next day, and she couldn't wait to get out of there. Outside her room, across from the nurse's station, the elevator doors opened, and an African American woman carrying flowers stepped out. She ignored the nurses behind the counter and proceeded to find Sandy's room on her own when a nurse stopped her and asked her whom she was there to see.

The well-dressed woman stopped her determined stride and looked at the pit bull in scrubs, forcing a smile to her face. "My sister, Sandy Storm," she said.

The look on the nurse's face was one the woman was used to—being African American and having adopted white girls for sisters had always been strangely controversial—and then there were the names given to them from their hippie parents. And she wasn't even in the mood to tell her about their *other* sister, Dusty Storm.

"I'll need to see some identification," the bewildered nurse demanded as she led her back to the nurses' station.

Hailey Storm placed the flowers on the counter and handed over her driver's license and uttered the single word she had used so many times before: "Adopted."

"Thank you," the nurse said and pointed down the hall. "Last room on the right."

Hailey took back her license, picked up the flowers, and made her way to her sister's room.

Sitting up in bed and reading a magazine, Sandy was surprised to see her sister open the door. "What are you doing here?" she asked, eyeing the flowers wide-eyed with suspicion and then looking back to her magazine at the article she'd been reading of the sorority girl who had gone missing at the same sorority Hailey had covered a while back when the murders had happened. She glanced at the spelling of her name in the article. "I see you still think you're *all that* using Halle Berry's spelling for your name, you fake."

Hailey let the door close behind her. "These are for you," she said, handing the flowers to her sister and letting them drop before Sandy could catch them. Together they watched them fall, hit the bed, and land on the floor. The women just stared at each other. "You never could do anything right, could you?" Hailey added.

"Get out!" Sandy shrieked.

"No, not this time," Hailey said, picking up the flowers and handing them to her adopted sister. "We need to talk."

Sandy took the flowers and could smell the lovely fragrances intermingling. To her own surprise, she smiled back. "Mom's favorites."

"Wendy's too."

Sandy averted her eyes from her sister and sighed. "Oh God, we tried. She tried," she said, placing the flowers on the bed beside her and then looking back to her sister. "You know, all she wanted to do was be close to you. She thought if she could get a big enough story, she could prove she was *as good* as you. That's really what drove her."

"Look, what happened between Wendy and me is over. We all know the past, but we don't know the future. And...well, Dusty and I have been talking since this entire Savage saga started and have decided it's time for us to come together."

"Dusty? How is she?"

"She's worried."

"Jesus, remember as kids we all thought we'd be some kind of superhero team with our names?"

"I remember. Shame we had to grow up too fast to enjoy it. When are you getting out of here anyway?"

"Tomorrow. And I can't wait to go home."

"I bet, especially with losing your insurance with the station to cover all this."

"I know, but as it turns out, it's all paid for."

"Really? How?"

"I think it's Sam Savage. Or one of them, anyway. Here, I'll show you." Sandy opened the small drawer next to her bed and pulled out the note left for her. She handed it to Hailey and watched her read it out loud.

"'Sorry for your loss, and the medical bill has been paid—S.' Who is this S?" Hailey asked, looking to her sister.

Sandy shrugged. "I don't know. I figured it was that pushover Sam Savage; he looks like the biggest pussy out of all of them."

Hailey turned over the note and handed it back to her sister. "So you didn't see who brought this to you?"

"No, I woke up and found it on my nightstand. It was a little creepy to think someone was in here watching me sleep. But I figured, if that's all it cost me—for some freak to get off—to get this paid for, then I got off easy."

"I don't like this," Hailey told her.

"At this point, after what we just went through, I don't care. All I want to do when I go home tomorrow is put this all behind me."

"I tell you what: tomorrow I'd like to pick you up from here. What time are you being discharged?"

"I'm not sure. The asshole doctor has to sign off on something."

"Asshole?"

"Well, he was, until the bill was paid in full."

Hailey nodded in thought as she pulled out her card. "Text me when you know, and I'll be here—if that's all right with you."

"Sure, we can go to my house and do each other's hair."

Hailey looked right back at Sandy and saw the smile cross her lips as she handed Sandy her card. "You had me there for a second—bitch."

Sandy started laughing, and Hailey enjoyed the moment with her. After saying their good-byes, Hailey left her room. Going back to the elevator, she wondered, *Just who exactly is this mysterious S?*

CHAPTER 12

The loneliness was everywhere.

The sound of his empty existence banged loudly in his head as Sam remembered driving over to his home in his truck. In every vehicle around him in those early hours, he saw happy couples, families with children and pets in packed cars, off on their merry way in their perfectly partnered lives. Her voice was in his ear, and her hand was on his thigh, a move she'd always done when they drove, telling him how protected she felt just touching the man she had fallen in love with all those years ago, the strong woman whose presence was one others admired but was secretly a shy creature, a woman in love with her man, who privately was the schoolgirl in love with her partner for life. "I love you," she said. And Sam remembered stopping at the red light and turning to the empty seat next to him to see her, belted in next to him as she'd always been. She was smiling, and she lifted her hand and wiped away the tear from his face. "I love you," she said again when the horn honked behind him, startling him from his memory of his beloved wife, Cara.

Viewing the now-green light, he remembered accelerating through the intersection and turning on his street to his house, away from the family at Zolie's compound. Pulling into the driveway and hitting the garage remote, Sam sat there with the engine running, watching the garage door open. His mind raced from his wedding to the moment the RV had gone over the road to being pinned behind the wheel, unable to move; he couldn't escape the RV to keep his wife safe. The guilt washed over him, and he was, once again, drowning in it. He turned off the ignition and sat there in silence until the light sensor determined there was no movement, and the garage went dark in the early-morning hours. The heaviness of losing his wife was insurmountable, and when he felt the surge of raw emotion within him when he'd woken earlier, safely in his bed in the guesthouse, he left the others at Zolie's in order to be alone.

He didn't remember opening the truck door, dropping his favorite photo from their honeymoon, or moving into the house. It was the sound of his cell phone that brought him back to the present to find himself sitting on the floor of his study. Photographs of his wedding to Cara were all around him. The happy moments of his life with his beautiful wife were nothing but empty pieces of paper lying around him. Like confetti from a parade of sadness, he looked at the memories around him and ignored the ringing of his phone.

The wind outside Sam's home blew the fall leaves from the trees in his unkempt backyard, and the shrub branches danced against the windows, startling him from his thoughts. Seeing the photographs of his beloved around him, he picked up a few and wiped his eyes. "My Cara," he cried.

Pulling himself together he gathered the photographs toward him, like sweeping a table of chips after a winning poker hand, and piled them back into the beautiful hand-painted box Cara had insisted they make together to hold the most precious memories of their lives together. Placing the lid back on the box, he got up from the floor to put them away when his phone vibrated with an e-mail notification. He placed the box on a table and pulled out his phone, noticing he had missed a call from Heather.

"Our baby," Sam whispered as his gaze fixated on the framed photograph of Heather and her friends from her birthday party the year before the trip to hell. Heather and Ava were the only two remaining survivors from the small group of friends. Nash, Jake, Noah, and Mia were gone. Like Cara in the photographs, the faces of his daughter's friends looked out at him from the innocent framed photo with smiles that would never appear on their faces again. Sam picked up the photo and held it against his chest as more purging tears fell.

He grabbed the box and moved to his desk and reopened it, pulling out the love letters Cara had enjoyed, letting them drop in front of him. Emotion blinded him as he pulled a yellow legal pad from the drawer and started a letter to his beloved wife. He wrote feverishly and didn't know how long he had been there, but when he stopped, he reached for a framed photo on his desk from their last trip to Martha's Vineyard together. It was the last photo she'd framed for him. As he grasped at it, his vision blurred, and he knocked several of the frames over, hitting the last photo she'd given him to the floor and shattering the glass. Panic streaked through him as he pushed back his chair into the credenza behind him and grasped the fragmented remains of his life, trying to piece back together the broken pieces, cutting his fingers and dripping blood on the photo. Seeing the blood staining his beautiful wife, he tried wiping it away, smearing it and making it worse.

"What have I done?" Sam yelled out in his home. Hearing the loud silence slap him back hard, he picked up the broken pieces and laid them on the desk, cutting himself further, watching the blood turn from a trickle to a stream.

CHAPTER 13

I n her high-rise apartment, Aisha Thomas finished up the article on her findings with Ed Savage for the *Hollywood Reporter* and printed out a copy to proofread. As the printer came to life, she started collecting all the notes from the whole adventure spread over her desk: the inflammatory stories from the Storm sisters, the other editorial comments from the different news organizations that had weighed in either spreading the garbage or slamming the Storm sisters on *their* reporting, the photographs from Patty's cabin, and the broken Latin she'd deciphered from the piece of paper found in the spine of the book *Spells of the Dead* they'd discovered in Patty's cellar.

The only new evidence she had was from the interview she had done with the woman Marcus Bowers had terrorized before scamming her out of her money. Not wanting to be identified because she felt so ashamed for being duped, she told her that not only did Marcus spend hours trying to mimic the puzzles of the Zodiac Killer, but he had tried in vain to learn Latin from books and listened to recordings to mimic the enunciation of the words he spoke.

She picked up the yellow legal pad pages she had written the words on from the note she had found in the spine and knew the work was of a Latin novice. She had told Ed all about this and had copied her notes and sent them to him. He had told her to omit this from her article because it was considered evidence on the upcoming cases the family was dealing with, and once it was out in the open, he'd tell her all about it. Hoping this would help him later, she obliged without a second thought.

When the printer stopped, she looked over at her finished article sitting in the tray and grinned. Picking it up, she read it again. Deciding it was ready to submit to her editor, she placed her copy in the folder on her desk. She then opened her desk drawer and saw the silver-framed photo of her and her ex-fiancé, Danny, from happier times. She pulled it out and traced her fingers over her body in the picture and sighed, shaking her head. Putting the frame back in the drawer, she lifted the folder from her desk to place with it. Under the file, written on her desk calendar, was the word *Appointment*, circled on tomorrow's date.

CHAPTER 14

Zolie pulled her Dawn convertible into the driveway next to Sam's truck and parked it, shutting off the engine. They could see his driver's door was ajar, and upon looking in, they saw the photograph of Sam and Cara from their honeymoon on the floor on the driver's side. The garage door to Sam's home was open, and both sisters looked to each other with worry before rushing into the garage. Pushing open the door, Maura called out for Sam, but only silence greeted them. Moving farther into the home, Zolie looked over toward Sam's office and saw through the open double doors.

"Maura," she almost whispered.

Together they moved into his office and saw the chaos across his desk—and the blood. They saw the leather storage box Cara and Sam had painted where they'd kept photos and all the love letters to each other. They were scattered about the desk, along with crumpled papers torn from a yellow legal pad. On the pad itself was a letter he had been writing to his beloved deceased wife. The last line read: *I can't without you.*

The framed photographs of their lives together were knocked over, and the glass was shattered in one of them. Adorned with bloody fingerprints, it looked like he had tried to piece it back together. There were drops of blood on the desk, and some had even soaked into the letter he had been writing.

"Oh God, no," Maura whimpered.

"Sam! Sam!" Zolie yelled, noticing the blood drops on the floor and following them out to discover more on the stairs. They headed up to the second floor, yelling for Sam, and as they passed a hall bathroom, they saw the first-aid kit open and thrown about the counter. There were torn wrappings of bandages and a few pills scattered on both the counter and the floor.

Seeing the slightly closed bedroom door at the end of the hall, they went to it. Pushing it open, they saw him. There on the bed, he was wearing the tuxedo he'd worn at his wedding. It was slightly ill fitting after all this time, and clutched in his arms was the wedding dress once worn by Cara Vanderran. His hand was poorly wrapped in gauze and bandages, and as hard as he must have tried, he was unable to keep his blood from staining her pristine white gown.

An empty bottle of Crown Royal XR had been knocked from the nightstand to the floor, and the man was close to passing out. He had a few blood smears on his face from wiping tears from his wet eyes, and his breathing was labored.

"Oh, Sam," Maura cried, as she moved forward to take the dress from his arms. Under the garment was another framed wedding photograph, and as she moved the dress into her arms to move the picture, Sam opened his eyes wide.

The blood from his fingers on the dress was showing in her arms, and Sam thought he was dreaming.

"Cara! Cara! You've come back to me," he cried. Crawling over the bed to his wife's twin, he put his arms around her and burst out crying. "I'm so sorry I wasn't able to protect you, my love. Please forgive me," he begged in his hoarse whiskey-laden voice.

Tears came down his face as Maura held him in her arms and rocked him. She fought back her own tears and noticed her sister was crying, too, as they joined together to comfort him.

"Sam...Sam, come on. Wake up, Sam," Maura repeated.

Zolie went and wet a towel and brought it into the room to wipe his face. The coolness of the towel seemed to wake him, and he focused on the women.

"Maura? Zolie? No—I'm so sorry."

"Quiet, Sam," Maura whispered. "Just let it out. Get it all out, Sam."

Sam swallowed hard and seemed to gather himself when he spotted the blood on his wife's wedding dress. "What have I done? I've ruined it," he cried.

"No, Sam," Zolie said. "No, it's not ruined. We can fix it."

"I want my wife back," Sam cried and reached for the dress, clutching it against his body.

Zolie went and rewet the towel and gave it to Maura. "I'll go get him some water," she said.

Maura watched her sister leave the room, and all she could do was rock her poor brother-in-law in her arms, offering comfort where none could be given to a man who'd lost his true love.

CHAPTER 15

When Trent York saw the headlines, he finally knew Ed Savage was his father. Over the years, stumbling into conversations between his mom and her sister, he began to question his paternity. It was the day he heard Jillian and her sister Marta talking about his love of photography and the impossible shots he would try to get "just like his father did" when they were first married. Trent had a love of Mother Nature's wrath, from storm chasing in the tornado belt of the Midwest to hurricanes whipping the East Coast to erupting volcanoes in Hawaii. His fearless drive never faltered in getting the best shots. And when he got his first drone to attach a camera to, he was like a child at Christmas. His love of photography started to pay off when *National Geographic* used some of his photos and videos in a documentary, and now he was planning an exhibition of his own.

That day he'd overheard words coming from Marta, the woman who he thought at the time was his mother; she mentioned she'd remembered Ed's fascination with planes, always building the toy models, a habit *his son* had also owned. When she saw him with one of his electric toy models, it seemed all too familiar. Of course, when he asked about it, he was told even more lies, causing the confusion to build.

Jillian's sister Marta had raised him as her own child after her divorce, but after many years of evading the questions and the newspaper story, she finally caved. Trent had asked repeatedly about his father but never got an answer from his real mother, Jillian. And now there was no turning back.

When Trent arrived at Jillian's penthouse later that afternoon, she was worried. Jeremy Bigelow was gone, and it was just the two of them. To say the meeting was awkward was an understatement. She had been hiding the truth from him his whole life. Trent was let in by her maid and told to wait in the main room.

In her bedroom in the midst of changing clothes from her earlier meeting with Ed, the phone conversation had been short. Ed had called to tell her he couldn't see her due to his schedule, but if Trent wanted to meet with him, he would arrange it for later this evening: either dinner at the house with everyone—including his wife, Marlo—or if Trent wanted to fly to New York for an overnight trip to get to know each other, then Ed would fly him back in the morning while he did his interviews.

It was all so lovely, the thoughtful plans Ed must have been thinking about in meeting his son—all without her. She had been kidding herself, she thought. She moved to her dresser and pulled out a demure cardigan. In the drawer, she saw it: the wedding photo of her and Ed Savage she'd thrown her purse against that awful day he'd discovered her infidelity. Slipping on her sweater, wrapping herself in the warmth of what she'd thrown away, she picked up the framed photo and held it against herself as the truth hit her. Being a stupid money-hungry fool, she had destroyed her life with the perfect man.

There it was, she thought: he had time for his son but nothing for her. Half expecting it was one thing, but to hear the truth was quite another. She looked to her bedroom door, and a hardened look came over her. The one thing she wasn't going to lose was her son. When she finally came out from her bedroom, she saw Trent standing at the windows looking out at the city, and she knew what needed to be done.

"Please don't hate me."

He heard the words behind him. He turned, expecting to see the woman he'd always thought of as his aunt dressed in the latest fashion, like he had always seen her, but today she seemed hurt, and her casual attire showed it. He was angry, and he had a right to be.

But, like his true father, he had a way of holding his cards close to the chest.

"Mother, I don't hate you," he said, looking at her with pain in his heart.

"Please sit down," Jillian said, pointing to a chair across from the sofa, where she moved to sit facing him.

"I've thought a lot about this," Trent said. "We've gone through this for quite some time, and now I want the truth—the complete truth. I deserve to know what happened."

The color in Jillian's face faded, and she truly felt ashamed. "All right then, the truth you will have," she said.

Jillian sat back on the sofa and sighed. "The first time the marriage got bad was after the miscarriage," she said, spinning her web of lies. "Your father blamed me, and the anger in him frightened me. I hadn't seen that side of him before. Things got good for a long while, and I'd forgotten about how violent he could get with his drinking until that damn business deal started it all over again. I didn't even know I was pregnant when your father kicked me out of our home." Pausing, she glanced at her son to gauge his reaction. "Your father *thought* I had an affair with Jeremy, and there was no going back with Ed."

"Well, you're married to him now. Did you?" Trent shot back.

Jillian was surprised *and angry* at the pointed question hurled directly at her, but she figured she had it coming after all these years of lying to him. "I am still your mother, and you won't talk to me that way ever again! But to answer your question, no, I did not," she lied. "What happened was this: Your father's company was doing business with Bigelow Construction at the time. I had simply met Jeremy at one of his properties, another hotel where they'd been doing construction on a new wing, to try to iron out a problem his father, Jacob Bigelow, and Ed's father, your grandfather, Nathan Savage, were having."

"What kind of problem?"

"Trent, that was so long ago; so much has happened since. Let's just focus on the now and go from there," she said, trying to keep the pleading tone from her voice.

"Not this time, Mother. I need to know this." Trent spoke directly at her.

"So long ago," Jillian said, turning her head to look out the window to gather her version of the story. "The Parkwood Plaza Hotel project." She turned back to him. "Jeremy's father, Jacob, had too many projects running at the time, or so I remember. There was a cash-flow problem, and Bigelow Construction was in trouble temporarily of course, but Jacob made a deal with the devil, Savage Construction, and Nathan was a real prince."

"The Parkwood Plaza? That's the hotel you have me staying in," Trent said.

"So it is." Jillian pulled one of the pillows on the sofa to herself and clutched it. She seemed to be brushing invisible wrinkles in the fabric of the pillow as the hurt emotion filled her face. "We arranged your hotel room months before all this started with your dad, and I completely forgot. See, it wasn't that important." Jillian layered another lie as she continued, "Anyway, months passed, and everything was going along as planned, I thought, when without warning, Savage Construction tried pulling the entire project away from Bigelow. The fighting between Jacob and Nathan was ugly, and Ed stood right at his father's side and did everything he could to destroy Jeremy and his family. Both families were at odds with each other. It was too much. I couldn't take the…" She paused, seemingly remembering something she didn't want to look at and most definitely did not want to say out loud. "I simply went to speak with him privately to see if anything could be done to stop the fighting, but Ed only saw red."

Jillian could see in her peripheral vision that Trent was hanging on her words as she continued, "We fought, and he…" She stopped, raising her hand to her face as she looked away from her son. "He struck me." She said it, releasing the final lie in her arsenal. She started to cry and wiped a tear from her eyes.

Trent was immediately angered. He had been raised with Marta's daughters, and even though he was a year younger, he had always protected them growing up, and one piece of morality he held tight was to never hit a woman. Jillian, of course, knew this and played on it in preparing her story, and it paid off big time. Trent seemed to believe every word she spoke.

"Now, Trent, you must not open this old wound again: not with me and not with Jeremy and certainly not with your father. Do you understand me?"

"Why not? We're going to meet soon. I want to see him. I want to know my father. Have you talked with him about meeting me yet?" he asked, full of hope.

"He said he would call later today and try to set something up, but knowing your father, well…just don't go and get your hopes up, honey," she lied, not wanting him flying to New York with Ed for the night.

"He'll call. I know he will," her boy said, and she could see the hope in him start to fade as she imagined his mind racing over what she'd just told him.

"Now promise me you won't mention the past. I don't…" She trailed off. "I don't trust him." She finally added an additional lie to the tale she was telling. "Now, I want you to meet with your father, get to know him, and just leave the past where it is. This is a new beginning for the both of you; please remember these words when you see him. Trust me—it will be better that way," she said. As she started to move her hand to her face, she stopped, taking her trembling hand and placing it in her lap, head bowed for full effect.

The wave of distrust and loneliness was gathering on the shallows in front of him, and as the tide pulled away from him yet again, he could remember all the times he never quite fit in growing up in the family that he now knew was never his. The feeling of finally being so close to the family he actually belonged in was at his fingertips, yet he could feel it all slipping away into the abyss just beyond the crashing wave of hurt moving closer to him. Now hearing that his father had put his hands on his own wife unnerved him.

Trent was deflated. He had read the stories in the newspapers of the Savage family nightmare playing out for all to see, and now he was questioning all of it. He even did an Internet search on the family he belonged to but never knew. He had been so excited to finally get to know his family that was taken from him, and now he just wasn't sure.

Growing up, Trent was popular in school, and he had many friends. But when he would go over to their houses, he was reminded of how different things really were at his home. He'd thought he was finally going to feel like he belonged, just as the wave came in from the shallows and swept over him. The distrust and loneliness he could now clearly see and feel reminded him of all the times he knew something was off growing up. That feeling of not quite being real was back, and it was sitting across from him on the sofa.

Trent got up from his chair and moved to the door.

"Where are you going?" Jillian asked.

Trent opened the door, looked at her, and without saying a word, left the room and closed the door behind him.

CHAPTER 16

D r. Stanley Sinardi may have hated his life once, but now he envisioned that things were about to change. Entering his office and leaving the door open, he saw his cat, a gray British shorthair with yellow eyes, aptly named Daughter, lounging next to his favorite bottle of tequila. Picking up the bottle of Don Julio Real, the cat hissed at him and jumped to its feet, scratching at him, catching his sleeve. "Fucking cat!" Sinardi yelled as he batted the animal to the floor. The cat hunched its back and hissed at him again, and he looked to see the cat's bowl was empty. "All right, Daughter, all right," Sinardi said, going to the glass hutch and opening it to grab the box.

Dr. Sinardi shook the box as the cat sat still, curling its tail around itself waiting to be fed. He had trained the cat well, he thought, as he went over and poured the cat its meal. Starving the cat to attack restrained patients was a specialty he'd read about from one of his favorite doctors, who also loved expensive tequila.

Pouring a glass of his favorite brand, he walked over to the window and looked out above the glass atrium at the East Tower, where Patty's room was, as the dark, threatening clouds moved in over the sanatorium. He laughed to himself, imagining all the previous patients that had dwelled in that very room before her, and he knew the drugs he'd given her would be a wild ride.

And it was so true. The voice Patty Galloway had heard when she'd arrived at Vreeland Hills Sanatorium came back to her once she was alone in her room. The pain medication Dr. Sinardi had given her left her in a hazy state, but the ketamine was wicked when mixed, and the hallucinations were unbearable. It was her mother's voice she'd been hearing when she'd arrived; only before the injections, it had been calm and inviting. Now it was loud and menacing: an evil mother shaming her slut daughter for the nasty things she'd *allowed* to happen with the Cullens in that mining shack. Patty screamed and pulled at her restraints, the long chains secured to the floor on each side of her bed and shackled at her wrists clanking against the bed's metal frame. She was alone in her dimly lit and frightening room with the heavy curtains shut against the light of freedom. But no one would come. At her door she saw the brief movement and the eyes of some stranger who looked in to see her. Then the abrupt sound came from the little peek-through viewing window slamming shut, leaving her alone in her room filled with doom, and she screamed for her life.

The phone in Dr. Sinardi's office rang, and he had a feeling what the call would be about. Hanging up, he took in the cold gray skies that had blown in, altering the day's happy sunlight, and he admired the eerie shadows of the gargoyles perched atop the building. He smiled. *Yes*, he thought—he was in a good mood now that he'd been told of Patty's torment. He sat down at his desk and stared at the newspaper, where an article was circled—about West Point parents' weekend—and dreamed about his revenge against Ed Savage.

Dr. Stanley "Stan" Sinardi's departure from Hollywood had been disgraceful. It'd started out so good, and somehow it'd all turned to shit as quickly as it'd begun. It seemed so long ago that a producer had sought him out and interviewed him for an upcoming TV show he was working on, and the two had hit it off. They needed a psych council for an upcoming series they were planning, and the part was small. Originally they'd cast him as the doctor that answered the questions about the current case they were working on for the upcoming "spook" series. It wasn't long before Stan started seeing stars in his eyes and worked his way into the lead position in the series, edging out the halfwit actor they had hired for the spot by drinking with him on the set and watching him fuck up his lines, causing expensive delays, and filling his head with psychobabble and lies that they were going to fire him on the nights he got him too drunk to think straight.

The first year the series started strong, but the numbers slid in the second season, and the network talked about canceling the show. That was until Ed Savage's agent, Rachel Shepherd, negotiated a spot for Ed to join the cast midway through the second season. Ed hadn't shot a movie in years, and his last one, *The King, The Witch, and the Maiden*, was never released due to a murder on set. With the film shelved due to the legal mess created by the horrific crime, Ed just turned away from filming and focused on his family and Savage Construction. When his agent broached the subject of the spook series, Ed immediately canned the idea until his agent talked him into it.

Slowly the ratings climbed, and soon the show was out of trouble, for a while anyway, until the trouble started up once again.

Sinardi had always thought the show was his, and Ed Savage, to him, was just some has-been sidekick that hadn't had a movie in years, and his last one was shelved. *Probably because it was a bomb*, he'd thought. True, he was a psychiatric doctor, and his knowledge from his past and brief time spent dispensing his brand of bullshit medicine was his draw. But the fact that he escaped with his license intact was sheer luck for this quack's quick-witted crap.

It wasn't long before Ed had had enough of working with his so-called costar, who was way too full of himself and was an annoying arrogant asshole to the crew. Toward the end of the second season, Ed's press surged when finally *The King, The Witch, and the Maiden* was released, and it shot to the top. Soon after it was all about Ed Savage, and Sinardi started making trouble.

The made-up stories leaked to the press accused Ed of being a total asshole on the set, screaming at stagehands and morphing into a megalomaniac. And his alleged sexual harassment of a young starlet to "put out or get axed from the show" was the last straw. When Ed saw this, he was done. He also didn't like the underhanded ethics of the show in its storytelling and knew it was time to go. Things had settled down at home with Marlo at the time, but the headlines had started another round of fighting.

With the last episode in the can and the rest of the series playing out on TV, Ed pulled the plug. They wanted him for season three, but he declined, and that's when he started *Savage Mysteries.* That was also the beginning of the war, according to Stan Sinardi.

The sound of the cat's bowl being knocked over pulled Dr. Sinardi from his fantasy of the ultimate payback, and he went over and righted the bowl. The cat was still hungry, and Sinardi shook the box, teasing it before putting it away. The cat hissed at him again, turned, and ran out of the office to hide in the darkness of the hospital's long corridors. Sinardi watched the cat leave and moved to close his office door before emptying his glass of tequila.

CHAPTER 17

T he phone conversation Ed had with his brothers on the way to the interview was heavy. They were all worried about Sam, and each of them had stories of seeing their other brother spiraling down to a dark place. It was decided that an intervention would be needed if things didn't change soon, and they had no idea of what was happening at Sam's house when they were talking about him that very day.

As the conversation came to an end, Logan, with Roman on the office speakerphone, mentioned that Sally Anne had come back to his office after he'd left with Jillian. She'd remembered a woman named Mingyu from the Philippines in their dad's office the day he gave her the instructions to mail a copy of his will to that PO box. Ed had never heard of her but said they'd discuss it later.

Disconnecting the call from his car audio, Ed silently added one more layer to the mess his father had left for him. His mind was still going in too many directions as he pulled into the local TV station parking lot; he needed to focus. *No,* he thought, *get this interview over with, and then deal with the rest.*

The earlier newspaper interview Rachel had set up for him didn't happen. Ed had driven to their old location, forgetting they'd moved, and when he finally figured it out, it was too late. If he went, which they wanted him to, he would miss out at the TV station. He said he was sorry and would try to reschedule.

The first live interview on Ed's list had him nervous. While he was as seasoned as any accomplished actor could be, he knew he was going to be asked about the senseless deaths, and he wasn't prepared for it. It wasn't one of his older movies or a play he had starred in or even one of his current TV shows. No, this was a vile attack on his family by a fragmented mind, and no script could prepare him for what was to come.

Surprisingly, the interview went well. The station manager had been lucky enough to get the first interview, and the parent company that owned the station warned them to take it easy on him. They were well aware of what had happened with the lawsuits from the Storm sisters' broadcast from hell that put several stations in court, and they proceeded with caution. The questions presented to him were made to be easy to handle and not as pointed and sharp as he'd expected. The plan was to get Ed Savage back after what they thought the other stations might have planned in their assaulting interviews that were coming.

The last of the questions took a different turn when they asked Ed about his acting history on *Phantom Finders*. It had been a long time since he'd even thought of that show—let alone the disaster it turned out to be.

The story that pitted *Phantom Finders* and *Savage Mysteries* against each other was strange. A woman who had visited her child in an institution claimed to have seen two younger women become possessed before her very eyes and demanded her child be moved to another hospital. And when the headlines hit the papers, it got worse. The younger women she had spoken of were two of the Brockman siblings who claimed they had not only been possessed when they murdered their parents, but their home was actually on the same block as the original home that was ground zero for the movie *The Exorcist*.

When the murders happened so long ago, the youngest Brockman— a boy who was traumatized over what'd happened in his presence—was separated from his older sisters and placed in a separate institution. At the time the three children living in the home had been seen by different doctors due to their experiencing such strange symptoms, and those were the only sourced stories that got released by neighbors way back when it happened. The murdered father was a pastor, and the actual stories of what happened in the house were buried due to the family's ties to the church.

It wasn't until the home had sold and a wall had been damaged due to a renovation that they found a closed-off room with torn, bloodstained clerical clothing and an ornate mask depicting a tortured soul that added to the Brockman murder case. The headlines again, went everywhere.

With the media attention covering it, both producers of Savage's and Sinardi's shows ordered episodes covering the original story: integrity was the approach *Savage Mysteries* used while covering all their stories—not so much with Sinardi's *Phantom Finders.*

The snowballing bad luck that followed was laughable. Sinardi's *Phantom Finders* aired first. The numbers were huge, and the production was over the top. The entertainment gossip shows reported it being the best and scariest episode to date. Sinardi rode the publicity wave and demanded a pay hike. This substantial increase was seriously being discussed by the powers that be—until the charges were filed.

The current episode he was filming in an old butchering plant was in its third day of shooting when production was halted. A young makeup assistant had filed rape charges on the first and only day she worked.

She'd been beyond happy to get the call to replace another makeup assistant who'd abruptly quit. That first night's shooting was exciting for her; she had been a fan of the show, loved it, and was thrilled to be there. That was until Sinardi got tanked. He was celebrating the huge surge in numbers for his show and took the bottle of Yukon Jack from his dressing trailer and walked onto the set that first evening of that young girl's career. When he ran into the young woman exploring the area, he cornered her. At first the heavy making out was consensual, but when she wanted to stop, he didn't. He raped her right there in the butchering plant on an old meat counter.

To make matters worse, the *Savage Mysteries* episode of the same story aired the following week but told the tale slightly different. Ed

Savage's team combed through every record and told the *true* story from the written accounts of what had happened to the Brockman family and the origins of *The Exorcist*. The episode was a truthful documentary, which was still scary, only not as overproduced for that tabloid scare factor.

With the headlines of the story making the papers, the comparisons between *Savage Mysteries* and *Phantom Finders* were top stories, and the two shows wound up in a showdown. Soon the talking heads were reinvestigating the original stories themselves, and Sinardi's was proven to be mostly lies.

Then the rape charges hit the papers, and soon after that Sinardi got a taste of his own medicine. A tape was leaked from a friend of the first makeup assistant that had quit. She told her friend on set that Sinardi had put the moves on her and scared her. Instead of reporting it, she just quit. The next day her friend brought in her own video recorder to film the out-of-sight pranks used for raising the scare factor. The video showed the wires used by the show to fake the moving of furniture and slamming of doors by the supposed 'ghosts' being reported to haunt both the Brockman homestead and the original home where *The Exorcist* was said to have happened.

But the jewel included Stan Sinardi himself on video, laughing at the gullible fans that worshiped him. The damage was irreparable; the irredeemable fool had been caught red handed.

The icing on top was the movie *The Witch of Carmen Castle*, the sequel to Ed Savage's *The King, The Witch, and the Maiden*, which had just been green lit. Everyone was interviewing Ed Savage to see if his character, the king, would be reprised in the new film. With the scheduled interviews and the headlines of the *Exorcist* stories, the entertainment gossip shows started the Savage-versus-Sinardi war, and the questions were unavoidable.

Ed Savage hated Stan Sinardi for the hell he'd put him through and wanted to eviscerate him in the press, but he didn't. Instead, he never said anything bad about the guy, nothing good, but he always dodged the questions like the true gentleman he was. There were rules in Hollywood and rules Ed followed his whole life, including the dictatorship of growing up Savage and his West Point and Secret

Intelligence Agency training. He had morals, and Ed played to win. His nonanswers to the Sinardi mess spoke volumes, and the press picked up on it. Soon the name Sinardi became a joke in Hollywood, and Ed Savage was the first person smart enough to see it, and the late-night jokes followed.

The fact that Stan Sinardi was a laughingstock infuriated him, and Ed Savage rose higher and never did a thing but share in a few laughs along the way.

What Ed did not know was what had happened to that miserable man he'd once worked with, and frankly he just didn't care. Of course, during his interview, he kept that part to himself.

The few questions from his *Phantom Finders* days were basically comparing the strife that happened when he left that set to start *Savage Mysteries* and how he'd picked himself up and started fresh. They also asked if he could take something from that long-ago experience and apply it to what was happening now to help him get through, even though it was completely different.

To Ed, the difference was night and day, and he could see the woman interviewing him meant it with kindness, not like that reporter who had cornered him coming out from an old jailhouse while on location at the time to grill him on the wild accusations his costar Stan Sinardi had thrown at him all those years ago—or those two Storm sisters, who seemed to double the hell when they blindsided him just as he was released from the sheriff's office recently. His mind was swimming in the past when he told her nothing that had happened during *Phantom Finders* could have possible prepared him for what he'd just gone through with his family, and that he was happy it was all behind them.

When the interview was over, she smiled and tilted her head back, reminding him of Ellie Collins with the way her hair was styled and how they used to laugh at the world and get along so well. He played along, answering her questions, and thanked her for the interview.

When it was all wrapped up, Ed left, traveling back to Savage Tower. Those last questions regarding *Phantom Finders* got him thinking of the past, and all sorts of things popped up in his mind. He needed to check in about meeting his son Trent and then get home and prepare for his overnight trip to New York. And yet his thoughts were on what Tallulah had told him in his office and what had happened between him and Thrasher on that case so long ago. *That case*...the one where everything had changed between him and Winston Weston Thrasher III.

CHAPTER 18

The TV station Ed had just left planned on running the interview as often as they could to get as much press as possible, being the first to get the story everyone was talking about. The sound bites they advertised promised an exciting interview, and when Dr. Stanley Sinardi saw it, his blood boiled. In the confines of his lair at Vreeland Hills Sanatorium, the mere mention of *Phantom Finders* was taboo. To hear it being brought back to life on TV was something he couldn't stand.

Shutting down the TV in his office, he dug in his desk drawer and spotted the two flash drives of different sizes, pulling out the larger one. He then loaded it into his computer and opened the file. There, he watched the movie reel that was transferred long after its time, like Patty Galloway talked about what she'd done with the filming of the accident that had started it all in the reports he'd read, yet the discovery of such tapes had never been recovered. Here, however, was something Patty never knew about. Dr. Victor Vreeland, a descendant of the Vreeland family of doctors that had run the sanatorium, had a "special patient" locked up in the very room Patty was now occupying.

The woman had been pregnant and in a tragic accident; she lost her husband and was declared dead at the scene. When the report was sent out, Dr. Victor Vreeland, who was also running a smaller ward at the time where he could hide his sick, less sadistic side of medicine aimed at the young, was near the accident. He heard the call and was especially interested in the fact she had been pregnant and wanted to inspect the body. He rushed to the morgue. Being well known in the medical arena, Victor was let in without so much as a question.

The day had been eventful enough with that horrific accident, and when the news was showing the burning gasoline truck on the expressway, the staff left the morgue to watch the TV in the break room down the hall, leaving Dr. Victor Vreeland alone with the bodies of both Melvin Galloway Sr. and his pregnant wife, Rose. And in that moment, something happened. Rose Galloway's death transformed into nothing but a trance, and she suddenly woke up on the gurney she'd been brought in on.

The blood that had pooled in the back of her mouth was spit out all over him as she gasped for breath, scaring the hell out of him as she attempted to rise up from the gurney. The people down the hall didn't hear him because they'd turned up the volume to watch the video playback of the burning truck that had been caught on the camera from a news helicopter.

There he was, alone with the bodies and splattered in blood from a partly burned corpse that had just been resurrected before his very eyes; his stethoscope was around his neck, his doctor's bag was knocked over on the metal stand next to him, and a bottle of smelling salts had fallen to the floor, releasing a vile odor.

Realizing what was happening and the small window of opportunity he had, Victor held Rose down and pushed her gurney out to the back, where the ambulance was still parked at the bay on the other side of the morgue's back double doors.

"Where? Where are you taking me?" Rose said as he restrained her inside the back of the ambulance.

"To the hospital. Hush, ma'am. You're weak, and you don't want to lose the baby."

"Patty? Where's Patty?" Rose cried, hearing the man slam the back door shut and get up front and start the engine. Driving back to *his* hospital, Dr. Victor Vreeland radioed the morgue telling them that he had selected her body to study the death of her and her baby more closely and would be back to inspect Mr. Galloway's body at a later time. And on that very day, he became Rose Galloway's savior, doctor, and, above all, her captor.

The woman screaming after she'd given birth in the doomed room on the top floor shown in the film Dr. Stanley Sinardi was watching had long gray hair. She was chained to her bed—the same bed her daughter Patty was now in.

A determined look came over Dr. Sinardi, and he grinned at the black television where Ed Savage's story had just been showing. Clicking on the file to close the video on his computer, he ejected the flash drive and dropped it back in the drawer, and then he grabbed both of them and looked up at the poster behind his office door from his *Phantom Finder* days. He then got up from his desk and moved to the window and looked up to see Patty's room on the top of the East Tower. He clutched the flash drives in his hands and knew he was glad he'd saved it.

Dr. Sinardi hated his life and this place he was in, and he thought back to what could have been. With nothing but the tattered remains of his psychiatric license left, Dr. Stanley Sinardi returned to the only job he could find, working at Vreeland Hills Sanatorium—the hospital no one in their right mind would want to work at. And Dr. Stanley Sinardi had a score to settle.

CHAPTER 19

That particular Vreeland doctor who had finally been set free from his abusive family felt like a new man. Life since leaving New York had been good for Dr. Todd Vreeland, until the earthquake in Chile, South America changed all that. It had been years since he'd left Vreeland Hills Sanatorium, and the strange part of his leaving was *how* his life had changed. It was like he was a different man; gone were the murderous thoughts that seemed to manifest as the long years went on working with his family—just being away from *that* building seemed to lift the heavy shroud from his thoughts until he felt like he was living like he was supposed to be, like everyone else, he thought. He'd even stopped drinking. It was almost like a feeling of having two personalities like *Dr. Jekyll and Mr. Hyde,* yet, in the many years away, not once had he ever had those horrible dark thoughts—even the nightmares had stopped.

Still wearing the clothes from the double funeral of his daughter and wife, whom he'd finally met in Chile, he got out from his car, leaving the door open so he could hear his radio playing. He walked up to his daughter's favorite climbing tree with the tire swing she'd loved to play on and where they'd picnicked in a park on a hill overlooking the city of Concepción. He then climbed up to the same exact branch where he'd sat with his new family, and he could see the old stone market in the distance—the market he'd sent them to that afternoon the earthquake struck, trapping them inside when the stone building collapsed, crushing them to death.

Todd looked back over his miserable life, from the countless countries he'd practiced medicine in to finally landing in Chile and feeling like this was the place he could call home. Getting work in the many hospital's he'd worked had been easy due to his schooling and skills. Even his practice had changed. All his years of trying to craft his neurosurgical skills to shine in his father's and *his brother's* eyes had been hard for him when his passion was orthopedic surgery. Since leaving New York, he followed that passion and became a top physician in that field and also taught in the many less privileged hospitals he'd worked in. And each time he gave notice they all wanted him to stay, but Todd had to move on, not wanting to stay in one place for too long. All that changed when he got married and celebrated the birth of his daughter, and as the years passed his feeling of needing to *run* evaporated—just like his new family did the day the earth shook.

As he sat quietly in the tree, his radio played "The Sound of Silence," a song he'd loved when he'd first heard it originally by Simon and Garfunkel. However, now it was angrier, like his mood, and the artist was named Disturbed, which was exactly how he was feeling. When he looked out in the park, in the distance he saw a father with his three boys flying a kite and heard them cheer when they got it to soar up into the sky. Todd smiled, thinking of his two brothers, Blake and Eric; listening to the lyrics of the song; and thinking back to his old life in New York—and how it all could have been so different from the hell it had been and why he'd left in the first place. The evil in his past life at home seemed like he was looking at a totally different person than he was now when he recalled the horrors of his past, and he felt that karma had come back to bite him back—hard—by taking his family.

The firestorm that had ripped through Wildwood Meadows near Vreeland Hills Sanatorium all those years ago was the perfect alibi for the sniveling little brother of the head of the hospital. Dr. Todd Vreeland hated his older brother Dr. Blake Vreeland, and even though he'd tried over the years to make things right, the two just never saw eye to eye for more than a short period of time. Dr. Todd, as he liked to be called because his mother always called him that, hated his self-righteous, superior older brother Blake, who was not only his father's "golden son" but the state's top brain surgeon specializing in his own secretly performed lobotomies. The coming fire had been unavoidable, but the choices made until that fateful day could have been entirely different.

Vreeland Hills Sanatorium housed the most violent criminals of the time, patients the Vreeland brothers loved performing midnight surgeries on in the hidden operating rooms of the basement. The cold, dark rooms were near the torture devices they kept down there for the unwilling madmen trapped in a hell of their own making. But one of the nastiest memory's came from the top-floor operating room, and it haunted him constantly.

It had been so perfect; no one would ever believe or care what these people had to say, and their sinister acts that played out in delivering them to the sanatorium were nothing compared to what was waiting for them once inside the dark and impenetrable walls of the hospital.

For a time, the brothers got along like Dr. Frankenstein and Igor. Dr. Todd was always studying his brother's notes and trying to please both him and their father, Victor Vreeland, with his own brand of midnight madness in the basement. But when Blake was called out of state to lecture on the so-called wellness he provided, Todd had taken it upon himself to step into his brother's shoes as leading physician.

The patient had been the sister of a prominent congressman whose father secretly took her in the middle of the night against his wife's wishes. Dr. Todd Vreeland admitted the influential patient into the hospital and gave her the best room there. He had assured her father that his brother would be back in a few days to perform the surgery and that it was best for her to be left there alone to get adjusted to the hospital without any outside interference. All this was for her benefit, he told them.

With the family away and a few days before his asshole brother would return, Dr. Todd went on a bender of tequila, cocaine, and sex (with some of his unwilling patients). And during his functional alcoholic behavior, he decided it was time for his name to be entered in the history of the hospital. By nightfall the next day, with hardly any sleep and sedatives laced in his patient's food, bringing the poor woman to the spacious operating room was the easiest part of the fiasco that followed on that tequila-driven night.

Entering the private sixth-floor operating room, Dr. Todd saw Nurse Pam and Bob, a part-time smart-alecky X-ray tech who had also helped out as an orderly. Bob was helping the anesthesiologist move the patient from the gurney to the operating room table. Seeing things were moving along well, he went to the scrub area and grabbed a mask, tying it behind his head. He could smell the tequila on his breath inside his mask as he went to the scrub sink and scrubbed his hands like he'd never before, focused on making sure everything was perfect. His nurse put on sterile gloves and began to prep the patient. He then came into the room, holding up his hands like he was the king; his scrub tech, Lorena Mason, was there to gown him.

Hearing the squeaking wheels of the gurney slowly moving away from the table, a habit that fucker X-ray tech seemed to love to do to irritate the esteemed doctor, Todd grimaced under his mask as he thought of the painful way he was going to murder him. "Hey, fuck stick! Hang around and watch this one. I may want an X-ray," he said, suddenly knowing he just wanted Bob to watch the horrifying surgery that would be the cause of his own demise.

"Why would you need an X-ray?" Nurse Pam said. "You've never needed one before for these cases."

"Fuck you, Pam!" Dr. Todd barked. "I will not be questioned."

"Question this," Pam said, holding up her middle finger.

Dr. Todd laughed, glaring at the woman he loved being a total dick to—when he wasn't giving one to her.

With the patient finally ready and Dr. Todd thinking the sedatives were strong enough until the cutting of her skullcap began, Dr. Todd ordered his obedient lapdog anesthesiologist, Marvin Newman, to keep it light because he wanted an awake craniotomy with lobotomy, so she could see it happening to add to her torment—and he wanted it to be painful. "No lidocaine with the propofol either. I want it to burn," Dr. Todd said, feeling the tequila lighting up his own blood.

The functioning alcoholic bastard moved about his patient like he had so many times before; sober or obliterated in a blackout drunk, he'd somehow managed to keep it under control over the years, but tonight he'd been snorting cocaine in order to make this the surgery of all surgeries.

After he sliced open her forehead and separated the skin from her skull, he turned on the electric cutting saw, watching it spin and testing it on the metal mallet from his surgical tool set in front of his patient so she could see the spark. He watched her eyes move in absolute shock and horror and paused to prolong the torment as he sang his tune for the operating room. Either he'd "Dooo-be-dooo-be-doo-doo " to the words of a song on the radio or make up his own tune under his mask; that was the only endearing trait the man possessed when performing the atrocities raging in his malignant mind. He then proceeded to cut her skull open.

The pain was instant, and she bucked on the table. Dr. Todd nodded to Marvin, who was reading a *Penthouse* magazine. "Hey, dummy! She's too light. Take her down a bit," Dr. Todd ranted. "But not too far down—I want her to *enjoy* this."

The flustered anesthesiologist dropped the magazine and quickly grabbed the filled syringe of propofol and injected more into the IV line; together they watched her movements subside.

"That's it, my dear," Dr. Todd cooed in his sinister, playful way. He then whacked her upside the head with the mallet and laughed under his mask when her eyes flinched open. He then raised the bone saw and began cutting away part of the skull to get to the frontal lobe of the brain.

Of course, he *had* to do it this way for the scar, to show the family how he'd performed the lobotomy. But what he preferred was the old-fashioned way—the icepick lobotomy method entering above the orbits of the eyes—and that's how he performed it. The other was just for show and terror and, of course, pain, like he did with his other failed surgeries. But this time would be different.

"Okay, the cutting's done. Bring her back up," Dr. Todd ordered.

Slowly he watched her stir to a heightened state when he looked to Marvin who nodded back from looking at the numbers on his monitor.

Carefully removing the portion of the skullcap, the tissue was pulled from his hands, and it slapped back on her open skull; her eyes shot open. Blood was dripping down between her eyes, and her arms raised from her restraints as the terror registered within her. She was seeing the madness of fingers grabbing at her skull and a small part of it being pulled away from her with strands of tissue snapping like bloody snot.

The alarming sound of the monitor indicated that her blood pressure was dropping. Dr. Todd silently fumed, waiting for the idiot administering the anesthesia—a man who'd kept all Todd's secrets—to do something about it. As he watched Marvin Newman fumble in the drug drawer and pick up the wrong drug—succinylcholine—his eyes blazed. "Not sux, you idiot. Ephedrine!"

Realizing his error Newman dropped the drug and grabbed the ephedrine and administered it. In the silence that followed (silent but for the shrill alarm coming from the monitor), they both watched their patient's numbers rise to a safe point to proceed with the surgery.

"Sorry about that, Doc," Newman muttered.

"Fuck you, Pam," Todd responded with authority and a quick, evil glance shot at Marvin as an insult—a joke he'd throw at anyone who raised his ire in the slightest, which came as a warning to most.

"I think you're making me wet," Nurse Pam said from her corner of the room, where she was charting the case. "And it's Pamela, asshole!"

"Let me know when I make your nipples hard!" Todd laughed. "Oh yeah, fuck you, Pam!" The doctor laughed and smiled under his mask feeling aroused when he gazed at Pam across the room. "I'll need you to report to my office after surgery," he said.

Pam looked up and saw his bloodshot eyes over his mask. "Not tonight! I won't be your sloppy third or fourth, and fuck you too!" She laughed. "Besides, I'd rather have a big one like your brother Blake's than your dwarf dick."

"Fuck you, Pam!" Dr. Todd shouted in anger, feeling the sting of her words in the room with all eyes on him. She knew he was overly blessed and commented on how she liked it being "beer-can thick" in bed several times, but the bitch was going to be taught a lesson, he thought, as his team of imbecilic misfits he lorded over obeyed his every command. He knew he couldn't trust a damn one of them to not run to his brother Blake once he returned, but with this case he didn't care. In fact, he wanted them to run.

"Have another ephedrine on hand, and I want no further interruptions! Now take her back down." Todd barked, happy that she'd seen him pulling away part of her skull. He watched Marvin Newman place another syringe next to his monitor as he adjusted the gas and injected more drugs into her IV. The moment seemed like an eternity for the doctor as he watched his patient's eyes roll back into her head, and he calmly continued the lobotomy portion of the surgery.

After he'd broken the orbital bone with the icepick and extracted a portion of the frontal lobe, finishing the lobotomy portion of the surgery, he went back to the top of her skull and removed the layers to the brain and suctioned out a portion. As the time passed and the chunks of brain were removed, he flung the pieces to the floor, where they landed amid flies. And as he removed the last of the infected part of her brain (what he'd told her father that his brother, the arrogant doctor, would be doing), he ordered the other patient to be rolled closer to the patient on the table.

Obeying his orders, Nurse Pam pushed back the curtain that separated the operating bays, and there was the lumberjack killer laid out on a gurney. Green sterile drapes covered his blood-soaked head, and as she whipped them back, she pulled a surgical sponge stuck inside his head with it—sending a chunk of tissue flying with the drapes along with a few flies that scattered from the dying man's skull.

"Easy there, Pam. I'm going to make you beg for it when we're done." Dr. Todd laughed as he lowered his bloody gloved hand down his belly in a pointing motion.

Pam did have a thing for the guy, and at one time Dr. Todd had told her he loved her. But Pam also enjoyed his brother, and the two of them would always laugh behind his back over it. Smiling with her eyes and smirking under her mask, she pushed the gurney over to the table. She then pulled the remaining drapes from over the lumberjack's head, revealing his open skull for Dr. Todd to select just the right portion of brain to be transplanted. He violently dug into the lumberjack killer's head and cut out just the right size, not noticing the maggots worming their way deeper inside the tissue. As he was doing this, the flies from the floor in the operating room landed in the young woman's brain. Two of them buzzed inside her, and when the good doctor moved back to her, he carefully placed the freshly cut brain inside her head over the two flies that had gotten caught in her bleeding tissue, completely missing the insects.

After carefully packing the new brain tissue inside her, he silently prayed the connective tissue would do its job. He then finished up and replaced the skull piece over her brain and stapled it together; then he drew back her scalp and closed the wound, stitch by stitch, all the while looking right into her open, terrified eyes, singing that usually endearing "Dooo-be-dooo-be-doo-doo" melody he constantly sang in the operating rooms. And when he was finally finished, he pulled down his mask with his bloody gloved hand and smiled at her.

After ordering Pam and Marvin to take her to recovery, he looked at the lumberjack killer still on the gurney and laughed when he saw the frightened look in Bob's eyes; he'd watched the entire thing. "Just think what I'll do to you when you really piss me off!" Todd shouted. "Now get the fuck out of here," he ordered.

Todd knew the little fucker would run right to Blake when he got back and tell on him, and he couldn't wait to put the blades to him for doing it. But, for now, he had to deal with the lumberjack killer. His lists were endless.

Admiring the instrument sticking out of his other patient's head, which he'd used to bore into his brain, Dr. Todd moved to an old elevator and pulled open its metal cage doors in the operating room with his favorite song "The Sound of Silence," in his mind. "Dooo-be-dooo-be-doo-doo," Dr. Todd sang the tune looking into the pitch-black darkness of the elevator shaft. The pit seemed to be hungry. Moving back to his victim, he grabbed the instrument sticking out from his patient's head and dug down with all his might, watching the barely alive man buck in his restraints on the gurney. He then dragged the gurney, hearing the wheels turn and squeak, reminding him of how much he wanted to kill that other fucker, until he was next to the open elevator door. Pausing a moment to admire his work, he released the restraints and reached down to the near-full syringe leading to the line in his patient's arm and injected the remaining contents into him.

It only took a moment for the drug to work, and when the lumberjack killer opened his eyes, Dr. Todd was holding something above his head, and it *hurt*.

Todd laughed, watching the killer's eyes look toward him as he pulled the instrument from his brain. Scooping out a portion, he then flexed his hand, letting the brain contents splat onto the frightened man's face. He then kicked the gurney sideways and slammed it up against the doorway, which was now a pit of sorts from the broken-down elevator shaft. He shoved the body from the gurney, listening to it fall from the sixth floor to the ground and hearing the cracking sounds of his bones when he hit the bottom.

Now he could celebrate. After stripping off his bloody gown and washing his hands, he reached in his pocket and pulled out a vial, giving himself a bump of cocaine before retiring to his private office on the same floor to retrieve his tequila. He turned on his "screaming devil music" (as Bob the X-ray tech called his heavy-metal tunes) and enjoyed the high of the evening, waiting for Pam to join him after she and Lorena cleaned up the mess in the operating room.

With the music blaring and enjoying it in his altered state, he had no idea that in the time that'd passed since he'd finished the surgery, the woman's father had arrived—along with his brother, the great Blake Vreeland.

CHAPTER 20

r. Blake Vreeland was surprised to see the congressman's father pull up behind him when he arrived home early from his trip. And when the man told him he was there to check on his daughter, he was equally surprised that she was already there. Seeing her empty grand room on the fifth floor for the special guests of the hospital, he'd then learned she'd been sent to the sixth-floor recovery ward, and they rushed to check on her. When they saw her, it was an epic fright.

In the hours since her surgery, she had regained consciousness from the light sedation but was in a drooling, rabid state. She had torn one of her restraints free and had dug at the itching in her eye, ripping it out, letting the maggots drip from inside her head. The infested slime had dried on her gown, and she was eating it.

Her father gasped at the sight, and Dr. Blake Vreeland knew exactly what had happened. He also knew he'd have to keep this horror within the walls of the hospital. In a panic he ran to the woman and held her down in her bed, ordering her father to assist him. Not knowing what was happening, her father aided the doctor. Blake moved quickly to the dispensary in the ward and procured a syringe, filling it with just the drug he needed.

He returned just as his younger brother Dr. Todd Vreeland entered the room.

"What the fuck have you done?" Blake shouted.

"Pretty impressive isn't—it." Todd nearly choked when he saw the disastrous results from the surgery he'd just performed. "How can this be?" he shouted back, realizing what Blake was trying to do. In the commotion, he ran to his patient, grabbing her father's arms from behind and pulling them back as his brother slammed the needle into his heart. Dr. Todd watched the man turn to him with the shocking and confusing events cross the poor victim's face, and he smiled knowing he'd told him his daughter would be in the best of hands. The young woman's father finally slumped over his own bleeding, mad daughter.

"Quick, get him on a gurney," Blake ordered. "There's not much time."

"There's time," Todd slurred. Blake could smell the tequila.

"You're killing me, Stubs," Blake shouted. "Now move."

Todd felt the wind hit his face, and when he came out from his thoughts, Disturbed's "The Sound of Silence" was nearing its end. He heard the young boys laughing with the kite not far from him, but all he could see was Blake's rage-filled face from that ugly day.

The anger and pain from the day he'd gotten that moniker "Stubs" ignited his blood, transforming it to acid. He remembered handing his brother the wrong instrument during a crucial moment when Blake was showing off for their father, Dr. Victor Vreeland.

"Not a fifteen-blade you idiot! A ten-blade! Blake shouted, throwing the blade at the metal mayo stand where Todd's hand was resting next to the ten-blade he needed.

Watching Blake grab the correct blade, he saw him pause, dropping the blade and grabbing the bone cutter, stepping on the foot-pedal bringing the deadly weapon to life, and nearly slicing off his hand on the metal mayo stand, where it was still resting.

Blood pooled at the top of his hand under his glove, and he pulled it back, watching his blood flow down his arm. "You bastard!" Todd cried, as he watched both his brother and father laugh at him when he grabbed a clean towel to stop the bleeding.

"You're worthless," Todd's father sneered at him. "Blake, cauterize it," he ordered, handing a clean Bovie to the operating field.

Blake peeled off his outer layer of bloody gloves to the clean ones underneath them. He then tossed the Bovie plug off to his father and watched him plug it in as he turned to his dimwit brother. "Move the damn towel!"

Todd winced but knew if he didn't follow orders, his father would kill him. He pressed the towel down hard to absorb as much blood as he could and then pulled it away as Blake took the hot cauterizing tip and seared the top of his hand where he'd cut him.

Todd cried out like a wimp to the laughter from the others but had no idea the worst was yet to follow. Blake despised his little brother, the darling of their late mother, and grabbed the alcohol prep sponge near the field and squeezed it out as he was cauterizing the wound for the second time. He laughed harder as the flames erupted on his brother's hand, watching Todd pull away, crying like a baby.

"Get away from the patient!" his father yelled. "You're contaminating everything!"

"Dad, I need you to scrub in," Blake asked, almost begging.

"That's *my* patient," Todd cried out as he ran to the scrub sink to put out the flames.

"Get that little prick out of my sight," Blake ordered.

Todd Vreeland grabbed a towel and wrapped his hand as he moved back to the operating room table. He could see his smug older brother standing over his patient. His muscled arms that his brother admired so much moved in a mad rush as their father grabbed Todd from behind and yanked him backward with a force that caused him to fall to the ground, hitting his elbow in just the right spot sending pain shooting through him.

Victor Vreeland then moved over to a scrub sink, sprayed some disinfecting hand scrub into his palms, and rubbed them together as he moved to the scrub table and picked up his gown.

Todd got up to tie his gown, but the anesthesia doctor shoved him out of the way and tied up the grand doctor of Vreeland Hills Sanatorium himself. With his hand stinging and wrapped in a towel, a nurse led him away from the table to a corner of the operating room, where she cleaned his hand and stitched him up.

The ugly memories flashed through Todd's mind—always being considered less than the great Blake Vreeland. He looked to the scar on the back of his hand that was his constant reminder. He then heard the children with the kite yell out as their kite dive-bombed to the ground, and they started yelling at the younger one who had been flying it. Watching the two older one's push the smallest to the ground, and the father rushing up to stop the quarrel. From high up in that tree, it was like he was watching a fight he'd lived through before.

Gritting his teeth, Todd remembered the rest of that ugly night when he'd grabbed a gurney, and together the brothers got the girl's father up and stripped him of his clothes. They then pushed him into the hall toward the operating room. In Dr. Blake's mind, he wanted to perform a partial brain transplant into his prized patient, the lumberjack killer. And when he called his favorite Nurse Pam to fetch the patient, the look on her face alarmed him.

"You!" Blake hissed at his brother.

"Fuck you!" Todd yelled back in defiance. "The surgery will still work."

"Are you fucking kidding me?" Blake yelled back. "Maggots are seeping from her brain. She's the living dead right now."

"We'll open her back up. Suction the shit out of her!" Todd pleaded.

"No, it's too late for her. Where's the lumberjack?"

Blake watched his brother's eyes look through the wide-open operating room double doors, straight to the door of the pit they threw away the dead in, which was still open.

Realizing his prized serial killer was dead, Blake charged Todd and slammed him against the wall. The two brothers fought and tumbled from the hall into the operating room. Grabbing instruments, they slashed at each other, drawing blood. Todd slashed his brother's face, slicing his cheek; Blake swung his arm, coming down like a hammer and hitting the back of Todd's hand, making him drop the blade and punched him in the face. Seeing him turn from the hit, he then grabbed him from behind and threw his vile younger brother into the darkness of the pit. And after catching his breath, he ordered Nurse Pam to select the next patient on his list to bring in for surgery.

"But your...face, Doctor?"

Blake reached up and felt the blood on his cheek where Todd had slashed at him. "Damn that bastard!" Blake barked, eyeing the blood on his hand.

"Let me stitch that up first; then I'll get your patient," Pam said, seeing the sadness within the man she mended.

Todd remembered feeling lucky that day, falling against the few remaining cables a floor below and hearing Pam with his brother as he hung on for dear life. Now he felt like his life was over, and he looked out over the city of Concepción and knew it was time to move on.

CHAPTER 21

When Ed arrived back at Savage Tower, he checked his messages and was surprised he hadn't heard back from Jillian. He remembered her in his office earlier and something she had said about an exhibition. Searching on his computer, he entered Trenten York's name and the word *exhibition*, and there he was. The firstborn son of Ed Savage stared out at him from his computer screen. Finding this so easily on the Internet angered him for not knowing about it sooner. But the anger melted away as he looked at the young man on the screen. Yes, it was his son, and the resemblance was strong. He could see it clearly, and the emotion flooded over him. "Teddy," Ed said out loud in his office, "my boy."

He didn't realize just how long his cell phone was ringing as he stared at the photograph of his son who'd been kept from him for all these years. When he did notice the ringing, he dug it from his pocket, and his voice was barely there when he saw it was from Zolie's home.

"Hello." His voice was shaking, letting the caller know something was off.

"Ed, honey, are you all right? You sound upset."

Hearing Marlo's voice brought him back, and he looked away from his computer. "Yeah, I'm fine; it's been a hell of a day. What's up?" he asked, not wanting to say what he was now feeling over seeing Teddy Trenten Savage.

"Ed, it's Sam," Marlo said, her voice now also filled with worry. "Zolie just called from his home over on our old street. He's bad, Ed. And they're bringing him home."

"Who's bringing him home with her?"

"Maura went with her; Heather called the Kellers, and they told her his truck was in their driveway. I don't know what time he went over there, but Zolie said his state of mind is bad, and they're bringing him home now."

Ed was torn; he looked at the computer screen, and everything in him told him to go to his son right away. Yet the closest person in his life was in trouble, and he needed to get to him immediately. "I'm on my way home, Marlo. Call me with any news, and I'll see you shortly."

Hanging up the phone, Ed printed the page with Gallery 26's address on it, along with his son's photo, and as he waited for the printing to finish, he took a photo of his son with his phone from his computer screen. His heart was heavy, but he knew where to find him, and once he made sure Sam was okay, he was going straight to find his son.

Just as Ed pulled the page from the printer, his cell phone rang again, and he saw it was Tallulah. Ed answered, eyeing his cane. "Tallulah, what did you find?"

"Are you on your way over here? I've got the physical address of the PO box and the name of the woman that opened it."

"Woman?"

"Yes, a Ming Yuki."

"Ming?"

"Yes, do you know that name?"

"Yes. Well…no. Sally Anne came back and told Roman and Logan she remembered a woman with a name similar to that, a Mingyu something…she couldn't remember her last name, but she was with my father in his office."

"Ed, let me have a talk with Sally Anne; I'll get everything out of her. Bring her over with you."

"Tallulah, no, now's not the time. Something's come up, and I can't. I'm headed home, and I have to go now." The tone in his voice told her it was important, and she knew not to pry.

"Call me when you can."

Ed hung up his cell and stuffed it in his pocket. Gathering together the printout of his son's exhibition and his cane, Ed hurried home to Sam.

CHAPTER 22

W hen Ed arrived home, it was a circus under the dark sky. He entered the main house and was immediately swarmed by the Savage children. All but one of the twelve Savage cousins was there. The french doors to the pool and guesthouses were open, and he could hear his brother's cries. He ran down the path to his brother and was stopped by his daughter Ava.

"Daddy, you have to help him. He's lost it," she said, looking scared.

Ed nodded and told her to get to the main house. Heading to the front door of the guesthouse, he opened it, startling everyone inside.

There Sam was, wearing his wedding tuxedo and clutching his dead wife's blood-spotted wedding dress. He was backed in a corner, and the hurt on his face was something Ed had never seen before in his life. His younger brother, his confidant throughout his entire life, was in a tailspin headed directly for a fiery crash.

When Sam looked past the others in the room and saw his other brother, Ed, the shame hit him at once, and he bolted for the stairs to the second-floor art studio with a beautiful view of the grounds. Gabby, Roman, and Logan were right behind him, and Ed followed, hearing the commotion of the door hitting a wall and Gabby raising her voice, telling him to stop.

Sam got to the sliding glass door and opened it when the others ran into the bedroom. He bumped into the balcony table and chairs, knocking them over as he tried to make it to the railing. He stepped onto a chair, and Gabby reached for him, pulling him back just as Roman and Logan got to him and helped keep their brother from going over the railing. Sam yelled out, losing his balance. In doing so, he let go of the wedding dress, and the wind blew it down into the garden, like an elegant ghost floating in the air. Unfortunately, the phantom headed down to where the sprinklers had come on, matting it into the muddy ground, furthering its destruction in front of every Savage cousin that had disobeyed their parents and had come to watch the misery play out. And as they watched from below, Sam Savage was pulled back from the railing just as they heard Ed get there. The brothers caught him, breaking his fall to the stone balcony floor below.

It was over as quickly as it seemed to begin for Ed when he opened the door downstairs. Sam covered his face and curled up in a fetal position. He was shaking all over, in part from shame and in part from the mixture of booze and whatever pills he'd taken at his house. When Ed pulled him up into his arms, pills spilled from his brother's torn pocket onto the floor, and everyone saw them.

Gabby picked one up and looked at it. "What are these?"

Maura, Zolie, and Marlo were the last to come up the stairs, and Maura remembered seeing some of the pills at Sam's home in the hall bathroom with the torn bandages covering the floor.

"Let me see that," she said, reaching out to Gabby for the pill. "These were at his house. I saw them on the floor of the hall bathroom."

Ed grabbed his brother's face and squeezed his cheeks. "What did you take, Sam? What pills did you take at home?"

"Found some of dad's old aspirin; my head was throbbing," Sam mumbled as the adrenaline left his body and the shaking grew more violent.

Ed could feel the rage inside his brother immediately abate and the frantic chills course through his body. "How many did you take, Sam?" Ed barked at his brother. "How many?"

Sam moaned and held up four trembling fingers in response.

"Are you sure that's all you took?" Ed said, looking right into his eyes.

But Sam's eyelids closed, and he passed out in his brother's arms.

"Come on, Roman, grab his feet. Logan, help me get him into bed," Ed ordered, feeling the cool wind pick up.

"Shouldn't we get him to the hospital?" Maura said.

"Yes, but it's too cold out here for him," Ed said, wanting to get him safely inside.

"Come on, let's get him downstairs on the sofa until we can get a car over here," Roman said as he and his brothers got Sam up and back into the guesthouse.

The women followed, and it was Gabby who found the open bottle of pills on the floor; she grabbed the small orange bottle. A single pill was still inside, and the label told her the medication was OxyContin. "Oh God, Ed, it's OxyContin," she cried. "It's not aspirin; this is so much worse. And he's been drinking!"

"Is someone getting a car?" Ed barked when Marlo came out from one of the downstairs bedrooms with blankets, and they covered Sam and stayed by him until Logan arrived outside, honking the horn on the side driveway to the guesthouse.

When they got him up yet again to get him in the car, the younger Savages had gathered and watched in horror as Sam was placed in the vehicle. Little Lisa was confused, and Marlo was mad as hell that Ava let her come down there. But it was Heather who saw her mother's wedding dress getting wet in the dirt from the sprinklers and using one of her crutches she pulled it away, trying to wipe the filth from her mother's beautiful gown.

Chet put his arms around his sister, and they all watched Ed, Roman, and Logan pile into the car with Sam and take him back to the hospital that too many members of their family had spent too much time in recently.

CHAPTER 23

Mia Delgado's family had been torn apart way before she made that ill-fated decision to go up to Black Ridge Falls with her friends, and now it was completely obliterated. Her parents had divorced when she was young, and after giving her daughter her maiden name wanting nothing to remind her of her abusive affair with her dad, her mom dropped her off at her aunt's house one day, never to return. Raised by her aunt Raquel Delgado, it had been the two of them against the world. In her grieving, Raquel saw the headline "Bastard Son Wins Daddy Lottery" and learned that afternoon that Ed's son had grown up just like Mia had.

To say misery loved company might have been appropriate had Raquel had someone to share her grieving with. After one bad relationship after another, with the last one resulting in a restraining order, it was best for her, or so she thought, to withdraw for a while and focus on raising Mia. Now alone at her home, she realized her "a while" time had turned into three whole years.

Sitting at home with her hair up, in her robe, watching the news with the curtains drawn, she got up and opened them in the living room and realized she'd never seen the sun that day. Eyeing the stack of mail on the table, more on the floor beneath the mail slot in the door, her clothes thrown over chairs, and the empty wine bottles too many to count, she shuddered. "Ay, Dios mio," Raquel said, holding her robe close to her chest. She picked up a bottle and moved to the kitchen. Throwing it away, she started to tidy up while remaining in her trancelike state.

An hour later she was upstairs adding bubble bath to her running tub, candles were lit near a full glass of wine, and behind her on her freshly remade bed were several pretty dresses lying out as if she were planning on going out for the evening.

CHAPTER 24

Across town at Zolie's compound, Zolie and Maura were having a private moment in Zolie's bedroom sitting area and enjoying some tea. The women were shaken after the day's events with Sam, and they were glad he was now getting the help he needed.

Looking at her tea in frustration, Maura pushed it away and sat back on the small sofa. "I knew he was having a time of it, but I never dreamed it was this bad."

The bond of the three sisters was strong, yet they also knew how much Sam and Cara had been in love with each other. "Maybe now that he got that out of his system, he can move forward," Zolie said as if wishing it out loud.

"I don't know what's going to be worse for him; the kids saw him up on that balcony, and he must have seen them too. Dealing with the grief is one thing; being embarrassed is quite another," Maura said.

Zolie put down her tea and looked away in thought.

"What is it?" Maura asked.

"Was I wrong?" Zolie said, looking at her sister, her face filled with concern. "Was I wrong to have everyone come here? If I hadn't, then no one would have witnessed that. The last thing I'd want is to add to Sam's torment."

"No, you weren't wrong, Zolie. But realistically it can't last forever."

"You're right about that. I overheard Marlo on the phone to her lawyer about that damn show. She's doing it, you know."

"Did you know Cara had signed on?" Maura asked.

"She talked to me about it." Zolie picked up her tea. "You know, I watched a few episodes with her, and I saw Andrew on it. He still looks as good as the day I left him," Zolie said with a laugh.

"Have you spoken with him since?"

"Not really. We crossed paths at a charity event some years ago, and he was with this new woman that's on the show, Marilyn Caspian. They're married now."

"I read about that name...wasn't she married to the man at Global Film and Television who got in trouble for insider trading?"

"Yes, she was, but I don't really know her."

At that moment there was a knock at her door.

"Yes," Zolie answered.

Amanda opened the door and peeked inside. "Here you are."

"Come in and have some tea with us," Maura suggested with a warm smile.

"I'll pass, thank you. I just wanted to tell you I was going out for a bit," Amanda said, entering the room and closing the door behind her.

Amanda sat down, and Zolie looked at the cast on her forearm. "I want that off you. I'm tired of seeing it and dealing with the memories that come with it."

Amanda held up her arm. "Oh, come on, Mother; I bet you have a Gucci scarf that will look smashing with my outfit."

Maura started laughing, and soon all three of them were sharing in the moment.

"Where are you off to?"

"I'm meeting Jacqueline for drinks at Gabby's place. She's celebrating the huge order she got from Donert's Department Store."

"Donert's! Good for her," Maura said.

"Yeah, not only are they doing it up with a big new display at their flagship store, but they're spotlighting several pairs in all their stores," Amanda said.

"And what of your clothing line?" Zolie asked.

"Nothing yet, Mother—one thing at a time."

"Zolie, Madeline Roberts is also on *Tycoon Wives*, isn't she?" Maura said, stirring the pot from their earlier conversation.

"I don't like where you're going with this." Zolie's quick wit read her sister's mind.

"I just recall Cara telling me how much she enjoyed meeting Madeline at a dinner with Sam; that was well before the company lost Donert Tower."

"I love Don and Madeline Roberts, but this whole *Tycoon Wives* business I want nothing to do with, Andrew Hart included," Zolie said, looking from Maura to Amanda. "But darling, your clothes would look wonderful in their stores."

"I don't know what web you two are spinning up here in your boudoir, Mother, but I'll be making it on my own," Amanda said with a laugh. "Anyway, just wanted to tell you I won't be here for dinner."

Getting up and moving to the door, she stopped and looked back to see the two women whispering to each other. "Enough, ladies!"

Caught like two virgins on prom night exchanging gossip, the two women laughed once more.

As the door closed and the laughter subsided, Maura leaned forward on the small sofa and adjusted the pillow. "Speaking of secrets, it was a complete shock to hear of Marlo's involvement with Cara and the restaurant."

"Cara always had a soft spot for that one," Zolie said. "Have you by chance spoken to Gabby about this? She's the one who knows more about restaurants than any of us."

"She was just as surprised as the rest of us. She and Marlo have always gotten along, and you know Marlo would sometimes help out at her restaurant in a crunch, but Gabby never heard a word."

"Marlo slinging hash—now, *that* I'd pay to see." Zolie laughed.

"What do you think of the new restaurant's name being Savages?"

"Savages!" Zolie paused for a moment. "Of course, this was before that massive mess in the mountains, but it might work, grisly as that was. Did Cara name it, I wonder?"

"I wanted to ask Marlo about that myself, but I really haven't had a moment with her. She seems a little distant."

"Hmm, distant is a word for it. By the way, I have a little dirt on Marlo myself," Zolie said, picking up her tea and prolonging the intrigue.

"Oh, get on with it already. I hate it when you do that." Maura laughed at her sister.

Zolie looked to the door Amanda had just been at; then she side-eyed her sister. "Seems Mandy's friend Jacqueline was at Donert's a short time ago, and she saw Marlo there. Well, she was about to go over to her when Jillian got in Marlo's face, and the two went at it."

"No!"

"Oh, yes, darling, a couple of turned-up fishwives having a go at each other right near ladies' shoes. I'm so sorry I missed it." Zolie laughed.

"What was said?"

"Basically that Jillian was in Marlo's face about her child, the one she kept from Ed."

"What did Marlo do?"

"She ripped that simpering bitch to shreds and walked away the victor."

"Hmm, maybe this show *Tycoon Wives* will be a perfect fit for her. From some of the episodes I've seen, she'll fit right in. She's sure been keeping that bit to herself."

"Marlo's good at keeping secrets; that I'll give her. But I also wonder what else Cara was keeping from us…if anything," Zolie said.

CHAPTER 25

The partnership of Don Roberts and his wife, Madeline Stone, went past just being married. They were a supercouple. They'd met when they were young and fallen madly in love. She was with him from the beginning in that small boutique with a dream. Now, through the hard times and the good times, they ran Donert's Department Store together—it really was the American dream.

In her office, Madeline was going over the new design plans Jacqueline Holt's new shoe line was going to be displayed in. Looking for a file, she got up and opened the cabinet and paused, seeing the familiar first photo of Jacqueline's store. Pulling out the large photo, she leaned on the cabinet and smiled.

"What's got you so happy?" Don Roberts said as he entered his wife's office.

Madeline held the photo to her chest, and the look on her face reminded him of the young woman he had met all those years ago and fallen in love with.

"Here, take a look for yourself," she said, almost childlike.

Don reached for the photo and looked at it and recognized everything all at once. "Oh, you sentimental little girl," he said, dropping his hand with the photo to his side. With his other, he reached for her. "Come here, my beautiful love," he said and pulled her into his arms and kissed her.

Madeline kissed him back and looked him in the eyes. "It's uncanny, right?"

"It sure is close." Don took a second look at the photograph and placed it on top of the file cabinet.

The small boutique Jacqueline Holt started her business in was eerily similar to the one Don started in the very spot they were now in. Only now, after several remodels and acquiring the block, it was a much larger department store.

When Madeline had been in New York last year, cast as a Tycoon Wife, she had gone shopping with one of the other wives. And when they turned a corner in busy Manhattan, she saw it immediately. There, like in Port Roberts, was the small brick building with the flower boxes and the barbershop right next door, exactly like the small building she had spent so many hours in with Don, dreaming of making it big all those years ago.

"And here I thought we were taking in her shoe line because of her parents," Don said.

"Honey, I have to tell you. It was meant to be. And while we're on the subject…no, this has nothing to do with Jacqueline's parents. The girl has a real eye; her shoes are stunning."

"As long as you want it, I want it," Don said with a wink.

"Now take me to dinner. I'm starved," Madeline said with a slight laugh.

"Your chariot awaits, my love."

Don Roberts may have his name on the chain of department stores operating in several key cities, but Madeline was the powerhouse behind them. There wasn't one SKU in the entire store she didn't know about or personally choose. The team of Don and Madeline went way past husband and wife: they were not only truly in love with each other; they made one hell of a business partnership.

CHAPTER 26

Jacqueline Holt ordered her Manhattan up at the bar and immediately felt at ease listening to the comfortable jazz music. The shoe order she received was huge, and when she called her parents back home in London, they were thrilled for her. She checked her phone and saw a text from Amanda saying that she would be there in ten minutes.

At the entrance standing next to the hostess, Gabby hung up the phone with a worried look on her face. She had not heard from Roman about Sam since she left the house and received a call about some problem at the restaurant. Taking her coat off, a waitress came to her with an urgent plea regarding a disaster in the kitchen—water was flooding the dishwashing area—and she hurried to attend to the problem.

At that exact moment, Raquel Delgado entered and brushed right past the hostess, straight into the bar. She sat down around the corner of the bar from Jacqueline, and immediately ordered a glass of wine. The last time she was there she hadn't looked her best, but tonight she was stunning, wearing a long, sexy red dress that was a far cry from the drab, dark clothing she had been wearing on her previous visits. When she looked down the bar to gain the bartender's attention, he looked to the hostess, Gabby's sister Kimberly, who nodded her approval. With a slight hesitation, he took Raquel's order and poured her a glass of her favorite chardonnay.

When Raquel finished her wine in record time and ordered another, it was poured and reported to Kimberly at once. The whispered conversations behind her back were of nothing but concern; the woman was grieving, and the staff at Gabby's Jazz Club knew it. It was well known that Raquel had gone through a nasty separation several years ago, and it was just the two of them, her and her niece Mia, living in that big house all alone. The savage death of Mia Delgado at Black Ridge Falls was splashed all over the news, and it was a wonder her natural mother, who'd left Mia with her all those years ago, was not at her side at this fragile time in her life.

Jacqueline didn't know Raquel but noticed her when she arrived. Minutes later, Amanda showed up and found Jacqueline at the bar, and the two shared a celebratory hug when the bartender came over.

"I'll have what she's having," Amanda said as the duo caught up and the music played, Gabby noticed Amanda and went over to her.

"Hey there. I didn't know you were coming."

"Hi, Gabby. This was so last minute. I'd like you to meet my friend Jacqueline Holt. This is my aunt Gabby," Amanda said, making the proper introductions.

"Jacqueline, good to meet you. I've heard good things."

"Nice to meet you too," Jacqueline said. "I met your husband at Donert's with Amanda the other day."

Gabby's eyes looked to Amanda, watching her smile.

"Yes, Roman was there with Sam," Amanda said, causing both her and Gabby to lose their smiles almost immediately.

"I'm sorry; did I say something wrong?" Jacqueline asked.

"No, not at all," Gabby replied. "I tell you what: let me go get you some appetizers." She then looked up to the bartender when he returned with Amanda's drink. "Frankie, two more, and this is a house account," she said, pointing to their drinks. "I'll be back with something good," Gabby teased.

The girls laughed and were enjoying themselves when only a few minutes later, a glass broke down at the end of the bar. The two looked over to see Gabby's sister Kimberly moving quickly through the bar to the woman in red.

"No, I'm fine. Leave me alone," Raquel pleaded with the hostess when Gabby came from the kitchen. At that moment the phone behind the bar rang, and the bartender answered it, all the while keeping his eyes focused on Raquel.

"Just another chardonnay," the woman in red said a little too loudly, causing everyone in the bar to look her way.

Gabby went to Kimberly's side and waved a busboy to come over and pick up the broken pieces of glass.

"No more, Raquel. Time to go home," Kimberly said with a kind heart of understanding.

Watching this scene play out, Gabby was reminded of Sam just as the bartender approached her. "Gabby, phone—it's Roman."

Gabby looked over behind the bar and saw the light blinking on the phone. She looked to the bartender and then to Raquel.

"Go ahead; I've got this," Frankie assured her.

Moving to the phone, she picked it up, already dreading the news. "Roman, is Sam all right?"

"Sam's fine. He's sleeping right now. But his blood-alcohol content was too damn high."

"What about the pills?"

"Doc said he had more than four pills in him. But Sam said he took aspirin. God, I hope he *thought* he was taking aspirin! I don't even want to think along the other lines."

"Just one more chardonnay!" Raquel ordered, extending the word in a loud slurred voice over Kimberly's suggestion of coffee.

"What the hell was that?" Roman asked.

"It's Raquel, and it's still happening. God, I hate this night. I have to go, hon."

"I'll stop by and see you soon," Roman promised.

"Yes, I'd like that," Gabby said, hanging up the phone.

Gabby rushed to Raquel to talk with her, but when she looked into the woman's eyes and saw the utter destruction that awaited her there, she hugged her. Raquel broke down in tears, and they were able to get her out from the bar.

"Gabby, I'm afraid to call a cab. I'm scared for her," Kimberly said once they were out of the main area and got her sitting in a chair.

"I know," Gabby said. "Go get my purse in my office. I'll take her home."

"Are you sure?"

"Tell Roman to call me when he gets here."

Kimberly knew the look on her sister's face and hurried to get her purse.

Back at the bar, Jacqueline was amazed. "Who was that woman?"

Amanda looked at the cast on her arm and fidgeted a bit. "You don't want to know."

"No? All right then—let's change the subject," she said, taking a sip of her drink. "I've been wanting to tell you something."

"Oh?" Amanda said, reaching for her own glass and taking a drink.

"When we were at Donert's, meeting Roman and Sam, maybe I saw something that wasn't there. But when I shook Sam's hand, I *felt* something, and maybe Sam did too."

Amanda nearly choked on her drink. "He's old enough to be your father, you little tart!" Amanda coughed and caught her breath. "And he was married to my aunt! Oh, girl, you're going to hell on that one!" she said, laughing.

The friendship between Jacqueline and Amanda was long and strong, and they told each other pretty much everything, so this slightly odd remark Amanda took as being worth a grain of salt.

Despite this, given the timing, Jacqueline was slightly embarrassed and turned a shade of red. "Well, you know I have daddy issues, and he is handsome," she said, holding her hand to her face in shame.

"You're as red as Raquel Delgado's dress," Amanda said to her friend, not thinking.

"Delgado? Wait, wasn't that the name of Ava's friend that—" She stopped herself as she realized Raquel was the aunt of Mia, the young girl who'd died on that horrible night in the mountains.

Amanda took a deep breath and nodded. "Yeah, I didn't want to bring it up, but she's not the only one having a bad time of it."

Jacqueline realized immediately that all the while she had been gushing on about Sam, it was Sam who was in some sort of trouble. "Oh God, Amanda, what was I thinking? Is Sam all right?"

Amanda looked up at her friend and shook her head.

"And to think one crazy woman started all this," Jacqueline said.

"Which one? The mother or the daughter?"

Jacqueline held her drink and looked Amanda right in the eyes. "You're right! I never thought of it that way before. Good thing that crazy Patty is locked up tight."

"I'll drink to that!" Amanda said, lifting up her glass and thankful Patty was right where she belonged and unable to harm anyone anymore.

CHAPTER 27

The ketamine dart dosage Dr. Stanley Sinardi had injected into her shoulder was strong, and the hallucinations started almost immediately. But the new round of shots the nurse injected into her seemed even stronger. The pain combination of fentanyl and Versed had all but stopped her thrashing about, but that second injection had her seeing and hearing all sorts of things. The special K high mixed with the other drugs had her sweating, and it felt like the heat in the room was on much too high. Swooning from side to side in her bed and drooling, she could smell the stench of her own fetid breath on her soaked gown as she cried out for help. Even the soft, calming voice she had heard earlier was now calling her from the open bathroom door in her room, and the voice was angry. A night-light was on inside, and she imagined she saw the shadows from *the being* that called her. It was a woman's voice, and the shadow seemed to have long hair.

"You let them touch you, you little slut!" The screaming shrew's voice from the bathroom mocked her.

"Who's there? Who's in there?" Patty mumbled, gasping for air in the overheated state she was in.

The sound of the gas radiator in the room whistled with a loud hiss, frightening her, and she looked in the darkened room toward the sound. As her vision blurred, she thought she could see a brush on the counter that reminded her of the one she used to brush her mother's hair with. But *that* was impossible.

Even though it had been hours since she thought she had arrived and been locked away in this strange room, it felt familiar, but the heat was too much, and she thought she was going to be sick. The radiator, the drugs…she thought she was going to pass out when the sound from the door relieved her torment. Little did she know it was about to get worse.

The small set of eyes peeking through the tiny window in the door appeared once again. "Help me," she cried through her drugged haze. "It's too hot in here." The small window slammed shut, and she could hear the heavy locks being turned. As the door started to open, she began chanting in Latin again. "*Incendes, incendes*," she repeated, hearing the voice return to its calm tone in her head, telling her to burn him—joining with Patty in her strange mantra.

The man entered her room carrying a toolbox. Closing the door behind him, he locked it. He then moved over to the radiator and slammed down his metal toolbox on the hard floor with a loud bang. Patty screamed, and the man smiled. "Sorry, ma'am," he said, turning toward her and looking sincere. "I'll just be a few minutes here, and I'll have that heat all fixed up for you."

The man turned away and bent down, opening his toolbox. He knew she could not see him put the small bottle of cooking oil into his pocket. He then looked at the heater and started to fuss with it. He tried turning the knob, but it was stuck, and he picked up a small jar and pulled out the applicator and painted a lubricant around the base of the knob, when she screamed behind him, causing him to spill it down his arm and in his lap.

"Damn it!" he yelled, shaking the flammable chemical from his hand and feeling it hit his face. He grabbed his rag in his back pocket, smearing it; then he turned the knob, hearing it squeak and then freely turning, shutting off the heat. As the hissing of the radiator started to lessen, he got up and moved closer to Patty's bed.

"Incendes, incendes!" Patty mumbled, fighting the drugs inside her and unnerving the stranger.

He looked to her with a question on his face. "Crazy bitch," the man said and moved over to Patty and nudged her. "Shut up with your batty bullshit, lady!" he ordered.

The room was still warm, and he wiped his forehead of sweat as he leaned down on his prey and held her face away, kissing her neck. The man then opened his pants and with one hand held himself; with the other, he grabbed the back of Patty's neck. "Incendes on this!" He laughed as he let go of himself and reached for the cooking oil, twisting off the cap to pour some in the palm of his hand.

Patty arched her back and tightened her muscles; she felt his grip tightening on her neck, and he got to his knees on her bed and turned her toward him. She was scared, and something in her mind moved. It felt like ants moving around in her head, tickling her at first, and then it hurt, like the banging of a drum within her brain. "Incendes, incendes!" she shrieked, and the temperature went up in the room.

The man felt it at once. A hot flash slapped against him like boiling water being thrown into his face. Only there was nothing there. He let go of Patty and pulled his hands to his face, splashing the cooking oil on himself as he wiped the burning heat from his eyes. He stumbled back off the bed toward the radiator, his eyes stinging when he heard her again.

"Incendes, incendes," Patty repeated as the voice got louder in her mind, screaming like a banshee to burn him.

He opened his eyes to see her staring at him; rage and hatred filled her face as he heard the squeaky radiator knob start to turn on its own. He looked to it and saw it moving; then the scream pierced right through him as the explosive fire erupted behind him. He felt the air of the hot blast blow by him, and he turned to see the older woman in the doorway of the now-burning bathroom. She was desperately trying to turn on the faucets of the sink for water as the flames caught her strange clothing on fire. She was dressed in something that looked like an old and dated patient gown. And when the fire caught her long gray hair as she was slumped over the faucet, she screamed and pushed herself away from it. Turning, she stumbled into the doorway.

The man was frozen in fear. When he looked back at Patty, she was laughing at him. The woman reached out her hand to him and screamed for help. And as he looked from Patty to the poor burning woman, he watched her face change from an older woman into a demonic creature with rotting flesh. Before he could utter a scream for help, the line from the gas radiator snapped off, and the flame shot out, igniting the lubricant on his face and pants.

The man screamed out as the flames enveloped him. He ran to the locked door and tried in vain to open it. He could hear people on the other side of the door scrambling to get the door open to help him. He saw the eyes peek through the small window and the stunned face looking in; a woman screamed on the other side of the door. Losing the fight of his life, he stumbled back and fell to the hard floor, burning. The woman on fire—was she there? Did he really see the fire come from the radiator? Was it all in his mind, or was it *her*? The last thing he saw was Patty laughing at him as he reached out his hand for help.

The locked door was finally opened, and the staff ran inside just as his arm slumped to the floor in white-hot flames. There, the charred, smoking body of one of the orderlies was on the floor, his one hand reaching out toward Patty's bed. The flames quickly went out, and embers began to glow from his burned remains. Patty was restrained to her bed but screaming with hysterical delight at the sight. The panic grew when they noticed nothing else was burned. Everything seemed to be just as it had always been. It was as if the man had spontaneously combusted right there on the spot. The only thing that remained was a black outline of the evil soul that'd come with malice now marking the floor.

"This place *is* haunted!" The woman that had screamed gasped at the sight.

CHAPTER 28

The arm reached out from the grave, and Ed shook the ugly thoughts away as he was sitting at Sam's side, watching his poor brother sleep. Ed's mind went to his father's grave. There he imagined his arm reaching out from the dirt to fuck with their lives once more, to mess with the only son that housed him after all the horrible things he'd done to them—and God knew how many others—during his miserable life on earth.

Logan was with him, and when he spoke, it was like he was reading Ed's mind. "The one who cared for him the most is now hurting the most," Logan said.

At that moment, when Roman entered Sam's room, Sandy Storm was walking the halls on her last night in the hospital and saw him go in. "Hey, Mia's aunt Raquel is at the bar causing a scene. I told Gabby I'd stop by," Roman said, seeing the worried looks on his brothers' faces.

The thought of the kids on that damn trip to the mountains caused Ed to think of his son with Jillian. "Jesus, I was supposed to meet my son tonight."

Logan and Roman exchanged a look.

"He's here?" Logan said.

"He's been here for quite some time. Right under my nose and I didn't even know it." Ed then raised his hand to his breast pocket and could feel the folded paper of the printout with his son's picture on it. Pulling his hand away, he looked at Sam. *This isn't the time*, he thought.

"That woman had him here this whole time, and she didn't tell you?" Roman said in a slightly raised voice, aware of Sam's condition.

"The whole time? That I don't know. But what I do know is where he's working, and I'd planned on seeing him tonight, but it'll have to wait."

"Aren't you going to New York tonight for the interviews tomorrow?" Logan asked.

"That too," Ed said.

"You guys go on. I'll stay here with Sam," Logan said. "I'll call you with any news the moment I hear it."

"You're sure you're going to be fine without a car for the night?" Roman asked. "I can come back in the morning, unless someone else is going to be here."

"I'm fine. Trust me." Logan said. "But what are you two going to do?"

Roman looked at Ed. "Want to grab some dinner at Gabby's place?"

"No, go on ahead; I'll grab a taxi and head on home," Ed said, thinking he wanted to stop at the gallery on his way home.

Ed looked at Sam, and then he looked to the floor, lost in the same ugly thoughts shared by everyone in that very room, and nodded. "New York—this couldn't come at a worse time."

As Ed stood from his chair, the door to Sam's room opened, and he was taken aback when he saw Sandy Storm standing there. She was dressed in sweats for the evening and had her IV on the portable stand she was pulling along with her.

"You!" Ed growled in disgust. "What the hell are you doing here?"

"I didn't know you were all here," she said, seeing all the brothers present. "I saw Roman go into the room, and I've been standing out there trying to get the courage to come inside." She then looked at Sam. "My God, what's happened to him?"

"Outside," Ed said as he moved her back into the hall, and Roman and Logan followed.

"Now what do you want?" Ed said, the patience all but gone after this insane day.

"I wanted to thank you," she said, smiling and looking at them like they should know what she was thanking them for.

Ed looked to Roman and Logan, and it was apparent they were all at a loss.

"Thank us for what?" Roman said.

"For paying my bill. I lost my health insurance when we got fired from the station, and I got your note—well, one of your notes." Sandy then knew she was right, that it had been that pussy Sam Savage who'd paid it and probably didn't tell anyone. *Damn rich people*, she thought.

The Savage brothers exchanged a look, and Logan shook his head. "Sorry, ma'am, but what are you talking about? We didn't pay your hospital bill."

"Ma'am?" Sandy shook her head. "Anyway, I didn't think it was any of you three that paid it. I thought it was Sam because the note was signed with an *S*."

"What note are you talking about?" Ed asked.

"It's in my room. I can show you."

"Lead the way," Roman said.

Logan opened Sam's door and peeked in on him; he then followed them down the hall. The hospital had two wings, and Sandy's room was at the far end away from Sam.

"I can't wait to get out of here tomorrow," Sandy said as she led them into her room.

"You're being discharged tomorrow?" Logan asked.

"First thing." Sandy opened her small drawer next to her bed. Pulling out a movie magazine with more Savage gossip splashed across it, she tossed it on the bed, seeing the note underneath it in the drawer. As the magazine hit the bed, a small flash drive caught between its pages fell to the floor, and Ed picked it up for her.

"Here you go," Sandy said, handing the note to Roman as Ed handed back her flash drive. "I found it after waking up from a nap. A little creepy if you ask me."

The men looked at the note as Roman read it aloud. "Sorry for your loss, and the medical bill has been paid—S." He looked to his brothers. "Had Sam mentioned anything of this to you?"

"No." Logan shook his head.

Ed took the note and looked at it closer. "With his shoulder healing, his handwriting's been a little off, but I don't think this is Sam's writing. I mean, what do you guys think?"

"We'll have to wait to ask him," Logan said.

"But if you three didn't pay this, and you don't think Sam did either, then who did?" Sandy asked, looking genuinely nervous.

"You don't know of anyone else who would pay this?"

"No! I don't have friends like that. But whoever did was standing in here watching me sleep!"

Ed pulled out his phone and took a photo of the note and handed it back to Sandy. "It's scary when someone messes with you and you have no clues. Isn't it?" Ed then flashed his signature devilish grin from his TV shows at her. "Pleasant dreams, lady."

Sandy watched the three men leave her room, and the protection she felt in their presence vanished before the door closed. Alone in her hospital room, she sat on her bed looking at the mysterious note.

Outside in the hall, the men were just as bewildered. "Glad I'm staying the night," Logan said. "I'm not leaving Sam's side."

The night was revving up to be more than Ed had first expected. On his way home, he had the taxi stop at Gallery 26 and park on the empty street. He got out from the cab, and noticed the paper on the gallery's windows covering them for the upcoming event inside; however, part of the paper had fallen down. There he stood, peering into the darkened building, and there he saw it. The security lights inside the building allowed him to see his son's face illuminated in the darkness. There, like one of his earlier shows, was a life-size cutout of Trent York standing in front of a monstrous wave he had shot during a hurricane in Florida. Ed gazed at the artwork, and it was surreal for him, realizing that his boy had grown up to be exactly like his old man. He got choked up a bit and swallowed hard.

The giant wave behind his son was foreboding, like a warning he could not see. Poor Ed Savage could not realize then that trouble was not only headed his way, but that it *was* planned.

CHAPTER 29

Jillian's phone alerted her that she had a text message. When she read it, she was filled with regret yet glad at the same time. It was from her son, Trent, and he simply asked if she had heard from his father.

As she was texting him back, Jeremy Bigelow came up behind her and saw the message she had typed out: *Sorry, honey, not a word.*

"Just like that Dudley Do-Right to screw everything up like he always does. Goddamn Savage," Jeremy said as he went to the bar in their penthouse for another whiskey. "You want another one?"

"No, I'm good," Jillian said, watching the text send to her son, and feeling guilty for keeping the New York trip from him.

Jeremy topped off his drink and looked to her. "I won't be much longer. It's been a long day, and I'll be in in just a minute."

Jillian got up and moved to a counter, plugging her phone in to charge for the night. She then went to the bedroom, passing the study, where Jeremy had his desk light on and many papers strewn about.

Jeremy waited a moment and then went over to her phone and looked at the messages. He read the text message from Trent; then he scrolled up to see what else was there. Just as he was about to place the phone down, he looked at her call log. There it was: a call from Ed Savage received earlier in the day.

He knew the situation going on with Trent and really didn't care that he was Ed's son. He had never taken a liking to the boy when he first knew of him all those years ago, and the fact that Ed was kept in the dark was all the better. He backed out from the phone log to the main screen and shut the phone down.

In his office, he closed the door and sat down, pulling out the police report hidden under the papers on his desk. There it was: the official police report from Black Ridge Falls and the highlighted fact that Ed Savage kept a gun under the seat of his Range Rover.

CHAPTER 30

With the day not going as planned and the long hours spent with Sam at the hospital, Ed was tired. When he finally got home later that night, Marlo had his dinner waiting, and he picked at it as he sorted out all the headlines he'd cut out from the various newspapers and magazines in his briefcase to prepare for his day in New York City. He was staying at their apartment in Manhattan for the interviews, and he also needed to check in at Trask Studios for a meeting. Getting all his notes for Trask in order, he picked up the phone and called Savage Tower to have the helicopter standing by, telling the crew that he was on his way.

As Ed headed back into town for that jaunt downstate, a different kind of movement of sorts was taking place.

Unknown to Ed at the time, somewhere in Port Roberts, New York, a flash drive was being loaded into a computer. The electronic data stored on that flash drive was explosive. It was the unaired portion of Wendy Storm's scathing report from Black Ridge Falls—and it was sent out everywhere.

CHAPTER 31

Maura Savage stepped off the elevator at the hospital and made her way to Sam's room. She tapped gently on the door as she opened it to find her husband, Logan, at Sam's side and a transporter preparing to take Sam for tests. "Good morning," she said, offering a smile, noticing the television was muted in the room. "Sam, how are you feeling today?"

Logan got to his feet from the uncomfortable sleeping chair where he had tossed and turned for the night, dropping the blanket to the floor as he reached for his coffee.

"Better," Sam said. "Except my shoulder where I got shot hurts like never before. Maybe I landed on it from the railing?" he said, looking embarrassed.

It was a wonder he'd remembered it, she thought, just as Logan mentioned he had filled Sam in on last night's misadventures.

"Where are they taking you?"

"Doctor ordered an MRI for my shoulder," Sam said.

"How long will that take?" Maura asked the transporter.

"Shouldn't be more than an hour, ma'am," he told her, moving the bed toward the door.

Logan put down his coffee and moved to help the bed navigate through the door as they watched the transporter push Sam's bed down the hallway to the elevators.

"Sam, the girls are leaving today. I'll come back after I see them off," Maura said from behind his bed.

Together they watched Sam lift his hand and wave to them. Seeing him go, Logan went back inside and grabbed his coffee.

Maura followed him in and looked to her disheveled husband and the chair he'd slept in. "Logan, I can't believe you slept on that. Come on—I'll take you home. You'll feel better after a shower."

Logan finished the last of his coffee. "You can quit pretending you care. No one's around to hear us."

Maura looked genuinely hurt by his statement, but it was sadly the truth. They looked at each other, and Logan remembered how happy he *thought* he had been before all this had started. When she was coming home to London, he had actually believed they would be able to work things out. Then the news of Nathan's death and the trip to the States had Logan Savage thinking *just maybe* he could salvage his marriage. Even after all they had been through on the Vanderran dining superyacht and what followed after with their hurt children, Macy and Ty, there was no change in the fact that she had fallen out of love with him.

Maura felt awful. She loved him, and she knew he loved her too, but her feelings had changed, and she wasn't *in love* with him anymore. That had been the main reason she had gone to the States in the beginning. She needed to be with her twin sister, Cara, who'd always been there for her. They spent so much time talking over all this that the day she was going back to London for Zolie's book tour, she had planned on telling Logan she wanted a divorce. Then the news of Ed and Marlo's accident in the mountains changed everything.

"Logan, don't. Not now," she whispered.

"Maura, I can't do this anymore. I'm done. It hurts! All of it hurts, and I can't go on pretending everything is fine when it's clearly not," Logan said, crumpling up his disposable coffee cup and tossing it into the waste bin. "How much longer did you think I could take this?"

"Logan, it's just that so much has happened, and this isn't the time for us to tell the others."

"Why not? Why isn't this the time? The worst is over, and we're all picking up the pieces after the hell this family has been through.

Besides, I found the divorce papers in the closet when one of your bags fell from the shelf as I was pulling down my old briefcase."

Maura's mouth dropped, and she moved to the window to stare out at the crisp autumn day. "You saw them? Why is it you're telling me this now?" she said, keeping her back to him.

"Maura, I picked up the bag, and the papers fell out. It was that innocent and it hurt. I guess these last few days since Ed got back with Marlo, and with Lana and Kate coming home, I needed some time to absorb that the end of our marriage is real."

"I'm so sorry." Maura's eyes, still fixated on the fall leaves littering the hospital grounds, began to well up with tears.

"So am I."

Maura turned around and took a look at the younger man she had married all those years ago, wishing she'd see a spark, something to tell her she was making the biggest mistake of her life. But nothing was there, and her heart told her so.

"I've got to get out of here," Logan said, moving toward the closed door.

Maura watched the man leave, and she felt terrible over all of it. Suddenly, she called out, "Logan, stop!"

Logan's hopes and dreams were instantly lifted. But when he turned around, expecting her to run into his arms, his heart sank. Instead, he saw Maura pointing to the muted television.

"Turn it up," Maura said.

Logan saw the news banner "Ed Savage's Sick Sex Games" across the bottom of the screen. Grabbing the remote, he unmuted the sound. There was Wendy Storm in her mud-splattered dress reporting from Black Ridge Falls. They thought they had seen the last from this smirking bitch, but there was obviously more—and it was ugly.

The worst of the news Wendy and Sandy Storm had shot slamming the Savage family had apparently been cut when it aired. However, a copy had leaked, and it was explosive. There was Wendy Storm telling the world of the sick sex games played by the Savage men with their wives, explaining the possibility of Lisa Savage not being Ed Savage's biological child but rather the child of one of his brothers.

"This is Wendy Storm reporting live from Black Ridge. Actor Ed Savage and his brothers are close—too close, if you know what I mean." Wendy gave the camera a self-satisfied smirk. "The lost little girl, Lisa Savage, may not even be his biological daughter. Reports of the brothers sharing their wives on their parents-only weekends at their lake home have been discovered. Sources tell me Lisa's father could be any of the Savage brothers. Furthermore, sources report Ed liked it rough, and so did Cara Vanderran, giving Ed's wife, Marlo Savage, a much-needed break."

The video then went to their lake home with a close-up of the address on the house, and footage was taken *inside* one of the bedrooms, where all kinds of sex toys were displayed on a bed with rubber sheets. The camera had blurred out most of the toys, but you could tell what was there. The camera then went back to the reporter. "This is disgusting," she said on air. "This is actual footage from the Savage lake home. My only hope is for that innocent little girl to be found. This is Wendy Storm reporting from Black Ridge Falls."

Logan and Maura were beyond shocked. The thoughts of his failed marriage dissipated with this fresh steaming pile of lies being flung at them first thing in the morning.

"Oh my God!" Logan said.

"Good thing that bitch is dead, or I'd kill her myself for tarnishing my sister's name," Maura seethed.

Logan pulled out his phone and punched in Ed's number.

"Who are you calling?" Maura asked, turning a shade of red from what she'd just heard.

"Ed! He's in New York on his way to those damn interviews today."

"Oh no! He'll be blindsided."

"I've got to warn him," Logan said.

Maura looked back to the television and thought of the lake house. "Logan, how did they get inside the lake house to film that?"

"I have no idea," Logan mumbled as he listened to Ed's cell phone ring and go to voice mail. "Ed, Sam's fine—just call me back before any interviews. It's important. Oh, and I asked Sam. He doesn't know anything about Sandy Storm's hospital bill."

Logan waved at Maura to follow him. "Come on—I know where this came from."

Putting his phone in his pocket, Logan bolted from the room, and Maura followed him past the elevators.

"Where are you going?" she asked, not getting an answer. She followed him to the other wing of the hospital to a room at the end of the hall.

"This was from you!" Logan said, opening the door to see an *empty* room.

CHAPTER 32

Ed Savage adjusted his mic; he was positioned on the set for the first news interview of the day. His cell phone was in his jacket in the dressing room they had given him for the occasion. He was tired from the late flight to New York City, and his thoughts were heavy with Sam and the son he had hoped he'd meet yesterday. As he sat there completely clueless to the missing news bite from Black Ridge Falls making the rounds, the interviewer, Vanessa Broomer, was in the soundproof booth. She could see it being played out from a cable news channel on a monitor. She looked up and waved through the glass at Ed with an innocent smile; she then picked up her notecards and turned to her assistant.

"Everything all cued?"

The assistant nodded, and Ed saw the big-haired former pageant princess emerge from the glass soundproof booth, reliving her second-rate runway walk toward him, just like she did every morning for the early news edition. He straightened up in his chair and smiled as a flutter of personnel surrounded her when she sat down on her throne. The lighting on set went up as her makeup, hair, and mic were adjusted, and the attendants were gone just as fast as they appeared.

"Ready?"

"As I'll ever be," Ed said, completely ready for the questions he *thought* were coming.

"We're live in three, two, one…" came the voice from behind the camera.

"Good morning! Today we have actor Ed Savage with us. What with all the headlines out there, we'll be getting to the real story from the man himself. Ed, good morning," Vanessa said, smiling.

"Good morning, Vanessa. Thank you for having me," Ed replied politely.

"Now, Ed, let's back up to *before* the trip to the mountains. What was life like at home? Were there any indications of what was to come?"

"Ah, starting off easy, thank you," Ed said, thinking this might not be so bad. "Life was good. My hours were getting hectic filming, and when my daughter's school had to close for electrical repairs, we thought it'd be a great time to get away."

"How close were you to your father, Nathan Savage?"

"We didn't see each other as much as we could have."

"Was that because of your busy work schedule, or was there something else? That inheritance hit the papers, and we got a lot of comments on that."

"Yeah, that was supposed to be kept private; I'm not sure how that story got out there. But my dad and I really didn't see eye to eye on a lot of things," Ed said, looking at her with hard eyes.

Vanessa stared down at her notes. "So...up in the mountains, when all this was happening, did you ever expect this was something stemming from the acts of your father?"

Ed knew about the letter that Patty had sent out to the papers, detailing the affair her mother, Rose Galloway, had had with his father. But the VCR tape they'd received was safely locked away, along with the copy he'd taken from her cabin. "Not once. We were blindsided, and my heart broke because I was jailed, and I couldn't search for my daughter or be at my wife's side."

"How is that cute little girl?" she asked as the monitor behind them showed little Lisa with the koala on the episode of *Archive Raiders*.

Ed glanced up and saw it. "She's doing fine, my little nugget. All the cousins are keeping a close eye on her." Ed smiled as he spoke about the love of his family.

"Ed, there were some live news broadcasts from Black Ridge Falls from a couple of reporters who were both hurt; one of them was even killed. Sandy and Wendy Storm—they threw out some pretty serious accusations and were not only terminated, but they paid the ultimate price. Was anything they reported truthful?"

Ed rolled his eyes. "Oh gosh, where to begin? I don't know where those two tabloid reporters were getting their *sources* from, but nearly all of it was a lie. The only factual reporting they did was my daughter being missing. Everything else was a flat-out lie."

"Now, Ed, I understand the defamation lawsuits filed against the reporters and the TV station that aired it. That information is all out there for the public to see, so I do have a few pinpoint questions to ask."

"Fire away."

"They reported your brother Sam got you released."

"Not true. The evidence cleared me."

Vanessa laughed. "Sorry, Ed, but they reported Sam was an ambulance-chaser type of lawyer. Has Sam ever practiced personal-injury law?"

"Never. Sam started in real estate, environmental litigation, contracts, and commercial construction. He later went on to try criminal cases, but never personal injury."

"So family money had nothing to do with your release?"

"No."

"Now, switching gears here a bit. Donert Tower had originally gone to Bigelow Construction, and now, according to an article in the *New York Times*, it's been awarded to your company, Savage Construction. How did that come to be?"

Ed was surprised she didn't bring up that whole "paternity of Lisa" insult those two bitches had spat over the air. "That building should have been ours from the get-go. We worked hard on that contract and were surprised when we lost it. Anyway, after that half-a-block lawsuit cleared, the bidding reopened, and we got it—fairly."

"Fairly? Is there something else you'd care to add to clarify that?"

"Vanessa, you follow the rules in life, and you don't get problems. We followed the rules."

"Following the rules," she repeated. "The murder of Parnell F. Bancroft is still unsolved. Ed, when did you see him last, and, in your opinion, did Parnell F. Bancroft follow the rules?"

Ed eyed this self-glorified prom queen and could feel the interview turning. "Parnell handled my father's estate, and I saw him last at the reading of my father's will. As far as following the rules, well, I didn't work with him directly, so I can't answer that, but Parnell certainly lived well."

"You can't blame a guy for that if he followed the rules," Vanessa said. "Now, I tried to get an interview with Patty Galloway, but according to her sister, Stevie, she's not seeing anyone. Stevie Galloway did tell me she intervened during the hotel massacre. Tell me, did she really help?"

"Yes, it was because of Stevie that both my wife, Marlo, and Aisha Thomas are alive. She intervened when something was about to happen. Understand I can't talk about specifics of the case at this time."

"And she was arrested?"

"She was taken in, yes. There's still pending litigation, so I really can't speak on this any further."

"Marcus Bowers had been able to access a few Savage bank accounts. Has all that been resolved?"

"Most of it, but again, it's pending litigation."

"And you were acquitted of his murder?" she pressed on, seeing Ed was getting pissed, and this was exactly what she wanted. She could see him getting uncomfortable and heard his tone change when he spoke.

"I was defending my family," Ed said, getting a bit restless in his chair. He shot her a look, and she winked at him.

"The timing of *Cosmopolitan*'s article and centerfold could not have been worse. Tell us about the day you shot it?" She asked the question as the centerfold appeared on the screen behind them.

Ed saw it, smiled, and turned a bit red, but he was thankful the questions from the murders seemed to be finished. "Well, I didn't want to do it at first, but my agent talked me into it, and I had to get my wife's approval. We shot it on the top floor of a closed department store with an outdoor area that was once a cafe, they wanted a look like you'd find at Restoration Hardware, which some stores have rooftop outdoor furniture areas. It was a fun, lighthearted shoot, given the nature of the photo."

"It sure got a lot of press."

"I think because of what was happening at home, it got more than it would have. And you're right on the timing—boy, everything seemed to be piling on all at once," Ed said, remembering how things had seemed to be coming at him from all angles at the time.

Vanessa dropped a few of her note cards on her lap, and as she picked them up, she looked at one that seemed to have been forgotten.

"So, Ed, one last thing: where on earth would they have come up with the paternity angle on your missing daughter at the time? The only things out there that anyone can search are the *Phantom Finders* articles from way back. And even those were proven false."

Damn, Ed thought. "I'll tell you something, Vanessa: the allegations thrown my direction lately have been off-the-charts wrong. They're not true by any means, and I have no clue where they came up with this garbage. And as far as *Phantom Finders* is concerned, that part of my life has been over for too many years to even address."

"Ed, the *Phantom Finders* allegations are eerily on par with what was reported. There were sexual assault charges alleged during your time there. And later charges were filed against your costar, Stanley Sinardi."

Ed hadn't heard that cretin's name in ages, and now it was everywhere. He certainly had no desire to talk about him. "I'm sorry, Vanessa; none of that is my concern. I was not involved with any of it, and I have no comment."

"And you are aware of the new footage from Black Ridge? Correct?"

Ed suddenly knew he was trapped, and he looked at her smiling face and knew *something* ugly was coming. "New footage? No, I haven't seen anything new."

"This was picked up early this morning, and it's all over the Internet. Now, some of what you're about to see is graphic, and we've blurred parts that were deemed inappropriate. Okay, Ed, let's take a look and see what you have to say about this."

The monitor behind them jumped to the interview of Wendy Storm in her mud-splattered dress. "This is Wendy Storm reporting live from Black Ridge. Actor Ed Savage and his brothers are close— too close, if you know what I mean."

As Ed watched Wendy smirk on camera, he glanced over at Vanessa, who was blatantly relishing the ratings coup she knew she was getting.

The Reporter of Bitches Past continued, "The lost little girl, Lisa Savage, may not even be his biological daughter. Reports of the brothers sharing their wives on their parents-only weekends at their lake home have been discovered. Sources tell me Lisa's father could be any of the Savage brothers. Furthermore, sources report Ed liked it rough, and so did Cara Vanderran, giving Ed's wife, Marlo Savage, a much-needed break."

Ed's mouth dropped hearing that garbage and seeing not only their lake home appear on the screen but the address as well; then the camera moved through the front door to a bedroom that looked like a sex play room. Ed shook his head, watching as the blurred sex toys were shown. "This isn't right," Ed barked.

"This is disgusting," Wendy Storm said, and she seemed to enjoy saying it on air, Ed thought. "This is actual footage from the Savage lake home. My only hope is for that innocent little girl to be found. This is Wendy Storm reporting from Black Ridge Falls."

The monitor froze over Wendy and her mud-splattered dress, and Vanessa leaned toward Ed with a smile. "So, Ed, care to retract your statement?"

Ed was angry and it showed. He turned away from the homecoming bitch sitting next to him and looked right into the camera. "I'm sorry to cut this interview short; the allegations reported in this video are false, and that's all I'm going to say."

"But the lake home is indeed your family's home, is it not?" Vanessa interjected.

Ed pulled his mic off, threw it into the chair, and left the set. Vanessa waved her arm and pointed for the camera to follow him offstage. And when he was gone, another camera focused on Vanessa. "The lake house shown in what could possibly be Wendy Storm's last broadcast is, in fact, owned by Savage holdings." She smiled and nodded. "We'll be right back."

CHAPTER 33

Ed Savage was fuming when he called his agent, Rachel Shepherd, and as he leaned against the building, he saw his next stop in the building right across the street.

In that building, Tabitha Tealey, of *Tabitha's Tea Talk*, was watching the fiasco play out on live TV, and she panicked. She immediately called Ed's agent to make sure her star interview was indeed still coming. As she was on hold, an assistant tapped her shoulder with a grim face.

"What?" Tabitha lashed out.

"Savage isn't coming," the terrified assistant informed her.

"You spoke with Ed Savage and didn't give me the phone?" she screamed.

"No, I spoke with his agent, a Rachel Shepherd."

"You get her back on the phone now, or you're fired," Tabitha yelled.

As the assistant tried recalling the number, Tabitha grabbed her phone from her as it was ringing and was surprised when it was answered in two rings.

"Hello," Rachel answered.

"Rachel, this is Tabitha Tealey, and, yes, I saw it. I'm so sorry. Please tell Ed to come to the studio, and we'll set things right." Tabitha crossed her fingers as she waited for the answer, and when she was met with a disconnected tone, she lost it.

Across town in Rachel's office, she had Ed on her cell phone and had held up the office phone, so he could hear. When he told her to hang up, she did.

"Oh my God! We're live in less than twenty minutes," Tabitha screamed at her now-frightened assistant. "Get that Black Ridge clip ready, and make sure Tonya is ready. We'll move her time slot up," she said, handing back the phone.

The assistant went pale. "Um, she's not here yet, Tabitha."

Tabitha's eyes widened in shock. "*Tabitha?*" she said, mocking the idiot in front of her. "It's *Ms. Tealey*! And where the hell is she?"

"I don't know. She hasn't arrived yet."

"Give me back your phone," Tabitha said, snatching it from her. She found the number to Randall Bishop of *Tycoon Wives* and hit redial, and the call went to voice mail.

"Ms. Tealey, you need to get on set," another assistant called to her from down the hall.

"Jesus," Tabitha cried.

Tabitha's part-time cohost, Carly Tilton, then came around the corner. "*Tycoon Wives* just called; they'll be here in ten."

"Oh, thank God," Tabitha said as she rushed to the set.

When the music started and the audience applauded, Tabitha was all smiles, sitting alongside Carly on set. They spoke of today's headlines and the surprising new development in the Ed Savage drama, and as she was telling her audience that Ed Savage could not make it today, the voice in her earpiece said that the assistant to *Tycoon Wives* was there, and the guest was ready.

The relief that both Tabitha and Carly shared from the news in their earpieces was short lived. Just as Tonya Lipschitz was introduced and the on-set wall was raised to greet their guest, Tabitha's heart jumped in her throat as she saw Marilyn Hart standing there, dressed to the nines, smiling and walking out. Tabitha side eyed Carly, who had a frozen smile plastered on her face. Both women were ambushed, and suddenly Tabitha knew exactly how Ed Savage must have felt only a short time ago.

"Tonya, you've changed," Tabitha said, hiding her contempt as she stood up to hug her.

"Yes," Carly added, "this is a complete surprise." She stood next in line for a hug.

"Randall told me it was all arranged," Marilyn said, knowing she'd pulled a fast one on them as she took her seat. "Besides, this would've been hard for Tonya—you know how she never gets up before noon."

"Well, that's a sound bite." Tabitha fake laughed, and the audience applauded.

"So, Marilyn, I'm sorry your skit lost last year and you had to work at Barn-Mart's Automotive for a day. But that was too funny watching you selling tires in their discount center. Can you tell us anything about this upcoming Cinema Shake-Up?

Marilyn looked at her manicured fingernails and pretended to rub grease from them. "Tabitha, that was one greasy day. What did *you* think?" she said, playing to the audience.

The audience cheered, and one member shouted, "Love you, Marilyn!"

Marilyn looked to the person that said it. "Love you too!" she said, laughing. "Seriously, ladies, if I told you anything I shouldn't, I'd get in a heap of trouble." Turning to the audience, she continued, "Well, first I'd like to thank the fans for sending in all your wonderful ideas. *Tycoon Wives* will be doing comedy this year, and there'll be a *Lucy* sketch reenacted."

The audience cheered, and when it died down, Tabitha deadpanned, "Oh, I do so hope you're getting grapes thrown in your face," she added with a grin.

Carly gasped, and Marilyn sneered at Tabitha. "I didn't say I was involved in that sketch, and you know, Tabby, dear, it's really too bad the producers passed on your audition tape. It'd be nice to bring you up in society. Who knows? Maybe you'd even land an acting gig?" Marilyn said, knowing the woman despised it when she was called Tabby and knowing of her wish to be in the guest chair. She watched her recoil at being addressed that way on air.

The war was on, and the nails were out, but Tabitha had to play this right. She still needed to get Ed Savage on her show, and she thought she still had a chance, so she played it nice. "Oh, that was years ago, when the TV series first started. Looking back at all the crazy drama you girls get into, I'm glad it worked out this way."

Marilyn was surprised Tabitha had backed down so easily.

"Marilyn, tell us, with the new cast members this past year, it seemed they were out to get you. Had something happened off camera that wasn't shown? Because Cassidy Meyer and Tonya Lipschitz really went at you," Carly said.

"No, nothing really. I did make a comment once on Tonya's dirty-blonde hair looking like, well, dirt and said that a little color would be a nice touch. Yeah, I suppose that was a little bitchy but not worth what she threw at me. I was actually just as confused as the viewers were when she turned on me."

"She certainly did. Now I want to ask you about Cara Vanderran Savage. We all know her sister Zolie was married to Andrew while you were married to Anthony Caspian. With the news of her joining the cast and her murder, can you tell me how that's affected the show?" Tabitha asked with the sincerity of a nun.

Marilyn looked to the audience, which fell silent. She clasped her hands in her lap and lowered her head. "Let me be clear: it was both a shock to learn of her joining the show and even more of a shock with what happened to that poor woman. My thoughts and prayers are with the Savage family as they are dealing with more than any family should endure."

"Have they recast her spot on the show?" Carly asked.

"I haven't heard anything yet, but we're usually the last to know about those things."

The theme music started, and the camera zoomed to Tabitha and Carly. "Stay tuned. We'll be right back," Carly announced.

Back across town in Rachel Shepherd's office, she was busy canceling all Ed's scheduled interviews. Her television was on, and the news was all focused on her poor client. The last call she made was to Trask Studios to advise them Ed would be there sooner than scheduled and to see if things could be moved up to accommodate him so he could get back home sooner.

CHAPTER 34

ogan and Maura arrived in her car from the hospital and saw the girls' bikes parked in the driveway; one of the cargo saddlebag lids was open, and a duffel bag was sitting on the seat of the red one. Exiting her car, they passed the bikes, knowing their daughter was leaving, and it was one more thing to feel sad about as they entered the home. Chatter from the kitchen welcomed them as all the cousins were busy making a farewell breakfast—without the help of the staff.

"What's all this?" Maura said, seeing the happy mess.

"Oh, they insisted," Zolie said. Noticing Logan's mood, she asked, "Logan, is Sam all right?"

"He's fine. I had a bad night's sleep, and I need a shower," Logan said, moving to his daughter Kate and opening his arms. "How about a hug for your old man."

"Daddy, you're not old," Kate said, wrapping her arms around him in a baby bear hug.

Maura felt the undercurrent of his comment and grimaced—a look Zolie caught.

"Love you, sweetie," Logan said. "Now don't leave until I get back in here."

"We won't, you big goof," Kate said. "Now go shower."

As Logan left through the kitchen terrace doors, he could hear the barrage of questions from the kids hit Maura about Sam. His poor brother, he thought, missing the love of his life so much and not being able to do a damn thing about it. Logan was feeling the exact same thing for a woman that was his brother's wife's twin. He shook off the cryptic similarities and was making his way to the guest-house they had been using, when Roman and Gabby saw him enter his home.

"Honey, I'll see you inside in a minute," Roman said.

"Sure," Gabby said, watching her husband follow Logan and knock on his door. She then continued on to the main house.

"It's open," came the loud voice from inside.

Roman opened the door to see Logan coming from the kitchen with a glass of orange juice. "Hey, things all right at the hospital?"

"You didn't see it?" Logan asked, looking surprised.

"See what?"

Logan finished his orange juice and put the glass down. "Wendy Storm strikes again. And this time we're all thrown into it in a sick and twisted way." Logan picked up the remote and tossed it to his brother. "Turn on the TV. I'm sure it's all over by now, or check the Internet."

"Just tell me."

"Ed must have gotten blindsided today at his interviews because I can't get a hold of him, and Wendy Storm is saying we swap wives."

"What the hell? Oh Jesus, Logan." Roman started searching for information on his phone.

"*And* someone broke into the lake house and staged a sex room in one of the bedrooms. It was all on the fucking TV!"

Roman stopped fidgeting with his phone and looked up in shock.

"Oh, and Maura is divorcing me," Logan said, slamming the door against the wall as he moved into the bedroom, taking off his shirt for his shower.

Roman's jaw dropped. "Wait—*what?* What's this about Maura?" He followed his brother into the bedroom.

Logan tossed his shirt on the bed and entered the bathroom, keeping the door open so they could talk. "That's right; she's divorcing me, and I'm not keeping it quiet any longer."

"Longer? How long has this been going on?"

"Several months before all this shit started happening."

"I had no idea. Why didn't you tell me?"

"I wanted to—several times. But it just didn't happen. Then she left me for the States prior to the Black Ridge hell."

"Gabby and I wondered why she was here so long. We thought it had something to do with her sisters."

Logan turned on the shower and raised his voice over it. "Roman, not a word yet to anyone. Let's get through this day getting the girls off in a happy way. I don't want Kate worrying about us; she and Lana have enough on their plates right now with West Point."

Roman knew exactly what their daughters were facing and wouldn't want either of them to be distracted with worry. "Fine, not a word. I'll see you inside," Roman added, raising his voice as he heard his brother get into the shower.

Leaving the guesthouse, Roman felt awful and saw the Wendy Storm article on his phone. He read the headline and shut it off when got near the terrace doors to the kitchen area; he could hear the family, and he put on a smile as he stepped through the doors.

"Good Lord, what a spread," Roman said, eyeing all the food.

"We made everyone's favorite." His daughter Danni pointed to the eggs being poached. "Even yours," she laughed.

Logan's daughter Macy was pouring herself a coffee and poured another for him. "Here, Uncle Roman."

"Thanks, Macy," Roman said. He looked over at the boys playing a video game in the next room. "Where'd Gabby go off to?"

Macy looked around. "She was here a minute ago; try Aunt Zolie's study."

Roman left his coffee and moved past the dining room, where Lana was setting the table; he stopped and hugged his girl. "Love you, darling."

"Oh, come on, Dad; West Point isn't that far."

Roman looked into her innocent eyes and kissed her forehead. "I don't care if it's in the backyard. You're still my little girl, and when I need a hug, you'll give me one."

Lana saw sadness in her father's eyes. "Dad, I'm sorry. I know it's been rough for us. But remember, parents' weekend is coming soon, and I can't wait to show off for you up there." Lana flashed her mile-wide smile as she hugged him harder.

"Love you, girl," Roman said, letting go.

Lana watched her father head to Zolie's study and quietly wondered what her father was keeping from her.

Eyeing the closed study door, Roman stood there listening for a moment before knocking lightly.

When Marlo opened the double doors, he saw the look on Gabby's face and knew the four were talking about the divorce. Smiling, he played dumb and reached for his wife. "Come on, let's be with the kids on their last day," he said, shooting a look right at Maura. "Let's see if Danni's eggs benedict doesn't kill me."

When they got back to the kitchen, the girls were rinsing off a pan when water sprayed them, and they all started laughing. Seeing the water spray into the air, Roman felt a stabbing sadness in his heart for his little brother, Logan, and looked out the window in the direction of his guesthouse.

There, Logan was in the shower, the hot water steaming around him and the shampoo running down his backside. He put his hand up to the shower and blocked the stream as suds ran down his hairy chest. Leaning against the glass wall, he started to cry.

CHAPTER 35

Knowing his agent had canceled all his remaining interviews in light of the newly resurrected news clip from hell, Ed called her back to ask her to call Trask Studios to tell them he would be there earlier; he wanted to return home as soon as he could. And when she told him she'd already done it and was planning on meeting him there, he actually breathed a sigh of relief. Thankful for the amazing woman in his work life, Ed walked over to the next block to grab a cab. He cringed reading the trashy headline on a newsstand tabloid: "Bastard Son Wins Daddy Lottery."

Once in the taxi, sitting quietly in the back seat, he searched his phone and found the article to see if any further garbage was mentioned about his son. And as the cab wove its way through traffic, Ed read the article. Seeing a pop-up advertisement announcing the new Wendy Storm video made him grow angrier by the block.

Conner Trask had assembled a team to welcome Ed into the fold of Trask Studios, and there was a lot to work out. First there was the rebranding of his shows into a package so fans could easily find them; then they'd restructure them in such a way that brought new excitement to the work Ed and his team provided.

Ed got out from the cab and passed security on his way to his new home. The newness of the studio brightened his day as his thoughts moved away from the morning's fresh serving of shit thrown in his face, when he saw the sign, which for a moment made him forget the ugly day entirely. There, with a big bouquet of balloons tied around it along with a welcome sign, was the posted wooden sign that read: "Don't even think of parking in Ed Savage's spot." The smile on his face widened at his private parking space, and he laughed it off as he made his way to the entrance.

Inside, he spotted Rachel, and she was happy to see him. "Welcome to your new home, Ed."

Judging by her knowing smile, Ed knew she wasn't going to bring up the morning's surprise with Vanessa Broomer, and he was glad. "Morning—it's great to be starting fresh here. I can't wait to get started."

"Oh my God, Ed, I just got here a few minutes ago, and you won't believe the size of the studio they have for us. You're in for a surprise," Rachel said as she walked him toward the conference area near the actual studio set where they'd be filming in the future.

"Rachel, um, no more surprises for me, okay? I've had enough to last me," Ed said and flashed his signature devilish grin.

"Oh, sorry—poor choice of words."

Together they dropped the conversation as they entered the conference room. There he saw the posters from his current shows, and at the end of the long table was an easel covered with a black velvet drape. Ed and Rachel both looked to each other and felt like kids waiting to see what Santa had brought them.

The sound of footsteps got their attention, and they turned to see Conner Trask and a woman coming to greet them.

"Ed, glad you're here," Conner said, reaching out to shake his hand.

"Glad to be here." Ed noticed the young Asian woman with him. *Don't let her name be Mingyu,* he silently prayed.

"Ed Savage, this is Kami Cho; Kami, this is Ed Savage and his agent, Rachel Shepherd." They said their hellos and shook hands. "Ed, Kami is one of my top producers, and she has been working on your new package here at Trask."

"Yes, it's been quite a project putting everything together, and I can't wait to get your thoughts on what we've come up with," Kami said. "Please sit down."

"Ed, I'm going to leave you all to it. Welcome again, and I'm really glad you're here." Conner patted Ed on his shoulder. Shooting him a knowing look, he winked as he left the trio behind.

Kami motioned both Ed and Rachel to sit down as she moved near the posters of his current shows. "Now, Ed, here's where our thoughts are on the rebrand. You've got several shows running with your name as the tie-in, and then you have your *Archive Raiders* on Sundays: *Savage Strength, Savage Mysteries, Savage Life, Savage Cases,* and finally, *Savage Past.*" She paused a moment and looked at the posters with them. "With your older shows in syndication and with *Archive Raiders* ending and the new series shooting, there can be some confusion over finding all your work as we move things around. To bring it under one umbrella, so to speak, we wanted to repackage everything in an easy-to-find format," Kami said.

Ed was nodding. "My thoughts exactly."

"Now, I've had several meetings with KBEX, and Sally Hayes, Tim Richardson, and Carol Simmons are all on board, so we just need to come together on the rebrand and decide on the sets." Kami paused, moving closer to the cloaked easel. "Any questions?"

Ed looked over. "Come on—you're killing us here."

"Going forward with Trask Studios, we have a new and exciting view on redistributing your work, and we added a twist. We also had to keep in mind *Precinct Wars,* which is separate, and there was a slight change from *Savage Mysteries* with a subtitle as we previously thought going forward. So we came up with this."

Kami reached up and pulled the black velvet drape, letting it drop to a chair next to it. There on the easel was Ed Savage standing tall with the words *Savage World* printed on a metal sign held in his arms in front of him. Around his standing figure were smaller images of him from his different shows with their names scrawled underneath each image.

"All anyone has to do is enter *Savage World* into their recording device, and they'll get all of your shows," Kami said, noticing both Ed and Rachel smiling.

"This totally works," Ed said. "I had a fan last year on Facebook tell me it was hard to record my shows because we had different titles in the specials we ran. I notified production and got them to look into it. I like this better."

"Ed, this is perfect. Kami, what about this twist you mentioned?" Rachel said.

Kami smiled. "We're mixing things up a bit. Instead of shooting one set of shows for a miniseason and then moving on to the next, we're shooting them out of order and airing them that way too. Each week will be *Savage World*, and then in the underline title will be the name of the show: *Savage Mysteries, Cases, Past*, and so on."

"Wait a minute: *Archive Raiders* is family oriented. I don't want that show tied in with the DVR crowd. I don't think the parents will like it," Ed said.

"While we do have many fans that watch everything Ed does, there is that small percentage that only watches *Archive*," Rachel added.

Kami also knew this and was waiting for this to come up. She looked to the easel and pointed to *Archive Raiders*. "We couldn't agree more, so what you see here was our first attempt." She then lifted the front poster off the easel and placed it on the table. Behind it was another poster with *Archive Raiders* missing; in its spot was the message, "Check out Savage Family for *Archive Raiders*."

"Savage Family?" Ed said.

"Exactly. This will be our initial advertising." Kami lifted the second poster and placed it near the other one on the table to reveal the last poster behind it. There, Ed stood holding a Pez dispenser on a globe. NASA and airships were above the earth and below; near his feet were the pyramids of Egypt and treasure spilling from a tomb. The NASA and Egyptian stories were always top favorites with his younger fans, and the candy factory stories were always a hit, especially the Pez story, and to Ed's surprise, the Pez dispenser had his head on it. It took him a minute to notice, and then he laughed out loud.

"No way! That can't be," Ed said, getting up to take a closer look.

Kami reached down to a chair where she had a small box and picked it up and placed it on the table just as Rachel joined Ed at the poster. Kami reached inside the box and pulled out a handful of Pez dispensers with Ed Savage's head on them. She handed them out. "Here, see for yourselves."

Ed and Rachel each took one and opened the plastic wrappers. Ed clicked back the plastic head, and a candy popped out. "This is too much. I love it." He popped the candy into his mouth.

Kami then reached into the box and pulled out the giant-sized Pez dispensers for them.

"No way," Rachel said, laughing as she reached for one.

"Pez makes the giant size for special occasions, and while we're not sure if we're going forward with the larger ones for mass market, we are thinking of placing a special order for your next Comic-Con. So what do you think?" Kami said.

Ed popped another candy in his mouth and looked at his mini-self in his hand. "I'm all in. Rachel, any thoughts?" he asked.

"Just one—with *Archive Raiders* finished airing new shows and Ed not doing any discovery episode specials in years, where's the draw for new viewers?"

"Good question, and I'm glad you brought it up. Ed, would you be interested in doing any further specials in this genre? I know you're spread pretty thin, but four a year to start would be all we need," Kami said.

"I like the idea, but it is a full schedule, especially with *Precinct Wars* being added. I'd like to…but we'll have to wait and see," Ed said, mulling over the idea.

"I understand completely, and we can address this at a later time. But as far as everything else covered here, do you have any other questions?" Kami said.

"It all sounds good to me. But I do want to go over the mixing of the shooting schedule you mentioned. Does this mean we'll be using the same sets for all these other shows?" Rachel asked as she pulled a candy from the Pez dispenser.

"No, we're using different sets for each show to give each its own identity." Kami reached for the folders sitting on the same chair as the box of dispensers. She picked them up and handed one to Ed and Rachel, and the three of them sat down at the table.

"We're using a larger studio space than what you were shooting in over at Titan. This way, we can build out the different sets and move as we shoot each series. Also, we're thinking of having you move from one set to another depending on the story we're doing; it hasn't been done before, but it could make for good copy." Ed and Rachel looked at each other and nodded at the brilliance of the concept.

"I don't think that's ever been done," Ed said.

"Not that we're aware of," Kami said. "Now, here are the thoughts we came up with and a few different designs we were thinking of for each show. Hopefully we nailed it, but Ed, it's your show, and you know what's going to work. So take some time here, and go over these, and tell us what you want. You have full rein, so if you want changes, just tell us."

Both Ed and Rachel were flipping through the pages and studying the different configurations of the sets.

"This is going to take some time," Ed told her.

"I figured as much; that's why I had lunch ordered, and I called them and told them you were arriving earlier. You two go through these, and I'll go check on the food. I'll also have the set designers come over so you can talk to them directly."

Ed stood up and shook her hand. "Kami, this has been weighing heavily on me for days, and I want to thank you for making it so easy and wonderful, especially today."

Kami smiled. "No problem, I couldn't wait to get my hands on this project; my kids love your shows. And don't worry about the news garbage. We're not."

Kami smiled at them and hurried off to see about the lunch.

"I didn't think they knew," Rachel said.

"They knew," Ed said as he moved over to the last poster on the easel and smiled at the Pez dispenser his image was holding. He then looked at the first poster on the table of him holding the metal sign and thought of Trent's poster in his gallery. "I'm afraid everyone knows."

CHAPTER 36

T rent wasn't the only one to see the latest news brought to light by Wendy Storm; it was broadcast everywhere.

In a diner upstate from Port Roberts, two men were watching it and reading the paper over a meal when the waitress brought over their filled thermos of coffee.

"Here you go, guys."

"Thanks, we'll take the check," one of them said.

Putting down the paper to add cream to the coffee inside the thermos, the other man noticed the article "West Point Parents' Weekend," and he grabbed that section and read about the day approaching where all the cadets would perform a jamboree. Below that was the headline "Bastard Son Wins Daddy Lottery."

CHAPTER 37

The cousins were enjoying finishing up their last breakfast together and were excited about the parents' weekend coming up at West Point. Their first month had been an adjustment for the girls, and with the drills and the schooling, they were exhausted every night and tired at every early-morning call. But they loved it and wanted to excel to be the best they could be—and the side bet they'd made with their cousins Tuc and Chet was worth a thousand bucks each, which they planned on collecting.

"The grades should be posted when we get back," Kate said to Lana.

The smile was back, and Lana glared at Chet. "I'll take my share in crisp hundred-dollar bills."

"Don't count on it, girly girl. We got you beat," Chet boasted.

Tuc laughed. "You really think you beat us? No way."

"Time will tell," Kate said.

Logan pushed his mostly uneaten plate away, got up from the table, and went and poured himself another cup of coffee.

"Dad, you're not hungry?" Macy asked when she and Kate looked at his uneaten breakfast.

Logan felt the knots in his stomach and told a white lie: "Had a bite at the hospital; sorry I ruined your breakfast, sweetie."

"It's not ruined," Macy said.

"Hey, Dad, we went and got Uncle Sam's favorite dessert, a blueberry pie at that bakery he likes," Kate said, getting up from the table.

"Oh?"

"Yeah, it's right here," she said, moving to the white box on the counter and showing it to him.

"Oh wow, he's gonna love that when he gets home."

"When is my dad getting home?" Chet asked.

"Surprisingly, he may get to come home today," Logan said. "He was feeling a lot better this morning, and the fluids they gave him all night helped with the hangover. His doctor ordered an MRI for his shoulder, and—depending on the tests, I guess—he said he'd release him later today."

"That's great," Chet said, feeling relieved.

"We'll make sure he knows the blueberry pie came from you," Tuc said to his younger cousins.

"How long until you ship out?" Lana asked the guys.

"We've got a few more days left," Tuc said.

"Well, leave our money here so we can send for it," Lana jabbed.

"You're not gonna win." Tuc grinned back.

The bet the cousins had made was on the total scores of both boot camp and their first round of tests combined. With parents' weekend approaching, the top ten candidates got two extra days off for the weekend, and the cadets really wanted the time to be with their families. Clearing the table, the excitement of beating their cousins filled the girls with happy thoughts as they finished with breakfast.

"So have you given any thought to where you want to end up after graduation?" Tuc asked.

"Oh, come on! You know how inundated we are right now. It's a wonder we're still loving it," Kate said.

"Wasn't it hard to transfer to the navy? I mean, didn't it take a while?" Lana said.

Both Tuc and Chet looked to each other and nodded. "Yeah, Chet got selected first; I'll never know why," Tuc said. "I had weeks of waiting until I got my approval."

"That's because I had to put in a good word for you," Chet teased.

Tuc turned to his cousin. "That'll cost you later," he said and laughed.

The years the girls had in front of them were enough to figure out what they wanted to do, like Tuc and Chet, who'd ended up in the navy on an aircraft carrier.

Both Tuc and Chet Savage, upon graduating from West Point, were able to transfer directly, with a waiver and approval from the secretary of the branch, from their commission into the navy, once they had approval there.

The only ones in the Savage family who had stayed in the army were Roman and Logan, and Nathan's dad, General Nelson Savage, who had later gone went into politics. Nathan transferred into the air force and became a colonel, and although he kept the brutal boot-camp ways raising his boys at home, the family had their roots in serving their country.

As the girls were clearing their plates to get ready for their ride back to West Point, the adults in the room shared the quiet gloom of the disaster brewing in the house and, unknown to the girls, of Maura's request for a divorce from Logan.

And others besides their commanders at the base were reading up on them too.

CHAPTER 38

D r. Todd Vreeland looked at his computer screen of the family hospital back home in Upstate New York and sat back in his desk chair. The sound coming from the television was disrupting his thoughts, so he grabbed the remote, muting the story of more depressing news of the earthquake that had claimed his wife and child. He then picked up his caramel triple-shot latte and took a drink, thinking back to the days of his life back home and the news articles of his old family hospital he'd been keeping up on.

The article had been brief; the State of New York was now running Vreeland Hills Sanatorium, and the lease they had was coming to an end. State officials were discussing the possibilities of signing another lease, and until that matter was resolved, all future spending on the facility was halted. The construction grant, however, was a separate bond the city had passed years ago, and the costs of maintaining the old buildings were in place, allowing the construction to support and repair the areas that required immediate attention for safety issues.

That damn building Todd thought, as he recalled everything and *everyone* he'd left behind.

The sixth floor of Vreeland Hills Sanatorium was strictly off limits to the staff with the exception of a select few, and Pam Porter was the nurse of choice. She was just as sadistic as the Vreeland brothers, what with her love of murder. Her goal in life was to kill as many people as she could and become the serial killer with the most victims of all time. Blake knew she had a thing for killing and always referred her to other institutions as a reward for her silence in the things he was doing. To her it was the best position to be in—being able to kill in other hospitals. And she *liked* being between the doctor brothers; her sick mind wanted to have sex with both of them at the same time, and she fantasized about that often. Enjoying her little secret, she ran off really not caring that Todd had finally gone too far after the fight she just witnessed with his brother Blake, besides she had to get his next victim to finish the surgery and she was tired, seeing that the sun had come up.

The so-called pit had been an out-of-order service elevator for a long time; the metal and wooden car had fallen years ago and crashed in the basement. The rotted car had split open, and the roof had caved in, making it easy for them to collect the bodies from the bottom of the shaft. They took them out in tunnels under a peaceful-looking chapel with a tall steeple so the patients couldn't see the countless bodies being removed from the hospital's vast grounds. Vreeland's Death Tunnel they'd called it. At first there was a quaint little cemetery near the chapel that housed the ill-fated patients. But when the numbers of the dead surpassed what it could hold, they were buried in the woods behind the sanatorium. There were 3,330 graves around the hospital: five sections of 666, to be exact. And this was all in the design from the long line of Vreeland doctors. Of course, the quaint cemetery had six rows of six graves on each side of the center path, and behind the chapel were six more rows of six. But underneath the chapel was where the final lot of losers would be buried. They figured another 558 would give them the number of dead they needed to complete the six sections of 666—and they were almost there, according to Dr. Corbin Vreeland, the grandfather of Blake, Eric, and Todd. The boys weren't allowed much time with their grandfather growing up, and at the time it was all right with them, being as they were terrified of the man.

The name Corbin was specifically given to the boy by his mother Cassandra, due to the name meaning "ravens"—and her lifelong association with the occult. And of course, when the monstrous sanatorium was built, the raven gargoyles were chosen with purpose. She liked the idea of the mythical tricksters looking down at you like a forewarning as you walked up the path to the intimidating structure—the ravens sitting ever so docilely like sentinels along the roofline giving you the false calm as they glared down at you like prey, to accompany the feeling of dread building within you as you gazed at the foreboding site—with the open-winged gargoyles greeting you at the entrances looking like they could swoop down on you and tear you to shreds if commanded.

Last night's surgery lasted hours, and Dr. Blake Vreeland never noticed his brother hanging in the cables of the elevator shaft; nor did he see him climb down and escape onto another floor of the hospital. When he finally finished, he was exhausted, angry, and fed up over the foolishness of his brother.

Wheeling the poor woman's father to the shaft, he dumped his body into the dark pit, hearing it hit the bottom, presumably on top of his dead brother. The partial brain tissue transplant surgery was one he'd hoped would change the behavior of the patient Pam had brought in, to be more docile, a medical study he'd been working on to cure the mentally deranged. And with the woman's father now dead, it would be another murder to cover up, and he added it to the long list in his mind. Of course, she'd have to be murdered too, and accidentally on the table according to the report he'd now have to write due to Todd's incompetence.

Moving to the scrub sink, he felt the sting from the stitches on his face, and after cleaning up, he replaced the bandages and gave himself antibiotics and a tetanus shot, just in case the blade was contaminated. He needed sleep, and retiring away from the patients to his sixth-floor private office and bedroom on the opposite end of the building, he went to the window to close the blinds—and that was when he saw his brother get into his truck and drive away from the hospital.

That bastard is alive! Blake picked up his bedroom phone and alerted hospital security that his brother was no longer allowed on the premises, and anyone caught allowing him back would be dealt with harshly—the punishment given out would be severe.

Knowing his brother's only option would be the clinic in the mountains that housed the children no one wanted, he banished him there permanently. Perhaps deep down he loved his stupid younger brother and thought maybe one day they'd work things out. But for now he wanted nothing to do with him.

CHAPTER 39

The muted news story of the earthquake had changed to the stock market, and Todd Vreeland glanced at it with his thoughts on his life from long ago.

The time spent away from Vreeland Hills Sanatorium had been pure torture for Dr. Todd. The hospital he'd been banished to was the Black River Children's Center, a prison for irredeemable kids who were troublesome bothers that were always getting into mischief. And Todd Vreeland hated it and despised his brother for banishing him there. The kids' only discipline was forced sedation, a tactic deemed too passive for the madness Dr. Todd wanted to inflict. Of course, there were the criminally insane adolescents that Vreeland Hills housed, but he'd never bothered to focus on them—instead he loved hearing the grown men and women plead for mercy at his hands. How he had dreamed of being able to bring about the atrocities of the adult facility on them, where things not only got a lot worse, but they had the scary contraptions they'd *show* the patients before torturing them with them.

The thing that bothered him the most was not being able to study his father's favorite patient, Rose Galloway. She was the prize that his father said had strange powers, and he was dying to find out what they were. She had aged quite a bit in that awful room, but without being there, he'd never see for himself the devil's tricks he'd been told she could perform.

His father, too, had aged, and as the years passed, the old man had become a bedridden nuisance, confined to his home in the lavish private section of the West Tower. It was after their brother Eric Vreeland had come home from Germany to check on their ailing father that he'd convinced Blake to let Todd come back to the hospital. Seeing as their father wasn't going to last much longer in this world, Blake agreed and told Todd he could come back under two conditions; he could only visit with their father, and the only patients he'd be allowed to see were the ones Blake hated the most—and that he'd need some time to think about him coming back to work there like he did before. And in that time of slowly gaining the trust of his brother and being back in the hospital, the nightmares that seemed to plague him his whole life intensified, and one morning he'd finally figured out what his revenge would be. He only needed the right moment to put his plan into action.

Todd Vreeland finished his latte and glanced at the muted television across from his desk. There he saw a story of confiscated cocaine from a passenger trying to board a flight to the States, and he unmuted the sound. Listening to the newscast reminded him he hadn't touched drugs of any kind since he'd left home—for more than a very good reason.

He still remembered that one night like it was yesterday; he was at his small home he'd rented at the time near the Black River's Children's Center, and there was a sudden loud banging on his door. Pam Porter was frantic, she was happy to learn he'd survived the elevator shaft, and said she'd been gone to another hospital and just got back earlier that day when she heard the horrible news. A patient had escaped and been shot.

Todd had been drinking hard and said he'd heard about the shooting yesterday, but really didn't care and invited her in, leading her right to his bedroom. The sex was intense; it was after when Nurse Pam, while cutting lines of cocaine with her switchblade, had mentioned the attack in one of the labs on the first floor near the basketball courts, that Todd took notice.

"Wait a minute—what attack are you talking about?" Todd said, remembering an awful event when he was younger at the basketball courts with his mother.

"Todd, it's your brother. That patient that was shot attacked Blake with acid; everyone knows about it. You said you didn't care."

Remembering his past with his mother and not hearing this part of the shooting story, he wanted to know everything she was talking about. "When and what exactly happened?" he asked, sitting up in the bed they were in.

"A few days ago. My God, Todd, your brother was severely burned."

Todd jumped out of the bed, his anger ignited by someone else paying back his brother besides him. "I called about the shooting; no one told me of this! I'll kill the little bitch that withheld this from me."

"No one's allowed to talk about it, and Blake doesn't want it getting out. He's worried about his reputation," Pam said, offering him the mirror decorated with the neat lines of cocaine.

"His reputation? That sounds just like that vain bastard. Where is he?"

"In one of the private suites. But you can't see him. He gave strict orders: no one is to see him until he says it's okay. His face is badly burned."

"We'll see about that," Dr. Todd said, leaning down and inhaling a line. Then he put on his pants and grabbed his shirt and shoes as he left his bedroom to his living room. Sitting down, he finished dressing and wondered how he had not heard of this. Picking up the phone, he dialed Marvin Newman's number. When Newman's assistant answered and told him Newman had gone on vacation, Todd was infuriated. The one night he needed his trusted lapdog and he wasn't around. Hanging up the phone with a loud bang, he saw Pam in the doorway.

"Pam, I need your help."

"What's going on?"

"Look, I know you're doing Blake, but now he's an ugly fuck. Help me tonight, and I'll pay you anything you want. Just ask."

"You've had a bit tonight. Are you sure you're up to it?"

"Don't you question me, Pam. I'm fine!"

"Well, I won't be climbing on him with that face anymore, with what's left of it. Besides, what's one more body? Sure, I'll help." Pam said, almost reading his mind.

"Get dressed; we're going to the hospital." Todd watched her disappear into his bedroom, and he reached for the bottle of tequila. Taking a huge mouthful, it spilled down his shirt; he didn't care. A few minutes later they were in his car leaving the mountain clinic. Considering how wasted he was, it would be a miracle if they even made it there at all.

Miracles happen. In the time it took them to arrive, the anger he possessed toward his brother had amplified. It was late when they got to the darkened floor of the hospital, and they quickly found his chart. They then went to his room and saw him lying in bed. His face was bandaged, and there were burn marks on his chest and arms. Todd saw that he was intubated and sedated.

"Damn you," Todd cursed. "All these years we could have worked side by side, and it was *you* who destroyed that."

Pam looked at him and took a few steps back.

He wanted to kill him right there, but he couldn't. No, he had a plan, and tonight was the night he was going to fulfill it. Quietly, he opened the door and looked down the corridors. The hospital was asleep in the dead of night, and he smiled.

Disconnecting all the leads and turning on all the battery-powered monitors; they got everything ready and wheeled his patient to the elevator, pushed his bed inside, and hit the third floor. The labs were located there, along with some of the less violent patients, and those were the ones he needed to be near. Getting inside the lab, which had a teaching surgical suite within it, he pushed the bed to the surgical table, and they moved him onto it. Strapping him down, he looked at the empty chair where the anesthesiologist would sit, and he gave Pam a look.

"Ah, this is what you needed me for. No problem," she said, hooking up the leads and equipment to the man on the table.

Leaving her to it, Todd left the room and proceeded down the hall to the patients' rooms, privately selecting the nastiest ones for the ultimate payback to his brother. Feeling the tequila, he swooned; his vision blurred for a moment, and he pulled out his vial of cocaine. Taking a healthy breath, he laughed. He was delighted in the fact Blake would hate this. Blake had been a toned and muscled man his whole life, strongest of the brothers and always beating up on Todd, even bragging that he was not only striking but better equipped than Todd below the belt, as well. He had constantly teased Todd about the fact that he was as handsome and smart as their father and far more loved by their mother than he would ever be. Blake had belittled him most his life and now…this was it. That innocent fair-haired child who'd never had a chance now had this moment: tonight was *his* for the taking.

Blake Vreeland was a strong man, worked out every day, ate right, and although he was a drinker of fine whiskies, bourbons, and scotches, he never went too far with the drinking—unlike his little alcoholic brother Todd. After years of being in his shadow, Todd was giving him what he hated most. The patients Blake allowed Todd to see were the gluttonous slobs that had got caught in a child sex operation. And when they pleaded guilty by reason of insanity, they were sent to Vreeland Hills Sanatorium. Blake not only hated having to treat these lazy people, but despised them for the crimes they'd committed against the children too. The fact that they were morbidly obese irritated Blake with his tight regimen of keeping fit—added to his hatred of them.

Dr. Todd didn't care one way or the other because they'd be dead shortly after he was done with them for Blake's surgery, and he figured no one would miss them anyway. With his selected patients (the ones Blake had allowed him to see) moved to a private intensive care unit near the lab, intubated and completely properly medicated and restrained to their beds per his orders, Todd knew they'd be ready for his plan, which would come at a moment's notice, just like tonight.

Seeing the lone nurse watching over the patients, Todd moved up quietly behind her, and when she turned, he slit her throat and pushed her backward to the floor. The room he was standing in smelled awful, like a sealed alcoholic's homeless tent, from the filthy patients he'd ordered to be left in their beds unattended. Grabbing a metal basin from a shelf, he then went to the drug cart and pulled the necessary drugs he'd need to keep the fat slobs quiet while he took what he needed knowing the light intubated patients would *feel* what he had planned for them. Finally he grabbed a few surgical blades and returned to the sleeping victims in front of him.

Injecting the succinylcholine into the IV to mix with the propofol and pain medications of his patients was the easy part. Waiting a few moments for the drug to take effect, he thought how much he loved the neuromuscular paralytic agent that stopped everything, including the ability to breathe, and he looked at the machine pumping air into his first patient's lungs and grinned, wishing he didn't need them so his patients would be wide wake to die of asphyxia and not be able to move or do anything to stop it in their paralyzed state. But *that* would be too quick, and bleeding out would be so much slower. Once he noticed the drug working, he injected the second drug to wake them, so they would *know* what was happening while being trapped inside their own bodies, and helpless to do nothing but watch. He then pulled back the sheet and nearly barfed when a vapor cloud of stench drifted up to his face. Holding his breath, he cut a large section of the fat gut that hung over the bed until it separated from the body and fell into the basin he'd placed on the floor beneath it. Picking it up, not caring about sterility, he placed it on a cart and proceeded to his next two selected victims and cut away the fat pieces and a goiter he needed for his brother's plastic surgery—the surgery to end all plastic surgeries.

"Dooo-be-dooo-be-doo-doo," Dr. Todd sang as he sliced off what he needed, getting sprayed in the face with blood and turning his head away in disgust. When he was finished, he continued his tune and moved to the beat in his head as he wheeled the nasty cart away from the patients he'd left to die a slow death and into his makeshift surgical lab, where Nurse Pam had already prepared the patient as best she could, adding a few more bandages to his swollen and seeping face, not knowing exactly what Dr. Todd had in mind.

The stench was awful, and Pam nearly puked going for the eucalyptus to dip into her mask to keep from smelling the foul odors from the cart Todd wheeled into the room.

When Todd arrived next to his brother on the table, he looked down at him, and a questioning look came over his face.

"Here, baby, I think you need some of this," Pam said, holding up the bottle of liquid cocaine she'd grabbed while dabbing her mask.

Todd smiled and went to her as she drew a syringe full of the drug and pointed it at his face.

"Open wide," she said, wearing a cunning smile under her own mask. She could only imagine what was about to happen, and being as sadistic as he was, she couldn't wait to enjoy the show.

With his mouth open, she pushed the plunger, and Todd could feel the potent drug numb his mouth immediately.

"What are you doing with that cart of shit?" Pam asked.

"You'll see," Todd said, feeling the high kick in and his vision blur for a moment before he gowned and gloved for surgery.

Back at the table, Dr. Todd looked at his brother's muscled body, which he'd worked on every day and was toned and tight, just like their other brother's, Dr. Eric Vreeland, who'd left the family practice to marry a European and had moved abroad. Todd worked out, too, but for some reason he was always the smallest of the Vreeland boys, and it infuriated him. He then took photos of his patient from an old instamatic before the fun began, not caring that the bandages covered his face, giving him comfort to not to have to look at him while he destroyed his beautiful body.

"Dooo-be-dooo-be-doo-doo," Todd sang as he pushed the cart over to his brother. And as he picked up the knife and held it where he was going to add the appendage, he had a moment of guilt wash over him.

"Shoo-be-doo-doo," he muttered. As he looked at the back of his gloved, scarred hand, the guilt disappeared and the hatred returned. He slashed his brother's skin in a feverish striking motion. The blood sprayed out from the vile slashing of his skin, and Dr. Todd went to work selecting the first portion from the cart, adding it to his side and over his stomach. He then spread his legs and added one to his pelvic floor, ball sack, ass, and thigh; then he moved to the other side of the table and sliced his left side, adding a piece from his abdomen to his thigh, then he lifted one of his arms and attached a nasty piece of fat to his underarm across his chest. Then for the crown in his surgery, he lifted the bloody goiter and peeled back the bandages under his patient's chin and sliced him open to apply the pièce de résistance.

"This is for sleeping with my first girlfriend, Connie, you fucking dick!" Todd said in a deadly calm voice, as the drugs he was on seemed to confuse him a bit. He leaned against the table, and all the while Pam was watching his every move. Then, as his vision blurred, he shook his head and lifted the bandages on his patient's burned face to see the swollen, bruised purple skin raised like a blistering wound under his jawline; his lips resembled those of a fish, and his nose and part of his cheeks were completely gone. Exposed bone and pus secreted from his wounds, and it stuck to the bandages. Seeing the tissue pull with the bandage, he dropped them and slashed him over his forehead. Blood pooled under the bandages and ran down the table, and he laughed.

He tried to focus, and Pam was at his side with the needle. "Here, babe, I think you need more of this," she said, lifting away his mask and pushing the plunger of liquid cocaine into his mouth.

Dr. Todd's eyes blurred again, and he looked back to his patient, staring through a haze to the bandages on his forehead turning red with his blood. Dropping the blade, he remembered Blake's *other* little trick and he grabbed the hot Bovie and cauterized the skin right through the bandage to form a vile scar, catching the bandages on fire to burn him. Thinking of every time his brother had one-upped him and made him feel like shit, he had burned him like a madman until his brother was a scarred monster.

With the surgery finished, he ordered Pam to clean up the mess he'd made in the other ICU and take the dead nurse with the patients to the basement, because he wanted to wheel *his* patient to his new home himself.

When Dr. Todd's patient woke from his drugged state, he was in a windowless room filled with many mirrors, and the lights were on as bright as they could be. He called out, raising his heavy arms to his face, pulling off the bandages to reveal his burning, pus-filled eyes, and tried to shield them from the bright lights above. The fluorescents hurt his eyes, and he could smell the stench of the fungal growth trapped under the heavy fat sacks. He could feel his once-chiseled frame now oozing pus that secreted from loosely bound stitches. He wasn't even restrained to his bed, giving him the thoughts to escape. But as he attempted to make out objects in the lonely room, he spotted the movement of rats scurrying across the floor. Then he noticed the photos. Photos of a toned and muscled Dr. Blake Vreeland were hanging everywhere, taped to the walls all around him. Then, he focused on the nightmare.

Photos of *his* finely toned body on the operating room table before it had been destroyed...his face covered in bandages...and other shots without the dressings showing a hideous beast that not even a horror movie director could create inside his own mind. This was *his* transformation.

He knew if he tried pulling the nasty appendages off from himself, he'd bleed to death, a fact his doctor knew well too he thought. His scream echoed through the sixth floor, sending the women into a panic, which was music to Dr. Todd Vreeland's ears.

CHAPTER 40

T odd Vreeland opened his desk drawer and pulled out a small family photo. It was a copy of the master portrait that hung in their home as a child, and he looked at his family's smiling faces before all the sad, depressing bitterness touched each and every one of them—like it had stretched tightly over their forced smiles as they grew older. The memories of that night continued in his head.

Dr. Todd settled into the sanatorium that very night. In the days that followed, everything was going to change, yet again, for the beleaguered physician. With his payback down the hall sick from the surgery and starving, Dr. Todd Vreeland ran Raven House and continued to treat his patients, especially the aged Rose Galloway and the other five women on the sixth floor of the east wing. And when one of the other pregnant women came full term, courtesy of the Vreeland brothers allowing their most mad patients into their room for sex to create the perfect child to sacrifice in the basement, his prized patient was dying of an infection in a locked room at the end of the hall.

Before the first baby was born, Todd's disfigured patient, in a last-minute fit of rage, was woken when a rat had climbed to his bed and began feeding from his open, seeping wounds. He thrashed about and was able to fall from his bed to the floor, ripping one of the fat sacks that had been sewn on to his body. Rotted fat tissue that looked like bloody macaroni and cheese secreting a sickly green pus seeped from the caught piece of flesh on his bed down onto him, splattering all over his face, where he succumbed to the agony of his surgery and died in that spot beneath his bed with the help of the hungry rats.

The death stench lingered for days, causing the other patients to grow ill and Dr. Todd to worry about the pregnant patients, whom he certainly couldn't lose to illness. When he finally unlocked and opened his brother's door, fluids from his body had pooled around and under him. The heavy vile odor sickened the orderlies, and they ran and vomited, but they had to get rid of the body or face Todd's wrath. Pushing a wheelbarrow into the room, they tipped it next to his body and then used shovels to lift and roll over the corpse into the wheelbarrow facedown. There, before them, remained an outline in dark body fluid staining the floor, a remembrance of Dr. Todd's saddest victim.

They covered him with a sheet and wheeled him to the pit, where Dr. Todd was smoking a cigar and enjoying his tequila. There was heavy metal music playing on the radio as he walked over to the wheelbarrow and proceeded to lift the filthy sheet, but a cloud of stench escaped, causing Dr. Todd to nearly puke, reminding him of the night he'd performed the surgery. Dropping the sheet, nearly uncovering the scarred and bloated face hanging over the edge of the wheelbarrow, he forced a smile. "I tried telling you our sick, bastard of a father was behind our mother's murder, but you wouldn't listen." And with that, he reached down with his cigar and pushed it into the back of the corpse's head, twisting it back and forth.

Singed tissue burned under the filthy sheet, and a foul smell choked Dr. Todd, and he stepped back, tossing the cigar in an ashtray. He then doused the burned tissue with the remains of his drink and lifted up the wheelbarrow and hurled him down into the pit. The splat that echoed up the chamber delighted him, and he returned to the radio and turned up the volume. As he enjoyed his moment, he was alarmed when he heard one of his patients screaming from her room. A smile crossed his face, and he knew it was time.

Rushing to deliver the first child, moving those few short steps away from the sixth-floor operating room, he heard the noise behind him. Looking back toward the pit door, a shadow of a man climbed out from the darkness and moved up the wall. Like a large cockroach, it disappeared into the ceiling like a bolt of lightning. Dr. Todd flinched. He blinked his eyes rapidly and dashed to the pit, staring down into the darkness. Seeing nothing, he distinctly heard the gurgling voice from below.

"Serve me," the voice said, turning into a faint laugh.

Excited, thinking he'd proved his basement shenanigans were finally paying off, he rushed to the insane woman screaming from her vicious contractions. He untied and grabbed her, and as he was lifting her up, she clawed at him, and he punched her in the face, knocking her out. He then picked her up and dumped her, slumping, into a wheelchair and pushed her to the working elevators running to the basement.

The night at the hospital was far from being finished, and on the far side of town, a fire had started in a factory that was going to interrupt the brilliant plans of the young, put-upon Vreeland that'd now claimed the sanatorium as his own. And when the wind picked up, the fire jumped the street to the fields on the other side and grew in ferocity as the nightmare played out in the hospital.

By morning's light, Dr. Todd emerged covered in blood and wore a crazed look in his eyes. He could smell smoke from a faraway campfire—a very big campfire.

CHAPTER 41

T
odd hated that he'd had some *missing* moments of his life, caused by the many blackouts he'd had in his old career of drinking and his free supply of medical drugs to sustain his choices didn't help. But *some* of the things he'd wished he could forget were forever locked in his battered mind, and they haunted him.

With the basement debauchery behind him, Dr. Todd passed out in his brother's sixth-floor private office on the sofa, and when he woke several hours later from his nightmare (about killing a nurse), he heard the sounds of terror. The TV had been left on, and the news was reporting the fire. As he focused on the old television set, a shadow of a man moved in his room, frightening him, and he heard the faint, desperate cries echoing down the long hallway from the women he kept enclosed on the opposite end of the building.

The sounds in his mind came from his patient pleading with him from his locked room down at the end of the hall, and the memory of his early years when he actually liked his brother flooded his mind. Panic took him, and the smell of the campfire grew stronger.

As he shook away the faded memories and the delusion of the shadow man, he sat up and enjoyed the cries from the women. But the shadow was still there, and it moved in the corner of his eyesight. "Who's there?" he cried out, turning on the sofa, seeing nothing. Panic started creeping in as he got up and turned to the light source, where he saw another shadow move across the wall and then...vanish.

"You're killing me, Stubs," came the whisper behind him.

Todd spun around and saw…nothing. "Blake, I know it's you," he yelled in the empty room. "You're killing me, Stubs!" Todd repeated in a disgusted tone. "I'll show you who's stupid now, asshole."

Todd slammed open the office door and saw the dead woman from his nightmare. She had a tourniquet wrapped around her throat, and her hair was wild and partly covered the bruise around her neck, which was huge. Her skirt was pulled down, and she'd been raped; there was blood on her white uniform, as well as on his pants. It was Lorena Mason, that stupid wench that always handed him the wrong instruments.

"No," Todd gasped, backing away from her body. Her dead, open eyes were fixed on the long hall leading to the operating room.

Then he watched her turn to him and smile. "You're killing me, Stubs," she said and laughed at him in a gargled voice, rising up from the ground with a syringe in her hand. "This won't hurt a bit," she gargled again. Spitting blood at him, she laughed as he stumbled backward and fell to the floor.

Todd got up and looked back at the woman as she slumped to the ground, dead. The black shadow of a man left her body, and the darkness moved toward him like a slow moving cyclone of black fog that whirled around him with a sickening heaviness. He could feel an evil soul touching his, and Todd's mind snapped. He yelled out for help as his eyes turned black.

"Dr. Todd," came the frightened voice from Bob the X-ray tech. But when he saw the doctor, he wished he hadn't.

Todd slumped over, and when Bob went to help him, he saw the vile deathlike mask emerging from his soul. Todd grabbed at Bob's throat but missed, able to catch only his scrubs. The fabric ripped, and Bob backed away, falling against an end table. Grabbing an ashtray, he smashed it against Todd's face, slicing his lower lip.

The mistake was huge—the blow seemed to give Todd *more strength* rather than slow him down. Bob got free and ran from the office to the hall, but Todd tackled him through the open door, sending him into another room near a medical supply cart; the lobotomy icepicks that fell nearby were perfect.

Grabbing one, he waved it in front of Bob's terrified face. "Remember this, you petulant prick?" Todd yelled, spitting blood from his busted lip.

"Pam said your brother's dick is bigger and tastes better, like everyone else's in this place!" Bob uttered and spit it his face.

Todd watched Bob's eyes widen as he grabbed his throat with one hand and brought down the icepick with the other, boring straight into the poor man's left eye. He dug in deep, and the eye made a popping sound in Bob's ears, or so it seemed. Todd then dropped the icepick and dug his fingers into his socket and ripped the eye out. Showing it to him, Todd then shoved it into his mouth.

Bob was gagging and bucking underneath him and reached up for the shelf; more equipment fell. And that's when Todd saw it. He grabbed a large bone-cutting knife and waved it in front of him. "Remember this, fuck stick? Remember asking what it was for in a below-the-knee amputation case you walked in on? Now it's for fucking fuck fuckers that deserve to die! Feel my big blade shithead! You probably always wanted to!" He screamed, spitting blood from his busted lip as he brought down the large knife into the man's abdomen and chest, stabbing him several times. On the last plunge into the dying man, he left it there and turned the blade. Bob screamed out as Dr. Todd grabbed the icepick with one hand, and his face with the other, and stared into Bob's one remaining eye.

"I want you to know I'm enjoying this, you belligerent little fucker!"

"No!" the man cried when he saw Todd lift the icepick above him.

"This is for asshole X-ray techs."

Bob screamed and spit up blood as his life was leaving him.

Todd's laugh turned into a rabid growl as his madness burned his blood. Bob tried to laugh to anger him more, but Dr. Todd saw his remaining eye widen with fear and knew he'd won. The last thing poor Bob the X-ray tech saw was Todd's evil grin as the icepick came down with such a blow into his other eye that his head bounced up off the floor, and Todd drove the icepick deep into the man's brain.

The whirling shadow around the doctor moaned with glee and moved down Todd's body to his feet and into the dying blind man. The force from it exiting Todd's body caused him to collapse and roll over the dying man. And when he opened his eyes, he saw the outstretched arm of Bob pull the squeaky supply cart near him. The sound seemed louder than ever as his blackened holes for eyes were staring at him with the icepick sticking out from his right empty socket dripping blood from its end. "Here's to Bob quality time, dick face." Bob's possessed body spoke in a monstrous voice. Then, as the shadow left the dying man, his outstretched arm slumped to the floor.

Todd watched the shadow man move from the body back to the hall and toward the operating room from where he'd first seen it.

"Sire, it's you!" Todd gasped, thinking it was the devil himself, making his acquaintance as the madness of the last twenty-four hours took its toll. "I'm sorry. The baby was stillborn," Todd cried out. Paranoia set in, and quietly he withdrew into himself thinking of what to do next, until his head cleared momentarily and he heard the news.

The night of the firestorm had been a blessing to Dr. Todd. And seeing the old news report of the missing congressman and his daughter being replayed panicked him, especially with the new report of the congressman's wife stating her suspicions that he'd taken her for a medical surgery she'd been dead against. Then he saw the reports; burning ash from far across the meadows was drifting to other structures, setting them on fire. This added to the panic, and he knew exactly what to do. It was the perfect plan.

Using the curtains between the bed bays on the sixth-floor psych ward, the good doctor got busy opening the windows and pulling the curtains, pushing the lower portions out from the barred section below. He then went outside to some leaves under the trees and gathered some in a bucket and carried them upstairs. Lighting them on fire he blew on them, waiting for bits of ash to rise, and throwing the burning embers on to the curtains. Being old, stained, and mostly rotted, they made for the perfect fuel. He then ran, tipping over laundry carts outside his patients' rooms and splashing highly-flammable alcohol prep solution in the hall at the doors of the patients, hearing the cries of the damned behind him. Then, for an added touch, he smashed glass ammonia bottles and splashed bleach all around and opened a few high-pressure oxygen tanks as he left.

The curtains caught fire immediately, and the beds went up in an instant. The mixture of ammonia and bleach combined to make a toxic gas that added to the hell that was unfurling.

When the fire hit the alcohol prep solution and the oxygen, the wind from the open windows stoked the fire; the roar built with the intensity of a tornado.

The five women trapped in their rooms panicked and tried to escape. Rose Galloway ran to her bathroom and tried to turn on the water, but it was useless. The lines had been turned off, and there was nothing they could do but see the freedom through the bars over the windows from their rooms.

As the fire burned through their doors and the first oxygen tank exploded blasting through the door down from Rose's room, the fire caught the peeling wallpaper aflame, and the two women that shared that room tried to run through it, catching themselves on fire and tripping over the burning sheets from the laundry carts in their way, stumbling and hitting the ground, struggling to escape.

Rose heard the second oxygen tank explode; she saw the patient through the small hole in her heavy door across the hall leap from her blown-out doorway. Her gown on fire, she landed in the smoking gas fumes of the ammonia and bleach. She was choking, and she opened her eyes and reached out to her; she then slumped over as flames consumed her body.

Rose screamed and backed away as more oxygen tanks exploded near her door, blowing it in and catching everything on fire. The flames caught her own gown, and she ran back to the bathroom and tried the shower, and as a few drops dripped down on her head, the flames entered the bathroom, trapping her inside. Her hair caught fire, and she screamed. Trying to escape the bathroom, she hit the doorframe and it splintered, and the top portion came down on top of her. Trapped and on fire, Rose Galloway screamed as she took her last breath falling to the floor.

Todd ran as fast as he could to his truck and drove to the Black River Children's Center. There he stayed until his staff alerted him that the authorities were on the property and wanted to see him; he was prepared.

Wanting it to seem like he'd been there for quite some time, he needed an alibi and wondered just who would be his goat for the sacrifice. Hoping he'd see that asshole who was always late and knocking off early, he knew *exactly* where to look.

Knowing that fat little pig's constant appetite, he saw Jonathan Holles standing at a patient's refrigerator, stuffing his fat face, not giving a damn that it wasn't allowed. Quietly, he pulled a white handkerchief and small bottle from his pocket and poured the liquid onto it. He then moved up behind the jackass and chloroformed the lazy asshole.

The orderly coughed up the patient's cake he was eating and gagged for help.

"Shut the fuck up, J-Hole; you're now my goat," Dr. Todd whispered in his ear as he smothered the little fucker.

The smile widened on Dr. Todd's face as he watched J-Hole's fat fingers squeeze the chocolate cake between them. As the man lost consciousness, Dr. Todd let him fall hard to the floor.

"Fuck! Now I have to carry Mr. Fat Ass!" Dr. Todd yelled in the empty room, and he picked him up and threw the bastard over his shoulder and brought him to surgery.

After getting that miserable man on the table, he positioned a metal triangle under his knee, a device normally used for positioning broken femurs and tibias during surgery. He then left the operating room and came back dragging in a sledgehammer. *This is going to be fun*, he thought. As he grabbed the sledgehammer, he noticed the chloroform starting to wear off and Jonathan waking up on the table. *Probably all that damn sugar in the chocolate cake the fucker ate*, his mind flashed as his anger grew.

"You've been a bad little piggy," he said in a mad rage. As he watched Jonathan's eyes open in fear, he smashed the guy's left knee on top of the triangle, denting the heavy radiolucent metal positioning device and rejoicing in hearing J-Hole scream like a little girl.

"No," Jonathan cried, "I'll tell!"

"Who are you going to tattle to you little bitch? I need a sacrifice and you're my goat."

For the encore, he swung the sledgehammer again and smashed his right hip; he then raised it once again and smashed him in the groin, busting his nut sack and his pelvis. The horrific scream that emanated was magic to Dr. Todd, and he decided one more swing was needed. Aiming for his right shin, he swung the sledgehammer one last time, splintering his tibia.

Jonathan screamed and tried raising his chocolate-stained hand up for help, which made Dr. Todd laugh as he watched it drop when the man passed out. He then slowly moved away from the soon-to-be corpse on his table.

"Dooo-be-dooo-be-doo-doo," Todd muttered with a grin, dragging the bloody sledgehammer away and throwing it into a large scrub sink, washing it in hot water before he hid it away.

He then took his time and didn't even scrub his hands before pretending to put the hapless young man back together. He later told the authorities that he'd slipped on the cliffs near the center after Dr. Todd caught him trying to rape an unconscious patient. "He even took a swing at me," he told them, explaining the fat lip he'd received from Bob the X-ray tech.

Yes, Dr. Todd Vreeland was a true fighter for the underdog in an unfair world, and the police wanted to question the man after he recovered. *Which, of course, isn't going to happen,* Todd thought.

It was then he was told the fire had destroyed most of the upper floors of the East Tower and a portion of the fifth floor. Although firefighters were able to put out the blaze, no one above the fifth floor had survived, and luckily the seventh floor with the beautiful glass skylights remained untouched as if the flames were afraid of the evil that emanated from that room.

Todd Vreeland got up from his desk and looked back to the tele-vision set. More footage of the earthquake was being shown, and he shut the set down. Moving to the kitchen, he opened a cabinet and pulled down the brand new bottle of Don Julio Real tequila, his favorite. It'd been too long.

CHAPTER 42

As he was leaving Trask Studios, Ed Savage called Logan. He was worried about Sam and told him he was all finished in New York City and couldn't wait to be on the helicopter heading back home. When he asked to say good-bye to the girls, Logan told him they'd just left for West Point and that Maura had driven him back from the hospital.

"Sorry I missed them," Ed said.

"Yeah, well, you've got bigger things to worry about. Hell, we all do."

"I got your message; you saw it all?"

"Ed, what the hell is this? I thought we'd heard the last from Wendy Storm."

"So did I."

"Do you think her sister Sandy leaked the tape? You were a little snarky with her."

"The thought crossed my mind, Logan; it's been a hell of a day."

"You don't know the half of it."

"What now?" Ed asked, thinking it couldn't get any worse.

"I'm headed for a divorce."

"What?"

"That's right, Ed. Maura's divorcing me."

"God, Logan, I'm so sorry. When did all this start?"

"Months before Maura left London for the States—before the Black Ridge mess."

"Can't you work it out?"

"Ed, I've tried. She says there's just nothing left."

"I'm so sorry, Logan. How are you doing?"

"Not good. It's killing me, but what choice do I have? I finally told Roman this morning, and I think Maura told the women, but we've kept it quiet from the kids."

"This family is falling apart. Listen, stay close to Roman until I get home, and we'll sort this out."

"Thanks, Ed, but Roman and Gabby are leaving for the lake house. They called the police and told them they'd meet them there. And how the hell did *that* get on the news, anyway?"

"You got me. Hell, I don't think anyone's been there in months," Ed said, thinking it was too late to call Tallulah due to the police already being involved.

"No one has! I've asked the family, and no one's been up there."

"We'll, I'm finished here, and I'll see you when I get home. And, Logan, I've got your back with Maura. Anything you need—just ask."

"Thanks. What time will you be home?"

"With traffic down here, a few hours."

"Fine. Maybe Sam will be home when you get here."

"They're discharging him today?"

"Good possibility. See you when you get here."

"Hang tight, brother."

CHAPTER 43

The Carlisle Consortium Nathan Savage had done business with in his earlier days had grown into a mega conglomerate, owning several companies around the globe by the time of his death. And the last time Nathan amended his will, he'd been in a rage. He'd had a fight with Ed about giving up his Hollywood life and returning to the company he'd built to give to his firstborn son one day. After hearing Ed wanted nothing to do with it, he and Parnell drafted the amendment, making Ed quit the Hollywood business.

When the completed will was drafted, it was sent right over to Nathan, and he had a copy made, sending it to the consortium as a backup. Over the years of doing business with Parnell, and the guilty nightmares he'd been having, he would change his mind and call him to change the will around. Thinking Nathan was losing it, Parnell decided to focus on Savage Construction and the millions he'd been making from the company and decided to play for himself.

The only obstacle with this scheme was the fact that Nathan was still as sharp as a tack, and soon, when the nightmares subsided, he was back to being his same cantankerous self. When the day came and Nathan arrived at his office, he was offered his usual brandy, and the two talked about the good old days. And when Parnell presented the amended will to his client, Nathan told him he'd changed his mind and to forget the new will. Nathan said to just keep the old one intact.

The problem, Parnell told him, was, seeing as Nathan had voided his old will when the new one was finished, that a new copy of the old one would have to be drafted, and he'd have to get fresh copies made and new signatures on them. Nathan would also have to have it signed by the end of the week.

Nathan agreed to stopping back by, and when he did, he signed all the lines he was told to. When the copy arrived at his desk, he'd meant to copy it and send it to the consortium, but the day it arrived he'd been in the hospital with heart murmurs, and it got filed away by a new part-time secretary when Sally Anne was visiting Nathan at the hospital.

The ticking time bomb in the file finally went off when Nathan's secretary, Sally Anne Cartwright, received Nathan's will from Parnell's office after he'd died and mailed a copy of it to a mysterious post office box.

Hours after Mingyu delivered the package from Nathan's post office box to the gloved man in the limousine, a team of consortium lawyers combed through every page. The slip-up Sam easily found in the language of the will giving Ed the ability to keep his Hollywood jobs and run Savage Construction at the same time, was also found by the consortium lawyers.

Calls were immediately made to the consultant Nathan had made his arrangements with who was on assignment in London—sitting in an office that was surprisingly not far away from Logan Savage's very own.

CHAPTER 44

Shortly after Kate and Lana left for West Point, Marlo threw her packed bags into her car and drove off to her doctor's appointment before heading to the train station. She had agreed to do *Tycoon Wives* and was headed to New York City for her first filming event. It was for her introduction and the Cinema Shake-Up.

The new cast additions were hidden backstage and brought in through a different section of the studio to a soundproof booth. Then when the current cast rejoined each other on the same stage where they'd shared their last reunion to add to the memorial fighting that always seemed to ensue, a large movie screen would come down from above, and drinks and popcorn would be served. The *Tycoon Wives* would then sit back and watch the film clips they'd be vying for, suggestions from fans that they'd be reenacting to start the next season.

When the lights came up, Randall Bishop would come out with the new ladies joining the show, and, depending on how many he brought out signaled how many could go—if any—once filming was done. The fans would vote.

Alliances were crucial, and a bit of game playing always pitted the women against each other, a fun tactic Randall thought of to get the drama started early in the new season.

The prior year it had been the glory days of black-and-white movies, and the top two clips were from two Joan Crawford movies. One was the scene from *Mildred Pierce* where her daughter, played brilliantly by Shamori Hanson, slapped Joan Crawford's character, Mildred, across the face, Crawford being played by Marilyn Hart. The clip was good, but it lost out to Cassidy Meyer and Tonya Lipschitz in their reenactment of a scene from *What Ever Happened to Baby Jane?* And that slap was all part of the following season's drama because Shamori really let her have it.

One of this year's categories had been reported to be comedy, and Marlo couldn't wait not only to watch firsthand but also to immerse herself in a character and act her heart out the way she used to from her early years with Ed. Marlo didn't know of any other cast additions, and she also had her thoughts about who she'd like to see fired from the show, but as she drove to her doctor's appointment, she let it all go because she was finally feeling like she had wanted to for such a long time. Too many years of watching her husband travel off for work, leaving her at home, had gone by, and now she finally had an entertaining job. She couldn't believe how lucky she was.

CHAPTER 45

K ate and Lana Savage were enjoying their ride back to West Point on the cool late morning in Upstate New York. The traffic was sparse, and the wind was blowing the fall leaves from the trees on the beautiful open country road. The clouds were intermittently blocking the sun, but the warmth of the engines kept them toasty. Pulling into a gas station, the girls went in and gave the attendant one of Lana's credit cards for both of them to fill up. As they grabbed a bottle of water, a service truck pulled in and parked near them.

The driver of the truck noticed the bikes right away and was impressed with them, but when he saw the bikes' owners pass him by as he entered the store, he looked back to check them out. "Hey, Greg," the driver of the truck said to the clerk inside.

"Lou! Hey, how goes it?" Greg said.

"Better now. The ladies with the bikes are hot!"

"You're telling me."

"Haven't seen them around. City folk?"

"I don't know—probably. The taller one's name is Savage," the clerk said, looking at the credit card she'd left inside the store.

"Oh yeah? I could get savage with that," Lou said, looking back to check out the girls once again.

"They're both hot," Greg said, lifting the blinds for another look and holding her credit card in his other hand. "I wouldn't pass up some Lana Savage." He laughed as he tossed her credit card on the small rack where he kept them.

"Lana Savage? I've seen that name somewhere," Lou said.

"Fill up?" Greg asked.

"No, we're good. Just came in to use the john."

"Here you go." Greg held up the key attached to the heavy plastic pipe.

Just as Lou was turning from the counter, he spotted the newspaper rack. "Wait a minute," he said, pulling a paper and thumbing through it. Finding the page he was looking for, he scanned the "West Point Parents' Weekend" article. He then glanced down to the article below: "Bastard Son Wins Daddy Lottery."

There he saw her name; the article was about Ed Savage's first-born son, some kid named Trent York. But below was a recap of his extended family and the murders that had happened in Black Ridge Falls. Those injured in the rollover were listed. Although a Gabby and Danni Savage made the list, the reporter stated that the oldest daughter, one Lana Savage, was not involved due to her being at West Point.

"You gonna be in there for a while?" Greg said, watching him.

"Sorry, no, just forgot something," he said, waving the key and putting the paper back.

He rushed to the john and quickly did his business. Returning, he dropped the key on the counter. "Thanks, Greg."

The clerk nodded and went back to his magazine, once again shutting out the world.

The girls saw the man walking out to his truck, and Kate gave a polite nod as she replaced the gas cap on her bike. He watched Lana continue to fill her tank as he got to his truck and quickly jumped inside, shutting the door.

"That was fast," came the voice from the passenger seat.

Lou started the truck and pulled out from the station. He stopped to check traffic and hung a right, speeding down the road.

"Hey, you're going the wrong way," Lenny said, looking at him like he was crazy.

"It's our lucky day, Lenny."

Lenny looked forward, scanning the road in front of them, and then turned back to him wondering what he was up to. "What do you mean? Where we going?"

Lou laughed and turned to his friend. "Lenny, if I told you, I'd have to kill you." He grinned as they drove down the road in the direction of West Point.

CHAPTER 46

At her doctor's office, Marlo Savage looked at her watch and was a bit agitated that it was taking so long. This was far past her appointed time. Her train was leaving soon, and she really didn't want to have to wait for the next one—or worse, drive into New York City by herself. She hated the traffic downstate, and when the receptionist told her she was next, she waited near the door, wondering who was taking up so much of her doctor's time. Impatiently flipping through a magazine, she looked up when the door opened and tossed the magazine onto the table next to her.

Standing quickly, she was surprised to see that instead of a nurse calling her in, Aisha Thomas had exited the back area, and the two literally bumped into each other.

"I'm so sorry," Marlo said. Realizing she knew the woman, she became startled.

"No worries," Aisha replied. Turning her head away, as if completely ignoring the woman, she moved toward the door.

"Aisha!" Marlo said, standing there, watching her try to leave. "What are you doing here?"

Aisha froze at the door; her first thought was to run, but that would look like she had *something* to hide. She quickly collected herself and turned around. "Marlo, so sorry—I've got too much on my mind, and I'm in a rush," she said. Wanting to scream in panic, she suppressed it and forced herself to keep a cordial expression.

"We're all in a hurry today," Marlo said as she put her hand on her belly. "Aisha, I didn't know you were expecting?"

Absolute panic was running through Aisha's veins, and she could feel her heart race in her chest. She looked to the reception nurse and grabbed Marlo's hand, leading her to the far side of the waiting room. Deciding she needed to say *something*, she gave her half the story.

"Marlo, Danny doesn't know yet. And, well...we've broken up, and I'm a complete mess over this."

Marlo was saddened by the news. "Oh, honey, I had no idea."

"It's bad, Marlo. Please keep this to yourself. I need time."

"I understand. I'm so sorry."

"Thank you."

"Marlo, you're next," came a voice from behind them.

"I really have to be going," Aisha said.

"Take care, hon."

"Thanks. And, remember, not a word to anyone." Aisha smiled and quickly left the office when Marlo turned toward the woman holding her chart.

She noticed her sunglasses resting on the chair and picked them up. As Aisha's last words ran though her head, she turned to the now-closed door and wondered, *Who would I tell?*

Not too long after her baby checkup, Marlo was at the train station and had plenty of time before her short ride to New York City. She was glad Randall Bishop had e-mailed and overnighted her contract to her and her lawyers, and she was going to do the show no matter what. But she also wanted to play out the intrigue that came with "having her lawyers take a look at it." While she hadn't heard from her lawyers yet, and was planning on signing after they called, she was sure everything was fine when she heard the announcement to board.

As she got situated on the train, she pulled out her self-assigned homework of catching up on all the latest gossip in the movie magazines for the show, when a very pregnant woman passed her by.

Marlo turned and watched the woman lumber back to her seat and thought of Aisha Thomas and how she didn't want her to tell *anyone* she was pregnant.

CHAPTER 47

B ack on their motorcycles, the temperature had dropped, and
the girls wanted to get there as quickly as possible. Pushing the
speed limit, they raced down the wooded area of Bear Mountain,
making great time until the sharp curve in the road met them with
disastrous results. What looked like a large dark puddle in the road
turned out to be mixed with motor oil, and when the girls hit it, the
accident was unavoidable.

Lana was on the inside of the curve when both bikes hit the
mass and started to slide. Her bike slid right out from under her, hitting Kate and sending her into the wooded area off the road. Lana
bounced off the grassy edge of the road and rolled into the ditch,
hearing her cousin scream in the distance.

With the sound of the engines in her ears, Lana leaned to her
side and sat up in the ditch. It was partly filled with water, and she
was soaked. "Kate!" she yelled taking off her helmet, climbing up
and away from the road. Standing, she could see exhaust from Kate's
bike and looked to the road for help. With no one there, she spotted
what looked like a carpenter's toolbox smashed on the side of the
road, as if it had fallen off a worker's truck.

"Lana!" She heard her cousin behind her. Turning, she dropped
her helmet and ran to the exhaust cloud to see Kate pinned under the motorcycle. When Lana's bike hit Kate's on the curve, she'd
tried to turn away and drove right off the road. Hitting the uneven

ground, she'd stayed on until the front tire hit a rut and she flew over her bike; it'd landed on top of her.

The eight-hundred-pound weight of the bike was atop her body, still idling. Lana quickly shut it off. She then got her footing and helped lift the bike away from her cousin, letting her climb out from under the heavy bike. The area was muddy, and in their frantic state, as they lifted it completely up while trying to keep it balanced, the bike fell over into the mud. Not caring and unhurt, Kate went around and tried lifting it up but slipped and fell back into a foot of nasty-looking mud that splashed up into her face.

Lana laughed, seeing her cousin in the mud. "Are you all right? Girl, you look awful."

Kate pulled off her helmet, letting her long hair fall, and tossed it beyond the mud to a grassy area. Mud had splattered up under her helmet, and she looked ridiculous. When she looked to Lana, she started laughing. "Oh my God, that was freaking insane! What happened?"

The fright and worry left Lana's mind as she stood there looking at her cousin. Instead, seeing her mud-caked face made her start laughing too. "Girl, I am going to beat your ass when we get out of here. You scared me!" Lana extended her hand to pull her up.

Kate put her opposite hand down for support, and it sank in the mud to her forearm. "Perfect," she said, lifting it up and shaking off the mud. She then tucked her feet under her and stood, with Lana pulling her up to stand. "Seriously, we really messed up."

"Yeah, let's see how bad it is," Lana said, moving to her cousin's bike. Together they pulled it up and saw the cracked windshield, the scratches on the gas tank, and a few broken spokes. But the mud was making it impossible for them to move it without help. "Come on— I'll get my bike, and maybe we figure out a way to pull it out."

The girls moved back toward the road to Lana's bike, and Kate saw the oil and the open oilcans. "What the hell is this?" she said, moving out to the road.

"Probably fell off a truck," Lana said, thinking she was looking at the broken toolbox she'd seen earlier as she was trying to lift her bike from the ditch that was several feet from where she'd landed.

"Like hell this fell off a truck," Kate said. "Look!" She pointed.

Lana turned to her cousin, and her gaze followed where she was pointing. There in the ditch were several freshly opened motor-oil cans.

The screeching of the hawk overhead scared them, and they jumped at the sound. "Screw this! Let's get the hell out of here," Lana said.

Kate rushed to her, and together they pulled her bike up and onto the road. She started it, and it roared to life. "What can we use to pull my bike?" Kate said, looking around the cold-looking woods and wanting to be on their way.

"I've got two belts; how many do you have? Maybe we can attach them together and then start your bike and get out of here."

"Just the one I'm wearing."

"It'll have to work," Lana said, opening her saddlebag and digging in her duffel and pulling out her other belt. "Got it—come on."

The two moved back to Kate's bike, and she lifted it from the thick mud and got on to start it. The bike roared with life, and the smiles on their faces returned. She tried to get it out on its own power, and the mud was splattering them, and they started laughing again. "Stop. Stop—this isn't working," Lana said as she took off her belt and fastened it together. When she was finished, Kate had taken hers off and handed it to her, and with the three combined, they had several feet of length. Then they gathered wood, leaves, and anything they could find to put under and in front of the tires for traction.

"That's good. I'll go get my bike," Lana said, and Kate spotted the tree.

"No, wait a minute. Lana, I think this will work. Let me slip on the end to my bike, then grab the other end of the belt, and pull it around that tree. When I gun the engine, pull like you mean it."

"Um, sure," Lana said, wanting to try anything.

Lana readied herself around the tree, and Kate got on her bike and revved the engine. She then nodded and gunned the engine, and Lana pulled like her life depended on it. The bike lurched forward with the help of the brush under the tires, and with a white cloud of smoke pouring out from the exhaust, the bike freed itself with a jolt, and she nearly fell off it again trying to stop it on hard ground.

Lana's arms were sore from pulling so hard, and she let go of the belt when she saw the bike lurch from its muddy trap. Moving to her cousin, she unhooked the belts from the motorcycle, and together they started walking it slowly, one on each side, over the terrain to the road. They were muddy, wet, and cold, but they had their sense of humor, and the worst was over—until the sound of the truck came speeding toward them.

They were a few yards from the ditch, and Kate recognized the truck from the gas station just as it slid to a stop, crashing into Lana's bike and sending it back into the ditch, severely damaging it. The girls screamed, and the men jumped out from the truck and ran toward them. It happened too fast, and the girls weren't expecting anything like this. They turned to run, and the men caught them and tried to knock them down, but what their attackers didn't count on was the fact that these cadets could fight.

The first one grabbed Lana, and she elbowed him in the gut as she turned and punched him in the face. He took a step back, regained his balance, and lunged at her, knocking her down and pinning her to the ground.

Kate heard Lana scream as she kicked the other man in the groin; when he bent over from the pain, she kicked him in the side of his head, knocking him down. She then ran to Lana, but the man was holding a gun to her head. She froze and then felt the hands of the other man on her from behind and the strange chemical-smelling cloth over her mouth.

Lana watched as Kate passed out, and the bastard let her fall right to the ground. He then removed a vial from his pocket and poured the liquid on the cloth and laughed as he got near her, placing it over her face.

The last thing she saw was his ugly face laughing at her. They were caught by an enemy they hadn't seen coming.

CHAPTER 48

When Maura got back to Sam's room at the hospital, he was sitting on the edge of his bed buttoning his shirt. "Sam, I'm sorry, honey; I thought I'd be back sooner. Everything come out as expected?"

"Not sure yet on my shoulder, but they're sending me home today."

"Is that a good idea, Sam?"

"Maura, I'm dealing with my loss as best I can. I just had to get that out of my system, I guess. Don't get me wrong; it still hurts like hell, but the worst is over," Sam said, pausing from buttoning his shirt and sighing. "I'll be fine."

Sam's doctor then tapped on the door and entered. "Hey, Sam; Maura, good to see you."

Maura nodded. "How is he?"

"Emotionally...I'd like to prescribe some medication."

"No pills," Sam barked. "I'm a strong man, and my feelings for my wife are mine. I'll sort them out."

"I know," the doctor said. "Physically, though, your shoulder needs to heal, and that fall on the balcony caused trauma to your ligaments that's going to cause you some muscle pain. Now, if you're going to take it easy for the next four weeks, I'd like to have you come back for another MRI and see if it's healing on its own. Otherwise, we may have to talk about another surgery."

"No more surgery," Sam said in a defeated tone.

"I can prescribe some mild pain relievers, but I don't want you taking anything else, like your dad's old meds."

"Nope," Sam said, "I'll pass on those too. Didn't you say there was some over-the-counter stuff I can take?"

"Sure, there are several brands."

"Then if you'd write those down for me, I'll be sticking to those," Sam said. "Maura, I called Heather and told her to go over to the house and throw out every pill she can find. I really thought I was taking aspirin, but obviously Dad had his own pharmacy, and I want it gone."

Maura smiled at the man she knew was coming back from the ugly despair she and Zolie had found him in. "That's good to hear, Sam."

"Fine then. Sam, call my office for an appointment in four weeks or so for that MRI, and I'll call you after I read the report," the doctor said with a smile at his patient.

"Will do," Sam said, standing to finish buttoning his shirt.

"And get some rest," the doctor added as he left the room.

"Yes, rest is the order for you," Maura said. "Sam, there's still that extra bedroom in the main house. Would you like to move in there?"

"Maybe," Sam said, thinking of the bedroom's attached bath with the huge soaking tub as a nurse arrived with his wheelchair to escort him out.

CHAPTER 49

E d Savage's helicopter landed on the roof of Savage Tower just as Sally Anne's text arrived telling him she remembered that Mingyu's last name was Yunt. Ed looked at the message and rushed down to his office. He had called Tallulah to have her meet him there, and she was waiting in his office at a table with a newspaper when he arrived.

"Tallulah, I'm glad you're here. Any further news on the *Manchester*?" Ed asked, closing the door and limping with his cane to his desk dropping his duffel bag on it.

"The news is deplorable."

Ed froze and stared at her, waiting for her to finish her statement.

Seeing his serious look, she shook her head. "The Wendy Storm news…sorry, Ed, I thought we'd heard the last from that insipid fool. As for the *Manchester*, intelligence picked up on a signal with the same words used when pinpointing the Eastern Seaboard attack— 'Old Suzanna'—coming from a private home near a ski lodge in the Catskill Mountains."

"The Catskills! That's not too far from West Point," Ed said, thinking of the girls riding up there today.

"Ed, the home's empty; we've got agents keeping a close eye, but the woman's name on the property is a Meiling Yung."

"Meiling Yung," Ed repeated. "Tallulah, Sally Anne remembered the last name of the woman who was in dad's office: Mingyu Yunt."

"What a peculiar name, Mingyu Yunt. She sounds like a real—"

"Tallulah!" Ed said, cutting her off. "I hate that word," he said with a chuckle.

Tallulah laughed, remembering the gentleman Ed Savage truly was.

"Besides, Sally Anne agreed with you."

"Oh?"

"She said she wasn't a very nice lady. Now, did you find out anything else about the address?"

"Just that the post office box was opened by a woman named Ming Yuki, and all this can't be a coincidence—and I saw the security footage the day she picked up and closed the PO box. Here, I have her photograph," she said, pulling it out of her bag.

Ed took it and studied it.

"Keep that one, and show it to that secretary; make sure that's the same woman she saw, Ed."

"Fine. What do we have? Let's say she's the same woman. She knew my dad, picked up his will from a post office box, and has a home in the Catskills. Then we have 'Old Suzanna.' Are you sure of all this?"

"It's the information that's coming in."

"'Old Suzanna'—a song of sorts. We need the lyrics, the artist, year it was released, all of it deciphered to see if it points to anything. What else does 'Old Suzanna' point to?"

"I don't know. As soon as anything comes up, I'll call you," Tallulah said.

Ed nodded in frustration and noticed the paper on the table next to her.

Tallulah followed his gaze. "Ed, you really need to have a talk with that woman I met here yesterday. These headlines have to stop."

"What now?" Ed asked, expecting the worst.

Tallulah unfolded the paper with the article she wanted him to see and got up from the table and laid it on his desk. "I had a feeling the ski lodge home would be a bust; it was too easy, but we'll check out the aliases of this Mingyu Yunt and find her. But something besides Wendy Storm's latest announcement and your ex-wife's 'Daddy Lottery' story in today's paper caught my eye, and I'm glad you called because I wanted to bring this to you myself. I've missed you, Savage Nine, and it's time you came home."

"Tallulah, you've been my one and only office wife," Ed said and winked at her as he looked to the paper. He gazed past Wendy Storm's story and below the "Bastard Son" story and saw the article she was talking about.

"The Dutchman!" Ed said with a wondrous smile.

"It's the perfect cover, Ed. It'll be like old times," Tallulah said with a familiar smile. "I'll leave you to it. And I'll be expecting a call when you've finished reading it."

Ed's mind was already thinking the same thing, although he didn't want to admit it. "Tallulah, part of me would love nothing more than to forget about everything that's happening now and focus on something outside of my life. We've had some good times. I just don't know if I can now."

"No worries, Savage Nine; I'm sure Thrasher will be fine without you." Tallulah's eyes seemed to flash as she said that; then she turned away from him and picked up her bag.

He watched her leave his office, and he clicked on his desk lamp to read the story.

The article about the Dutchman was not only a story he'd done on *Archive Raiders*, but it was also ground zero in the Catskill Mountains right near where the mysterious home was located near a ski lodge.

Ed picked it up and began to read: "Following the second destructive storm, a group of Scouts helping to clear a blocked stream found an iron box containing rotted cash and double eagle coins from the 1930s. Authorities have taken the evidence from the Scouts, and no further word had been issued. Could this be part of the stolen millions prohibition gangster Dutch Shultz, commonly known as 'the Dutchman,' supposedly hid in the Catskill Mountains?"

The article went on to delve into the past of Dutch Shultz, but Ed knew it like the back of his hand. He sat back in his chair and wondered if this could be true. He remembered the episode he'd done on *Archive Raiders* about prohibition years ago, covering the Dutchman and the lost treasure in the Catskills; if this was indeed the treasure, more was to be found. And Tallulah was right when she said it'd be exactly like old times with an undercover role being filmed while he did what he was *really* there for.

Ed started to close the paper when he saw the vulgar headline about his son winning the "Daddy Lottery" and tapped the mouse on his computer. The screen woke up, and there was Trent's face and the article on his exhibition. Ed stared at Trent's image. No more delays—it was time to meet his son.

CHAPTER 50

When Marlo's train arrived in New York City, she took a cab to the Plaza Hotel and checked in. Randall had a room reserved for her, and when she saw it filled with flowers, she was thrilled. Her view of Central Park was perfect; even the chilled bottle of sparkling cider was a nice touch due to her pregnancy.

When the bellhop left and she finished hanging her things, she noticed the note in one of the flowers. Opening it, she read, "Welcome to *Tycoon Wives*! We haven't met yet—but may your first season with us bring you the joy it did on my first season." It was signed by Madeline Roberts.

Marlo was touched; she knew the cast was kept in the dark on the new cast additions, and she had met Madeline before. She inhaled the scent of the beautiful bouquet and then placed the card on the bar near the cider. Opening the bottle, she poured herself a glass. She then went to the window and stood looking out over the park. She placed her hand over her tummy and smiled at all the good things before her since that horrible experience she never wanted to revisit again.

Going to inspect the other flowers, she found a note from Ed, telling her he loved her and was thrilled beyond belief over her success and the baby. Then she saw the one from Randall Bishop filled with a warm welcome and a reminder to check her e-mail for instructions regarding tomorrow's event. Excitement filled her as she pulled out her laptop to read what was next. Seeing the e-mail, she clicked on it, forgetting the last of the flowers in her room.

CHAPTER 51

When Maura pulled onto the grounds with Sam, it was strangely quiet. Everyone seemed to be out as she pulled up to the house and parked where the girls' bikes had been earlier this morning.

"Where is everyone?" Sam asked, looking around the quiet grounds.

"I'm not sure," Maura said, closing her door. "Come on—let's get you in bed."

Maura opened the front door and called back to him, "So you'll take the bedroom upstairs then? I had it prepared in hopes that you would."

Sam smiled at his wife's twin. "Thank you. That would be nice, but before bed I'd like something to eat," he said, entering the home.

"Oh my, that's right; you've had nothing today."

"Yeah, I had to fast for the blood work this morning; then I had the MRI."

"Sam, Zolie had some of your things brought over, and they're up in your new room. Why don't you go get settled, and I'll get something started. What would you like?"

"I know it's late in the day, but breakfast sounds great. How about some sausage and eggs?"

"I'll have them get on it then. Would you like a tray brought up?"

"No, I'll be back down in a little bit," Sam said as he reached for the railing of the stairs.

Maura hurried to the kitchen and found Benjamin coming in from the terrace.

"Benji, where is everyone?"

"Ms. Zolie left shortly after you did this morning; she told me to tell you she's working on her next book. As for the younger Savages, after the girls left this morning for West Point, they seemed to scatter like the wind. Except for Lisa—the nanny took her to the zoo per Mrs. Marlo Savages wishes."

"Well then, would you have a breakfast prepared for Sam? He wants sausage and eggs, and have them do it up with bacon, pancakes, and fresh fruit. Benji, Sam's been through a lot."

Upstairs in his new bedroom, Sam pulled off his shirt and looked at his shoulder in the floor-length mirror in the corner. He rubbed it where it was bruised and decided a hot shower was in order. Tossing his shirt on a chair, he saw one of his small suitcases opened sitting on a small chest of drawers in the walk-in closet. He pulled some fresh clothes out and went into his adjoining bathroom and eyed the separate soaking tub, but turned on the shower knowing breakfast would soon be ready. Getting undressed and about to step in the shower, he noticed the flowers in the vase on the counter, just like Cara had always insisted on having throughout the house. He went over and caressed the rose petals as gently as when he would lightly brush them over his wife's naked body in the mornings after an evening of lovemaking. He inhaled deeply and looked into the bathroom mirror at his naked reflection and sighed. "I love you, Cara, and I always will. I'm sorry I was weak, but I'm better now, stronger. I know you're with me, and you will always have my love." Sam then smiled at his reflection, caressed the rose again, and looked to the steam from the shower.

A short time later, he could smell the breakfast as he descended the stairs and was glad Maura had decided more than just sausage and eggs were needed; he was starving, and he sat down truly feeling better, and his appetite grew stronger.

"Have you figured out where everyone is?" Sam asked when Maura came back to check on him.

"Kids are off God knows where, except Lisa is with the nanny at the zoo, Zolie's out working, and Marlo was off to New York City this morning. Ed's due back soon. I'm not sure where Roman, Gabby, and Logan are," she said, eyeing his filled plate. "You *are* hungry. I'm so glad you're home."

"I'm glad to be home, too," Sam said, digging into his breakfast.

"Sam, I've wanted to ask you something, and if this isn't the time, just say so."

"Okay, shoot."

Choosing her words carefully, Maura spoke around the subject. "This restaurant Marlo has been talking about: I have to tell you this came as a complete shock. Had you known of it?"

"With everything that's been happening, I completely forgot about it. And to answer your question, yes and no." Sam took a drink of his coffee, thinking back before the trip to the mountains and Maura's long visit from London.

"Yes and no?" Maura repeated.

"Maura, I thought it was you and her that had something going on. I remember walking in on countless conversations with you two and feeling like I was walking in on something I shouldn't. You remember those occasions. Then there was the property and the buildings she was looking at, and she did run them through me legally, but again I thought it was the two of you."

"No, Sam, that wasn't what we were talking about."

"Well, now you know what I know. Now why don't you tell me what you and Cara were talking about?"

Maura moved past him to the window on the far side of the table, dreading the thought of even telling him she was divorcing his brother. "Sam, I'd rather not. Not today, anyway—it can wait. What's important is you're home, and we love you."

Sam watched the color drain from Maura's face as she turned away from him toward the window, and his worry set in at once. "Are you sure?"

Maura turned back and smiled at him. "I want today to be beautiful for you, Sam. Now, eat up, and I'll see you later. I have an appointment, and I should be home in two or three hours. Call me if you need anything, you hear?"

By marrying a twin, Sam had dealt with their privacy for years and not only respected it, but their British manner of keeping things to themselves reminded him of his and Ed's private meetings and their upbringing, so it didn't bother him as much as it could have.

"Will do, Maura; we'll talk about it when you're ready. Enjoy your day. I'm finishing my breakfast and spending the day watching TV like a kid. I think a James Bond marathon is in my future," Sam said with a smile.

After Maura had left and he'd finished eating, Sam went to sort through the DVDs and turned on the television, when he saw the latest report from Wendy Storm. He was floored at the audacious statement that sorry bitch was saying about his family yet again. He went to reach for his phone and realized he didn't know where it was. He went upstairs to his room, thinking Zolie might have placed it there for him. Not finding it, he went to his guesthouse and saw that the entire place had been cleaned and aired out. He looked in the usual place where he kept his phone and his keys and saw they were gone too.

He sat on the bed and remembered he had driven to his home. Getting up, he went to the garage, and his truck was gone. Ed's Jaguar was there, along with his prized classic Challenger Convertible polished to a high shine and a few others.

"Can I help you, sir?" the chauffeur said behind him upon entering the garage.

"Albert, yes, thank you. Where is my truck?"

"Yes, sir, when I went to get it with Benjamin, the engine didn't start right away. We thought to have it checked out and serviced if necessary. We should be getting it back tomorrow."

"Albert, was my phone in the truck?"

"No, sir, we didn't see a phone."

"Albert, we need to drive over to the house and get it. Have a car brought up to the house, and I'm going to grab a jacket."

"But, sir, I don't think Ms. Zolie or Ms. Maura would like that."

"You let me worry about that, Albert," Sam said, already leaving the garage.

Coming out from the house, Sam had changed completely, warmer for the cold October air, and the limousine was waiting for him. Sam got in the back seat, and Albert closed the door, and soon they were off to Sam's home, where his breakdown had gone into full swing.

CHAPTER 52

arking in front of Gallery 26 was impossible, and Ed had to circle
the next block. Not finding anything, he made a loop and caught
a car exiting a parking spot way past the gallery. He pulled up
and put on his turn signal for the spot across the street from Berman
Park. Getting out with the excitement rushing through him, he forgot his cell phone in the console, and he breathed in the cool air as
he headed toward his son's exhibition down the street. The closer he
got, the more nervous he became, and when he eyed the gallery only
a few shops away, he froze. His palms were wet, and for the first time
he could remember, he was as nervous as when he'd proposed to
Marlo. Looking toward the gallery, he saw some service men loading
lighting fixtures inside, and before he knew it, he was there, pushing
his way through the doors.

Standing at the life-size cardboard cutout of his son—just like
the ones for his own TV shows—unnerved him, and when the polite
young woman's voice asked if she could help him, he swallowed hard
and turned to face her.

Her expression changed immediately, and not because she recognized Ed from his celebrity life but because he looked so much
like Trent it was scary. She didn't know all about Trent's drama at
home, but she had seen enough in the news to figure out the man in
front of her was Trent's father, Ed Savage.

"Sir, can I help you?" she said, keeping everything else inside.

"I'm looking for my, um…I'm looking for Trent York. Is he here?" Ed said, hearing the nervousness in his own voice.

"I'm sorry; he just left a short while ago. Can I give him a message?"

"Will he be back soon?" Ed asked, now sounding a bit sad.

"He had some…stuff to work out—said he'd be back later."

Ed looked past the young woman into the gallery, and in the far corner was a radio reporting the news. "Stuff to work out, huh?" Ed said, thinking Trent had heard the disgusting news brought to the world by the biggest bitch in the East. "No, no message, I'll try back another time. Thank you," he said and was gone, feeling a little defeated.

Walking away from the gallery, his head was filled with images of his son hearing that garbage and thinking the absolute worst of him. He was angry, and it reminded him of the past weeks when everything seemed to be against him, and it felt like it was happening again.

The block across the street was longer due to Berman Park, as it sat on three city blocks joined together, and as he got to the midway crosswalk, the light changed, and he crossed the street to the same side of the park, deciding to keep going on the warmer, sunnier side of the street and cross back at the end of the block near where he had parked.

He could see kids playing and couples enjoying a coffee at a stand as he moved down the street, and then the sound of an electric plane came to his ears. Looking up, he saw the plane fly from over the trees above him and out over traffic before turning back and disappearing over the trees again. He felt the smile on his face and was reminded of his youth and how much he used to enjoy building the toy models and later flying them near the Cliff House Restaurant not far from his old home, with his son Tucker, just like the one that now flew over his head. Stopping and turning around, he entered the park and decided to watch the plane for a bit.

The park was large enough for the small field that sat in the center, where people would picnic and events would take place. There, alone in the field, was a young man holding the controls for the electric plane, and as the plane circled the sky, Ed moved toward him just as the young man turned to watch his prized toy obey his every command in the sky.

Ed's heart stopped when he saw his face; it was his firstborn son, Theodore Trenten Savage, working the controls of the plane, just like Ed had taught his son Tucker to do so long ago. He watched him look in his direction for a quick second and then back to his plane. But he looked back at Ed in an instant, and the moment lasted longer than it should have because when the sound of the plane changed to a dangerous dive, both Ed and Trent looked up as Trent tried controlling the plane.

Ed's instinct was to rush over and help him out, and he did move to him but was pleased when he watched Trent land the plane in one piece.

"Good job there. I thought it was a goner," Ed said with a smile that wouldn't leave his face, as he watched Trent stop the plane and drop the control into his backpack on the ground.

Trent looked up to the man he instantly knew was his father as the awkward silence surrounded them. "You know what? I've thought about meeting you forever; now I'm a dumbass and can't think of a thing to say," he said, putting out his hand.

Ed reached out and grabbed his son's hand and shook it, pulling him into a hug. "Trent, I'm so sorry. I didn't know." Ed couldn't believe this was happening. Taking a step back, he moved his hands to his son's shoulders. "Let me get a look at you."

Trent could feel the emotion of seeing his father for the very first time well up inside him, and he took a deep breath, watching Ed wipe the wet from his eyes. "Oh God, we're a couple of girls," Trent said with a short laugh.

"Come on—grab your stuff; let's go somewhere we can talk."

Trent looked to the man he'd always known was out there somewhere and nodded. "There's a bar on the corner; I think I'm gonna need a drink."

"That makes two of us," Ed said.

"Um, one more thing." Trent stopped and looked Ed right in the eyes. "What do I call you?"

"You're going to call me Dad, and that's final, but what about you? Jillian tells me you prefer Trent to your given name, Theodore. Okay, I get that, but you could go by Teddy or Ted? I kind of like that. Don't you?"

"Yep, we're gonna need a drink," Trent said, side-eyeing his father with a laugh.

The scandalous news of Ed's wife swapping had played out over the radio at the gallery and fed into what Jillian had told Trent at her penthouse, and he'd left to go cool off at the park with his plane. He didn't know what to think and was tired of hearing all the negative things about the stranger he'd longed to know. As they left the park, the stories Jillian had told him of the past filled his mind and gave him pause. He was unsure of how to handle himself. Having his father show up and catch him off guard had him unprepared, and when he found himself in situations like this, he'd always pulled back, listened, and chosen his words carefully, keeping his private thoughts to himself, a trait he'd had his whole life, unlike his stepmother and her daughters, who always lashed out. The other thing he knew was that his mother had *lied* to him for years, and the one thing he'd hoped for his whole life was to know his dad, and he wasn't going to let his mother come between them, unless what she'd told him recently *was* true.

Leaving the park, they walked across the street and turned in the direction of Ed's Range Rover, which was parked near a bar on the corner. It wasn't that busy inside, and when both men ordered IPA beers, they looked at each other and laughed. Ed then paid for the beers, and Trent moved to a table far away from the few people inside and placed his plane and backpack down on the empty chairs at the table.

When Ed handed him his beer, Trent started to take a drink and then stopped and looked Ed right in the eyes. "Shouldn't we drink to something here? Being such an awkward and strange situation all at the same time?"

"Here's to awkward and strange," Ed said, reaching to click his beer with his son's as he took his seat. Together they both took a healthy drink, and when they finished, they both stared at each other, and the silence was too funny not to laugh at it.

"Oh, this could be a real messed-up first encounter," Trent said, laughing.

Seeing his son attempt to break the ice between them warmed his heart, and Ed put his beer down and smiled. "Gosh, Trent, I really didn't know, and now that I do, I don't want to ever lose you," Ed said, trying his best to convey his love for a son without scaring him off. "I guess what I'm saying is the news Jillian blasted from here to hell and back came at a time when my family—*our* family—was at our lowest point, and I'm sorry I didn't find you sooner."

"Mr. Savage, don't—"

"Dad," Ed said.

Trent adjusted in his chair and placed his beer down on the table near Ed's. "Dad—wow, that's going to take some getting used to. But don't be sorry—please don't. Can I call you Ed until it feels right, sir?"

Ed smiled and appreciated his son not letting anyone railroad him into anything he wasn't comfortable with, even if it was his own father, and for that he happily agreed. "Deal," Ed said, raising his beer and toasting his son again.

"Thanks, Ed," Trent said, reaching for his beer. "God, when I read what had happened, I was scared for you, for everyone…I wish I'd met you sooner; then maybe none of this would have happened."

"No, Trent, I'm glad you weren't part of any of it. I'm glad you're safe."

"I guess this is better," Trent said, rethinking the situation.

"No, Trent—it is and it isn't. I'm angry at Jillian for keeping you from me, and I'm not sure how this will all get handled. But I'm glad we're here now."

"Good, I'm glad too," Trent said, taking a swig from his beer. "So you first knew when the article came out?"

"That damn article." Ed slapped the table. "Don't get me wrong—yes, that's when I first knew. But I was worried about you and how that was affecting you in your life," Ed said, looking Trent right in the eyes. "Is that when *you* first knew?"

"Confirmed, yes; knew, no." Trent sat in his chair, thinking back to that moment in time. "Dad, er…I mean Ed," he laughed. "Sorry, but this is going to take some getting used to. Anyway, I've known for quite some time that my stepmom, Marta, wasn't my natural mother. It just never felt right."

"She had Marta raise you?" Ed said. Trent could see the questions in Ed's head being answered and the concern showing abundantly clear in his father's face. "Were you treated well?"

"Oh yeah, had everything I wanted and then some, and I love Marta and my stepsisters too. It's just…Mother—she always had an answer for everything, and then everything changed."

"Changed how?"

"I don't know *the why* exactly. But I did hear your name once, your first name. And when I asked about it, I was basically ignored or told lies. But when it hit the papers, I finally found out the truth— well, for all I knew, anyway. But what I don't understand is this: Why did everything change around the time all these horrible things were happening? What was it that made her wait until *now* to put out that article? That's what I don't understand."

"That's a good question, Trent, and one I hadn't had the time to think of," Ed said, filing that one away for later dissecting.

"Good luck with that one," Trent said, finishing his beer. "Want another one?" He waved his empty bottle toward Ed.

Ed smiled and called out to the waitress for two more. "So, where are you living? Are you here in Port Roberts?"

"I have a place in New York City; it's small, but it's home. Mom's got me in one of Jeremy's hotels he built while I'm here for my exhibition," Trent said, remembering the story Jillian had told him and wishing he hadn't mentioned it.

"A hotel? Trent, I don't want you in a hotel. Why don't you come to my home? We've got bedrooms sitting empty, and the family wants to meet you."

"I don't know…isn't this a little fast? Besides, I have to be close to the gallery."

"You're where? Which hotel did they put you in? His Bedford Towers Hotel is his newest. The estate we're in is half an hour away," Ed said, wanting to spend time with him.

Trent looked to the waitress as she returned with the beers and took away the empties. "Parkwood Plaza—it's not too far from the gallery," Trent said, taking a drink from his beer.

Ed had reached for his beer and was about to take a drink himself when he heard him and stopped. Both men looked to each other and wondered what the other knew. "Yeah, that one is closer to the gallery than Bedford Towers is," Ed said, keeping his thoughts to himself.

Trent wanted to open the conversation and get it all out and over with, but he also saw the hurt cross his father's face and decided this wasn't the time. "I'll tell you what, Dad—and I mean *Dad.* I've got to get back to the gallery tonight, and tomorrow morning I've got deliveries I have to be there for. So if it's all right with you, can we meet up tomorrow? And yeah, I'd love to meet the family," Trent said, offering a friendly smile and seeing the hurt disappear from his father's face.

"So you'll come to the house?" Ed said, his voice suddenly filled with hopeful expectation for the future.

"I'd like that. Let's plan on it tomorrow—that way you can prepare everyone at home." Trent laughed.

Ed was elated; the conversation had started out a bit awkward, but now it was finally turning out to be a good day for Ed Savage and his son. Ed's phone, however, was ringing in the Range Rover, and the messages left would change the path of that "good day" very soon.

CHAPTER 53

Sam entered his house and found his phone charging in his office. The place had been picked up, but he noticed the glass inside one of the picture frames on his desk had been broken out, and the photo inside had dried blood on it. He thought for a moment and remembered being in there and the rage he had been under.

Calmly, he picked up his phone and left his house, picking a few flowers from the garden Cara had planted as he went to the limousine waiting outside for him. "Albert, can we stop by the cemetery on the way home? I'd like a few moments."

"Yes, sir," Albert said, closing his door for him.

A short while later, with the car parked, Sam got out on the peaceful grounds of the cemetery and made his way to his wife's grave. He placed the flowers down against the headstone and prayed not only for strength but also for forgiveness for losing it so badly and not being strong enough for his family. As he stood up, his heart was heavy, and that's when he heard her crying.

In the distance, the woman was kneeling at a gravesite, and she was utterly alone. Sam turned his head away, thinking she needed *her* time, but when he heard her cry out, he looked back and recognized her. Moving closer, he walked up behind her and saw the photos on the ground she had brought with her.

There was his own daughter, Heather, in the photo, standing with Mia Delgado in his own backyard. Sam kneeled down next to Mia's aunt Raquel Delgado, and she looked to him as a tear rolled down her face. He then put his hand around her waist, and she leaned into his strong body. Her own body was shaking, and he raised his other hand up, reaching across her shoulder to hug her. "Shush, you're not alone," he whispered to her, and she nuzzled her head into his chest.

Raquel's body was shivering, and the temperature outside was cold for the way she was dressed. Sam gathered the photos and stood with her, walking her back to his car, which was parked near hers. And when she dropped her purse, digging for her keys, he told her he would drive her to her home. He picked up her things and got her into the passenger seat of her car. He then yelled to Albert to follow them.

When he got to her home, he waved to Albert in the limousine and raised his voice, telling him he'd be a minute as he walked her inside. There, in her home, he saw the photographs on the table of her decimated family; her sister and the child she'd left in her care were gone. The sadness inside her was also emanating inside her home, and his heart hurt for her.

"You're going to be fine, Raquel; you need time," Sam said, putting her keys on the table with the photographs. "Do you need anything?"

Raquel shook her innocent head, and Sam could feel the hurt welling inside her, but he was also hurting and knew she had to get through it like he was doing. And as he turned to leave, she reached out and touched his arm ever so gently. He froze in his steps, and his heart filled with both hurt and love; he turned to her and saw the beautiful woman standing before him equally in pain. He wasn't over Cara, but he ignored his thoughts and embraced her, kissing her passionately. She unbuttoned the top of his shirt, and he slid the shoulder of her dress down her arm, wanting nothing more than to make love to this woman.

He paused and pulled away from her and put his finger to his lips. He pulled his phone from his pocket and called Albert and told him to go on home; he would take a taxi. He then returned his phone to his pocket, and she led him upstairs to her bedroom.

Passing a window, he saw the limousine pull away from the home as Raquel moved toward the bed; her long hair hung down over her breasts, and he pulled it away as he lowered the other shoulder of her dress, letting it fall to the floor. Her naked body stood before him, and she opened his pants, letting them drop to the floor with his boxers. She then finished unbuttoning his shirt, and he pulled it back and tossed it aside and looked into her eyes. She admired his muscled, hairy chest and ran her hand over it; as she looked down farther, she gasped. He reached for her chin and raised it and nodded as he kissed her, and she moved into his arms, feeling the warmth of his body as he kicked off his shoes and pants and picked her up and lowered her to her bed.

He stared into her eyes, and they each knew exactly what the other's pain was. It was like kindred spirits in a war finally coming into the presence of a comrade, finally feeling love, peace, and maybe a little safety in the hell they were living in.

Tightly, they held on to each other, and Sam kissed her passionately as he slid into her. In the hours that passed, they never let go of each other as each of them was in a way not only grieving but also growing from the ugly past that haunted them.

CHAPTER 54

T he greeting waiting for Roman and Gabby Savage at the lake house was ugly. The home had been vandalized, and when they pulled into the driveway of their family's lake house and parked, they were disgusted when they saw the word PERVERTS written in spray paint across their front door. Getting out, they saw the eggs splattered on the home, and they felt uneasy. They looked to each other with worry before they went to the front door. As Roman reached in his jacket pocket for the key, Gabby tried the door, and it was unlocked. She let go of the door and stepped back as Roman moved in front of her, raising his arms, protecting her as he pushed the door the rest of the way open.

"Hello," he yelled into the house. He then rang the doorbell a few times and stepped inside the home, listening as the sound of the doorbell faded to silence.

Together they entered, leaving the door open, and searched the home. Moving into the kitchen, they noted that the window near the breakfast table had been broken, and the breeze was blowing the curtain.

"Well, now we know how they got in," Roman said.

The dining room, den, and living room all seemed to be untouched; then they moved down the hall to the partly closed door of the master bedroom, where the news report videos and photos had been taken. Roman glanced to Gabby, and she nodded as he pushed open the door with his foot, and they were horrified to find the sick display inside.

The king-sized bed had been stripped of its usual bedding and replaced with black rubber sheets, and a black leather spread was thrown to the floor like someone had kicked it off. Greasy sex toys were on the bed, and different lubricants lay strewn about the floor, which was also littered with used condoms. In the sitting area, the furniture had been removed, and a sling had been hung from hooks drilled into the ceiling, and under it was another black rubber sheet.

"This is disgusting," Gabby said, wanting to light a match and burn it to the ground as she stepped toward the master bathroom, following the path of clothes in a trail along the floor from the closets of the home.

"Gabby, don't touch anything," Roman said as he pulled out his phone to call Ed. Getting his voice mail, he left a message and followed Gabby into the bathroom. There on the counter were small plastic zip bags with traces of white powder inside them, and marijuana was left in a pipe next to some burned-out matches in an overfilled ashtray.

"Call the police," Gabby said, mad as hell at the filth she was seeing in the home she'd enjoyed over the years with her family.

"Let me try Logan first." Roman's phone began to ring in his hand.

When Kate and Lana Savage didn't show up at West Point at the time they said they would, their fellow cadets and new friends reported it to their commanders. Calls were sent out to Zolie Vanderran's home, as well as to their parents, Logan and Maura and Roman and Gabby, for any news regarding their whereabouts.

Recognizing the area code, he figured it was their daughter. "Lana must be calling from the academy," he said to Gabby as he answered the phone. "Hello. How was the ride up there?"

"Mr. Savage, this is Commander Richton of West Point," came the authoritative, deep voice on the other end. "I'm sorry to ask this, but what time were your daughter and her cousin Kate due to return to West Point?"

Roman's face changed at once, and Gabby tensed up. "Commander, they should be there by now. What's happening there?" Roman asked, his voice matching the other man's in authority.

"Mr. Savage, one of the cadets said she was expecting them hours ago; she said they had called from a gas station not that far from here, and they've yet to arrive."

The panic every parent feared most entered Roman's blood, and he looked to Gabby. "Hang on. I'm with my wife, and I want to put you on speakerphone." Tapping the phone, he held it between them.

"My daughter—where is she?" Gabby asked fearfully.

"Ma'am, they haven't arrived, and they called one of their friends here a couple hours ago and said they'd be here within half an hour. They should've been here by now," Commander Richton said. "By the way, the friend they called is one of my good friend's daughters that I've known since she was a little girl. Now I know sometimes the cadets go AWOL, and normally we'd wait a bit to start calling, but I promised I'd look into it right away."

"Commander, we're not at home now; we're up at Rye Lake. Have you talked to Logan or Maura? Have they any news?"

"I've called the home of Zolie Vanderran; no one was there, and I left a message with the staff. I then called you. I haven't called Kate's parents yet; they're next on my list."

"Commander, this isn't right. Can you send a car to the gas station and look for them?" Roman asked.

"They were riding up on Indian motorcycles, a dark-red one and a black one. Um, what were they called, Roman?" Gabby asked, wanting to give as much information as she could think of.

"Commander, they were matching Springfield motorcycles, new ones, so keep an eye out for those, can you?"

"We'll send some men out, Mr. Savage. But call us if you find out anything."

"Commander, I will. Is the number on my cell a number I can reach you at?"

"Yes, but I'll text you my personal cell when I hang up in case I'm off the base."

"Thank you, sir."

"Not a problem."

Roman and Gabby saw the call disconnect from the screen, and Roman grabbed his wife, and together they left the crime scene in the master bedroom of a home they dearly loved. Moving up the hall to the front door, Gabby went outside and turned to see Roman standing in the doorway.

"Come on. We have to go home."

"The window," Roman said. "We can't risk anyone coming in here and contaminating the evidence. Call Maura; see if she's heard anything while I board up the window."

Roman then went into the garage, where the old cabinets from the backyard outdoor bar were still waiting to be taken to the dump. He selected one that was close to the size of the window and found some duct tape with some electrical supplies. It was all he could find, and it'd have to do. Getting inside, he propped the cabinet door in the windowsill and quickly taped it in place. "Did you get through to Maura?" he asked his wife as she was punching in another number into her phone.

"No, I left a message. I'm calling Zolie. Maybe she knows something."

"Hang up, and call her from the car. We're leaving," Roman said as he pulled the curtains closed over the boarded window. They locked the door and drove away from the home as a police car passed them by and pulled into their driveway. Roman called the police to tell them they couldn't wait.

CHAPTER 55

After putting Trent's plane in the back, Ed and Trent got in the front, and Ed started the engine, completely ignoring his phone as father and son drove down the street and parked behind the gallery, where Trent had parking spaces assigned to him off the alley. Trent's rental was there, and he pulled his keys from his backpack just as Ed was pulling the plane out from the back.

"So what's your day like tomorrow?" Trent asked.

Besides the bullshit of Wendy Storm's latest assault, Ed needed to touch base with Tallulah about the *Manchester* and everything else he now didn't care about. He knew Sam was home, and Marlo was in New York City shooting her new reality show, and the last thing he wanted to do was think of Savage Construction with Trent here.

"I've got a few meetings tomorrow to take care of, but I don't see anything keeping me from picking you up," Ed said, closing the back of the Range Rover, not wanting to say good-bye.

"Great—well, here's my card," Trent said, handing him one from his backpack in exchange for his plane as they moved toward the front of the vehicle.

Ed took it and glanced at it. "Great. Let me give you my number." Ed reached into the console to grab a card of his own and saw his phone, which he'd forgotten all about. Ed handed his son his card; Trent looked at it and joked, "Wow, I've got—Ed Savage's phone number!" as he stuffed it into his pocket.

Ed laughed with him. "No, not *that guy*—your dad's number," he said.

Trent started to turn away, and Ed reached out and grabbed him and hugged him once more, wanting to leave one important lasting impression on his son. "Trent, we've got a lot to talk about, about your mother and myself. And I want you to know you can ask me anything you want, and I'll give you the honest truth. I'll never lie to you."

Hearing that, Trent thought of the lies his mother had told him and wondered if there were any others he didn't know about yet. "Yeah, we do have more stuff; thanks, Ed."

"Oh, do you need any money?" Ed asked, going into father mode.

Trent laughed. "No, Dad, I'm good. Dad? Ed? Oh, hell—now go on, and I'll see you tomorrow," Trent said, beaming with a smile.

Ed smiled back as he nodded and got in his car and waited to watch his son use his key to enter the back of his gallery safely. Seeing the door close, Ed knew this was a moment in time he'd never forget. The amazing time he'd spent with his son was the best present the world had given him since finding Lisa safe and having his family home with him.

Backing out from the parking space, he took the alley back to the street, and as he circled the block, he looked over to his son's gallery, and all the problems in the world melted away. Ed Savage was beyond thrilled and happy over meeting his son and couldn't wait for tomorrow to bring him home. He turned on his radio to find his favorite song playing, and he put down the window as he drove past Berman Park. When he got to the end of the park, he turned left, circling it, and across the street from the park, he saw the old apartment buildings that had once been slated for demolition, and a new sign was posted.

The 2008 crash hit everyone back then, and just before it all went south, Savage Construction was in talks with the Berman family over the purchase of the buildings and the land. The Bermans talked of either extending the park or building an extension to the family medical center they owned at the other end of the park, but the woman that owned the entire block wasn't budging.

"Damn it!" Ed thought as he tried pushing the work from his mind. He wanted to focus on the wonderful time he'd just spent with his son, but instinctively he slowed to read the newly posted sign: "Grenning Towers: The New Name In Luxury Living—Coming Soon."

"I'll be damned," Ed said out loud. *He did it,* he thought as he drove past the sign. Tasker Grenning was not only a spoiled Wall Street wizard but also the son of that woman who wouldn't sell to the Bermans. Grenning lost his ass and nearly his job back in 2008 and tried to get his mom to sell. But the woman who had raised him was smarter than that and quickly put an end to it. Besides, those apartment buildings had been in the family for way too long to sell on a whim.

Grenning Lumber was located in Vermont, and the family was loaded, Ed remembered. He also recalled Tasker's father to be a shrewd businessman and possibly the real reason the apartments never got sold.

But now the new sign was posted, and it got him thinking in yet another direction on his way home—forgetting his phone in the console and not even thinking of the many messages that could be waiting for him.

Trent York was in an equally good mood. The news he'd heard on the radio earlier confused him; he was tired of all the lies that he was now thinking all originated from his mother—and he knew exactly who he could get the truth from. He looked around the gallery, making mental notes of what still needed to be done, and then he pulled out his father's business card and looked at it—and the to-do list in his mind was growing. He looked at his cardboard cutout like the ones his dad told him he had and smiled. *I've been going about this the wrong way*, he thought.

CHAPTER 56

The Carlisle Consortium Nathan Savage had been a part of was the type of business only the wealthy and influential were associated with. The money that flowed within the several shell companies and actual businesses was in the billions, and that was only the beginning. From rigged stock market exchanges to presidential elections and wars in foreign countries, the Carlisle Consortium was smack-dab in the middle, making huge profits. They had offices all over the world, and back in the late nineties, they had even allowed one of their buildings in Venezuela to be bombed as payback to the bank within that owed them money.

When the Carlisle Consortium contacted Nathan Savage to construct a tower in Miami, it was a cash blessing at a time Savage Construction needed it most. Nathan had loans from a savings and loan that'd gone under, and they were *that close* to completion on another major high-rise. The stress everyone was under to find money fast felt like a one-way step off the top floor of Savage Tower down to the sidewalk.

While Sam and Roman had seen and *felt* their father's wrath growing up, the stress in the office was pure fright, and when they told Ed and Logan about it, they were glad they were far away. Firings were happening left and right over the loss at the savings and loan, and as each day moved them closer to a construction halt, which would cost millions, Nathan and Niles's shouting matches grew. And then, it was over.

The large sum of money transferred into Savage Construction accounts overnight and the next day was business as usual. Sam saw very few documents on the loans and questioned his father at the time, but Nathan was vague and told him these loans would be paid in full and on time no matter what. That was the time Sam remembered *the shift* of contracts he'd usually see and the beginning of more secret meetings with Parnell F. Bancroft, Nathan's old friend from the early years of starting the business.

The consultant Nathan had made his arrangements with at the consortium all those years ago was one of the few men Nathan first feared himself. But as time passed and more deals were made, Nathan had become "one of the boys." And it wasn't long before he felt *he* was calling the shots. After Savage Construction had paid its last payment back to the consortium, Nathan started making a profit from them in various construction projects they'd bring him in on.

Yes, Nathan had a new friend in that young consultant named Hermann he'd met all those years ago, and together they not only raked in several millions in commissions for both Savage Construction and the Carlisle Consortium, but they also formed a plan. And when Nathan died and the discrepancies in his will were found, the consultant knew exactly what needed to be done.

CHAPTER 57

The sound of Ed's phone and the illumination of it in the console and the dashboard brought Ed back from his thoughts, which had shifted from construction to his marriage and the ugly divorce that followed with Jillian York. He'd been driving with his head filled with all the what-ifs, and his anger ebbed and flowed when he thought about the years raising his own flesh and blood that had been stolen from him. Looking at the caller ID on the dashboard, he hit the car audio button.

"Roman, what's up at the lake house?"

"What's up! Where have you been? I've left messages."

Ed picked up his phone and saw there were several messages waiting for him. "Sorry, Roman. The most amazing thing happened today. I met my son."

The happy tone Roman heard coming from his brother was something he knew Ed had been in short supply of over the news of his son with Jillian, and he hated being the one to change that. "Ed, that's great! Really, it is," Roman said.

"Tell him about Lana and Kate," Gabby said in a raised voice Ed could hear in the background.

"Roman, what's Gabby saying about the girls?"

"Ed, there's trouble. The girls didn't make it to West Point."

"What are you saying? Was there an accident?"

"I'm not sure."

"What the hell does that mean? You're not sure?"

"Ed, their commander Richton called and told us the girls were late checking back in. They should have been there before lunch, and there's no sign of them."

"Has anyone heard from them?"

"No—well, yes. They called one of their friends at the base, saying they'd be there in half an hour. That's it. No one else has heard from them. *And* we drove right there from the lake. They sent out a car and found something strange. There's an oil spill on a curve in the road, and it looks like the girls hit it and crashed their bikes off the road. There's a partially broken windshield and tracks in the mud of one of them getting stuck. They also found Lana's necklace near an area that looks like a scuffle took place."

"Jesus! What's this about an oil spill?"

"Ed, it looks deliberate. They found several empty oilcans thrown off in the ditch."

"Oh God! Where are you now?"

"West Point. The academy is out looking for them, and we're talking to their fellow cadets trying to find some answers."

"Roman, you said you found a broken windshield and tire tracks. No bikes?"

"Nope, nothing."

"Could they have driven away?"

"Ed, where would they have gone? West Point is close to the crash site. Here is where they would have gone—if they could."

Ed could hear the fear rising in his brother's voice. "Roman, I'm almost home. Let me make a few calls, and I'll call you right back."

"Ed, I talked with Logan, and our daughters are out there; they could be hurt or worse," Roman said with dread filling his words.

Ed immediately flashed back to being in that jail only a short time ago, wanting nothing more than to search for his own daughter. And when he didn't respond right away, Roman knew what his brother was thinking.

"Ed, it's starting again, isn't it? My God, you just went through this. Now Lana and Kate?"

"No, Roman, that can't be. Patty is locked away, and there's no one left out there. Now I'm pulling up to the gates. I'll be in the house in a few minutes, and I'll call you back. Have Commander Richton call me. Will you?"

"As soon as he gets back, I'll tell him. But, Ed, that doesn't explain the lake house? If Wendy Storm reported it way back then when this nightmare began, how do we know there isn't anyone else still out there?"

"I don't know, Roman. We still need to figure that out."

"The lake house was broken into through the side kitchen window near the breakfast table. I don't know what happened in there, but the master bedroom is disgusting."

"You saw it?" Ed said, hitting the button on the remote to open the gates.

"Ed, Gabby wants to burn it down, and I'll never use that master bedroom ever again after what I saw in there."

"Then we'll sell it or have it razed and build a new one! Hell, I can't think about that right now. One thing at a time, Roman," Ed said, pulling past the gates and up the long driveway to the house. "I'll call you back soon."

"Ed, one last thing—the police showed up right after we got the call and left. I saw them pull into the driveway. I called them and told them we had to leave, so that's where that was left."

"Thanks, Roman. I'm home now, and I'll call you soon."

"Be waiting on it," Roman said, disconnecting the call.

Ed parked in his spot and shut off the engine; grabbing his phone and duffel bag, he rushed to the house. Opening the door, he wasn't expecting what he walked in on.

"Oh, Logan!" Maura shouted.

"Don't even try sounding upset. I'm done pretending," Ed heard his brother shout back.

"Did you know that little tramp who died in the rollover had a thing for you?"

Logan remembered Lucy dropping her top in the hall of Chance's home, showing him her breasts, but decided not to mention it. "What are you talking about?"

"Don't you dare insult me; you know what I'm talking about. Just like you told Roman of our troubles. It wasn't time!"

"It wasn't time? Maura, how long were you planning on dragging this out? I can't take it anymore."

"Hey! Hey, guys. Enough," Ed said, raising his voice as he entered the room the argument was coming from.

Both Logan and Maura turned to see him standing there.

"The girls—they're missing!" Maura cried.

"Ed, I'm so glad you're home," Logan said. "This is madness! No one's heard a word from them, and it's late."

"I just got off the phone with Roman. Now whatever you two are arguing about can wait," Ed barked.

"Don't you dismiss me in my own sister's home," Maura snapped back, still amped up from the fight she had been having with Logan. "My daughter is missing!"

"Stop!" Logan cried out.

Ed's anger rose as the tension in the room grew; hearing her speak of her daughter being missing sent a knife through his heart. "I don't know what I walked in on, but let's put it aside and focus on Kate and Lana."

"You said you just spoke with Roman. Is there any further news?" Logan asked.

"He's at West Point. They're out looking for them, and it looks like they could have had some sort of accident on the road."

"Oh God," Maura cried.

"Logan, pack a bag; we're driving up tonight," Ed ordered.

"I'm going with you," Maura said.

"No, Maura, you're not," Logan said. "Someone has to be here in case they call."

"I've got a call to make myself," Ed said, turning away from them and swinging his duffel bag over his shoulder as he headed to the stairs.

Logan gave one last look to Maura and turned away from her, rushing to his guesthouse to pack a bag.

Upstairs in his room, Ed tossed his bag on his bed, unzipped it, and emptied out the clothes from his trip to New York City. He then pulled out his phone and punched in a number.

"Tallulah, we've got trouble." Ed put the call on speaker so he could repack.

"What is it?"

"Kate and Lana are missing. Looks like they were in some sort of accident near West Point. I'm driving up tonight."

"Wait. Looks like? You don't know?" Tallulah asked, hearing the frightened tone in Ed's voice.

"There was oil poured on the road; empty oilcans were found nearby and evidence of the girls' bikes off the road. Someone caused this to happen." Ed threw clothes in his bag.

"I'll send a team down from the Catskills at once, Ed."

"Negative. Roman's there, and West Point has men searching the area. A team would be too invasive. Didn't you mention Thrasher was up there?"

"Yes, he's at the ski lodge in the Catskills."

"Just him, Tallulah. I want only him on this for now. And have him call me when he gets down there. Oh, and I want a small team sent out to our lake house."

"I'll send one over, but, Ed, it's been on the news. The police may be watching it."

"They *are* watching it! They were just there, but Roman left just before they arrived and called telling them he had to leave. Now, I don't want to wait on this, so can you get a small team down there? And if there's any problem, have them call me. And get Thrasher to West Point."

"Yes, Ed, I've got too many looking into the *Manchester* so I'll send a team. And I'll call Thrasher. As you know he'll be there, but... it's almost his anniversary."

Ed froze as he dropped a shirt into his bag and remembered the fire. "Oh God, Tallulah, what's he doing working?"

"It's his way."

"Fine. Thanks for reminding me."

Ed heard the call disconnect and watched his phone's illumination go dark. He sat on his bed and thought back to the day everything had changed between him and Agent Thrasher.

CHAPTER 58

Waking up, the smell of the salt water hit her. Lana opened her eyes, and the faint light from the porthole in the side of the old boat they were in illuminated the cold, damp room. As she attempted to move, she pulled on the chain that was binding her to a railing along the wall, and she pulled at it. Realizing what had happened, she saw Kate across the room chained to the railing behind her.

"Kate," she whispered loudly, hoping no one else would hear her. When her cousin didn't respond, Lana stood up and tried to look through the porthole that was above her. She could make out another old-looking boat close by and heard a gull's cry in the distance, somewhere in the sky above them. Looking back at Kate, she saw she was coming out of her drug-induced daze and waited patiently for her to wake.

"No," Kate slurred from her altered state as she became aware of her surroundings.

"Kate...Kate," Lana whispered. "Shush, Kate, I'm here."

Lana watched her cousin wake and sit up. Then she saw the same confused look she felt herself only moments ago.

"Lana? What's happening?" Kate said as she pulled on the chain binding her to the railing.

"We've been kidnapped. That has to be it."

Kate shook off the deathlike slumber she'd been in and stood in the gloomy bowels of the nasty boat. The rocking of the boat and the sound of it hitting against something told them they must be docked.

"I can see another vessel next to ours," Lana said, pointing to the porthole above her.

Kate could see through another porthole on her side and saw yet another vessel. "There's one over here, too," she said, pointing with her free hand.

"If there are boats on both sides of us, then where's the dock?" Lana tried to get a better view. "Do you remember anything?"

Kate's head hurt. "Just the accident...I think."

"That was no accident," Lana told her.

"Try to find something to break these chains," Kate said, looking around the ugly room as the sound of a door slamming met their ears. "Quick, get back down," Kate said.

As the door to their room squeaked open, the girls watched in horror as a man entered carrying two paper bags of takeout and a corrugated tray with coffee. He had a bandanna tied around his face and dark sunglasses on, and he saw they were indeed awake.

"I'm only gonna say this once. Do as you're told, and you won't get hurt." He then placed the takeout down on a drum between them and separated it just enough so each of them could reach it.

"We have money we can get now if that's what you want?" Lana said to the stranger.

"I'm sure you do, but it certainly won't be enough." The man laughed as he left the room, pulling the door closed with a loud bang.

Hearing the sound of locks meeting metal, the girls looked to each other in utter fear.

CHAPTER 59

When Zolie Vanderran arrived at Vreeland Hills Sanatorium, she took one look at the place and almost got back in her car and left. The place was an atrocious eyesore, and a menacing foreboding feeling seemed to emanate from the haunting place at that. She looked around in the parking lot and checked her watch. She then pulled her phone from her bag and checked for any new messages from the person she was meeting, when she heard a car on the road. She looked up and saw the blue car described to her drive onto the grounds and park near her.

The door of the old Chevrolet sedan opened, and Zolie was reminded of that first moment walking into the Vander Place Hotel and meeting that beautiful, bold blonde woman behind the counter. Eve Blakely had greeted her, and now Stevie Galloway was standing in front of her, her boldness gone; in its place was the meekness of someone deceived and searching for redemption.

"Thank you for meeting me," Zolie said with a cautious smile.

"Mrs. Vanderran Kenowith, I'm so sorry for all of this," Stevie almost pleaded.

"Oh, save it, darling." Zolie was curt and unforgiving. "Ed dropped the charges since you tried to stop your sister from killing Marlo and Aisha, but she shot my sister's husband, a good man, right in the shoulder. He could've been killed."

Stevie lowered her head in shame as Zolie passed her on the way to the entrance to the hospital. Watching her pass, Stevie raised her head and gave her a dirty look. When Zolie realized Stevie wasn't following her, she turned back. "Well, I haven't got all day. Come on," she ordered.

The look on Stevie's face sharpened; a bit of the boldness raised its ugly head. "Look, lady, I can just as easily get back in my car and drive out of here. Then where would you be? A few insightful pages short for your next novel?" Her tone had now changed from the Girl Scout to a rebellious little vixen in need of a sharp slap to her face.

Zolie gasped at the little bitch standing up to her.

"That's right, Vanderran; you *need* me. So cut it with your high-and-mighty act, and let's get this over with," she said, holding out her hand. Obviously the meekness had been just a ruse.

"I'll pay you once I see your sister. Not before."

"Have it your way," Stevie sneered and marched past her getting a few feet in front and glancing back. "Come on, I haven't got all day." She mocked Zolie's British accent.

Inside, after checking in, they were led to a waiting area. The few minutes there seemed dreadfully long for Zolie; Stevie could tell she was irritated and frankly didn't care. And when Dr. Sinardi finally arrived, he was glad to see Stevie and met her with open arms.

"Good afternoon, Stevie," the doctor said, giving her a light hug.

"Good afternoon, Dr. Sinardi," Stevie said. "How's Patty doing?"

The doctor looked to the strange woman next to her, and Zolie reached out her hand.

"Dr. Sinardi, Zolie Vanderran. Pleasure to meet you," she said.

"Vanderran?" the doctor said, looking to Stevie.

"Yes, I'm Cara's sister," Zolie said. "I know this may seem unorthodox, but I'd like a few moments with Patty. It would help with getting closure the family needs, and perhaps it could help Patty too."

"Patty did have a rough night last night," Dr. Sinardi said as he gazed down in thought.

"What happened to her?" Stevie asked.

Looking up and lying through his teeth, he told her she'd just gone through the usual antics of being in a new and strange place and carried on throughout the night. Neglecting to tell them with the new day, and the higher dosage of drugs he'd ordered for her, she was *exactly* in the state where he'd wanted.

"I'm sorry you drove all the way out here, but she's in no condition for visitors and today is out of the question," Dr. Sinardi told them.

"I see," Zolie said, sounding a bit disappointed.

"I tell you what. Why don't you call me tomorrow morning before driving out? And if she's in a better place mentally, then visiting will be just fine. I'd like her to have company," the doctor said, pulling his card from his pocket and handing it to Zolie. "Here you are; my private line is listed."

"Sorry, Zolie," Stevie said. "Why don't you wait here? I'm going to visit with her for a bit before I go," Stevie suggested, knowing Zolie hated to wait.

Zolie was angered, but there was nothing she could do. In any case, the doctor interrupted Stevie with news saying she couldn't visit either.

"What do you mean? I'm family," Stevie said.

"Your sister is in no condition for visitors—family or otherwise," the doctor informed her. "Stevie, it'd be best if you called too before driving out."

Zolie saw the peeved look on Stevie's face and felt the karma slapping that little bitch hard where she deserved it. "Doctor, thank you for your time," Zolie said. "I'll give a call in the morning."

"Thank you. Believe it or not, Patty would thank you too if she could right now," the doctor said with a kind smile.

Walking back out to their cars, Zolie ignored Stevie and opened her car door.

"Aren't you forgetting something?" Stevie asked.

Looking to the tattered woman, Zolie shot her a cold stare. "If you think I'm paying you for nothing, you have another thing coming, my dear," she said, getting in her car.

"Zolie, wait!" Stevie said, rushing to her car door. "Look, I don't even have enough to get back with," she said, pulling her wallet from her purse and opening it to show her the two wrinkled one-dollar bills and some change inside.

Zolie looked at the sad woman and sighed.

"I'm sorry I snapped at you," Stevie said. Her eyes becoming wet, and she glanced away in shame; the meekness had returned. "Mrs. Vanderran, I'm sorry. I have no one and nothing—and if I could've, I'd have brought you here for free. I just needed some help and thought this was the only way."

"You should have thought of that in the beginning. I would have given you ten times what you're asking had you done this out of the kindness you should've had after what your family has done to mine," Zolie said, starting her car. "Ed may have forgiven you, but I haven't." Driving away, she left a trail of dust behind her.

Zolie drove down the road, and the anger for her lost sister was choking her, and she started to cry. Pulling over and putting the car in park, she caught her breath and opened her purse, pulling out a tissue to wipe her eyes. Adjusting it and dabbing at her eyes as she looked in the rearview mirror, she saw Stevie back in the distance open the trunk of her car and pull out a blanket. She stared into the mirror and then watched her pull out an old pillow then close the trunk of the Chevrolet; she then opened the back door of the sedan and tossed them inside. Quietly Zolie sat there watching as Stevie got in and closed the car door behind her.

Zolie had left the Dawn convertible at the house and taken the hardtop Rolls-Royce for the long drive to the sanatorium, wanting the feeling of more protection. Now sitting in her luxurious car and witnessing the sad life play out behind her, she closed her eyes and prayed. "Cara, I miss you so," she said, and when she opened her eyes, Cara was sitting in the seat next to her. It was like old times, and Cara put her hand on her sister's arm and told her to remember to love. "But I miss you." Zolie blinked her eyes, and in that moment Cara was gone.

Zolie sat there looking at the empty seat, and a sympathetic feeling came over her. She looked to the mirror and sighed once more as she shifted gears and turned the wheel of the car and drove back up the driveway to the blue Chevrolet sitting alone in the dreary parking lot.

Parking farther away than they were moments ago, Zolie got out of her car, leaving her door open, and walked to Stevie's car. Looking inside, she saw the car was a mess. There were takeout containers and clothes piled in the front passenger seat, and when she knocked on the glass, Stevie was startled and popped her head up.

Opening the door, she got out and faced Zolie; the shame was evident, and the woman was the polar opposite of the expensively dressed and rich woman who stood in front of her. She was embarrassed that Zolie had seen inside her car, and there was nothing she could do to hide it.

"How much gas is in your car?" Zolie asked.

"I think I can get back down to that gas station I passed getting off the freeway, but I don't think I'll have enough to get back tomorrow," Stevie said. "I just can't risk it."

"Nonsense," Zolie said. "You can't stay the night out here—it's too cold. Where do you—" She stopped herself, realizing the woman was living in her car. "Never mind. Get in your car, and I'll follow you to the gas station. We'll fill the tank, and I'm checking you into one of the hotels we passed before the exit."

"But…"

"But nothing. Just do as you're told, and we'll discuss this tomorrow. Now come on."

"Evicted. You were going to ask where I lived a second ago," Stevie said, watching her walk back to her car. "I have a small storage locker."

Zolie stopped and turned back. "We'll talk about this later."

Stevie watched her get in her car and start it; then she shut the back door and ran around to the driver's side and got in and led Zolie back to the gas station.

After filling up her car, Stevie followed Zolie to a Holiday Inn not far from the sanatorium exit and parked. She followed her inside and was surprised when Zolie booked her a room for a week.

"A week!" Stevie said, the smile returning to her sad face as she finally felt hope after a long road of hell.

"Sir, I'd like full restaurant privileges added to my credit card for the week's stay," Zolie said to the front desk manager processing the room.

"The dining room opens at six every morning, and the last meal is served at ten every night," the manager informed them as he handed Stevie the registration card for her car information.

"Are there laundry facilities?" Zolie asked.

"Down this hall to your left," the man said, pointing.

"Thank you." Zolie watched Stevie give the man the information card as he handed her the key cards.

Back outside Stevie couldn't wait to tell her how thankful she was, and when Zolie handed her three hundred dollars and told her to call her if she needed anything, she started to cry.

"Oh, stop it," Zolie said. "Pull it together and get some rest. We'll talk in the morning."

Stevie watched the fancy lady with the British accent get in her expensive car and drive away, leaving her in the best condition she'd hoped for—at least for now.

CHAPTER 60

In New York City, Marlo Savage woke up in her luxurious suite. The smell of the flowers filled her room, and she smiled as she rose from her bed. Moving to the windows, she opened the drapes to the magnificent city that seemed to smile back at her with a crisp autumn day. Today was going to be her first day of shooting for *Tycoon Wives*, and she was ready for it. She had been drained after her first day there, filled with private photo shoots since she hadn't been introduced to the ladies yet and the seemingly endless meetings, and when she got back to the hotel she was exhausted. But after a good nights sleep, she was ready to start her new day. She looked at the clock and noticed her scheduled room service was due any moment, and she put on her robe just as a slight knock came at her door.

Looking through the peephole, she saw the young man standing behind the cart with her breakfast, and she opened the door. Yes, today was the beginning of her new wonderful career, and she was thrilled beyond belief it was now happening in her life.

Just as the man was about to push the cart into her room, panic grabbed her by the throat, and her mind flashed to being alone with that man in the RV. She grabbed the edge of the table with one hand; with the other, she reached out and stopped the cart midway through the door.

"Ma'am, is there a problem?" the young man asked with surprise.

"No, I'll take it from here; thank you," Marlo said, signing the check and handing it back to the attendant.

"Yes, ma'am." Taking the check, he then bent down and smothered the Sterno flame underneath the cart and then turned away, leaving her to pull the table into her room herself.

Getting the table inside, she closed the door and locked it immediately. She turned and leaned against the door and held her stomach as the shaking began. Pure fear was running through her body, and she hadn't seen it coming. Moving past the table to the bed, she climbed back inside and pulled the covers over herself until her nervous shaking abated.

"You're okay," she said to herself in the beautiful room in the city—far away from everyone she loved.

CHAPTER 61

The taxi drove up the familiar roads to his old home away from home. It had been too many years since Dr. Todd Vreeland had been back. Now older and never charged or implicated in the fire that had killed so many all those years ago, it was time to return to *his* hospital.

Dr. Todd's time away in South America was exactly what he needed. Being the skilled physician he was, he had been welcomed in every hospital he went to. After the fire, he was running the sanatorium *his* way without Blake looming over his shoulder. It would have stayed that way, too, until their other brother, Dr. Eric Vreeland, called looking for Blake and said he was coming for a visit at the end of the month when he could arrange it.

With everything that had happened, including the death of their father, Todd had lied when he told Eric he was excited to see him and was glad he was coming home. He reminded him Blake had leased the hospital to be run by the state of New York due to the hard times the old family hospital had been facing at the time, and that he'd gone on a trip to New Zealand. He also told him he was leaving for Canada in a few days for some skiing himself. He remembered the conversation well.

"Skiing? When will you be back?" Eric had asked.

"Not sure. I need some me time," Todd lied, wishing the conversation hadn't happened.

"When will Blake be back?"

"He called and said he was going on some cruise. Not sure where, though."

"Hmm." Eric's tone had been full of doubt.

Todd remembered having the feeling Eric knew he was lying and wanted nothing more than to get off the phone. "So why don't you hold off on coming back here until I return? That would be better, and maybe Blake will be back then, too," Todd suggested, hoping he'd take the bait.

"Well, I would, but I don't like the idea of the state running the hospital without a Vreeland there. Someone should be there to oversee things until it's running smoothly. No, better I get there, and the sooner the better," Eric had said before hanging up the phone.

The waves of guilt that came and went in Todd's life had never ended since that horrible and wonderful night he'd become the lead Vreeland running the hospital. His drinking increased, and the blackouts erased the ugliness, but he'd get flashes of memory from that night he could barely remember. With the thought of his only living family member left coming back home and the guilt mounting on the shores of his mind, Dr. Todd broke down. He looked at the hospital like it was a curse, and that was the last time he'd spoken with his brother Eric before leaving for South America.

With the taxi driving away from the home Todd had left under the caretaker's attention, he pulled the key he still had with him and unlocked the door, dropping his bag in the dusty, musty-smelling old home. He'd missed his old farmhouse, it was nothing like the small house he'd rented after Blake had banished him away from the hospital. Walking though the home brought back many memories, and going to his kitchen, he found his truck keys in the drawer where he'd left them all those years ago, and later he found his prized pickup had been left idle for far too long. Never being the ostentatious type, like Blake, who always had to have the newest Mercedes, Todd had a sense of humility his whole life; he appreciated the things he had and took great care of them. And anyone from the outside looking in would have definitely seen that in him—had he only been given the chance.

Alone in his garage, he tried to start his truck, and when he finally gave up, he left the garage and went around back to the old ambulance parked under a carport in the backyard next to the work shed. It was older than his pickup, but the engine was new, at least at the time he'd had it put in.

It only took a few tries, and the engine roared with life, and he noticed the gas gauge was low when the engine died. Shutting off the key, he tried it again and heard the familiar clicking sound of a dead battery that had miraculously started once after being dormant for too many years to count. He looked to his wonderful old home, knowing he'd need to get a new battery and some gas in the tank along with an oil change before driving to the hospital. Deciding to stay there for the night, he got out from the ambulance and stared at his old life, looking back to where everything had changed. The memories of his abused and murderous life played like a movie in his mind. And one event in his young impressionable soul forever scarred that innocent child he'd once been.

The beating Todd Vreeland had just endured was nothing compared to what was coming. Slamming the back door of their home closed, not far from the Vreeland Hills Sanatorium, Todd passed a mirror and saw the dirt encrusted on his face—a parting gift from brother Blake to remember him by. Stumbling into the bathroom near the kitchen, he reached for some rubbing alcohol under the sink and poured some on a washcloth and dabbed at his face. The sting from it caused him to flinch, and he yelled out and swooned, leaning on the counter to keep from falling over and nearly spilling the alcohol.

He lifted up the bottle and took a healthy drink and nearly puked as he spat out the nasty taste from his mouth. A mixture of blood, alcohol, and spit sprayed the mirror, and he started to heave. Moving to the toilet, he lifted the lid and lost the remains of his insides; sucking in air, he choked on his own vomit, making the day even worse. Getting up and flushing the mess away, he leaned toward the mirror and wiped his mouth. In doing so, he bumped his nose with his hand, causing fresh blood to wash over his lips. Holding a towel to his face, he moved to the stairs and saw his father's bar in his study. Eyeing the Don Julio Real tequila, he went and opened the bottle and downed a shot, smiling at the smoothness of it. Proudly, he took it with him and went back to the stairs to escape to his room to hide out before their father came home.

Moving down the hall past his brother's room, he noticed the door was ajar, and Blake's aquarium caught his eye. He kicked open the door and went to the large tank next to his brother's desk. There he saw a beautiful partially drawn picture of one of the fish—the one their mother had given him. Then when the blood dripped from his nose and hit the drawing—that was the only inspiration poor Todd Vreeland needed to add to this miserable day.

The rage flowed in Todd's veins as he looked over to the fish tank, and he smiled watching the exotically colored fish swim innocently by. That's when he put the bottle of tequila down and opened the top of the fish tank. He then leaned over the drawing and removed the towel from his nose, holding one nostril closed, and blew out the bloody mucus all over the drawing. Seeing his added touch to the picture, he blew the other side onto it and laughed. He then picked up the bottle of tequila and poured most of it into the fish tank.

Standing there, he watched as the fish closer to the top swam into the heavy alcohol as it came down upon them—snuffing out their lives. He smiled as the fish one by one turned over and floated to the top of the tank—not even hearing his bastard brother sneak up behind him.

The hockey stick collided with the back of Todd's skull with a crack. The same stick that had been used on him only a short while ago was back in action. Todd yelled out and fell forward, and Blake grabbed the back of his head and slammed it down on his desk—on top of the destroyed drawing. Banging his head against it several times before lifting him up and dunking his blood-soaked face into the aquarium, he held it under as his younger brother's arms were flailing about. Todd panicked, and the adrenaline shot through him, and he pushed back against his brother with his legs, bringing the aquarium down on both of them.

Todd was choking for air when he saw his father holding a baseball bat appear in the doorway and lean against the frame as Blake regained the upper hand and grabbed his collar and began punching him in the face.

"That's enough," came the gruff voice of their father.

Todd opened his eyes and saw his father was still standing there as his brother's fist hit him again.

"I said, that's enough!" their father yelled as he grabbed Blake from behind and forcibly threw him across the room into the wall. Blake hit the wall hard and fell to the floor but was up as the fire inside him was at an all-time pitch. Advancing toward his brother—and his father—he didn't expect the baseball bat would come swinging toward him, hitting him hard in the left arm, breaking his humerus with a loud crack.

Blake yelled out as he hit the dresser and fell back to the floor, and Todd's reaction turned to fear as their father moved closer to him and squatted down, holding the bat in his hands in front of him.

"Was that a smile I saw on your face just then? You deserved what he gave you for this mess in here, but no son of mine will raise a hand to me—ever!" Todd watched as his father stood; then the crash of the bat came down on him—breaking his left humerus like his brother's. "Here's something to smile about. You damn girl."

Todd cried out, rolling over, clutching his broken arm, and saw his father throw the bat across the room, hitting the far wall and floor like his brother had. He and Blake both flinched at the sound as they saw him move to the door of their room.

"You've got five minutes to get to the back of the truck for a ride to the hospital, or you'll crawl there," their father said in the calm and scary voice they'd heard their whole lives.

Todd rolled over and reached for the end of the bed, and as he leaned against the edge of it, he saw his brother staring at him. Not a word was said between them, and Todd watched his older brother get up from the floor and move toward him. Fear gripped his heart, but when his brother reached his hand down to pull him up with his good arm, his heart broke wanting nothing but peace with his older brother, whom he'd secretly always admired.

The fight they'd had earlier really wasn't Todd's fault at all, and it all stemmed from the time Todd accidentally left a door at his father's laboratory open and a patient escaped, or so he had been led to believe. The patient should've been restrained *entirely* and nowhere near him to begin with, and Todd hadn't even known he was there.

·The entire day had been strange. Todd was to meet their mother, Claire, at the hospital after school, and when he grew bored of waiting, he left a note and went outside to shoot baskets in the court, thinking she would find him out back.

By the time Claire did show up, the patient in the adjoining room at the end of the hall had managed to unfasten his restraints, and as he was making his escape through the open door to the basketball court Todd had left open, he saw her alone and killed her. She was found with the note shoved down her throat, and the patient had gotten away and was a menace in the headlines.

Yes, everything prior to that day had been fine, even between the brothers. Blake knew his younger brother idolized him, and even Eric would share their discoveries in the lab with him. All Todd wanted was for everything to be as it was. And when he broke his mother's favorite vase, the vase Blake and Eric had pooled their allowances for, they used that as an excuse to beat the hell out of him over the loss of their mother, which they blamed Todd for, and chased him outside with Blake's hockey stick to do just that. Poor Todd Vreeland was outnumbered, and after getting a few good hits in himself, Eric held him down while Blake pummeled him.

Feeling his brother's help for the first time in what seemed like an eternity since their mother had died felt like a blessing to the younger Vreeland as they moved down the hall. The pain from the beating was there, but maybe finally, Todd thought, he could find a way back into both his brothers' good graces. The happy thoughts filled his mind as he looked over the bannister to the open front door below. He heard their father's truck start in the driveway and knew soon they'd be on their way.

Blinded by his sheer idolization of his older and smarter brother, the happiness didn't last long before they passed the family portrait at the top of the stairs. Poor Todd Vreeland really didn't see it coming when Blake tripped and pushed him from the top, sending him spiraling down the stairs to the foyer below just as their father had walked back to the house and saw the whole thing.

Eric's laughter filled Todd's ears when he opened his eyes from his place on the floor; he watched his brother Blake leap past him and dash out the door past their father, and in that moment Todd saw a look of compassion on his father's face—it was the last time he ever wore it.

"Eric! Get over here, boy," their father ordered in his calm, frightening tone.

Todd tried lifting himself off the floor against the stairs to see Eric glance at him, hesitating as he approached their father.

"Yes, sir." Eric's heightened state sounded in his voice.

"You better have Blake's room cleaned when we get back."

"Yes, sir," Eric said, glad that was all it seemed he wanted, and as he turned away, he heard his name. Slowly turning back Dr. Victor Vreeland backhanded the boy hard, knocking him down.

"Now you're excused." The abusive bastard grinned.

Victor Vreeland then helped his youngest son, Todd, up, and together they got to the truck.

"You touch your brother like that again, and I'll break your other arm and every bone in your hands," Victor snapped at Blake, instilling the fear in the boy just like he'd instilled the lies of his mother's death he had told him earlier.

Driving the short distance to the sanatorium where he'd repair his sons' injuries, avoiding all police reports, Victor Vreeland thought about the plan he'd devised of murdering his wife so he could keep all his holdings and be free to whore about without all the fighting at home. The day Todd was to meet his mother at Vreeland Hills Sanatorium was the day the trap had been set, and maybe Todd was paying too high a price for the crime he was hiding from everyone.

Yes, it had been too long since Dr. Todd Vreeland had been home, and with his brother Eric, the smartest one that got far away when he could, back in Germany running his practice there, he was now curious about one Dr. Sinardi—the man Todd had learned was running *his* hospital.

CHAPTER 62

The morning at West Point would have been filled with good memories for Ed Savage had the situation been different. His short time there in his youth and coming back to enjoy all the graduations of various family members had all been lovely occasions.

After he and Logan had gotten there late last night, and after passing the spot on the road being searched in the dead of darkness, their plan was to go and search it themselves in the light of day. Roman and Gabby were set to go back there with them until they got a call about a pair of motorcycles with "For Sale" signs on them at a gas station not far from where they were. They decided to split up, and Roman and Gabby would touch base with them later after checking out the gas station.

Watching Roman and Gabby pull ahead of them when Ed and Logan pulled up to the curve in the road where the girls were last thought to have been, the feeling of dread swept over them. Remembering the yellow sheriff's tape from their campsite in the mountains, Ed pulled over and parked behind a squad car. Shaking that image from his mind, he opened the door and got out and stretched, feeling like he didn't need his cane he left it in the SUV.

Two West Point officers were standing guard and greeted them as they moved near the crash site. Ed immediately noticed the oil in the wet area was evident from the rainbow effect on the asphalt where the water in the road had receded a bit. The forensics team was there and just about finished up when Ed and Logan saw one of the oilcans still lying in the ditch.

"Mr. Savage, Glenn Marshall," the lead investigator said, standing near the oilcan.

Ed shook his hand. "My brother Logan," Ed said. Logan nodded and exchanged a handshake as Ed continued, "Anything new since yesterday?"

"We got a tire track and some broken taillight pieces that were buried. They came from an Indian Springfield motorcycle, sir," Glenn said.

"I need to see them," Logan said, the desperation clearly evident in his voice.

Glenn motioned them over to another vehicle, an SUV with the back opened up. There they saw everything the law had found—all bagged and tagged.

"Go ahead; I'll leave you to it. If you need me, I'll be back over there," Glenn said, waving to where they were just standing.

Ed nodded as Logan picked up the red glass fragments of the taillight inside the plastic bag. Looking beyond it, he noticed the bag containing a woman's belt. He picked it up and recognized it as his daughter Kate's. "Ed." Logan held up the bag.

Ed could see the frightened look on his brother's face, a look that had become all too familiar, since many of his family members were wearing it. "Logan, we'll find them," he said.

Logan got emotional and waved him away, and Ed knew his brother needed some time. As he walked away, a text vibrated his phone in his pocket. Ed reached for it and saw it was from Thrasher. As he looked back to check on Logan, he noticed his brother walking away from the SUV toward the side of the road. He then read the text: *Was there earlier—sorry, nothing of value to report except the handyman's plumb bob they found in evidence.*

Putting his phone back in his pocket, Ed moved back to the SUV and found the plumb bob in the plastic bag. "Hey, Glenn? Where did you find this?" Ed asked with a raised voice.

Both Logan and Glenn moved back toward him, and Glenn read the sticker on the evidence bag. "Marker eight. Right over here," he said, moving to where Logan was just coming from.

Together the men followed him to the paint mark on the side of the road. There, only a few feet away, they saw splinters of wood like something had hit the ground and broke into pieces. "You find any other tools out here?" Ed asked.

"Nope. Just this," Glenn responded.

Ed looked down and saw a splinter of wood a few feet away. He crouched down and saw it was fresh like it hadn't been out in the elements for a long time. "How far down did your men search?" Ed asked.

"A few feet past here."

Logan was already moving past the spot it had been found and was looking beyond the shoulder of the road for anything he could find. And when Ed followed behind, Glenn waved to his men to come down and assist in widening the search area. It wasn't long before Logan found a screwdriver about sixteen feet past the spot where the plumb bob had been found.

"Ed! Over here!" Logan yelled.

"Don't touch it!" Ed barked back, moving toward him.

Both Ed and Glenn rushed to Logan's side and looked at the object partly hidden underneath some leaves that had collected on the side of the road.

"We're looking for someone with a truck who uses these tools," Ed said as he reached for his phone.

"Who are you calling?" Logan asked.

"Roman—he needs to know this, and I want to find out about that gas station."

When the call went to voice mail, Ed looked to his phone and saw he had service but thought Roman might not out here in the mountains, which was another reminder of why he was starting to hate the damn forest.

"Roman, call me when you get this. We found some handyman tools—a plumb bob and a screwdriver. Looks like they fell from a truck, which we also have a tire track they're checking on."

As they watched the team glove and bag the screwdriver, Ed and Logan moved back to where the bikes had gone off the road. They followed the tracks to where it was apparent one of the bikes had gotten stuck, and scouted the area where a suspected scuffle took place. Saddened by all of it and scared for the girls, they realized there was nothing left for them to do there. "Ed, let's go to that gas station and see for ourselves what's going on. I'm worried about Roman and Gabby," Logan said.

"I was just thinking that myself." Ed checked his phone again.

They moved back to the road and got directions from Glenn, and soon they were on their way.

CHAPTER 63

When Marlo Savage arrived at the set of *Tycoon Wives*, the excitement and magic of being back in the profession she'd missed for so long made her forget the panic attack she'd had earlier at the hotel. Today was a big day with the series starting anew. The way they filmed and introduced new wives was intriguing to her, not like that carbon-copy rip-off show titled the *True Homemaker* of whatever state they happened to be in at the time!

Marlo was introduced along with Carmen Reynolds, whose husband was a champion race car driver, for the first time with the other ladies. She couldn't wait to talk about the film clips they were also shown backstage and find out which part she'd get. With only a week for everyone to get ready, the introduction wasn't as bad as she thought, with them being seen as possible replacements for any of them, and that's how each season started. This way, at least she thought, before all the hair pulling and snapping at each other began, the new ladies joining the cast were also there to help the ones on the outs, should any of them *want* any help.

With comedy being one of the topics this year, as the current queen bee of the show, Marilyn Hart, had revealed on air, Marlo had been floored when she not only saw the film clip, but also when she saw the set already built on another stage; it had taken her back. It was an exact replica of the *Designing Women* living area, complete with staircase and furniture.

How she used to love that show and all the characters that played on it. And when Randall Bishop introduced her to the other ladies, it was nothing but a warm moment, especially from Madeline Roberts, whom she'd met with her husband, Don, along with Ed, Sam, and Cara quite some time ago. The greetings were everything she expected until she came face to face with Marilyn Hart.

The coldness behind her eyes was blatant; her smile was indeed forced. Marilyn Hart may have been Marlo's favorite *Tycoon Wives* star when she only watched the show. But after meeting her after she'd studied up on her, Marlo knew exactly what this bitch's story was, and she didn't care, because she had arrived, and *no one* was going to spoil her return to the spotlight.

CHAPTER 64

rriving at the gas station, Ed and Logan saw the motorcycles for sale and immediately knew they weren't the girls' bikes. The two Yamahas were older and in pretty bad shape. Realizing this was a dead end, Ed pulled into a spot near the convenience store entrance and switched off the ignition.

"Want anything?" Ed said, opening the door.

Logan noticed the local newspapers displayed near the entrance. "I'll take a water, but in the meantime, maybe our handymen advertise?" he said, motioning over to the area.

Ed looked over and quietly realized his little brother had one-upped him in the detective zone. "Hey, when did you become Dick Tracy?"

"Come on, Ed—you're not the only big dick in the house."

"Yuck, that's an image I don't want in my head. Thanks."

"Don't mention it." Logan winked at him, giving him a taste of his own brand of humor.

Ed glanced at the newspapers and entered the store, seeing more inside and leaving Logan outside; he walked to the cold section and grabbed water and an iced tea for himself. Bringing them up, he placed them on the counter and noticed the grease-monkey shirt the man behind the counter was wearing with his name opposite his pocket.

"Will that be all today, sir?"

"What can you tell me about those bikes out there?"

"The owner just finished working on them in the garage, tuning them up, and he's trying to sell the pair. But between you and me, he'd sell just one if that's all you were looking for."

"They look a little worn; get any newer ones around here?"

The man stopped ringing up the drinks and looked at him. "You're the second one today asking about newer bikes. Damn, they're never going to sell," the man said and laughed.

"Hey, Greg, you'll sell them," Ed said, looking right at his name on his shirt.

"That'll be three eighty-nine," Greg said. "Need a bag?"

Ed fished out four bucks and handed it to him. "Nah, I'm good."

Greg handed him his change, and Ed picked up the drinks. As he was leaving, he turned back around. "Oh hey, by the way, I've got a back porch that's sagging on one end. You don't know anyone that does that kind of work, do you?"

"As a matter of fact, I do. Here's a card right here," Greg said, reaching near the register and grabbing one to hand to the nice gentleman.

Ed took it from him and read the front of it: "Lou and Lenny's Repair?"

"A couple of good old boys. You tell them I referred you, okay?"

At that moment Ed's mind flashed—and Patty Galloway was now standing behind the counter like she had in that little mountain store dressed in Greg's grease-monkey shirt. The name on the shirt was hers, and her hair was wild, like that night in the cave.

"You'll tell him I referred you, okay?" Patty repeated.

Coming back from his thoughts, Ed flinched as the horrible vision melted away, and he smiled. "Yeah, sure thing. Thanks, Greg."

Leaving the store, he got to the Range Rover and opened his door, handing Logan his water. "You find anything?"

"No," Logan said, taking a drink as Ed got in and closed the door.

Ed took a drink from his iced tea and placed it in the cup holder. "Well, don't worry, Dick Tracy. I covered it," he said, handing him the business card.

Logan took the card and read it. "Lou and Lenny's Repair?"

"Name, number, and address. It's a long shot, but if it pans out, you can hang up your detective hat." Ed grinned devilishly at his brother.

"You're such a dick," Logan teased.

"That's *bigger* dick." Ed laughed as he backed out from the spot and onto the road back to West Point. Coming around a bend to a clearing, Logan's phone beeped with a message. Checking it he saw the message was from Roman.

"Ed, Roman says they have another lead on the bikes up at a ski lodge, and he and Gabby are on their way there now."

Ed's mind raced from Patty behind the counter to the surveillance from Tallulah of this mysterious Mingyu Yunt at the ski lodge. "Is there a name of the lodge? An address?" Ed asked.

"No," Logan said, doing an Internet search.

"They shouldn't have gone up there without us."

"Why not?"

"I've got a bad feeling," Ed said as he increased the speed back to West Point.

CHAPTER 65

The ransom call for the girls arrived at Savage Tower shortly after Ed and Logan left the gas station. The caller was obviously confused when he asked to speak directly to Kate's father, Ed Savage. Being on alert and aware of the missing girls, the Savage family had a police unit at the building set up in an empty office to intercept any and all calls related to them. A skilled female detective answered the phone as Ed's secretary and tried to keep the caller on the phone for as long as possible for a trace, all the while asking a barrage of questions to confuse and get as much information as possible. When the caller tried ending the conversation, the detective would ask more incessant questions. Fed up, the caller finally disconnected the call.

The amount of money they were asking for was absurd considering the money the Savages had inherited from their father, which was plastered in the newspapers and online everywhere. The caller asked for one million dollars for the release of both girls and said that instructions would follow on how it was to be delivered.

On the plus side, the recording picked up two distinct background sounds: the cry of a gull, signaling they were near water—possibly the exact opposite direction the girls had been going on their way to West Point, unless it was picked up over the Hudson River—and a distant foghorn that was heard over a static interruption. The trace only gave them a radius from Savage Tower in Port Roberts to as far south as New York City and north to the Catskills.

The news wasn't the best, but it was a start, and the detective picked up the phone to call Roman and Logan Savage.

CHAPTER 66

When Ed and Logan arrived back at West Point, they met with Commander Richton and were going over everything Roman and Gabby were looking into.

"Who exactly called in the report?" Ed asked.

"Two reports actually. First, an Indian motorcycle was spotted in the parking lot of the Catskills Ski Lodge. Shortly afterward we picked up a call on the radio. Catskill police reported an accident involving an Indian motorcycle and an automobile," Commander Richton said.

"Oh God," Logan said, placing his hand over his heart. "Was it one of our daughters in the accident?"

"No plate on the bike. The female driving it wasn't carrying any ID, and she was taken to Catskill Cliffside Medical Center."

"What color were the bikes? The one in the accident?" Logan asked.

"The one in the accident was black; the other one was listed as red in color."

"Ed, Kate picked out the black one," Logan almost cried.

Ed remembered the girls riding up to him on the bikes that day he drove in to the office, and he could feel exactly what his brother was feeling. "Do we have a description of the girl from the accident?" Ed asked, as Logan's phone started to ring.

"Midtwenties, long dark hair," came the answer.

Both Ed and Logan sank deeper in their fear as Logan's phone continued to ring.

"And Roman and Gabby went to the hospital?" Ed asked as Logan pulled out his phone and looked at it.

"Roman called and checked in after investigating the gas station, I'd given him the report and he said they were going to check it out and go to the ski lodge," the commander told them.

Logan recognized the number from Savage Tower and answered it with excitement. "This is Logan; what do you got?"

"Logan, this is Detective Mallory O'Shea; the ransom call came in."

"Hang on; Ed's with me. I'm putting this on speaker." Logan continued, "Go on—we're here."

"Couldn't keep them on the phone long enough for an exact trace. They can be anywhere from Port Roberts as far south as New York City and up near the mountains where you're at. However, they're asking for one million dollars and said they'll call back with instructions."

Ed had wished the police hadn't gotten involved and that Agency One was handling the case. But with West Point calling Roman, and his getting the police involved, there was nothing he could do but ask, and he gave it a shot as he looked to his brother with fear on his face. "We'll pay it. No police. Let us just pay the ransom and get our girls back; then you can do whatever you need to do," Ed said praying the feds hadn't been called in yet.

"Sorry, sir, if they've crossed state lines, it's a federal offense, and the entire tristate area is on alert."

"Ed, you know more about this stuff than I do. What do we do?"

"We'll want the usual proof of life when they call back. Is there anything else?" Ed said, staring at the phone in his younger brother's hand.

"Yes, sir, we picked up the sound of a gull in the background."

"A gull? They're near water!" Logan said.

"Yes, sir. That and the sound of a distant foghorn—we're now analyzing the recording for more. Oh, Mr. Savage, something the caller said didn't make sense."

"Oh?" Logan was afraid of what was coming next.

"They asked for Kate's father, *Ed* Savage, not Logan Savage. Does that mean anything to you?"

Both brothers looked at each other and shook their heads.

"This is strange," Ed said into his phone. "Either the girls are trying to tell us something, or we're dealing with amateurs. When they call back with the drop instructions, we'll know better, but until then I want you to send that recording to my cell the minute you hang up. That's *my* cell, not Logan's; you have the number. Do you understand?" Ed said.

"Sir, I'll have to get authorization. I can't—"

Ed interrupted her, "Text me your lead detective's name and contact information now while we have you on the phone. We're not hanging up until this is handled."

"Hold the line a moment, sir."

They could hear her shout out the orders in the background as they waited, and he looked to Logan and the commander. "I'll get that recording," Ed assured them as he pulled out his phone to wait for it.

"They're sending it now, Mr. Savage."

The text alert vibrated his phone, and he saw the message bubble pop up on the screen. "Sergeant David Johnson. Got it. Hang on," Ed said into Logan's speakerphone.

Ed sent a quick text to Tallulah at Agency One. He then punched in her number and moved away from the men.

"I got the text," Tallulah said. "What do you want me to do with it?"

"This is Ed Savage," Ed said into the phone, knowing Logan and the commander could hear and that Tallulah would understand. "Detective Mallory O'Shea is handling the now-confirmed kidnapping of my nieces, and she requires authorization to forward me the ransom recording."

"Unclear to talk, understood. Ed, you'll have it; hang on a second." A moment passed and Tallulah was back. "It should be coming in any second, but while I have you on the phone, we've picked up a wire transfer. A sale is taking place, and it's big—twenty million."

Detective O'Shea's voice came back on Logan's phone.

"Are you there?"

"We're here," Logan said.

"Just spoke with Sergeant Johnson; we'll be sending the recording now."

"Thank you; they're sending it now," Ed said into his phone.

"Ed, forward it to me, and we'll work on it from our end. And Agent Forester just landed at Kennedy. I'll be assigning all this to him once he gets here."

The recording e-mail notification popped up on Ed's phone. "Robert, huh? I haven't seen him in ages—good call. The recording just came in. Thanks." Ed hung up and forwarded her a copy.

CHAPTER 67

Pulling into the parking lot of the Catskills Ski Lodge, Roman and Gabby Savage parked and made their way inside the beautiful, warm lobby. They'd hit a few patches of black ice on the way up, which made them worry more for the girls. Eyeing the front desk and the familiar-looking gentleman checking in, Roman wondered if he'd seen the guy before.

The consortium consultant Nathan had been dealing with took his key from the front desk associate and carried his one bag with him to the elevator just as Roman and Gabby arrived at the front desk. As the elevator doors were closing, he noticed the mixed-race couple checking in but didn't recognize Roman Savage at all.

"Checking in?" the associate asked politely, admiring the beautiful and expensive-looking necklace the African American woman was wearing.

"Maybe. We don't have a reservation. Are you full tonight?" Roman asked.

Gabby looked at her husband but did not say a word.

"We have rooms available, sir," the associate said.

"We'll take a suite—the best you got." Roman placed his black American Express card on the counter with his identification.

"How many nights will this be for, sir?"

"Just for tonight for now. But call us should you start to fill up—we may extend. Can you do that?"

"Yes, sir, that will not be a problem," the associate said, happy to have booked their most expensive room. "Are your bags outside?"

"They're not here yet. But thank you." Roman offered a flirtatious smile.

With everything signed they took their keys and made their way to the elevators, and once the car door closed, Roman turned to his wife. "How'd I do?"

"How'd you do? What the hell was that all about?"

CHAPTER 68

The voice mail messages Roman had sent to both Logan and Ed arrived seconds apart, almost thirty minutes after he'd called. They had been to the Catskills Cliffside Medical Center and confirmed the woman in the motorcycle accident was not Lana or Kate. Further, they mentioned they were headed to the Catskills Ski Lodge to check out the report of the other Indian motorcycle seen there.

"Thank God," Logan said, hanging up his phone.

"This doesn't make sense," Ed said, looking at his watch. "The messages should have been here long before now."

"It's probably the damn mountains."

Ed grimaced recalling the text message they'd received from Mia's phone in the mountains sending them right into harm's way. "Come on—we're going skiing."

Ed turned away from his brother, and Logan followed him to his Range Rover.

CHAPTER 69

When the elevator opened on the top floor of the Catskills Ski Lodge, Roman put his hand against the doors and waited for Gabby to exit the car first. They paused as they looked at the room numbers and arrows on the wall directing them to their suite and turned left to their room at the end of the hall.

Passing the maid's cart as they got to their room, Roman slid the key card into the slot; the green light illuminated, and they heard the sound of the door unlock. Opening the door to the luxurious suite, they were not only impressed, but as they were entering the room, they saw the same man from the lobby exit his room up the hall from them and move toward the elevators. And as Roman paused and studied the man, Gabby noticed and looked as Roman closed the door.

"Gabby, have you seen him before?" Roman asked.

"No, not that I can recall. Why, Roman? Who is he?"

"I've seen that man before, but I can't place him," Roman said as he moved toward the windows framing the majestic view. He then looked down to the parking lot and saw the motorcycle. "It's not hers," he said with a saddened heart.

Gabby moved with him, and together they looked down at the bike.

"Honey, I don't understand what we're doing here. Why'd we check in?"

"Call it a hunch, but I've seen that man before, and I needed time to think," he said, pulling out his phone. "Damn it, why hasn't Ed or Logan called?"

Roman started punching in Ed's number as he moved away from the window, and Gabby turned back to look at the motorcycle again; the man they'd just seen in the hallway was now standing next to it.

"Roman, that man! He's next to the bike!" Gabby said, full of excitement.

Roman hung up his phone and moved back to the window to see the man move past the motorcycle toward a trail that led to private lodges on the property and a scenic viewpoint.

"Stay here. I'm going to find out just who this asshole is," Roman said, moving toward the door.

Gabby followed and watched him move down the hall, passing a maid with her cart, to the elevators. She watched him push the button, and as the elevator opened, he turned to her and waved. Closing the door, Gabby moved back to the window and saw the bike alone in the parking lot and got an idea—an *awful* idea, spawned from all her conversations with Marlo over the years about *Skirt Squad*, that long-ago TV show she'd done one season, where she'd played an undercover cop.

Moving back to the door, she opened it slowly to see the maid's cart alone in the hallway. She then opened her purse and grabbed a wad of cash; lifting her skirt, she tucked it into her garter. She then tossed her purse behind her, closing the door, and moved to the elevators to push one of the buttons. *Don't come out, don't come out,* ran the thoughts in her head until the elevator car arrived, and as it did, she stepped into it just as the maid was coming out from that man's room.

"Oh thank God—my key! I forgot it," she said as she rushed down the hall, getting to the maid and standing between her and the door. "I can't thank you enough," she said, lifting her skirt and pulling out the cash. The three crisp hundred-dollar bills she counted out and handed to the maid did the job. The maid took the money, and she quickly looked up and down the hall and then let the kind and generous woman into the man's room—no questions asked and thankful for the tip.

Just as Gabby thanked the maid one last time, the door of the room beside her opened, and an Asian woman with long, straight black hair stepped out. She saw the strange African American woman enter the room of the man she knew was staying there and then watched the maid begin pushing her cart to the service elevator. She then moved to the guest elevators and waited for the maid to leave the floor.

CHAPTER 70

ownstairs, Roman exited the lodge and hurried to the motorcycle. He hesitated a moment and looked up to his hotel room window high above in hopes of seeing his wife, but between the glare of the sun and the trees reflected off the windows, he couldn't make out a thing, so he moved toward the trail to the lodges and the scenic viewpoint.

With each step he took, the foreboding in his heart increased as he passed tourists by, and the shortness in his breath was something he hadn't experienced before. He worked out daily, and he couldn't understand where the heaviness was coming from.

Upstairs in the lodge, Gabby made her way to the window of the man's room and saw her husband move from the motorcycle to the sign marking the viewpoint. She then started looking around the room and searching everything she could find. She opened the closet doors and found the lone bag sitting on a luggage rack. She squatted down and opened it, flinging the top portion back, and rummaged through it, digging her hands in under the clothes to find the smaller case inside. When she opened it, she gasped.

There was the empty sponged case that held a gun.

Her heart jumped into her throat. "Roman!"

She never heard the door of the hotel room open or the sound of the woman enter the room, but as she turned to escape to warn her husband, the woman's fist clocked her in the jaw, knocking her against the closet doorframe.

Gabby's lip busted, and the blood hit the clean white wall as the Asian woman advanced. Gabby started to fall to the floor as the woman grabbed her by her hair and pulled her from the closet into the room. But the one thing the Asian woman didn't know was Gabby could fight, just like her daughter, Lana.

As Gabby screamed from her hair being pulled up behind her, she turned and hooked her arm between the woman's legs, and with her other hand she grabbed her hair and pushed with both her legs, lifting the little bitch up and body slamming her against the edge of the dresser. Her back hit with a crack, and her shoes hit the mirror, shattering it. The Asian woman screamed, and Gabby let go, letting her hit the floor.

Gabby felt the pain inside her and realized she hadn't healed completely from the rollover accident and knew she needed to get away and get away fast. She then rushed to the door and tried opening it in vain to see the swing lock engaged. It only took a second to push the door closed, but that Asian bitch was up and slammed against her, pushing her face into the door. Gabby put both hands on the door and head butted her in the face, feeling her fall back, but the woman had a hold of her, and they both hit the furniture together.

Tumbling into the desk, then hitting and breaking the coffee table, Gabby felt herself roll away from her attacker. In that moment, as she tried to stand, she looked back as the Asian grabbed a lamp, ripping the cord from the wall, and swung it, hitting her in the face. The ceramic lamp base shattered, and Gabby screamed, spitting blood as she fell back to the floor. Dazed and disoriented, her vision blurred. Seeing a writing pen on the floor, she grabbed it as that bitch with the long, stringy black hair grabbed her by the back of the head and pulled her hair hard, standing her up. Gabby then swung around with the pen and slashed under the woman's jaw.

The scream Gabby heard rattled her ears as blood spurted out the woman's neck, and she watched her double over, her hair falling over her head. What she didn't see was the woman grabbing the vase that had been knocked to the floor from the desk because when she came up, she brought it with her, hitting Gabby under her jaw with a crack.

Gabby's mind went blank, the room went dark, and she felt her life slipping from her. Her last conscious thought was that she wished she'd never seen that man near the motorcycle. But when the woman grabbed her for the last time, she charged her toward the floor to ceiling window and pushed.

The cracking glass of the window shattered, and Gabby screamed as her face met the glass and the cold wind from outside. With her arms swinging for anything to grab on to, she fell from the top floor in a death scream—straight to the parking lot.

Everyone on the property heard the scream.

Even Roman heard her as he turned back from the viewpoint trail to see his wife being thrown from the window of the top floor of the lodge, her innocent body flailing helplessly in the air as sharp shards of glass showered down around her. He watched as his lover, his wife, and his life landed on a car's windshield near the motorcycle they were there to investigate. Gabby Savage was dead.

For that moment in time, everything froze in Roman's mind. He didn't realize that his mind was like a camera, taking memorial images of every last detail of the last moments of his beautiful wife's life, including the vision of an Asian woman looking down from the broken window above.

Mingyu Yunt ran to the bathroom and grabbed a towel to stop the bleeding. The lashing from the pen wasn't deep enough to stop her, and she ran from the room back into hers. Inside, she picked up her phone and quickly sent a text: *Grab the package, get my car, and leave now!*

The large white Tahoe SUV with the blacked-out windows came to a quiet stop on the far side of the lodge, and Mingyu rushed out and opened the door. Inside was the assassin who had murdered Parnell F. Bancroft, the same man Roman had recognized from checking in just a short time earlier.

"What the hell did you do?"

"Shut up and drive, Hermann," came her curt response as she slammed the door shut. And as they drove off and away from the ski lodge, the panic on the other side of the lodge was growing, with the exception of the agents left there by Agent Thrasher.

Earlier while he was there, prior to learning of the girls' kidnapping, his team had recorded every license plate at the lodge, and Thrasher had assigned agents to watch all the exits. So when the Tahoe left the premises, a car quietly followed.

CHAPTER 71

The emergency crews passed Ed and Logan on the way to the lodge, and when they got there, they were shocked to learn what had happened. There in the parking lot was the familiar yellow police tape blocking off a crime scene, and sitting on the back of an ambulance, exactly as Ed himself had been after Cara had died, was Roman.

His skin was pale white, and he had a blanket around him as a paramedic was checking his vitals. Both Savage men rushed from the SUV and ran to their brother to be stopped by police.

"That's our brother!" Logan yelled.

Roman heard the commotion and looked over at them; his face was broken, his eyes were red, and his cheeks were wet with tears. He nearly collapsed just seeing them, and both Ed and Logan pushed through to him as the paramedic was holding him against the vehicle.

"Good God, Roman, what happened?" Ed said.

Roman turned to his brother and burst into tears. "My Gabby, she's...she's gone," he yelled out and fell into Ed's arms.

Ed could do nothing but hold his poor broken brother as the sound of the gurney being wheeled by caused Logan to look and see the bloodied arm of Gabby Savage fall from the side and hang down, as lifeless as the fall leaves around them.

He swallowed hard and grabbed Ed's shoulder, causing Ed to turn and see the paramedic stop, lift her blood-streaked arm back on to the gurney, and continue to wheel her to another ambulance.

CHAPTER 72

The Catskills Ski Lodge parking lot was a circus, and after hearing Roman tell them what had happened and with Logan at his side, Ed saw Agent Thrasher and quietly moved away so the two men could distance themselves from the chaos.

"Jesus, Ed, I'm in shock. I didn't see this coming at all," Thrasher said.

Ed could still feel his heart racing for his family and leaned against a tree. "What room did she fall from?" he asked, looking up at the shattered window.

"The name registered was Noah Franklin. Does that mean anything to you?"

Ed furrowed his brow, looking away in thought. "Noah… Noah was the name of one of the kids who was murdered in Black Ridge, and Franklin…" He trailed off; then it hit him. "Franklin: Parnell's middle name, Parnell Franklin Bancroft—this can't be a coincidence."

"The credit card used for the room has been frozen, and we're checking into it. And, Ed, we found a gun case inside the room and ammunition. It's the same caliber of bullet that killed Parnell."

"You're telling me the man who murdered Parnell is linked to the sale of the stolen warheads from the *Manchester*?"

"It all ties in, Ed."

"The man from that room—this Noah Franklin—Roman said he recognized him but couldn't tell from where. He said they saw him from their room, and he came downstairs to follow him to see where they had met before. Then all this happened," Ed said, waving his arms in the direction of the mess before them.

"So we have at least two people we're looking for. I'll check hotel security for his photo when he checked in and see if he was with anyone," Thrasher said. "Unless he was alone, we're at a dead end on this other person."

"Maybe not," Ed said, seeing the forensic squad he and his brothers had spoken with earlier exiting the lodge. "Come on."

Thrasher followed along at a listening distance and watched Ed wave down the team.

"Hey there! Before you approach my brother, I'd like to know what you found." Ed looked toward the plastic evidence bags the woman was holding.

"So far we've got a bloodstained hotel pen," she said, holding up the bag; then she turned her hand over, revealing the second bag with the long black hair strands in it. "And this."

"God, I hope that's not Gabby's," Ed said, feeling the glow of something possibly positive creep back into his empty heart.

"We'll let your brother know what we've found, and you'll all know the results as soon as we get them," she said.

Ed nodded and watched them move toward Roman and Logan; he turned back to Thrasher. "Mingyu Yunt!"

"I beg your pardon?"

"I'll bet money that hair belongs to that mysterious woman my father's secretary spoke of."

"Ed, if that's true, and the gun case upstairs is a match for Parnell's murder, then your father was in deeper than we thought."

A chill ran down Ed's spine as he looked back to his brothers. "Call it in to Tallulah," he said, moving back to his family.

Agent Thrasher watched Ed move quietly back to his brothers; he noticed the sadness in in his slow stride, and when he pulled out his phone, the date on the display reminded him that this week was his anniversary. Thrasher sighed as he wished the thoughts away, and he punched in the number.

His call was patched right through, and Tallulah was grateful to hear from him.

"How's Ed? Have they found anything further on the girls?" Tallulah said.

"No, but it's bad."

"Bad? Agent Thrasher, Agent Robert Forrester is here from London, and I'm putting this on speakerphone."

Thrasher heard the familiar beeps, and then Tallulah was back. "Okay, Thrasher, what do you have?"

"Robert, it's been a long time," Thrasher said.

"Yes, good to hear from you, albeit I'd prefer under better circumstances. So let's get on with it: How bad is it?"

"Gabby Savage is dead."

Thrasher listened to the silence from the other end of the phone.

"Good God, Wes, what the hell happened?" Tallulah finally said.

"Thrown from a top-floor window of the lodge. Forensics found a bloodstained hotel pen and strands of long black hair. Ed mentioned a Mingyu Yunt as the possible owner of the hair. Who is this person?"

"Thrasher, is there anything else?" Robert Forrester said.

"An empty gun case and bullets that match the caliber fired into Parnell F. Bancroft. Oh, and the room Gabby was thrown from was registered to a Noah Franklin. Ed said Noah was the name of one of the kids murdered in the mountains, and Franklin is Parnell's middle name."

"Where's Ed now?" Tallulah asked.

Thrasher looked over to see him with his brothers. "He's with Roman and Logan right now."

"Thrasher, I've been on the hunt for an assassin for years. And this guy likes to play name games. If it's the same guy, he's tied to a consortium with so many shell companies that when one closes, another opens, making it impossible to track them," Forrester said.

"Do you have a photograph of the guy?" Thrasher asked.

"A partial. I'll send it now," Forrester responded.

"I'm checking hotel security for any footage of this guy too."

"Great, I need a full image of the guy," Forrester said.

"Has any further word on the kidnapping come in?" Thrasher asked, taking another look at the Savage brothers.

"Nothing yet," Tallulah said. "But on another subject, how are *you* doing, Agent Thrasher?"

"All things considered, just peachy," he said sarcastically, hanging up his phone.

That damn fire, he thought as he glanced over at Ed and moved away from the crowd.

Ed's phone vibrated, and he saw the text message from Trent. It read: *Hey, Dad! Boy, I can't wait to meet everyone. But is it possible to reschedule? Today's turning into more than I thought—Trent.*

Ed closed his eyes, thinking how so much had changed from his wonderful meeting with his son such a short while ago. Seeing his brother Roman in front of him falling apart, he was glad Trent had sent a text instead of calling. His emotions were running high, and he knew it would show in his voice. Texting him back he told him how his day was turning more hectic too, and they should touch base later and figure things out.

CHAPTER 73

he closer the old ambulance got to the menacing sanatorium, the more the heaviness increased over Dr. Todd Vreeland like he was caught in a downpour of misery on a cold and overcast day. Parking and standing outside, he looked up at the daunting building and was torn. He could slightly feel the instinct to turn and go back to South America, yet his feeling of being *pulled* back inside was stronger, and before he knew it, Dr. Todd entered his old hospital like he had just left it yesterday. He noticed things hadn't really changed that much in the old, partly crumbling structure. Staff recognized him immediately from all the large wall portraits hanging in various parts of the hospital and jumped in surprise because most thought he was dead.

Dr. Todd had no problem finding his way, only just being in the place seemed to bring about an anger within him—buried deep inside he had no idea he still possessed. It must have showed too, because most seemed afraid of him. And the farther he got inside, the more he realized that the place had changed a bit since his time there. A slight remodel had taken place since he'd left due to the decay of the building, and construction support beams were added in places while the work was underway. Seeing a young nurse walk by, he grabbed her and demanded she take him to patient receiving near the ambulance bays. Frightened by his intimidating presence, and after hearing the ghost stories about the place and seeing the older man's portrait, she obeyed and couldn't wait to take him where he needed to be so she could run and hide.

Arriving at the reception area, she was nearly shoved to the ground as he pushed by her to the counter. "I want to see this Dr. Sinardi at once," Dr. Todd said, slamming his hand on the counter.

When he was told Dr. Sinardi hadn't arrived yet this morning, he told the staff he would be in *his* office, and he was not to be disturbed unless it was Dr. Sinardi himself.

Recognizing the man from the many portraits in the building, a senior staff member made the call to Dr. Sinardi's phone, which at the time was of no use, seeing as the good doctor was probably passed out in a cathouse after a night of carousing, or so the hospital gossip expected.

"I need current access codes to the computers and a current list of all patients in house sent to my office—STAT," the stranger ordered. He then turned to see that the young woman who'd led him there was gone, and it infuriated him. "How dare she leave without my permission?" he hissed under his breath as he turned back to the counter, eyeing the staircase he recognized; he took it up to the fourth floor. There, everything was how it was when he'd left, exactly how he remembered it. The only detail that was sickening was that his main office had the nameplate reading "Dr. Sinardi" on the door: *his* door. He reached up and pried the metal nameplate off, cutting himself on the edge of it. "Damn it," he growled. "Now I'll need a tetanus."

Reaching down, he turned the doorknob to find it locked.

"Bastards!" he growled again as he stormed back down the hall to the stairs. Moving down them, he pushed open the door and went back to patient receiving. The staff saw him coming and jumped up in attention as a new employee appeared from a back office.

"My office is locked, and I need security to open it at once," he demanded.

"You have an office?" came the smartass remark from the new idiot now behind the desk, thinking the guy in front of him was nuts. "Whose patient is this?" he said, raising his voice with laughter and noticing everyone was suddenly standing there silent, just looking at him.

Dr. Todd stared at the imbecile like he was a new infectious plague and slammed down the metal nameplate on the counter. "The key to my office, *this office*, now." He spoke in his father's deadly calm tone he'd acquired long after he'd murdered him. He then smiled at the young fool and grabbed his name badge off him, leaving a blood smear from his cut hand on his pristine white jacket; he then glanced at his badge before putting it in his pocket and held up his cut finger. "Kumar, get me a tetanus for this, will you?"

Kumar looked to the others and knew this most definitely wasn't a patient, and he broke out in a sweat. "Yes, sir," he said before disappearing behind the back area. He came back out almost as fast with the small drug vial and a syringe in hand.

Dr. Todd grabbed them from him and ordered security to meet him at *his* office immediately.

A call went out, and a guard who was making rounds on the third floor in the lab responded and rushed to Dr. Sinardi's office.

When Dr. Todd exited the fourth-floor stairs, he saw the man down the hall fumbling with the keys to his door, and when he arrived, he had just opened it.

"Thank you. I'll take those," Dr. Todd said, snatching the keys from the fresh-out-of-high-school, scared-shitless kid. Entering the office, he slammed the door shut behind him and locked it.

The office had changed. Structurally it was the same large room with the smaller file room off the side where he'd kept his *private* things. Nothing like the second offices they'd kept up on the sixth floors—complete with private bedrooms—but the furnishings had all been updated. He started toward the desk when he looked to the windows and moved toward them to see the upper corner room on the sixth-floor of the East Tower, where his father had kept his favorite patient locked away, and he smiled at the memories that flooded back into his mind of the stories his father had told him of her terrified state the night she had gone into labor.

Dr. Todd smiled at his past and turned away from the windows and noticed the side table with his favorite bottle of tequila sitting on it. Above was a portrait of his father standing tall, with him and his brothers, Blake and Eric, at his side. Dr. Todd stood there a moment, and then he looked below the table, and on a lower shelf were *his* old journals. He picked one of them up, and a grin came across his face. Looking back at the portrait, he noticed the white lab coat with a name embroidered on it hanging on a wooden hanger off a hook on the side of a bookcase next to it. The lab coat was *his*. Putting down his old journal, he took off his jacket and tossed it on a chair at a table across from the desk. He then eyed his old lab coat and took it off the hanger and put it on—sliding back into his old life.

Standing in the gray light of the windows, Dr. Todd's faint shadow seemed to fill his office in a more menacing way, and he felt a familiar darkness touching his soul. Looking to a mirror, he stared at his reflection and smiled, feeling his old self coming back that he hadn't felt in a long time after paying for his debts like a prison sentence and now finally feeling he was where he was supposed to be—and he *liked* it. *I've been gone too long,* he thought. He then looked over at the desk. Moving to it, he sat down and began going through it: reading the notes and memos and the stacks of charts on the desk that must have been of some importance to this Dr. Sinardi. The minutes passed, and the light knocking at the door startled him. Looking up, he noticed the strange poster behind the door about a show called *Phantom Finders,* and as he approached the door, he saw the names on the poster: Sinardi and Savage. He looked at Sinardi and nodded as the person outside the door knocked once more.

Angered by the impatience of the person outside his office, Dr. Todd unlocked the door and whipped it open so fast it startled the person behind it, and he watched her drop one of the journals she was carrying. When the young woman quickly reached for the journal and stood up, he noticed it at once as she was straightening up the notebooks—she looked strangely like his mother had in photos before her wedding to his evil father. He was immediately reminded of his lost daughter in South America.

"I'm so sorry, dear. Let me help you," Todd said in the cheerful voice of a gentleman.

"Oh no, sir, I've got it." The young woman wore a kind smile. "Is there anything else I can do for you?"

"You know, there is. I've had an early morning. Can you bring me up a tray? Whatever they have for breakfast will be fine, and coffee, please," Todd said with a sigh.

"Oh, you poor dear—you must be starving. I'll rush it right up."

"Thank you. Tell me, what's your name?"

"Kayla, Kayla Bennet. And I'll be back shortly, sir," she said, almost adding a slight curtsy.

Dr. Todd took the journals from her into *his* office and shut the door. He then went over to the desk and began thumbing through them. All the while that girl's last name was repeating in his mind. "Bennet," he said out loud to himself and began paging through the journals for the name. He then looked to the smaller room at the side of the office as if something or someone had just materialized and was calling out to him.

Getting up from the desk, he entered the smaller room and stood at the doorway. Surprisingly the old file cabinets were still where he'd last remembered them—only they were in shambles. Files were pulled out and stacked on a table, and he went to search for the young girl's name. *Bennet,* he thought. Why did that name mean something to him? With so many patients he'd worked on and killed over the years, it was hard to keep any of it straight in his mind. And when the phone rang in his outer office, he jumped, smacking his hand against an open file cabinet and reminding him of his cut.

He went back to the chair and grabbed his jacket and brought out the tetanus drug and syringe, along with Kumar's name badge from his pocket, then answered the phone. "Hello."

"Yes, Dr. Sinardi? This is Zolie Vanderran. Is Patty Galloway allowed to have visitors today?" came a soothing British voice.

Galloway! He immediately remembered his father's prized patient and had known she'd had a daughter named Patty. She was here? His pulse raced. "Mrs. Vanderran, yes, of course she's ready. Please come to the hospital to see her. I'll be expecting you," he lied on the spot, planning on getting every detail out of this British fool on the Galloway woman.

"Perfect. I can be there in a little over an hour."

"I'll tell Patty you're coming." The doctor hung up the phone.

Dr. Todd dropped the items in his hand on the desk and opened the top drawer. Not seeing anything to pique his curiosity, he opened the larger drawer below, and there, as if by some sort of miracle, were his father's files on a patient named Galloway. It was like finding gold, and his excitement showed as he pulled them out and opened them on the desk, wanting to refresh everything in his mind that his father had written about her; just then someone knocked at his door. Closing the top file and putting them back in the drawer, he opened the door to see the lovely Kayla Bennet standing there with a tray.

"Here you are, sir," she said.

"Just place it on the table across from my desk, please," the gentleman said while admiring the young girl. He watched her move into his office and set it down.

"Your desk? Is Dr. Sinardi moving to a new office?"

"I wouldn't worry about that if I were you."

"Yes sir. Will there be anything else?"

"Tell me, are you from around here? You remind me of someone."

"I think so," she said, seeing the confused look on his face. "I'm sorry. I was an orphan. My parents died when I was born, or so I was told. I grew up around here."

"I'm so sorry," Dr. Todd said, sounding like the nice Dr. Jekyll instead of the cruel Mr. Hyde that seemed to be taking over.

"That's fine," she said as she moved to the door. "Now eat up while it's hot."

Watching that cute young woman smile at him as she closed his office door, Dr. Todd actually felt human for the first time since the earthquake.

Moving over to his breakfast, he lifted the tray covers and saw all the wonderful things she'd brought him. Lifting the smallest one, he saw the fresh mix of raspberries, cut banana, and blueberry—his father's exact favorite.

He placed the tray lid to the side and took off his old lab coat. Moving to the desk, he rolled up his sleeve and prepared the tetanus syringe and injected it into his upper arm. Then he moved to the tray, dropped the needle on it, and picked up a piece of toast and began to eat, all the while staring at the fruit cup and remembering his father's last day on earth.

CHAPTER 74

hat day had been peaceful, he recalled. It had been a long time since he and Blake had seriously fought, and they were tolerating each other, even working side by side at times like he'd dreamed about his whole life. And he remembered the symphony music that his father liked to listen to the day he died—and the secret he'd told him alone in that miserable room.

The confession of the ailing Victor Vreeland telling his beleaguered son about what *really* happened the day their mother was killed was meant to unburden him of the guilt he'd been carrying all these years and maybe get forgiveness from the son who'd received the worst effects of that horrible decision. Instead, however, it brought swift retaliation.

Victor had grown old and needed care from the boys, and in a moment of clarity and guilt, he'd told Todd everything, every last detail of putting that deranged patient who killed women he'd thought were irredeemable sluts and whom he'd been showing naked pictures of his wife to in the room close to where Todd was meeting his mother. Victor told of how he'd wanted a divorce and wanted to tear a page out of history, after finding his grandfather Cornelius's diary, of how he not only murdered his first wife, Greta Von Staller, but his cheating whore of a second wife, Cassandra Le Fey, too. And when Todd's school called telling them he'd been in trouble and that they were sending him home with a note for his parents to sign, Victor told the principal to have Todd meet his mother at the sanatorium, and that he'd told his brothers *Todd* had said to meet there—setting the trap that would ruin his son's life forever.

There were two things wrong with what he'd told him that day. One, Todd had never seen or heard of his great grandfather's diary; and two, they were alone, and Blake was not there to hear any of the confession. And when he asked his father to tell Blake and Eric the truth, his father shook his head.

"I can't break Blake's heart," the old man in bed said to the only son he'd betrayed. "He's the only one who still believes in me, the one I've left the hospital to, the one groomed to take my place and carry on the Vreeland legacy. Eric is good too, but I just don't see *as much* in him as Blake. No…*he* means too much to me."

He means too much to you, Todd thought as the truth hit him. At that moment the alarm beeped in his room, alerting him that it was time for his father's medication. In shock, finally learning the truth, Todd Vreeland moved to retrieve it. He went behind his father's bed to the far counter to where the large partially filled syringe was, right next to a small paper cup of pills. Opening the cabinet above, he pulled the morphine vial from the shelf and filled the large syringe to its capacity. Then, as he was putting it away, he saw the cyanide and arsenic tablets. Grabbing the deadly mixture, he replaced the pills in the paper cup, put the cyanide bottle in his pocket, and brought the poisonous potion to the bastard who had made his life a living hell. Standing over his father, he noticed the tears in his father's eyes; all the while the beeping of his medication alarm filled the room.

"You understand, don't you? Blake thinks the world of me, and you do of him. You always have. He'll keep you around. He's my favorite, and we can't hurt Blake, can we? Now turn off that incessant alarm; it's annoying me, Stubs!" Victor spat at his son, giving him a nasty self-satisfied smirk. He had finally cleared *his* conscience, and *he* felt good.

It's always been about you! Todd thought. He looked toward the beeping alarm, past the nightstand where his father's water glass sat next to his comb and the mirror his nurses would use to keep up on his grooming. Todd saw Victor watching him, giving him a cryptic smile as if part of him was enjoying hurting his son with these true tales from hell. His lucid mind was back, and Todd knew *now* was the perfect time before he drifted away completely to his vile, cantankerous self.

"No, Father, you're right. Blake's brilliant," Todd said with a smile as he placed the syringe on top of the mirror and grabbed the glass of water. He then held the paper cup of pills to his father's mouth and forced them down his throat; holding his nostrils, he made his father swallow the water and send the toxic concoction throughout his body. As he watched him swallow the cyanide and arsenic, he picked up the syringe and held it in front of his father so he could see that it was full.

Victor Vreeland's eyes widened with fear and started thrashing in his bed; grabbing his urinal, he swung it at his son, splashing him with the sickly sewage of his body. Todd grabbed his arm and threw his muscled body over his father's to hold him down as he grabbed his IV line to inject him with the lethal dose.

"You bastard!" Victor shouted as the poison erupted inside him, and he felt the morphine hit him in an instant. His throat tightened up, and his saliva thickened in the back of his throat. He started foaming out the mouth and slurring his speech, spitting the sickly yellowed mucus mixed with foam as he yelled. Todd then pulled out the bottle of cyanide and waved it in front of his father to see.

The seizures and gasping for air started, and he was choking on the slime now filling his throat like a clogged, overflowing toilet. One of the last things he saw was the hurt face and the death behind the eyes of that once-innocent fair-haired boy whose life he'd destroyed all because he had feared his own wife would destroy his if given the chance in court.

As Victor gasped for air, Todd gently picked up the mirror and held it in front of his father so he could see his reflection—his ugly sin-filled face now old and dying, watched over only by the hate-filled face of a son excited to see him go straight to hell.

"And to think I once looked up to you." Those were the final words Dr. Victor Vreeland had heard. And Todd remembered them well.

As the memory of that day faded and Todd came back to the reality of the present, he noticed that the entire breakfast tray had been consumed—including the fruit dish.

CHAPTER 75

T he sharp knock at the door was nothing like the light tapping from the lovely young girl who reminded Dr. Todd of his mother, and when he opened it, he was surprised.

"You couldn't stay away, could you?" The familiar nurse's voice was sour.

Dr. Todd took a step back and almost gasped. It was Stacey Porter, Pam's younger sister, who had not only been at the hospital the night it'd burned but was now the charge nurse of the operating rooms, according to her badge. He remembered the last time he'd seen her, when he'd dumped her for her sister, Pam.

"I think you'll find these of interest, sir," she said, showing him three medical charts.

"Stacey? You're still here?" Dr. Todd said as he opened the door and watched her brush past him to place the charts on his desk. He was floored and didn't know quite what to make of this as he watched her slowly turn to him.

"Shut the door," she said as she reached up and unpinned her long highlighted hair, letting it cascade down over her shoulders.

Todd pushed the door closed and locked it. When he turned back, she was there, looking up into his blue eyes as her hands moved over his groin. Her smile was alluring, and he placed his hands on her backside and pulled her against him, lifting one hand he unbuttoned her blouse and reached inside, grabbing one of her breasts as he pushed her down on the sofa. Lowering himself on top of her he kissed her passionately as she reached down and unfastened his pants.

Letting his fingers explore under her uniform, he ripped away her clothes and teased her, making her moan. The smile crossed his face as he moved up and positioned himself and looked into her beautiful green eyes, "I've missed this," he said sliding into her.

The sex was hard and rough, and when she suddenly realized it was a huge mistake, he put his large hand over her mouth and continued to have his way with her. She pleaded with him, but he didn't care, and when it was over, he looked down into her eyes and smiled.

"Fuck you...Pam," he said releasing his grip, knowing saying her sister's name would piss her off. Grabbing her chin, he squeezed. "Was it good for you, baby?" He laughed planting a parting sloppy kiss on her as he quickly jumped to his feet. Fastening up his pants, he moved over to the charts she'd brought in and glanced back to see her dressing. He smirked as he flipped a file open and read the newspaper article inside. The headline stated: "Exorcist Murders!"

"What's this about?"

"They're here," she said, buttoning up her uniform.

"Who's here?" The doctor looked at her, intrigued at what she'd brought him, as he thumbed through the chart.

"The three sick teenagers who killed their parents and claimed they were possessed when they did it. Don't you remember?"

Dr. Todd looked to her with wonder.

"You really don't know, do you?" she said, moving slowly toward him. "They were admitted here long before the firestorm, and the headlines were everywhere."

Dr. Todd looked down at the girl's chart he had opened. "It says here she was admitted well *after* the fire. What are you getting at?"

"Oh, that's right. The boy came here directly from jail. It was his two sisters that were transferred here later. Anyway, that bullshit doesn't matter; the fact is they're here."

"What's so special about these"—Dr. Todd paused to look at the chart—"Brockman children?"

"Oh, for God's sake!" Stacey moaned. "With all your basement shenanigans and your favorite movie ever being *The Exorcist*, I'd think you'd be interested in a case where the defendants not only murdered their parents, claiming they were possessed by the damn devil, but also lived in a home on the same damn block as the original story that was the source for the movie!" Stacey saw the smile appear on the doctor's face, and she continued, "So let's just say, what? With your past here, I figured you'd want to see these patients personally, especially with the poster from that show in here," she said, pointing to the one behind the door.

Dr. Todd eyed the poster of *Phantom Finders* and again noticed the man front and center with the name Sinardi. His mind flashed back to his family's basement rituals, a practice he'd long forsaken, and he remembered the shadow man who had appeared to him that night and couldn't wait to see these so-called possessed patients. His smile grew as he looked again at the poster and noticed another man, one who went by the name of Ed Savage.

"What is this show, and what does it have to do with the patients here?"

"That's for you to read up on tonight; tomorrow I'll take you to see them if Sinardi doesn't take you first," Stacey said as she moved to the door. "And next time I say stop, Doctor, you *will* stop, or I'll slit your throat."

Dr. Todd grinned, and the fire in his belly grew, pushing the blood back to his groin. "You have seconds to leave before *I* go for seconds, you little bitch."

"Glad we see eye to eye, asshole," the slutty little nympho said as she disappeared from his office with the banging of his door.

CHAPTER 76

Zolie Vanderran's Rolls-Royce moved up the long road to Vreeland Hills Sanatorium. The weather had turned bad when she'd picked up Stevie Galloway at the Holiday Inn, and the first thing the women noticed was the building's disturbing presence; giving off a scent of pure terror. The wind was blowing the remaining fall leaves from the trees, and the mounds gathered beneath them. When the women pulled onto the grounds, the gargoyles seemed to be smiling at them as if welcoming their prey.

Getting out from the Rolls-Royce, the wind blew Zolie's beautiful long hair, and she grabbed her Birkin bag and looked to Stevie sitting in the car. "Come on—it's too cold out here," she said as Stevie opened the door, and the wind hit her. Together the women rushed to the hospital entrance and raced through the doors, glad to be safe from the elements outside—too bad, really, since what was waiting inside the building was far worse than anything Mother Nature could throw at them.

CHAPTER 77

"I found them!" Sandy Storm's voice emanated from her office closet.

Hailey Storm moved from her sister's bedroom down the hall to see Sandy holding the keys to their sister Wendy's apartment in one hand and a jacket in the other.

"I totally forgot I was wearing this when she gave them to me," Sandy said, holding up the keys for her sister to see, and remembering she'd done the same thing when she gave her cardigan to Lucy after the yachting disaster.

"Finally! Jesus, I was beginning to think we'd have to break in. Come on; it's been too long, and I want to find out about this mysterious S. person who paid your hospital bill."

Sandy paused a moment. "Do we really *need* to know?" The vision of Wendy being stabbed right in front of her and then dragged to the swamp and drowned on that wet and nasty night played in front of her eyes.

Hailey could see the torment on her sister's face. "Hey, if you want to sit this one out, that's fine. I'll just go take a look and let you know what I find."

Thinking Hailey would once again beat her to the biggest story of her own career, she pushed the thoughts away, and a tight smile crossed her lips. "No, I'm good; let's go."

Sandy put the keys in her purse and moved to the TV in her living area to turn it off when she stopped. There was Wendy, on air, a rebroadcast from the mountains of the sound bite they'd omitted the first go around. She stood frozen, watching her sister like the moment had played out just yesterday, and when Hailey turned off the TV with the remote, she turned to her in an instant.

"Why'd you do that?"

"You know what that's about; you were there! So why'd you leak the footage?"

"What? I didn't leak any footage! That was kept off the air by the station."

"Yes, at the time the station didn't allow that segment of your reporting. But you later leaked it, and I want to know why."

"Hailey, I didn't leak the segment. I don't even have it!" Sandy's voice rose to a shrill pitch. "The station has all the film." Sandy was so flustered that Hailey remembered that specific trait in her sister's voice that came out when she was absolutely telling the truth, when caught up in one of Wendy's schemes growing up.

Hailey tossed the remote on the sofa. "I believe you, Sandy. I do. When I first saw it, I thought you'd done it, but now we have a bigger problem. Who did?"

CHAPTER 78

T he lovemaking lasted as the daylight faded through the entire night, napping in between and going at it again, and they held on to each other throughout; the morning was no different. The first thing Sam noticed before waking completely was Raquel's perfumed hair, her warm body against his chest, and his right arm around her shoulders with his left hand on her breast, and before he knew it, he was aroused.

Sam didn't want the moment to ever leave him. He was spooning Raquel, and as he kissed her neck, he watched her turn slightly to him, murmuring his name as he rolled on top of her. The protection she felt from his weight on her was a welcome emotion in her lonely world, and she could feel him between her legs.

"Ay," she moaned as he entered her in the early-morning light streaming through the bedroom curtains.

"You okay?" Sam whispered back.

The smile she gave told him she was—along with her hands lightly caressing his backside. Her light touch made his body tingle, and he kissed her passionately as he made love to her once more.

CHAPTER 79

When Zolie Vanderran asked to see Dr. Sinardi, she was told to wait in that same depressing room she'd been relegated to before, except this time there was fresh tea and coffee waiting for them in the overly air conditioned room. Wanting to just get on with it, she bit her tongue and moved to the windows, staring out at the wind-blown tree branches in their most rabid state. "It's really picking up out there," she said to Stevie, getting a shiver and feeling the dread of the building as she moved and poured herself some tea.

"I hate this place," came Stevie's almost frightened reply as she reached for some coffee.

The minutes seemed to last forever, and when Zolie finished her tea and placed it down, the door opened, and another man dressed in a white lab coat entered the room. Zolie immediately stood and looked at his badge.

"Mrs. Vanderran, Dr. Hollerman—Jack Hollerman," he said, reaching out his hand. Zolie looked at the young, handsome man with the kind face and shook his hand.

"It's nice to meet you, Doctor."

"I understand you're here to see Patty."

"Yes, however, I'd prefer to use my married name, Kenowith, especially where Patty Galloway is concerned."

"I understand completely. Did you have an appointment?"

"Yes, I called Dr. Sinardi this morning, and he told me it was fine to see her today."

"Hmm," the man said. "Dr. Sinardi hasn't been in today yet, and we can't get a hold of him. Where did you call him?"

Zolie opened her bag and pulled out the business card he'd given her. She looked at it and handed it to the young doctor. "Here, the number to his private line."

Jack studied it in her hand but did not take the card. "Strange... that's his office number, but no one's seen him today."

"Well, is that a problem? Can we still see her?" Stevie asked.

"Shouldn't be a problem at all. Come with me," he said, leading the women from the room.

CHAPTER 80

Vreeland Hills Sanatorium was a monstrous edifice. With the carbon copy sitting across the courtyard, anyone inside felt how disturbing the campus was—as if you were trapped inside with no way out.

These thoughts ran through Zolie Vanderran's mind as she took mental photographs; these were her internal tools when it came to writing her endless novels. The skyway from the West Tower to the East terrified her. The windows had grids on the outside, and when she felt the cold wind suddenly hit her, she saw the broken window and the partly pushed-out portion of the metal grid.

"What happened here?" she asked Dr. Hollerman.

"We're short on maintenance crews. It'll get fixed eventually," he said, turning back with a plastic smile.

"But that doesn't answer my question."

"It wasn't supposed to. But it looks like someone tried to escape." The arrogantly officious man suddenly showed his true colors.

Zolie winced at his curt remark and realized the charming man she'd met earlier was far more insolent than she'd first realized.

Exiting the skyway he stopped at a bank of elevators and pushed the button for the sixth floor. Moments later, when the doors were opening on the upper floor, Zolie and Stevie set eyes on a world they weren't prepared for.

The strange musty smell hit them immediately, and both ladies shot a look at one another.

"This place needs a good airing out," Stevie said, almost choking.

"With all the windows sealed, fresh air up here is luxury—not to mention this particular wing of the hospital has always been off."

"Off?" Zolie asked, determined to get an answer.

"Here, I'll show you." Dr. Hollerman led them to a room near the elevators. "Ever since the fire burned this section of the hospital, it's never been quite right."

"Fire?" Zolie repeated.

"Some factory fire years ago. But that's what computers are for, Mrs. Kenowith. I won't bore you with the details; it's all online for you to find."

Zolie was seriously questioning his words, watching him closely as they followed him to a sealed room.

"Here we are," he said, unlocking and opening the door.

The room was pitch black, and both Zolie and Stevie stopped dead in their tracks, just like Dr. Hollerman knew they would. "Here, allow me," he said, entering the room and hitting the light switches on the wall.

The strange odor was stronger, and it had a burned smell associated with it. They saw the few remaining working fluorescent lights flicker and then come to life in the cold and lonely windowless room. There sat a single bed. On the walls were mirrors arranged in a strange pattern. It looked like some of the mirrors were even missing, leaving spaces that were cleaner than the walls around them.

"So what's the deal with the room besides the god-awful smell?" came the quick, smartass question from Stevie.

Zolie heard her words, but her investigative mind was scanning the room, and she spotted the strange smeared marking staining the floor.

Dr. Hollerman looked at the blonde and quickly dismissed her tone as he moved to the bed. "This is where it's believed *the haunting* started," he said, pointing down at the strange stain Zolie was studying. "The fire is thought to have started in the psych ward a few rooms over."

Both women moved closer and saw the stain in the shape of a human form.

"What exactly are we looking at?" Zolie asked.

"We don't know. We don't know who, and we don't know what. But what we do know is that you can't get rid of it."

Both Zolie and Stevie looked to each other.

"We've painted over it, as you can see by the surrounding paint markings, but by morning the next day, the stain is back. Some believe it's the missing Vreeland brother, Dr. Blake Vreeland, who haunts this place. No one really knows what happened to him." Dr. Hollerman seemed to be enjoying his little tale. "So we keep this room closed off," he finished and turned back toward the door.

"You mentioned something about the fire starting in a psych ward, but it sure feels like a fire started in here," Zolie said.

"There are reports of spontaneous combustion cases in the hospital, including one recently; however, I've never encountered any," he said, moving to the door.

"Recently? Where?" Zolie asked.

"You'll see," he said, turning back.

"Wait for us!" Stevie rushed past him.

Their tour guide paused long enough to allow the women to pass; then he followed, shutting off the lights and closing the door behind him. Right as the lock engaged, the trio heard a woman scream—a distinct sound of fear that came from the end of the hall.

Both Zolie and Stevie jumped and looked to the doctor. "She's awake," he said, leading them toward the sound.

The quiver of the fluorescent lights from under the door caught Zolie's eye, and she reached for the doctor, brushing against his shoulder. "You turned them off. I saw you!" she said, pointing to the floor near the door.

What looked to be a shadow seemed to move within the flickering light. "Old building." The doctor shrugged as he moved away from the door.

The women quickly followed, and soon they were led down a corridor to the last room on the left, where the man opened the small door cut into the steel to peek inside before knocking.

"Hello, Patty—you have company," the doctor said gleefully as he unlocked the entire door, opening it inward to light the dark world that now belonged to the woman who'd made the Savages' lives hell.

Zolie and Stevie were both a bit nervous following the doctor into the horrifying room, but when they saw her lying in the bed, with chains from her wrists to the floor and a look of desperation on her face, they rushed to her side.

The sound of the door slamming behind them caused them both to look back just as the sounds of the lock announced that they were being sealed in with the monster they remembered. Shock ran through each of them, and Stevie immediately ran to the door and banged on it. "Open this at once!" she screamed. "What the hell are you doing? Open it now!" She continued to pound on the impenetrable door.

Zolie saw a lamp on the dresser and turned it on, bringing light into the awful room they were now stuck inside.

Stevie shook the handle of the door, when she heard the sound of chains clanking on a hard surface behind her. Then, the sound of the old woman's voice, a voice much older than Patty's, came from behind her.

"I've been waiting for you, Stevie."

Stevie Galloway froze at the door and slowly turned her head to face her sister, only when she focused her eyes at the woman in the bed, she saw her mother.

Zolie also turned, but it was Patty who was still in her view.

"This can't be happening!" Stevie said, her voice cracking in fright as she looked at the old hag in the bed. She looked older than that miserable day of the accident—wrinkled—and her hair had gone from gray to almost white. She didn't know what she was looking at when the old woman held up her bony finger at her.

"You're a selfish little hussy running off with that boy, leaving your brothers and sister. You're gonna pay for that," Rose Galloway whispered into Stevie's mind.

"No...Mother? It can't be you," Stevie said to the woman in the bed.

Zolie looked to Stevie like she'd gone stomping mad, witnessing Patty Galloway sit up in her bed pulling the long chains shackled at her wrists along the metal edge of the bed and shake her finger at her sister. "Stevie," she said in a raised voice.

Stevie took another step away and felt for the door handle; she then turned and tried frantically to open the door. "Let us out!" Her screams had turned into a frenzy of fear.

"Stevie!" Zolie shouted, moving and grabbing her, pulling her away from the door. "Stevie, what is it?"

"Let me go," Stevie shrieked. "That's not my mother!"

"Stevie, it's not. It's your sister, Patty!" Zolie pleaded.

"No, let me go, bitch," Stevie screamed in Zolie's face.

The slap Stevie received was long overdue, and it seemed to work when Stevie burst into tears and fell into Zolie's arms. "That thing is *not* my mother!"

"Stevie?" Patty said in a voice Stevie knew was hers, and when she looked back at the bed, Patty was the only figure in sight. "Stevie! Thank God you're here!" Patty cried out.

Shaking her haunted thoughts away, questioning the event she just *thought* she'd seen, Stevie looked to her sister. She then saw the hurt in her sister's face and ran to her. Seeing the chains on her arms that were shackled to the floor on each side of the bed, Stevie felt terrible for her sibling.

"My God, what are they doing to you?"

"You have to get me out of here! I'm so sorry for all of it," Patty said, looking from her sister to the strange woman with the English accent. "Wait...I know you, don't I? You look familiar."

Zolie's mind was overfilled with thoughts: being locked in, Stevie's peculiar behavior, and now seeing the insane woman chained to the bed being *sorry* for murdering her sister—none of this seemed real. "No, you don't know me; we haven't met. My name is Zolie Kenowith," she said. "I'm a writer. I'm doing a story on what happened, and I'd like your side of it."

Patty narrowed her eyes suspiciously at the well-dressed woman and looked to her sister, who was wide eyed, and nodding.

"Patty, Zolie's a good person. She's helping me now; she's given me a place to stay and money to live on. It's okay to talk with her."

"You're helping my sister?" Patty asked, looking right at Zolie.

"Yes, I want to help you too."

"Why?"

"I told you. I'm a writer, and that's what I get paid for."

"Bullshit! You sound like that bitch in the mountains who killed our brother. You even look like her."

Zolie knew the only way out was to tell the truth, and after finally meeting this vile woman, she'd seen enough and wanted nothing more than to cut through the bullshit and get what she needed so she could leave and never return.

"My name is Zolie *Vanderran* Kenowith. And yes, Cara was my sister, and I'm a writer trying to put an end to the insanity once and for all."

Zolie watched Patty absorb the news. It seemed to be sinking in when Zolie nodded, and when she looked down, she saw the discolored flooring like burned remains of another human form on the floor in Patty's room. "Stevie," she said looking to the floor.

Stevie rose from her sister's side and saw what Zolie was looking at. "Patty, what happened in here? What caused that mark on the floor?"

Patty shook her head, "Nightmares—burning nightmares."

Zolie felt a chill and looked away, spotting a faint red light blinking in the corner of the room—it was from a camera watching the whole scene.

In another room down the hall, Dr. Jack Hollerman was enjoying the show, until Dr. Stan Sinardi saw the open door and came up behind him and saw what he was looking at.

"What have you done?" Sinardi's sudden interruption made Hollerman jump.

"What do you mean? You knew they were coming. The English lady said she'd called you, and you said it was all right they come for a visit. And where've you been all day, anyway? We've been trying to contact you."

"Where I've been isn't your concern, and I haven't spoken to *anyone*. And Patty Galloway was not to have *any* visitors! They lied to you, dumbass!" Sinardi yelled at the man as he looked back to the monitor.

"No, they didn't." A stern voice came from behind them, and both men turned to see the strange man standing there in a white lab coat. Slowly the tall man moved into the light, and Dr. Stanley Sinardi's mouth dropped.

"It's you—Dr. Vreeland," Stan said, shaking away the shock and feeling the sudden luck hit him like a slot machine jackpot. He smiled, moving toward the man and extending his hand. "Dr. Todd Vreeland, I had no idea you were...here?" Sinardi then turned on Hollerman with a look of sheer contempt. "Why didn't you tell me the great Dr. Vreeland was here?"

Defiance crossed Dr. Hollerman's face, and he moved forward, slightly nudging Sinardi aside in order to meet the "great man" himself. "I tried, but you were too busy being your asshole self and not answering your phone," Hollerman shot back as he extended his hand. "Dr. Vreeland, Dr. Jack Hollerman, and it's a pleasure to meet you, sir."

What a jack-hole Dr. Todd mixed up his thoughts of asshole and jackass as he looked at the surly fool with the stupid smug grin on his face and was immediately reminded of that fat lazy orderly he'd murdered with the sledgehammer so long ago. *What was that fucktard's name?* he wondered as he looked at the man's badge in front of him. *Jack...James? No, Jonathan, yes, Jonathan...Holles.* He remembered how much he'd enjoyed killing that lazy J-Hole. Seeing this new man's last name, Hollerman, in front of him, all Todd could do was smile. *This is going to get fun.*

"Let us out!" The voice came through the small speaker of the monitor they'd been watching, and the three men looked to the screen.

"It shouldn't take much longer," Dr. Todd said, waiting for the payoff of watching the two women collapse from the drugged drinks he'd arranged for them to be offered.

"What shouldn't take much longer?" Sinardi asked.

Annoyance seared across Dr. Todd's face, irritated with his stupid question and gave him an insipid look. Waving it away, he saw that Zolie was the first who seemed to lose her balance and move to a chair, collapsing into it and dropping her bag on the floor. Then, following her lead, as Stevie rose from her sister's side to see what happened to Zolie, she fell to the floor next to Patty's bed.

"Prepare rooms for my new patients," Dr. Todd ordered as he left the two in the room.

CHAPTER 81

The morning ritual on the nasty boat remained the same, with the delivery of some takeout food, except this time the other man delivered the breakfast, and the girls had been unchained to use the bathroom located at the bow of the vessel before they ate. They were even given their duffel bags from their bikes to change their clothes.

When Kate came out from the filthy bathroom and reached for her takeout bag, Lou noticed the heavy bruising on her wrist from being chained so long. Watching Lana go to the bathroom and close the door, Lou felt the guilt. "You can't get out from here," he said, looking at the heavy chains secured to the wall railings. "You don't need to be tied up." He then stepped out the door and slammed it shut, locking it behind him.

When Lana came out and saw he was gone, she was scared. "What happened? I heard the door shut."

"He's having second thoughts," Kate said, rubbing her wrist.

"What do you think that means?"

"I think he saw my bruises and realized he's not as big of a jerk as his pal. He said we can't get out from here anyway, so he's leaving the chains off."

Quietly they began to look out the portholes to find out exactly where they were. The girls didn't know how long this guilt trip would last, so they wanted to take advantage of it as fast as possible. Hearing his boat start, they moved to the portholes in time to see the wake from his boat move past their view.

"Come on—let's find a way out of here," Kate said, grabbing a rotted board from a cupboard and breaking it off to try to break down the door.

Looking for a weapon, Lana started searching around the foul place they were in when she spotted an oar behind a barrel. Moving to get it, she leaned against the barrel, knocking it over. The top snapped off, and the contents inside were startling. Lana stood in fear, looking at the torn-open backpack filled with women's clothing.

"This isn't working!" Kate said, dropping the useless board with a loud bang. Turning to Lana, she saw her standing still as a mouse. "Lana? What is it?" Moving to her, she saw the clothing and looked to her cousin as the reality hit them both. *They weren't the first ones to be stuck here.*

Slowly crouching down, Lana began sifting through the items, looking for any identification. Kate joined her search when she found the old, folded paper medical bracelet like you'd get when admitted to a hospital caught in the fold of the backpack. Pulling it free, she unfolded it and read the name: Emily Waters.

"Oh God, no." Kate cried showing her cousin.

Lana recognized the name at once and was just as horrified as Kate. It was only last year, and the news of the girl was everywhere. She had been reported missing, and when the family was finally contacted about a ransom drop that got screwed up, the girl had later been found dead.

CHAPTER 82

T he sixth floor of the sanatorium certainly had its share of frights over the years, but the bowels of the hospital were even worse. And the torture that happened there outdid the fire in spades.

The "hotbox" was one of Victor Vreeland's favorite contraptions when he was alive, to be used only on the patients who *dared* defy him. It was brought into play usually after a severe beating with a bullwhip. His henchmen would then salt their wounds and drag the screaming victims and toss them into the hotbox to bake. Triple-thick lead glass protected the ones on the outside who watched the poor souls struggle until they burst into flames. He especially liked to let others view this tool of fear to keep his patients in line. That was just *one* of the hideous things that waited for the unwilling down in that filthy place.

The cells that housed the current special patients were down a separate corridor, away from the torture area, and as Dr. Sinardi led Dr. Todd Vreeland to his prized patients, Dr. Todd reveled in seeing all of his old favorite toys.

The *Exorcist* murders were now old news, of course. The court case had been a circus. The two older sisters wanted their rich parents dead for the money and killed them. Their younger brother, however, was also blamed when he was found trying to bury the murder weapons in the backyard, and it all stemmed from the hype of a scary movie they'd seen, or so the jury had ruled.

As they neared the first cell, the small bench on the far wall opposite the cell started shaking on its own, bringing a slight grin to Dr. Todd.

"Parlor tricks," Sinardi said. "They're just warming up."

The darkness within the cell before them was foreboding. Even Dr. Todd took a step back at the uneasiness he felt radiating from behind the thick glass.

"No need to worry, they've never escaped these impenetrable cells, and they never will."

Dr. Todd nodded.

"Are you ready to meet the Brockmans?" Sinardi said, really not caring about the answer as he turned on the lights within the cell.

The woman was...beautiful. Her dark-brown hair was perfectly brushed, her skin glowed radiantly, and her patient gown was impeccable, with the exception of the tear she'd added between her breasts. She was sitting in a chair pushed away from her small table with her meal on it, and Dr. Sinardi smiled when he saw Dr. Todd take a step forward, watching her stand.

"She's performing for you, Doctor," Sinardi whispered with a side-eyed glance.

"Good evening, Dr. Sinardi," the woman said. "Who have you brought to meet me?"

"Belinda, this is—"

"Dr. Todd Vreeland." The woman finished his introduction, and wearing a polite smile, she moved up to the glass. "Doctor, the walls tell many stories about you," she said, reaching up and pulling her long hair back away from her chest. She then started caressing herself, reaching inside the torn part of her gown, partly exposing herself, and leaning into the glass.

Dr. Todd watched the glass fog near her face as she breathed out on the other side of it.

"Murder any fish lately?" she said with a smile, as the lights in her cell went out for a split second. When they came back on, she had transformed into a version of his dead mother wearing the dress she'd been murdered in.

Her skin was scarred, and her neck was bruised black, just like his mother had looked after being strangled. Decomposing flesh covered her neck and half her face, and her teeth had been knocked out.

"Look what you did to me!" She laughed behind the glass, spitting blood from her mouth.

Dr. Todd stepped back and knew things had changed completely from when he'd been there, and he couldn't have been more scared or happier all at the same time.

"Come on, Dr. Todd, this is only the first act," Sinardi said, seeing his reaction to what he himself could not see. He spoke in a gleeful tone, as if proud that his prize patients were performing so well for the famed scientist. He then nudged the man he'd hoped to impress to the next cell down the miserable corridor.

The length between the cells was substantial due to the severity of the patients held within them. And just as they approached the second cell, the lights inside came on by themselves.

"Hmm," Sinardi muttered. "Belynn never likes to be seen. She hides when I come down," he continued as they stepped in front of her cell.

The first thing Dr. Todd noticed was the color of her hair: it was darker than the first woman he'd just seen, and it was arranged in a tangled fright. She was lying facedown on her bed, and her head was turned away from them.

"Go away, Vreeland," came the sarcastic voice from within the cell.

"Belynn's the middle child," Dr. Todd heard Sinardi say as he moved to the glass and put his hand to it.

"You'd be wise not to give me orders," Dr. Todd barked, feeling the scorn rise within him for being spoken down to.

"Or what, asshole? You'll perform another botched lobotomy on a helpless woman?" The tone was hard and angry, and they watched her move to the far side of the bed.

"Show me your face!" Todd ordered.

"Ha-ha-ha," the woman laughed as she stood, facing away from him. She then turned, letting her tangled hair hang down over her face as she stumbled along in a strange gait toward the window.

"What are you going to do if I don't? Rape me with your dwarf dick like you did with Lorena?" The woman laughed, tilting her head back and whipping her wild hair around for Dr. Todd to see her new form—Lorena Mason, the scrub tech he'd murdered in that very hospital on that horrific night. Her uniform was torn at the crotch, and it was stained with blood.

"Why don't you come in here and rape me some more like the night you strangled me in a blackout?" She laughed as she touched herself behind the glass, and then she looked away, her hair falling across her face. When she looked back, Lorena was gone; a new woman stood there. She looked like a younger version of the first—except something within her was strangely familiar.

She dashed to the glass, putting her hand exactly where Todd's hand was on the other side. "Come play with me. I dare you," she said, exposing her chest and adding a sinister laugh.

Dr. Todd stood his ground and slammed his other hand to the glass. "Be careful what you wish for, bitch!" His voice was strangely deep, making the woman behind the glass flinch. She even stepped back, as if she was afraid of what type of demon *he* could let loose.

Dr. Todd laughed, and a sinister look flashed behind his eyes. He could see his own reflection in the glass; his blue eyes were now black and menacing. The thing behind the glass saw that too and bowed her head.

Starting to shake, she looked to her left and then her right and then bolted back to hide on the far side of her bed as the lights inside her cell went black.

Dr. Sinardi marveled at the strength of his telepathic patients, wishing he could see the malignant horrors their intended victims were seeing in their minds, and judging from Todd's reaction, they'd struck his deepest fears. All the same, Dr. Sinardi was in awe; he'd never seen that vulgar behavior in her before, and his smile brightened as he got a snapshot of the filthy mind of Dr. Todd Vreeland standing in his own presence, looking at the amazing talents that sat inside his cells.

"I knew one day I'd show off my fabulous brilliance," he said, almost giggling.

The giddiness and self-worth within the pompous man was flat-out embarrassing, and it infuriated Dr. Todd; he turned on Sinardi with a look of disgust. "These crass bitches don't interest me with their amateur tricks, you imbecile. This is nothing but a simple mind game." Dr. Todd shoved Sinardi in the direction of the next cell. Having studied the telepathic Rose Galloway from his father's notes years ago, he knew quite well their *powers* were nothing more than the ability to search their intended targets' minds and replicate their ugliest memories to make them *think* they were seeing them—like they were standing right in front of them. *Demonic possession*, Todd thought. *This guy is a total idiot.*

Sinardi found his footing as he tripped against a support beam between the cells, and dirt from the old building fell from above; he was momentarily at a loss for words. The women were the only ones who showed abilities, powers that possibly came from demonic possession, and the younger brother was the only Brockman child whom Sinardi thought was sane, not that his sanity mattered. After all, the poor man would forever remain behind bars in this godfor-saken place.

Realizing Todd had obviously studied these types of behaviors, he worried he'd not be able to impress the great doctor like he'd planned. "Then I must say I'm sorry; their younger brother you're about to meet never did amount to much."

Dr. Todd looked back at Sinardi with contempt, remembering similar hateful words coming from his father, and started to wonder exactly *how* he was going to murder him.

Moving to the next cell, Sinardi switched on the lights to see the youngest of the Brockmans lying in bed with the covers pulled up over his face. Dr. Todd looked in and saw the man's black hair stick-ing out from the top of the blanket; and for some reason he started thinking of Blake. The more disturbing note, however, was the fact that this Brockman also bore the same first name as his own vile brother.

"Blake, you have a visitor," Sinardi announced.

Just hearing his brother's name caused Todd to cringe.

"No." A voice that sounded all too familiar to Dr. Todd came from beneath the blanket.

"You want the punishment again?" Sinardi growled. "I *want* you to meet someone."

"They made me do it!" the younger man cried as Dr. Todd watched the blankets start to move away from the youngest Brockman's face. Slowly the blankets fell away, and Todd watched him lumber out from bed. He was naked, and Todd watched the poor hairy man turn and reach for his robe.

The robe was too big for him, and the hood covered most of his face, yet something about the man's jaw…

"What? What do you want?" the man in the depressing room muttered as he got to the glass separating them and lifted his hood to view his visitor.

Dr. Todd was shaken as he realized *exactly* who he was looking at. The man behind the glass *was* his brother. Blake Vreeland was standing before him, just younger, with the kinder face he remembered from those few occasions before they'd been turned against each other.

"Sir, nice to meet you," came the timid voice behind the glass. "I don't care what you've been told—I'm not like my sisters."

Dr. Todd was in shock; he was seeing and hearing his brother's raspy voice come out from this younger man. It was impossible, he thought, not sensing the same menacing vibrations he'd felt from the older sisters.

The younger man had the look of innocence as he stood near the glass, peering into the eyes of the speechless man on the opposite side. "Please, sir, it happened so long ago, and all I wanted to do was fit in."

Dr. Todd blinked his eyes in amazement. Was it a trick like the two little bitches before him tried to do? It was like seeing himself in his own brother many years ago when all *he* did was try to fit in.

"I've seen enough," Dr. Todd announced like a seasoned dictator. Turning on his heel, he walked away from the much younger man and marched down the corridor, leaving the cells.

The women were laughing behind the glass when he saw them. "What's the matter?" Belynn spat against the glass. "Afraid of another game of bash the skull with a hockey stick?" She screamed as she rocked back and forth, illuminated by the lights of the corridor. "You think you're smart—we're *many* and *we're* smarter." She continued to laugh at the man.

Dr. Todd was unnerved, and he hurried to rush by her, passing the first cell and seeing the ugly face still pressed against the glass. Her fingers were clawing at her breasts, and when she pulled them away, he saw the lines of blood appear and drip down her chest.

"You're killing me, Stubs!" the deranged witch behind the glass laughed as she quickly moved along the glass to follow him. She suddenly ripped her nails over the top of her other hand, drawing blood, like Blake had done to Todd with the bone saw when he'd been performing for their father from hell.

Dr. Todd winced at the memory, seeing her laugh behind the glass, and rushed down the corridor. His mind had too many thoughts in it to figure out exactly what was happening, and when he passed the torture devices he'd loved over the years, he stopped, seeing something that'd come in the handiest. It was the broken elevator shaft leading to the upper floor of horrors that'd been his playground for years. He remembered Blake throwing him into it and how he had to hang on to the remaining cables in order to climb to safety. Todd looked inside and saw the few remaining broken bones left behind by the damned.

With his past looking him right in the eye, a powerful inner strength whirled up inside him, and he watched a strange shadow of a man emerge from the elevator pit and disappear into the crevice in the corner where the walls met.

CHAPTER 83

Pulling up in front of Wendy's townhome, Hailey parked her car, and the two sisters got out as the cold wind hit them, freezing them on the spot.

"Damn, it's getting colder," Sandy said, wishing she'd put on a heavier coat.

"Come on," Hailey said, rushing past her up the steps to Wendy's door.

Following, Sandy pulled out the key and opened her dead sister's front door, and the two entered, closing the door and shutting out the cold wind. The interior, however, was also freezing, and Sandy felt it immediately.

"Burr! It's colder in here than out there," she said as she moved to the thermostat and turned on the heat, setting the control to ninety degrees.

The women looked at each other and could see each other's breath as they heard the ticking sound of the heat coming alive. "Thank God, it's still working," Hailey remarked as the air vents roared. She watched Sandy move down the hall to the kitchen and followed. "What are you doing?"

Entering the kitchen, Sandy grabbed Wendy's teapot on the stove and emptied out any remaining water inside. She then rinsed it out, filled it with tap water, and placed it back on the stove and turned it on high. "I'm making tea," she said as she opened a cupboard and pulled down some teabags.

"Fine, as cold as it is in here, I'll take anything." Hailey turned away and moved to Wendy's office to begin rummaging through it.

Sandy looked back at Hailey and leaned against the counter, eyeing the photograph that was hanging on her refrigerator of her and Wendy at the station they used to love working at.

"Come on—what are you waiting on?" Hailey's voice came from down the hall.

Sandy looked at the stove and saw the burner turning hot and quickly followed her sister to Wendy's office. It was time to search for any clues that could help them figure out just who this mysterious S. benefactor could be.

CHAPTER 84

Sam finished his shower and stepped out dripping wet, grabbing for the towel Raquel had left out for him. He dried off and found the fresh cup of coffee waiting for him on the counter and saw his clothes laid out on the newly made bed. He picked up his coffee and took a drink, placing it down next to the toothbrush left by the woman he'd made love to more times in one evening than he could remember. He picked up the toothbrush, opening the brand-new package, and saw the toothpaste on the counter. Catching his smile in the mirror, he thought back to the first time a woman had done this for him in his early life as a single man.

Getting dressed, he smelled the delicious scents coming from downstairs, and when he descended to join her, he saw the table had been set with orange juice.

Raquel was still in her robe, but she'd pulled herself together and applied a little makeup; she'd fixed her hair to look beautiful for the man who had saved her last night, and when Sam saw her in her kitchen with the light shining from within her soul, his heart melted because he was feeling the exact same warmth.

Moving to her, he put his coffee mug down on the counter and stood behind her, and as she prepared breakfast, he reached around and hugged her. Turning to him, she let go of the spatula she was using to prepare the scrambled eggs and snuggled into his arms. He then lifted her chin and kissed her as the frying pan crackled with heat, and she pulled away, worried about the meal.

"Ay, no, I don't want to ruin it," she said, mixing the eggs and lifting the pan from the hot stove as the toast popped up next to them. "You! Butter and jam the toast—that's your job," she insisted with a demure smile.

"Yes, ma'am," Sam said with a happy grin, feeling a sense of togetherness that he hadn't felt in quite some time.

He placed the toast on a plate and buttered it as he watched Raquel divide the eggs onto plates with bacon and sausage. She then moved to him so that he could add the final touch. "Grape or strawberry jam?" he said, pointing to the jars on the counter.

"Ay, I forgot the apricot," Raquel said, putting the plates down and opening the refrigerator. Grabbing the other jar, she watched him pick up the plates and move to the table.

There they sat down, and Sam saw the light shine within her eyes; he knew there was something more than the shared loss they both had in common flowing between them now. "You're beautiful," he said to her as he reached for her hand.

"You are, Mr. Sam."

Raquel's heavy Colombian accent turned him on as he felt his lust for the beautiful woman sitting in front of him start to return. "Nantucket," he said. "Have you ever been to Nantucket?"

"No, I hear it's beautiful."

"Let's go. We have a home there, and we can just be alone for a while. God, I need that type of peace, and I hope you do too," Sam said, wanting nothing more than to take Raquel away for a few days and just be in a place where they could enjoy each other and be alone.

"Yes." The reply was quick and simple, delivered with a smile that told him she trusted him, which made him want her even more.

CHAPTER 85

A gent Robert Forrester was working in a recording booth at Agency One with a technician trying to get the static portion of the call cleaned up to increase the clarity, but when he hit the play button, the static was still partially obscuring the actual sounds on the recording, with the exception of a chiming sound.

"There, right there," he said. "Back that up five seconds, and increase the sound, and if you can clean that portion up right there, I think we'll find something."

The technician worked the controls, and in a moment the video screen in front of him flickered, showing the wavelengths of the sound as it was playing. The sound was now as clear as it could be. The ringing bells in the background during the call were distinct. Agent Forrester then checked the time of the call and knew the bell was ringing at approximately noon. He then added up all the information gathered to figure that the call came from an area with a school nearby ringing a lunch bell; it was close to the water from the cry of the gull and the clear sound of the foghorn.

He had the date, time, and the foghorn in front of him, along with the manifests of every vessel in the area at the time.

With the new information, Agent Forrester quickly went to work, and with the help of Agency One's best, anything on the Hudson River was ruled out, which meant the call had come from someplace near New York City.

Zeroing in on the locations, two spots came up: a school near La Guardia by the water with a view of Riker's Island, and another school near a tugboat graveyard on Staten Island.

"Gotcha!" Forrester said, looking at the monitor of the abandoned ship graveyard. Picking up the phone next to him, he punched in Tallulah's number.

"I think I've found where the girls are being held," he said, looking at his monitors.

"Forrester, that's good news. I was just about to call you. Ed found a small-town carpentry business, and, although a long shot, Ed has a hunch this may pay off. I'll send you the photo of the business card."

Agent Forrester heard the e-mail come in on his computer and opened it, clicking on the image. "Lou and Lenny's Repairs?"

"That's it," Tallulah said.

"Give me a minute, and I'll call you back." Agent Forrester hung up the phone.

Selecting to print the e-mail, he heard the sound of his printer and went to work searching their names, previous addresses, bank accounts, family members, and anything else he could find, including pulling their social security numbers, which made it easy to track their job histories.

Paging down the excessive lists for both men, Agent Forrester smiled when he came to a six-month gig Lenny McCoy had worked. Approximately a year ago, he landed a job at a marina, working on the different boats, and he had repaired the wood floors on an old yacht located near the school bell he'd zeroed in on, not far from a small bay that now was home to the rusted history of New York's water taxis and tugboats on Staten Island.

Pulling up satellite imagery of the yacht's location, he printed the map and circled an area where he thought the kidnapped Savage girls just might be located.

CHAPTER 86

When the ransom drop-off location was finally called in to Savage Tower, all agents were focused on the marinas of Staten Island. And when they were told to leave the money in a backpack on board the Staten Island Ferry during a time when a nearby school was letting out, they knew his information was correct.

They'd been told to board the three-o'clock departure from Staten Island and place the backpack on the top-floor garbage can near the stairs located on the starboard side of the ferry. The location made sense since it was near an exit. With the access to the stairs, anyone picking up the backpack could escape off the ferry and disappear into the bustling city. The problem they faced was the ferry would be packed not only with passengers but students as well, and they couldn't risk anyone getting hurt.

The plus side of the last phone call they'd received, however, since they had an idea where to look, was that they'd been able to trace the number to a phone booth located in the area Agent Forrester had mentioned.

CHAPTER 87

The sound of the door slamming behind her caused some of the flower petals to drop from the many arrangements in her room, and Marlo Savage turned to the door she'd just swung shut, worried and angry for the noise she'd just made. Rushing back to the door, she opened it and looked out into the hall of the Plaza. Not seeing anyone in either direction, she closed the door and sighed, happy that the first day of shooting was over.

"God, what a bunch of bitches!" she said out loud to herself in her beautiful room as she moved away from the door and took off her coat and tossed her purse on the bed. She then moved to the window and pulled the sheer curtains back and looked at the coldness of the coming winter in Central Park. Turning away, she kicked off her shoes and eyed the minibar in her room. *I really want a drink,* she thought and put her hand over her pregnant abdomen, trying to push the thought away.

Outside of Madeline Roberts, most of the wives from the show were nasty in their own way when the cameras weren't rolling, but, my, how they'd turn on a dime once the "lights, camera, action" went into full swing. She could still hear Marilyn Hart's nasty voice *ordering* her to check with *her* regarding wardrobe. There were certain things *she* wouldn't allow the others to wear or *do*, upstaging her; never stand between *her* and the camera; and there was a pecking order around there, and she *always* got her way. Shamori, however, seemed the most genuine, and later in the day, when her husband had arrived with their child, she watched her turn into the young mother Marlo remembered herself being with Tucker all those years ago. The memory brought a smile to her face, and she opened a bottle of water and picked up the room-service menu to order in for the evening.

Her mind wandered to her and Ed's early life when Tucker had been their only child and how beautiful everything had been. She kept remembering seeing Shamori lifting her beautiful child up in the air for kisses, just like she'd done with her little Tuc. With the memory so vivid in her mind, she tossed the menu aside on the bed and reached for her purse. Opening her wallet, she thumbed through her few photographs inside and found the photo of her holding Tucker when he was born, with Ed smiling by their side, not really noticing the appointment card fall from her wallet to the bedspread.

Her smile was glowing as she recalled those tender moments, and as she closed her wallet, she noticed the card on the bed. Picking it up and seeing her follow-up appointment scheduled, she remembered seeing Aisha Thomas at her doctor's office.

"Don't tell anyone I was here." The tone of her voice in that office had been filled with fear. She then envisioned Shamori, an African American with a Caucasian husband, just like Gabby and Roman, and Marlo's jaw dropped.

No, she thought, as the clues seemed to be piling up at the doorstep of her battered mind. She then began to rethink everything since this entire nightmare for her family began, and the more she thought about it, the more she believed it.

Getting up from the bed, she didn't know where to turn. She began to pace back and forth, thinking the absolute worst. Staring at the flower petals littering the floor, her gaze moved up to the arrangement on the table and noticed the small white card still attached to the holder within the roses.

It seemed to be calling her, and something inside her told her not to go near it; the almost-pure-white card perched innocently among the thorns of the roses felt like a warning.

"You're being silly," she whispered to herself as she remembered back to that horrible moment when the bathroom door in the motor home had burst open and that horrible man with the hunter's mask lumbered out and attacked her. Perhaps it *was* the fear still in her body from that nightmare in the mountains, but before she could think any further, the card was in her hands, and she was opening it.

The card read: *Marilyn—May you savage your reputation from last season with those two horrible bitches! —A fan.*

Marlo blinked and reread the note. *Savage?* She read it again and figured it was a typo for the word *salvage.*

The uneasiness crept into her soul just like that night she'd found Lisa's doll in the woods before the attack. And when she looked back at the card, it became an evil tool of some sort, and her instinct was to open her palm and let the disgusting filth fall to the floor. But she couldn't—she read the note again and turned it over. She then looked at the flowers it had come in and rummaged through them, knocking more petals to the floor, not giving a damn. *No,* she thought. *This was written to Marilyn—that cold witch she'd just filmed with! These weren't addressed to her.*

Were the flowers sent to her room by mistake? If not, then was it a typo? Her mind went back to Shamori with her husband and seeing Aisha with her dirty little secret she didn't want anyone to know about.

Marlo's mind filled with ugly, horrible thoughts of her husband with another woman, and she started to cry. *Not after all we've gone through,* she thought, remembering that pregnant woman from the train. It was if signs were coming at her in all directions.

The sadness of the horrible moments her family had just endured returned to her in spades, and she leaned against the bed and slumped to the floor, pulling a pillow with her; she clutched it as her mind painted an ugly portrait of the things she didn't want to look at and she realized she'd missed certain clues over the last few weeks.

The torment was back, and her anger flared, but she couldn't lash out, not *really,* not until she knew the whole truth. She had to find out, and she had to keep it together because tomorrow the cast was taking a charter to Martha's Vineyard to Marilyn Hart's second home for the first episode of the season. To the cast it was a nightmare, having to leave the comforts of the studio where the Cinema

Shake-Up was still being filmed, just for her damned luncheon. Of course, Marilyn had connections and had told Randall about the award she was receiving, a tribute that she insisted be filmed for the show. And to ease timing for the Cinema Shake-Up, she had demanded they use Pier Productions on Martha's Vineyard for any segment they chose as long as *she* got to be filmed receiving her bullshit award.

Marlo knew like everyone else that Marilyn had Anthony Caspian in the background supporting her whims and knew she was a manipulator, but to watch her on television, you'd never believe all the rumors and gossip about this overbearing woman. And to think she had longed to come back to this business for all these years.

What the hell is wrong with me, she thought.

CHAPTER 88

Ed Savage heard his cell phone ringing and opened the shower door and stepped out, dripping wet, to answer it. He picked up a towel to dry his hand and answered it on the third ring.

They'd all been waiting for news, anything to help them move forward, and the events that played out at the Catskills Ski Lodge had been draining for the Savage men. Roman had become a complete basket case over the loss of his wife, Gabby, and had taken a heavy tranquilizer to calm down. With Roman needing to get home to tell the children before they heard it on the news, Logan drove him back to Zolie's compound in Roman's car, leaving Ed alone to see if anything further could be found out at West Point.

Seeing Tallulah's number, Ed felt hope, and it was something he was in short supply of. "What do you got?" he said into the phone.

"We're getting close, Ed. We narrowed it down to a small area on Staten Island."

"Staten Island? Where?" he said moving from the steam in the bathroom to the next room.

"The marina on the far southern end, not far from where a tugboat graveyard is located. Thrasher has all the details, and he's on his way to meet with you. I've arranged a helicopter to take you from the base back downstate, and by the time you arrive, we'll know where they are," Tallulah said with the knowing authority he'd heard from her in the past. "And leave your keys. I have someone coming to bring your Range Rover back to Savage Tower."

Ed knew exactly where the tugboat graveyard was located because he'd kayaked out there with his brothers years ago for some exploring. Now the images of his nieces being locked up within one of those tetanus traps sent chills over his wet, naked body.

"How long before Thrasher arrives?"

"He should be there now." Tallulah said the words, and Ed suddenly heard a knock at his door.

"He's here," Ed said, looking at the door to his private barrack on the base. "I'll call you when we get there, and I'll leave the keys on the dresser." Hanging up, Ed rushed to the door.

Opening the door just a sliver, Ed saw Thrasher standing there and swung the door wide open. The reaction on Thrasher's face was a mixture of shock and embarrassment, seeing Ed Savage standing there completely naked and dripping wet.

"Come on, there's no time," Ed said as he turned and dashed back to the bathroom, grabbing a towel to dry off. "Shut the damn door," came Ed's voice. "It's cold out there."

Thrasher moved inside, closing the door, and stood looking at the partially open bathroom door; he could see Ed with the towel over his head drying himself off in the mirror. His mind blurred, and the image of that awful fire and the even worse mistake he'd made that day flashed before his eyes.

Ed finished up. Tossing the towel over the shower rod, he looked in the partly steamed mirror and saw Thrasher's reflection looking at him. *It's his anniversary,* came the sound of Tallulah's voice in his mind as he grabbed a fresh towel and wrapped it around his waist. "Be out in a minute," Ed said, closing the door as his own thoughts went back to the day of the fire.

Ed Savage remembered feeling the intense heat from the inferno all around him as he ran up the hotel stairs. The explosion of flames had engulfed the upper floors, and he saw the angry fire burn through the walls of the stairway in front of him. Seeing he couldn't go any farther, he opened the door to the floor he was on and escaped the stairwell as part of it collapsed behind him.

Moving down the smoke-filled hall, he got to the room directly under the princess's room and inserted his room key into the lock.

The lights stayed dark on the device, and he kicked in the door to find the flames had moved down and into the room the agents had occupied while tracing a lead for the missing *Manchester* after a tip that the Royal Family could be the target.

"Thrasher!" Ed yelled into the smoke and fire-filled room. Keeping low and moving inside, he got to the double doors of one of the bedrooms and saw that part of the ceiling had come down, crushing someone underneath it. The smoke was thick, and Ed waved his hands in front of him; he saw the man was unmoving, flattened beneath the debris, and a wall of fire separated them. Ed saw there was nothing he could do when the second explosion rocked the building, and he heard the princess scream from upstairs through the broken windows; as he moved away from the fire, the man buried under the debris stirred.

Backing away, he searched the agents' second bedroom for survivors (which had been an adjoining room) and seeing it empty, he went back into the hall and moved for the opposite stairwell he'd come up from. Moving up to the princess's floor, he felt the door before opening it. Checking how hot it was, he knew it was safe to open, but when he did, he was horrified. There on the floor just a few feet from him was Agent Winston Weston Thrasher III. The walls around him were burning and partly caved in, and his head was bleeding. Shocked at seeing his fallen friend, Ed moved to him when he heard the princess scream from somewhere down the smoke-filled hallway in front of him.

Ed grabbed Thrasher and nudged him, felt for a pulse, and saw he was alive.

"Come on, buddy. Wake up," Ed yelled over the sound of the fire, and that had been when Thrasher opened his eyes. Blood, sweat, and soot had pooled in the corners of his eyes, and it stung as he blinked it away. In his deluded state, he looked up through the smoke and saw his partner, Freddy, looking back at him as a window blew out in a room on the other side of the wall, feeding oxygen to the hungry explosions, and the fire roared like thunder sent down from an angry god.

"Fred, thank God," Thrasher had mumbled as more debris fell near them, banging loudly in the inferno. He then reached up and grabbed Ed's shoulder and pulled him to him, kissing him passionately.

Caught off guard at the action, Ed pulled away. He knew Thrasher was gay and never had a problem with it until he kissed him—but he couldn't for the life of him understand why he'd kissed him at all.

"Thrasher, wake up! It's Ed!" he continued to yell as he watched his friend's eyes focus through the thick smoke and the look of sheer fright and embarrassment cross his face as he tried to stay conscious.

"She's here," Ed said, dragging Thrasher back into the stairwell. Propping him up against the wall away from the fire, Ed moved back down the hall and disappeared into the smoke.

The suite the princess was in had been huge, bigger than the rooms below that the agents had taken, and this room had many additional main hallway doors leading into several adjoining rooms. Ed got as near to the fire as he could, and then kicked in the closest door and entered.

"Princess!" Ed yelled.

"Here! I'm here!" she screamed, and Ed followed her cries until he could see the door to a bathroom move back and forth, getting caught from the partially collapsed ceiling that split the doorjamb inward.

"Hang on!" Ed moved to her and saw her hands on the edge of the door trying to pull it open.

"Princess Nina, are you all right?"

"Oh my God! Yes, please get me out from here."

"Back away from the door," Ed yelled.

"Okay," Princess Nina cried from behind the barrier.

Ed kicked in the door. It opened partway, and he tried one more time, finally splitting it so the door swung open. The princess rushed into his arms, and he took her back out to the hallway, making their way to Thrasher, who had been in no condition to move on his own.

"Oh my God," Nina cried when she saw the poor man lying nearly unconscious against the wall. "Come on—help me," she said, reaching down to grab him on one side. Ed grabbed his other side, and together they moved down the stairwell and away from the fire. When they got to the next floor, Agent Thrasher's eyes shot open, and he lunged toward the door leading to the hallway to his room, opening it slightly as another explosion rocked the burning building. Thrasher's voice could barely be heard over the explosion, and Ed heard his friend call out his name. Then he pulled his friend back, telling him it was no use as he passed out in his arms, and they rushed him down the stairs to the approaching paramedics moving up from the base of the building to meet them.

Ed stood in the mirror looking at his reflection, thinking of that awful day, and his mind went to hearing him call his name—at least, he thought he had.

"I'll be outside," Thrasher's voice came from behind the closed bathroom door, bringing Ed back to present, out from his memory from that awkward day his friend kissed him and their solid friendship changed forever. *He did call out my name, didn't he?* Ed thought. Hearing the outer door open and close, he opened the bathroom door and grabbed his clothes from his open bag on his bed and quickly got dressed.

Minutes later he opened the front door and saw Thrasher standing a few feet away.

"Come on, the helicopter's waiting," Thrasher said, motioning Ed to follow.

Getting in the agent's car to the helicopter, Thrasher immediately started giving Ed the information gathered on the girls' whereabouts. Ed absorbed every word. Yet when he seemed finished and had glanced at a folder next to his seat, his mind was still focused on that fire.

"I thought you said 'Ed' that day—but what you really said was 'Fred.'" Ed looked over to the man who had shot and killed that lunatic woman who had nearly killed his wife only a short time ago.

Thrasher's hands physically tightened on the steering wheel as he tried to continue the briefing, but Ed saw the corner of his eye become immediately wet, and he remembered seeing that dead man lying in the room below the princess's.

"Thrasher...I'm so sorry. I had no idea. Why didn't you tell me the man in your room was your partner? I would have understood," Ed said, seeing that man in his mind under the debris, his dark hair and the black soot and blood from the explosion masking his features, features Ed now realized were similar to his own.

"Not pertinent to the case, Savage Nine," came the official answer from the man who had *never* been open about his personal life.

Ed watched him wipe the corner of his eyes and reach down between his seat and the console. Reaching for a folder, he handed it to him.

"Here's what we have," Thrasher said as he glanced over at Ed, the look of truth finally coming to the surface between the old friends clearly written on his face. He dropped the file on Ed's lap. "Here, this is where the girls are," he said, pointing to the photograph sticking out from the folder before looking back to the road.

Ed felt terrible for all the times he'd bashed Thrasher, thinking the guy had a thing for him, guilty even over his remarks about *not being his type* when he had been changing clothes in the 4-Runner en route to save Lisa—when in actuality the guy had been—and still was mourning the loss of a loved one, and probably holding back hostility toward him at the time. "I'm sorry," Ed said, respecting the man as he opened the folder and picked up the photograph, recognizing the tugboat graveyard.

He then noticed a second photo from the Catskills Hotel. It was of a man checking in; he held it up. "Thrasher, is this the man Roman was looking for?"

"Meet Noah Franklin." Thrasher nodded. "I sent Forrester the photo before I picked you up."

"Anything on the woman?"

"Nothing."

"Damn it!" Aggravated, Ed stared at the photo.

Winston Weston Thrasher III focused on the road ahead and bit his lower lip, knowing Ed did not know the *entire* story. The lives of his nieces were at stake at the hands of probable amateurs, and he couldn't take any risks. The fact that his partner Fred had been alive under that pile of debris and had managed to get past the flames in the room *after* that second explosion when Ed had left him was only part of it. The fact his body had actually been found a few feet from the stairwell door he'd tried to lunge through when Ed had stopped him—stopped him from saving his life partner—had eaten at him ever since. He was angry for the mistake he'd made in allowing Fred to come by that day, angry over all of it, and he couldn't bring himself to tell Ed because no good would come of it. But the tragedy Ed unknowingly could have averted had brought the hostility between them, and too many years had passed.

CHAPTER 89

When Logan and Roman opened the door at Zolie's home, they found Maura in hysterics, and she rushed to the door.

"Zolie, thank God you're—"

Both Logan and Roman saw the surprised look on her face turn to one of dread when she realized it was the men.

"Maura? What is it?" Logan asked his soon-to-be ex-wife.

"Zolie! She's...she's gone," came her panicked reply.

"What do you mean *gone*?" Logan said, taking her in his arms like he'd done so many times to calm her.

"I'm sorry. I thought you were her coming in. I've been worried, and it's not like her to not call me back!" she said, moving away from him. "First the girls—now Zolie! My God, the girls! Where are they?"

"Where's Zolie?" Logan said, raising his voice.

"I don't know," Maura said, turning a shade lighter.

"When did she leave?" Roman's voice broke through, half the strength of his usually deep, confident tone.

"Yesterday, to go work on her new book," Maura said, turning to him and seeing something was off about the man. "Roman, what is it? You look awful." And as her words left her mouth, she saw the brokenness that she'd once seen in Sam emerge from the depths of Roman's soul.

"Maura," Logan said, shaking his head and looking down.

Maura looked from Logan and back to Roman. "My God...the girls," she said, clutching her chest as she watched Roman break down and Logan guide his brother to a sofa. "Gabby will tell me what's going on," she blurted out and looked toward the still partly open door when the wind blew it slightly, as if a ghost was entering the home, and it hit her. "No, not Gabby!" Maura cried as she rushed to Roman's side.

"She's gone—just like Cara," Roman cried in her arms.

The emotion whirled inside her as she looked to her husband; the tears in his eyes, first for her, were now for his two brothers—it was abundantly clear. Not knowing where the girls were and now with Zolie missing added to the news of losing Gabby weakened her, and she sank into the sofa next to Roman and hugged him as hard as she could. "I'm so sorry, Roman; what happened?"

"We're not even sure yet, but she was thrown from a window."

"What?" Maura gasped as Roman lost control and started crying in her arms. There was nothing she could do but hold him.

"Where're the kids?" Roman finally said, gaining some composure.

"Lisa's in her room, and the boys took off on their bikes. I was up late worrying over Zolie, so I'm not sure when they left. I think the girls are out planning a goodbye dinner for Tucker and Chet."

"Do they know about Zolie being gone?"

"No, I didn't say a word last night. I thought she'd be home later."

"She just said she was working on her book?" Logan asked.

"Yes, that's it."

Logan looked to Zolie's office and moved toward it, leaving Maura with Roman. Going behind her desk to search it, he looked back and saw her watching him.

CHAPTER 90

When Zolie Vanderran opened her eyes, she was confused, and when she realized what had happened, it was too late. She was bound in a bed in a different room she'd not seen earlier. In the darkened room, there was a nightlight emerging from the floor against a far wall, and she screamed for help.

"Zolie! I'm here," Stevie screamed back from the next room, her voice carrying through the air vent near the ceiling.

"Stevie? What's happened? What's going on?"

"I don't know. I just woke up in here, and I can hear *her*!"

Zolie's mind cleared from the fog she was under and realized they were now unwilling *guests* in the sanatorium. "Patty? You can hear your sister?" Zolie shouted back.

"No, not my sister, *my mother*!" Stevie shrieked, scaring Zolie and causing her to remember how strange Stevie had been acting just prior to when she started feeling like she was going to faint.

"Stevie, no! It's not your mother; it's some trick they're playing. The tea and coffee we drank—they drugged us! Stevie, think!" Zolie shouted as she heard someone at her door. "Quiet, Stevie, someone's coming." She muted her tone as she heard the locks turn on the door to her ugly room.

When Nurse Kumar entered, he turned on the main lights, and Zolie blinked away the shadows of the room and saw the man wheel in a breakfast cart. His instructions had been to deliver the cart and leave it by her bedside *just out of reach* from her, in a mind game the hospital loved to play, and then leave the room—just like he was to do with the other cart waiting in the hall for Stevie. But when he took one look at the woman, he recognized her immediately.

"Zolie Vanderran? My God, it's you! What are you doing in here?" Kumar asked, bewildered and flustered at the same time over seeing his favorite author bound to a bed.

"Help me. Please help me get out of here," Zolie pleaded, seeing the broken hospital equipment stacked on the far side of the unkempt room like it was used for storage.

The sound of approaching footsteps came from behind them, and Kumar lifted his finger to his lips, nodding. "We never spoke," he said, backing away and turning as the men entered her room.

"Breakfast delivered," Kumar said, shooting a smile to the two men.

Dr. Todd switched the camera views on the monitor and saw that idiot and recognized him from when he'd first arrived. Recalling his insolence toward him, he made a mental note to murder him at some point as he watched him step away from Dr. Sinardi to wait to be dismissed from the room. *God, it feels good to be home,* he thought. He then looked to Dr. Hollerman, whom he'd assigned the new moniker of J-Hole to, just like that lazy asshole he'd had so much fun killing all those years ago. *Yes, I've missed my old life and I've got some catching up to do.* He smiled.

"Dr. Sinardi," Zolie pleaded, recognizing him as a man *she thought* she could trust. "Untie me from this bed at once," she demanded.

"Yes, Mrs. Vanderran." He started to loosen the restraints. "I'm sorry about all this, but you weren't supposed to see Patty the other day, especially on *this* floor."

This floor, Zolie thought, now knowing exactly where she was in the monstrous building and wanting nothing more than to get out.

"You must have been exhausted because when we found you, you were asleep in Patty's room."

"You mean locked in her room."

"That's a precaution that's always taken around here."

Not believing a word spewing from this monster's mouth, Zolie knew to placate him. "And binding me to the bed?"

"Another precaution," came the swift lie. "Look at this room you're in; it's a fright, and we couldn't have you hurting yourself in your condition."

Zolie's mind went to her phone call to Dr. Sinardi and realized she'd been talking to someone else, someone who had *acted* like he was Dr. Sinardi.

"I'm so sorry for the confusion," came the familiar voice from the man who'd led her into the trap.

Zolie looked over at that bastard Dr. Hollerman, who'd drugged them when they'd gotten there, looking now like an innocent observer in his crisp white coat. "It was you I spoke with about coming out here, wasn't it?"

"Ma'am?" Dr. Hollerman said. "I didn't see *or speak* to you until you arrived."

Zolie listened to his voice, trying to remember if it really was him or another game he was playing.

"After I let you in to see Patty, I learned no one had heard from you and figured it was a ruse to get in to see her for that story you mentioned you were writing, Mrs. Vanderran, or should I say, Mrs. Kenowith? That was when I kept you locked in Patty's room—*after* I'd found out you'd been lying."

"I wasn't lying!" Zolie raised her voice.

Getting the last restraint untied, Dr. Sinardi lifted her hand to help her from the bed. "Come with me; this room is too dreary for you."

"I'm not going anywhere but home!" Zolie removed the blankets from her body. "And I'm taking Stevie Galloway with me."

Just hearing his father's prized patient's name on the speaker sent excitement throughout Dr. Todd as he eyed the beautiful woman on the screen.

"Yes, of course, Ms. Galloway will accompany you home," Dr. Sinardi lied through his smile. "But there are some *things* you need to know about Patty and why you're still here."

Zolie didn't quite know what to make of the strange statement, and she watched the well-dressed physician turn his head to that prick who must've drugged her with a look of scorn on his face.

"Dr. Hollerman! You'll report to my office at once and wait for me until I've returned," Sinardi barked, raising his deep voice over a buzzing sound. He then pulled out his pager and read a message just sent to him: *I'm coming in.* Noticing Zolie's odd look at his ancient device, he held it up. "Bad reception in this place. Now I have another patient to tend to right after we're finished," he lied kindly to Zolie, putting his pager away.

She noticed Dr. Hollerman's uneasy look.

"You," Dr. Sinardi said in a louder voice to the younger doctor. "You really messed up here, and I'd suggest praying I don't fire you." He teased the fool for pure entertainment and to impress his newest guest.

Dr. Todd enjoyed pulling Sinardi's strings and smiled when he tapped the monitor screen over Dr. J-Hole's face with his large finger. "That may be for show in there, fucker, but wait until you see what *I* have in store for you." His smile turned to a smirk as he remembered bashing Jonathan's legs with the sledgehammer.

As Dr. Sinardi helped Zolie from the bed, she watched Hollerman drop his head as a third man entered her room.

"What is going on in here?" came the deep and authoritative voice.

Just as Zolie's feet touched the ground, both men turned to see the distinguished and handsome man enter the room. His white coat seemed like one of a doctor who had been busy helping his patients, not starched like that Hollerman ass carrying his air of superiority like he was playing a doctor on TV.

"Dr. Vreeland," Dr. Sinardi said, full of surprise, just like they had planned before entering her room.

"This woman is not a patient! Why is she here?" he demanded.

Zolie's heart filled with hope as she watched the powerful man the hospital was named after move to her side.

"I've got this covered, sir," Sinardi said.

"You're just covering your ass!" Vreeland barked as he took Zolie's hand. "I'm Dr. Todd Vreeland, madam. I just now learned of this, and you have my apologies for all of it," he said, raising his voice and turning his head to the others in disgust.

"Bad move, gentlemen, bad move," he said, looking at the men. "Well?"

Dr. Hollerman sighed. "Sir, it was believed she lied to gain access to—"

"I read the report! Do you think I'm stupid?" Dr. Todd barked, interrupting him. "This makes me sad, gentlemen, and when you make me sad by not doing what I expect, horrible things happen." His thoughts turned to how much more he was going to enjoy murdering Hollerman.

Zolie watched both Sinardi and Hollerman flinch at his words.

"I want to leave; I want to go home now," Zolie said to the kind stranger as she lost her balance getting up and fell into the doctor's arms.

"As soon as you're strong enough, and if that's not soon enough, I'll drive you myself," Dr. Todd said like the hero from a fairy tale. "I can't wait for you to see the beautiful room you *should've* woken up in, a room I'd like you to use to recover until you're ready to go home," Dr. Todd continued, helping the still slightly drugged Mrs. Vanderran from that dark and hideous room.

"Wait—we need to get Stevie," Zolie said.

"Stevie? Who is this Stevie?" Dr. Todd's kind face glared at the men.

"Sir, she's Patty Galloway's sister," Dr. Hollerman replied. "She arrived with Mrs. Vanderran."

Zolie saw Dr. Todd Vreeland's eyes close and anger fill his face, and when he opened his eyes, he seemed to have calmly arrived at the response, as harsh as it was.

"You've confined *another* innocent visitor? That wasn't in the report. Thank God, I've come back to *my* hospital when I did. Someone's getting fired for this."

Both men lowered their heads.

"Please accept my apologies for all of this, and yes, of course Stevie will be joining you," Dr. Todd said, slightly flirting with her. "You there," he said to Kumar, still standing at attention. "Take a tray to the *other* Ms. Galloway and tell her she'll be joining Mrs. Vanderran soon."

Zolie felt Dr. Todd's strength as he helped her toward the door, passing the other two doctors.

"Sinardi, I want you and Hollerman in my office now!"

Dr. Hollerman smirked, feeling the weight of Vreeland's words, even though they were acting, but when Dr. Todd saw him, his words were swift.

"You think this is a game, Hollerman?"

The look on Todd's face told Hollerman otherwise, causing him to rethink the situation as Vreeland left the room with Zolie.

Moving outside, Zolie saw the second breakfast cart waiting to be delivered to the room next to hers, where she believed Stevie had called to her from. She was then led past the elevators with the newly "Out of Order During Construction" sign posted in front of it, to the grand staircase that ran up to the sixth floor of the building, and she had a moment of relief, feeling that *something* awful had been corrected by the handsome man leading her down the stairs, away from the nightmare she'd just endured, to safety.

As they turned on the landing to the fifth floor, the mood of the building changed dramatically. Gone were the dark and ugly walls that spoke of untold horrific nightmares; now brightly papered and freshly painted corridors resembled the finest hotels. Zolie even felt herself sigh in relief as she marveled at the beauty of it.

They turned back in the same direction they'd come, and she realized they were one floor down from exactly where she'd been bound up in a bed. *Terrifying for someone to know what was above them, should the patients on this floor ever find out,* she thought. She was then led to the last door on the left like when they first arrived with Dr. Hollerman upstairs, and when they stopped, she realized she was directly under Patty Galloway's room when Dr. Todd opened the door to the magnificent suite.

The first thing she noticed was there was no lock on the door, and a sense of safety swept through her. The room was beautiful and well lit, and the two king-sized beds looked like a pair of dream beds sitting next to each other with the separation curtain pulled back and tied between the matching night tables. There was a seventy-inch flat-screen TV on the wall, which was set on the menu provided by the hospital, like the finest hotels she'd stayed in showing her the finest of selections.

"My apologies again, Mrs. Vanderran, please select anything you'd like for both you and Ms. Stevie Galloway to be brought right up," Dr. Todd said as Zolie swooned again and nearly lost her balance. Feeling the man's strong arms hold her up, he guided her to the edge of the bed, and she leaned back on the pillows, feeling the room start to spin a bit. He then moved across the room as the amazing foods were appearing on the TV screen and slid open the door of a large closet.

"Please, should you require anything here, it's yours for the taking," he said as she saw the beautiful clothes hanging within. "I'm sure you and the Galloway woman will find *something* here," he said with a magician's smile.

"Wait. Where's my bag?" Zolie realized she hadn't seen it.

"Bag?" Dr. Todd was confused. "I'll find it and bring it to you."

Zolie was dumbstruck. *What is happening?* she thought as she surveyed the room. And when she turned away from the beautiful decor to stare at the doctor, he was closing the door that shut with ease and without any foreboding locking sounds.

Wanting to leave, she sat up on the bed, but the drugs were still in her system, and in response to the spinning of the room, she leaned against the many pillows and clutched one to her chest.

CHAPTER 91

D r. Todd stopped a few feet from her room, feeling the anger fill his mind to a bursting point. Harnessing his anger brought upon by the incompetent imbeciles running his hospital, he spun completely around, glancing at her door and back to the stairs, rolling his eyes to almost shutting them and bringing his fists to his chest and wrapping one over the other as he went into his thoughts. His fingers moved slightly, and his eyelids twitched as he formed his plan, and when he opened his eyes, he rushed back to the stairs and climbed up to the dreaded sixth floor.

Quietly he looked down the hall to see Kumar exiting Stevie's room and move down the hall, stopping to pick up another discarded breakfast cart. He then watched him go to the service area where the employee elevator was, near the single operating room. Entering behind him, he saw Kumar clear the trays from the cart and place it all in the dumbwaiter located on the far side of the employee elevator. He looked around and saw the familiar space he'd spent so much of his life in, and the bitterness of what his life could have been added to his anger. He noticed they still used the operating room when he saw the blood on the floor and a mop bucket alone in the room waiting for someone to return to clean it up. His anger then shifted from the seemingly countless losses of his life as he zeroed in on the pompous idiot who had disrespected him in his own damn hospital. Picking up the blood and tissue-covered drill from a dirty case cart near the elevator, he advanced on his victim.

"About that tetanus shot, you little bitch," Dr. Todd said, holding the drill behind his white coat.

Kumar spun around, and Dr. Todd's large hand was on his throat, pushing him back against the cart, knocking dishes to the floor, to finally pin him against the wall.

"Fuck with me in my home, and this is what you get!"

Kumar gagged and began to choke as Dr. Todd pulled his other hand from behind him and pointed the nasty blood-soaked, tissue-covered drill bit in his face.

"Say, ah," Dr. Todd said, squeezing the trigger.

Kumar screamed and tilted his head back as he struggled under Todd's strength, but the doctor rammed the filthy drill into his open mouth, pushing with all his might. The drill's battery pack started to smoke from the pressure Todd was placing on the device when the drill bit bore through the top of his mouth and broke through the back of Kumar's skull and into the softer wood of the wall, and his flailing arms fell to his side.

Kumar's shaking body convulsed, and his arms twitched like a puppet, and Dr. Todd stood back to admire his work. A wave of adrenaline shot through his body, and for the first time, he felt like he was home, *and it felt good.*

Eyeing the operating room, he wandered through the open doors to see his favorite place in the hospital. Outside of the slight remodel, everything seemed to be as it had been when he'd left, everything except for the old broken elevator shaft that'd come in so handy for discarding the dead over so many years. Shelves now stood where the old elevator had once been, and the wall paneling behind them looked cheap.

Moving over to them, Dr. Todd passed the surgical viewing room, which had been remodeled into an office where it looked like research was done. Medical journals filled the shelves behind a large desk, and there, the majestic golden hue from the light hitting the bottles of tequila caught his eyes, bringing a smile to his face as he grabbed on to one of the shelves in front of the elevator shaft and moved it away from the wall; then he knocked on the structure behind it and grinned, hearing the hollowness echo back at him. He quickly moved the other shelf, then stood and looked about the soul-less room and lifted his foot, kicking in the wall. The cheap paneling broke away, falling into the dark depths within the hospital. And he knew it would be hungry.

"Dooo-be-dooo-be-doo-doo," Todd sang to himself with a smile while grabbing a nearby gurney, hearing the wheels squeak like they had when that asshole Bob the X-ray tech used to annoy him turned his smile to a sneer. He wheeled it over to where Kumar was still hanging on the wall, dangling from the drill, like his brother's draw-ings he'd hang in his room. "Fuck!" Dr. Todd yelled, thinking of the constant reminders of annoying assholes in his life. Between his hatred of his brother Blake, Bob, and the fat idiot who had eaten his patient's food, he was going to have a blast murdering Dr. J-Hole Hollerman. Just seeing the dead man in front of him brought back so many mixed feelings of his past, and he smiled. He then shoved the end of the gurney next to his latest victim and grabbed his ankles, lifting them up until he could slide the gurney underneath him.

"Come on, darling," Dr. Todd teased as he tugged on Kumar's legs, rocking him slightly and then pulling as hard as he could, hear-ing his skull crack and his brains splatter up against the wall as his body hit the gurney, leaving a portion of his skull still attached to the wall, his brains dripping down the once-pristine paint.

Wheeling the gurney to the pit, Todd stopped and looked into the darkness of it.

"I'm home, Sire," Dr. Todd said as his face lit up like a Christmas tree.

He then grabbed Kumar by his shins and pushed him headfirst into the pit. The thumping sounds of his body hitting God knew what reminded him of his vague memories from the last night he'd seen Blake in this very room.

It angered him that the blackout he'd had after the deed was done kept him from recalling all the details he thought he remem-bered. The problem he'd been having were the nightmares he'd had from that night, and finding Lorena dead seemed to merge with what he was doing that wonderful night when he'd sent his muti-lated asshole brother careening down the shaft.

Good thing I'm not wasted tonight though! It'll be fun to recall murdering Sinardi and this asshole he thought as he kicked over the mop bucket spilling the contents across the floor as he left the room.

CHAPTER 92

Mingyu Yunt applied more makeup to her bruised face and wiped the last of the blood away from where it'd started bleeding again after she'd gotten away from the ski lodge. Grabbing a fresh tissue next to the discarded bloodied ones, she dabbed under her neck and held it there, moving away from the bathroom mirror. She was in her negligee, and she saw a few blood drops on her pillow.

"She really gave it to you, didn't she?" the naked man in her bed said as he pulled the covers away and got up, grabbing his robe.

"The bitch had fight in her," Mingyu said, putting her own robe on.

"We don't have much time," the consultant and assassin of Parnell F. Bancroft said, tying his robe and moving to the room-service cart to pour a cup of coffee.

"Relax, Hermann—we'll be fine."

Hermann Stangl turned his head toward her as he placed the coffeepot back on the cart. "You got sloppy, and we can't risk any further embarrassment," he said, picking up his cup.

Mingyu knew he was right, and she also knew retribution would be swift if this wasn't handled in just the right way. Moving to him, she untied his robe and hugged his bare chest. As she looked up at him, she smiled. "We have just a little bit more time, don't we?" she practically purred as she lowered to her knees in front of him.

Hermann Stangl took a sip from his cup and closed his eyes as a smile crossed his face. "You give good coffee, Mingyu," he said as he lowered his cup to the table and placed his hands on the back of her head. "I'll give you that."

Outside the hotel, the car that had followed them downstate from the ski lodge was parked, and the agent inside was looking at some photographs on his laptop. His camera was on the seat by his binoculars as he paged through the photos he'd taken of the suspects coming back to their SUV. They had come to collect the few things they had bought at a shop down the street and entered back into the hotel. He looked at one of the photos he'd taken, and his mind flashed to that moment when the male suspect had paused and seemed to scan the area, as if counting the cars parked there and keeping that data in his head.

He then clicked on the file minimized at the bottom of his screen, it was the photo showing the partial view of the man Agent Robert Forrester had sent to Thrasher and his team. It was a match, and the agent reached for his binoculars and lifted them up to look at their window.

CHAPTER 93

Maura joined Logan in her sister's office as he was looking through the notes piled on it. She glanced back at Roman, who was clutching a pillow from the sofa, and turned back to her husband. "What are you looking for exactly?"

"Anything that can tell us where she is."

"I've looked through all this! How can you think I hadn't?" She was slightly annoyed.

Her tone was a reminder of their lives lately, and he stopped what he was doing. "Maura, I'm not in the mood for any of it. Now think: What was she talking about? Where in her new book was she? Did she even say?"

"No, that's just it. She didn't say a word to me—only that she was leaving to work on the book. It's a thriller she's working on this time, though," she said, watching Logan turn to check the credenza. To his right was the bag she'd used when they'd gone to get Sam. *Zolie must have switched bags,* she thought, moving toward it and picking it up.

Rummaging inside, she found a crumpled-up credit card receipt. Pulling it out and placing the purse down, she opened it and read it out loud. "The Holiday Inn?"

Logan turned to her. "Let me see that," he said, reaching out for the receipt.

Instinctively she handed it to him and watched him move to Zolie's computer, which was on a table near the window. He hit the mouse to wake up the monitor. Within moments he had typed in the hotel's address and clicked on the map view.

"That's near the hospital Patty Galloway was taken to," came Roman's voice.

Both Logan and Maura turned away from the computer to see him standing in the doorway. His eyes were red, and he looked like a broken man who was attempting with all his might to wake up from a nightmare.

"That hotel is next to a restaurant Ed and I ate in after viewing the hospital our little psycho friend was committed to." Roman almost sounded a bit like his old self. "Why are you looking at that?"

"Why would Zolie have that receipt in her purse?" Maura asked, pulling the clue from Logan's hand and picking up Zolie's landline in her office and punching in the number.

"Yes, I'd like Mrs. Vanderran's room please," Maura said to the woman who answered at the other end. Pausing, she looked at the Savage brothers as she waited for the call to be transferred. She listened to it ring and ring before coming back to the front desk.

"I'm sorry; they're not answering," came a man's voice.

"Can you have my sister phone me the minute she gets back?"

"Yes, of course, I'll give Ms. Galloway the message," he told her.

"Galloway?" Maura said, frightened and confused, causing both men to take steps closer to her.

"Yes, ma'am, Ms. Stevie Galloway—that's your sister? Right?"

"No, my sister is Zolie Vanderran. Is she there, too?"

"Hang on a moment please," the man said.

Maura could barely hear him speaking to the woman who had first answered, and then she was on the line.

"This is Mary. I'm the front desk manager. May I help you?"

"My name is Maura Vanderran. I'm holding the credit card receipt from my sister, who checked in to your hotel, and I was just told Stevie Galloway is in the same room."

"I'm sorry; we're not supposed to give out that information, but since you already know, yes, the room has both their names on it, ma'am."

"And neither of them is there?"

"They're not answering. I can leave a message."

"Have Zolie Vanderran call me the minute she returns."

"Is the number on my caller ID a good number to reach you at?"

"Yes." Maura slammed down the phone. "The hotel room is empty. What in bloody hell is she doing there with *that woman?*"

"She's at the hospital to see that crazy bitch who tried to kill our family," Logan said, moving toward Roman.

"And her sister, Stevie, is with her." Maura shoved the hotel receipt in the pocket of the slacks she was wearing. "Come on—nothing good can come of this."

Roman watched the two of them leave Zolie's office and followed behind them to the front door. "You got this, little brother. I'll call Ed and let him know what you're doing. I need to be here when the kids get home."

"Oh, Roman...I'm so sorry," Logan said, wishing he could take the pain away.

CHAPTER 94

The helicopter took off behind them as Ed and Thrasher ran to a waiting car and quickly got in to see Agent Robert Forrester sitting inside the limousine waiting for them.

"Robert, good to see you," Thrasher said, getting in first.

"Wes, it's been too long, buddy," Forrester said. "Hello, Ed."

Ed nodded. "Robert, I'm glad you're here. What do you got?"

"Amateurs," Robert said, handing them surveillance photos.

Ed and Thrasher looked at the first one of a single man carrying takeout with three cups of coffees from a diner. The next showed an old pickup truck with paint marks on the back panels that matched the colors of the girls' bikes, which Ed spotted immediately, tapping them with his finger as he showed it to Thrasher.

Agent Forrester was nodding. "Ed, these guys gave it a shot, but we're better. Meet Lenny McCoy; I'd say he's the tagalong in this one."

"Why do you say that?" Ed asked.

"Because the other one, this Joe Pesci–looking fellow, Lou Sabello, he's the one making the ransom calls."

"How'd you find them so quick?" Thrasher asked, handing the photos back to him.

"That business card you found was really all we needed," he said, addressing Ed. "The ransom call had enough clues in it to narrow it down, and when I added in the information from Lenny McCoy from their handyman service card, it was only a matter of time before we spotted the truck."

"Have you spotted the girls?" Ed asked as Forrester's cell phone started to ring.

"Tailed him from a café with takeout. We've got thermal imaging on one of the tugboats," Forrester said before answering his phone. "Forrester."

Ed and Thrasher watched him intently as he spoke on the phone.

"Really! That's great. Send it right over," Forrester said, hanging up. "Seems our luck is changing," Forrester continued as he opened his laptop on the seat next to him.

Quietly they watched him find the e-mail he was looking for and smile. "Gentlemen, meet Parnell F. Bancroft's assassin and Gabby's murderer," he said, turning the laptop screen for them to see.

The photograph was of a man next to a white Tahoe parked at a hotel, and the woman with him had long black hair and was clearly of Asian descent.

"That's her!" Ed practically yelled. "That's the woman who worked with my father, and she killed Gabby!"

"The man is the one who was at the hotel, and he's the one who killed Parnell—I'm sure of it. He also looks like the partial photo we sent out—but who is this woman?" Forrester said point blank.

"Take your pick," Ed said. "Mingyu Yunt for starters! Along with several other aliases, like Meiling...something. Tallulah has the dossier. Anyway, she was with my father before his death; his secretary told me about her. But what's this guy's story?" Ed said, looking at the man on the screen.

Forrester turned the computer back to him and scanned his e-mail. "Facial recognition identified him as Hermann Stangl. He's the assassin I've been chasing for the last decade. He likes to use other names, names of his own victims—usually the first of one and the last of another as his own version of dead man's Scrabble, I guess, only I hadn't been able to trace him to your father and Parnell until now, with this Asian woman." Forrester closed the laptop. "But using Noah's name from the mountains—that's new to him unless one of his other victims is named Noah."

"And this ties in with the missing *Manchester* and its payload of warheads because the house near the ski lodge, the one leased to this Mingyu whoever she is, was confirmed a short while ago as the location of the twenty-million-dollar buy for the warhead," Thrasher said. "It was absolutely traced to that house."

"So the kidnapping of the girls is unrelated to the *Manchester*," Ed said. "The only similarity is that the location they were taken is also near where the traced call was made."

"Yes, Ed, we're confident in that," Forrester said.

"So what's our plan?" Thrasher asked.

"Get my girls free—then deal with that Asian witch who killed Gabby." Ed's phone alerted him of a text message. Leaning back in the seat, Ed dug in his pocket for his phone.

CHAPTER 95

Pacing back and forth near the window of the Hyannis Ferry Terminal, Marlo Savage was preoccupied with her own thoughts and had disengaged from the other women in the cast. Their flight had been diverted to Hyannis due to fog, and the ferry for Martha's Vineyard was leaving soon. She eyed the departure times, noticing the ferry to Nantucket, where her family had a lovely home—a home she now wished she could run to and hide.

For her and the cast, the day had started way before the sun had risen, when they'd taken a private flight to Massachusetts. The filming schedule was daunting because Marilyn Hart had arranged that damn self-serving luncheon where she was receiving an award on the island and wanted it filmed for the show.

Marlo thought back to all of Ed's traveling, which was the downside of the business, but the puzzle in her head that was building was something she hadn't seen coming.

Finding a window seat away from the others, she opened her briefcase and pulled out the documents inside. Paging through them she saw the contract to *Tycoon Wives*, the dossiers Randall had given her on each of her costars, and finally the divorce papers she'd filed against Ed.

Bringing them to the top of the stack, she looked at the documents as her mind pieced together the ugly puzzle she'd stumbled onto. She felt like a fool yet guilty at the same time for everything that had happened since the mountains and being raped by those two men. Her breakthrough had come too late, she thought, but when she'd gone to Ed, *then* he'd fixed everything like he always did. But in her mind *now*, it had been too late, and he didn't tell her.

The pain she was feeling in her mind was nothing to the sharp pain she felt in her stomach. *Is it the baby or stress?* she thought as she dropped the papers on the seat next to her briefcase and rubbed her belly. Stretching her legs out, she felt the pain subside as she played back the first piece of the puzzle building in her mind.

She only knew (thought?) it was Ed when that woman had said, "Don't tell anyone." Those were the words Aisha Thomas had said to her at her doctor's appointment. Then she had seen that pregnant woman on the train lumber by her to her seat.

Marlo glanced out the window at the ferry to Martha's Vineyard as the thoughts in her head continued, the thoughts of seeing Ed catch Aisha, saving her from falling off the ladder in the kitchen at the Vander Place Hotel that awful night after the boat crash. Yes, her suspicion had been piqued that day, but not like it was now.

Is it all in my mind? she wondered as someone came through an exit near her, sending the cold breeze across her flesh, chilling her, like the cold feeling she had building in her heart.

Alone and away from the family and finally pursuing her own dream of the career she'd missed so much, she recalled how cruel she'd been to Ed and how she had suppressed the rape as she lashed out, letting the guilt creep in. But when they got Lisa back, when she'd finally realized the truth and they had come back together, that had been the time for everything to be let go, she thought.

He was keeping this from me, her mind teased as it found the last piece of the puzzle. She nearly knocked her briefcase from the chair to the floor as she remembered her own son Tucker, asking her about Dad being nervous about meeting his son with Jillian—and the fact he'd been talking to Aisha Thomas on the phone when he had heard it.

Her mind froze, and she didn't recall her movements when she pulled her cell phone and sent the simplest and meanest text message she could to her husband.

CHAPTER 96

*T*hat baby Aisha Thomas...

These were the first words Ed Savage saw of the text when he looked at his phone, and his blood froze in his veins. He hesitated to open the message, and when he did, he visibly cringed in the back of the limousine.

That baby Aisha Thomas is carrying is yours, you bastard!

"Not now!" Ed cried out as the color in his face vanished, and both Robert Forrester and Wes Thrasher were startled when they saw it.

"Ed, what is it?" Thrasher asked.

Ed looked from his phone to the men, who were both concerned as he stuffed his phone in his pocket.

"I fucked up! I fucked up big time, guys," Ed said as the heat of embarrassment washed over him, and he put down his window, letting the cold breeze hit his face.

Both men looked to each other as an awkward silence fell in the car.

"I knew I should have told her," Ed finally blurted out as he looked back to the men. "Guys, I screwed up back when I thought my marriage with Marlo was over, and I—"

"Stop." Thrasher put his hand on his friend's shoulder.

"No, I need to get this out," Ed said. "I just want it out."

Thrasher could see his friend hurting and fought back his secret from the night of the fire, a secret Forrester knew all about.

"I slept with Aisha Thomas after getting those damned divorce papers from Marlo." Ed hit the button to close the window. "Goddamn secrets! Damn it, why didn't I tell her?"

Forrester glanced at Thrasher, and when Wes eyed him back, the two friends' thoughts were on the secret Wes had shared with him.

"How did she find out?" Ed continued as he turned his head and caught the strange look being passed between his friends. "She's in New York filming that damn TV show."

The sound of Forrester's phone ringing was a relief to all of them, and he quickly answered.

Ed wondered what that exchange was about and silently questioned the men he was riding with.

"Forrester," the agent answered. "What do you have?"

"Where are you? We have the money, and we're ready to make the ransom drop," Tallulah said.

Forrester looked out the window to gauge their location. "We should be on the water in approximately thirty minutes."

"Thermal imaging still has the girls in the same spot."

"We'll get them," Forrester vowed.

"Call me when you're in sight," Tallulah said, hanging up.

Forrester put his phone in his pocket, pulled his gun, and checked it. "They're ready with the money drop, and thermal has the girls in the same location," he repeated as the limousine sped down the road.

"Come on, let's just get there already!" Ed said, pushing the thoughts of his marriage away and putting a laser focus on saving the girls, a trait he'd learned many years ago when training at the British Intelligence Agency.

CHAPTER 97

A rriving at Vreeland Hills Sanatorium, Maura placed her bag on the floor in the back seat when Logan stopped and parked his vehicle. Getting out from the Cadillac Escalade, they stood looking up at the foreboding buildings, and the tension was palpable, and when Maura yelled out, pointing toward Zolie's Rolls-Royce parked beyond the glass atrium overhead, the fear spiked in both of them.

They rushed to it and looked inside to see everything intact, yet an uneasy feeling settled within them.

"Come on," Logan said as he moved back toward the entrance. Opening the door in the West Tower, they were surprised the place seemed empty, which was strange since security had always been present.

"Where is everyone?" Maura asked, eyeing the vast, empty entryway and the construction just beyond the area. "Maybe we need to go in the other building."

"No, this is it," Logan said. "Ed and I came here to make sure Patty would be secure, and this was where we came in. We were shown the sky bridge leading to Patty's room in the other building." He moved farther inside. "Here!" He pointed to the sign that read: "Closed to the public while under construction." It was staked into a terra-cotta planter where several dead plants had been pulled out from the pots and thrown on large plastic tarps. He moved farther along the lobby and looked to the far back of the building where the grand staircase began its ascent up the massive building's interior. "Hang on a minute," he called back. He then hurried to the stairs and looked up its winding first flight, which curved to the front of the building and it was blocked off with yellow construction tape that draped across the entrance to the stairs. Lifting the tape he moved underneath it and went partly up to see beyond on the first landing, there he saw several more empty terra-cotta pots and spilled dirt on the steps. Rushing back down the stairs and moving back to Maura's side, he then spotted the reception counter and the plastic clock with the movable arms telling him whoever was on duty would be back in an hour.

Maura moved behind the counter and began looking through a directory, and he joined her picking up the phone when Maura looked up and noticed another sign behind him: "Holiday staffing is in effect during construction."

"There's no one here," she said, motioning to the sign.

Logan looked at the sign and hung up the phone.

"Now where?" Maura asked. "Do you know where Patty's room is?"

"She's somewhere on the sixth floor," he said, looking toward the elevators.

Logan reached them first and pushed the button, watching the car's doors that'd been sitting there open in front of them. Getting in, he pushed the top floor, but the button would not stay illuminated. "So much for taking the sixth floor sky bridge."

"Are these things working?" Maura asked, slightly worried.

Eyeing the key panel, Logan pushed the third floor, and the light stayed illuminated, and the doors started to close. He then hit the fifth and fourth-floor buttons and saw they would not illuminate as the doors sealed them inside. "Looks like some of the floors are locked."

The elevator rose slowly, and the fear of the place crept into their souls as they arrived at the third floor.

Stepping out onto the lonely corridor, they saw the sign on the far wall telling them the directions to the stairs and the third floor sky bridge to the East Tower.

"Hello?" Logan shouted, but no reply came.

"I don't like this," Maura mumbled, staying close behind him.

"Neither do I." Logan pulled out his cell to text Ed but saw he only had one bar of service. "The service in here is shitty," he continued, thinking of the missing girls.

"Nothing," Maura said, looking up from her nonfunctional phone. "Maybe the signal's better at the sky bridge."

"Yep, two bars now," Logan said as they moved toward it.

"Hey, I just got full service," Maura said as Logan opened the doors to the sky bridge. Entering the battered walkway high above the glass atrium, Maura paused a moment and sent Ed a text message: *Any news on the girls?* Accidentally hitting send, she sent another: *At Vreeland Hills Sanatorium with Logan. Did you know Zolie was here with Stevie Galloway? Call me.*

Looking up and seeing Logan several feet in front of her and noticing the haunting place they were in, she felt the panic creep toward her like a spider moving toward its prey. "Hold up, Logan!" she said, putting her phone in her pocket as she hurried to catch up with him.

On the far side of the sky bridge, Logan opened the doors, and they entered the foyer. The hallway ran in both directions, and they had to make a choice.

"Which way?" Maura asked, not seeing a directory and really wanting to turn around and leave in the poorly lit area.

"I'm not sure. Maybe we missed a sign in the sky bridge," Logan said, turning back to watch the doors they'd just come through slam shut behind them. The loud noise made them both jump, and Logan grabbed at the door to find it now locked. The spider was creeping closer in Maura's mind, and her heart dropped as she lunged toward the doors to help him. With a last effort, they let go, and the echoing of the doors banging against the lock faded to a cold silence.

"You're not supposed to be in here," a voice came from behind them, scaring them to their very core.

Turning, they saw a young nurse moving toward them up the hall.

"Thank God," Maura said. "The door locked behind us, and we got trapped."

"Trapped?" the nurse said in amusement.

"'Scared' would be the better word," Logan said. "We're locked in."

"Hardly." The nurse smiled back at them. "The doors lock on this side for extra security, but you're not the first to get scared."

"So the sky bridge doors just slam shut on their own?" Logan clarified.

"Oh no, sir, all the electronic doors on the third floor do. Must be the old wiring." She broke into a smile. "Or all those old ghosts that supposedly haunt the place!"

Maura eyed the woman's badge. "Thank you, Kayla Bennet. Now can you take me to my sister, Zolie Vanderran? She's here, and I need to see her at once."

"I'm sorry; I'm not familiar with that patient."

"She's not a patient! She's here visiting one," Maura assumed. "Patty Galloway—she's here visiting Patty Galloway."

Kayla Bennet knew *that patient* and also knew trouble came when anyone had anything to do with her.

"Can you take us?" Maura asked.

"I can lead you to her nurses' station. I'm not allowed on the sixth floor," she said, slightly nervous.

"Then lead on," Maura said, happy that finally they would be getting some answers.

Following her to the rear of the building where the grand staircase of the East Tower rose from the third floor, they saw the sign for the temporary closure of those elevators near it for maintenance and another telling them the sixth floor was the psych ward. Moving up the stairs, they paused, realizing the nurse wasn't following them.

"Are you coming?" Logan asked.

"No, sir, I'm not allowed above the third floor. But when you get to the fourth, you'll need to stop and ask to be taken to the sixth," she instructed.

Logan glanced at Maura, and they looked up the brightly lit stairs. Its cheeriness lifted the dreariness they'd felt moments ago, and they heard people upstairs. "Thank you, Kayla; we've got it from here," Logan said.

Moving up the stairs, they got to the landing and turned, looking back down to see that Kayla was gone. They then moved up the second flight to the fourth floor. There they saw a nurses' station, and down the hall they could see an orderly pushing a patient into a room in a wheelchair.

The relief hit them both as they approached the station. "Hello," Logan said. "Can you tell me where I can find my sister-in-law? She's here visiting a patient, and we've lost track of her."

"Sir, there are no visitors here now. We're closed to the public for a few days for the construction downstairs," the nurse behind the counter said.

"She was here yesterday, and she hasn't left," Maura said. "Her car is still here."

"She might be in one of the guest suites up on the fifth floor. You're welcome to go take a look, but let me call first and tell them you're coming. Like I said, we're closed, and we have a skeleton crew today."

Maura and Logan watched her grab the phone and enter an extension. Her call was answered quickly.

"Hello, this is Gwen from Four East. Do you have any guests staying up there?" She paused and covered the phone. "I'm sorry; I didn't get the name."

"Zolie Vanderran," Maura said.

The nurse repeated the name and paused to listen. When she did, she smiled. "Thank you. I'll send them right up."

"She's here. Take the stairs behind you up one floor, and check in at the station; they're waiting for you."

"Thank you," Maura said, returning the smile as she looked to Logan.

Together they went back to the stairs, and at the second flight past the landing, the fresh paint and beautiful wallpaper eased them even more as they reached the fifth floor.

The floor was like a hotel, brightly lit and elegantly appointed, and was a complete surprise to both of them.

As they moved farther down the hall, looking for any kind of reception desk, Dr. Sinardi came around a counter along the wall from a recessed reception area. The phone call of the unplanned guests had caught him completely off guard, and he knew he couldn't let any of them leave.

"Hello. Can I help you?"

Turning quickly, Maura smiled. "Yes, my sister, Zolie Vanderran, is here, and I'd like to see her. The nurse downstairs told us to come right up."

"Ah, the English lady, yes, she's down at the end on the left," he said with a smile. "Go on; I'm sure she'd like your company." The doctor kept moving to a chart stand on the wall. Grabbing one and opening it, and looked to them. "Is there anything else?"

Logan and Maura looked to each other in wonder and shook their heads.

"Have a great day," the doctor said as he moved away from them with the chart.

"This is weird," Logan whispered. "Maura?" He turned to see her moving down the hall to her sister's room.

Maura stopped at the door, and as she raised her hand to knock, she paused just as Logan arrived next to her. When she knocked, Logan pushed it completely open.

There on one of the two large beds was Zolie; her breathing was labored, and she was clutching a pillow.

"Zolie!" Maura screamed, and she rushed to her sister. "Zolie, what in bloody hell is going on? You had me worried half to death," she said, noticing the condition of her sister. "What's wrong with you?"

"Thank God you're here," Zolie finally said. "I've been drugged, and I feel weak, and I want to get the hell out of here."

"Drugged? What do you mean?" Logan asked.

Catching her breath, Zolie continued, "Stevie and I came here yesterday. We were served some drinks before we saw Patty; then I woke up in an atrocious room upstairs not far from where Patty is."

"You came here with that Galloway woman's sister?" Maura asked. "Why?"

Zolie nodded. "For answers. They were supposed to bring her down here to join me, but they haven't, and I'm terrified to know what they've done with her."

The sound of electric equipment resounded within the walls around them, and they watched the door to the room swing shut with a solid bang.

Logan rushed to the door and pulled on it, but it wouldn't budge.

Seeing him try to open it, Zolie's jaw dropped. "But…there are no locks on the door. I saw that clearly when I came in here."

"Magnetic," Logan said, feeling along the metal edge of the door. "Help me up."

Getting up in a sitting position, Zolie reached for the phone on the night table and found it to be dead. "Logan? What's happening," Zolie said. Remembering the similar experience at Chance's home near her hotel, she dropped the phone back down.

Maura pulled her phone from her pocket to find no reception. "Logan, try your phone," she said moving toward the thick glass of the window. Watching him pull his phone and shake his head, she tried getting a signal as he rushed next to her with his phone. Together they saw their useless phones in their hands and turned back to Zolie, realizing they'd been duped.

CHAPTER 98

T he agents moved like stealth fighters outside the hotel that the suspects from the ski lodge had been tracked to. They were so good at their job that not even the guests had a clue of their presence. Behind the hotel at a strip mall, the agents filled the parking lot and descended on the property like fleas to a hound hiding inside—getting ready for possibly one of the most dangerous targets in recent memory.

A clear and very present danger was directed at the United States of America, and the men outside the hotel knew that failure was not an option.

Upstairs, the uneasiness filled the room, and the one thing Hermann Stangl knew was to trust his instinct. He looked to the window from the table he was at, and that gut feeling that always kept him in front of the law was gnawing at him in a way he'd never felt before. Placing his phone on the table next to his laptop, he rose and went to the window, scanning the area. He saw the white Tahoe parked where they'd left it and looked at the cars parked around them. He quickly counted the cars, a habit he'd picked up in his early days when he staked out a hit—seventeen, exactly the same as when they'd gone to get their things. But that gnawing feeling continued to grow. *It's nothing—probably just spooked due to that careless bitch*, he thought, moving toward his computer on the table.

Hermann took another glance out the window before going around the table to look at the screen. "She's right on target," he told himself with a smile when the sound of the window shattering caused him to practically jump out of his skin, knocking the table to the side and spinning the laptop around in the gunfire.

The men on suspension ropes came down feet first, breaking the glass as they crashed into the room.

Hermann reached for his gun and aimed, shooting at the men as he dived to the floor. The bullets sprayed the room as the sound of canisters being shot hit the wall and fell to the ground, releasing the thick smoke clouds within them.

The men shot back, and Hermann grabbed a semiautomatic placed around the corner in the room and stood, firing away. Bullets hit the computer screen flipping it over, and more destroyed its base. Hermann got hit more times than he shot; his body contorted as the bullets hit, with the last rounds spraying his face in a diagonal pattern, blowing off the upper portion of his head just when agents kicked in his door.

Mingyu had been downstairs before the attack. She'd worn a red wig and changed her makeup and was casing the place out preparing for an escape with her heavy bag, like she practiced each time she was in a new location. She was checking out the lower floors when she heard the bullets ring out above her. Reaching into her bag for her gun and eyeing a lone maid cart in the hallway near an open room door, she bolted down the hall and entered the room, pulling in the cart and slamming the door shut behind her. She locked the swing lock and grabbed a chair, propping it against the door.

"What's happening?" came the heavily accented voice behind her.

Mingyu looked to see the Jamaican maid standing there in absolute fear.

"A man!" Mingyu said in a horror-stricken voice. "I was just attacked!"

"I heard gunfire! I'm calling the police," the maid said as she turned to rush to the phone beside the bed.

"Oh great, here we go again," Mingyu whispered out loud as she dropped her bag and raced behind her, ripping the phone cord from the wall and strangling her with it. Feeling the life leave her heavyset body, she let the poor woman fall to the floor, her life taken from her in a moment when she thought she was being a heroine.

Leaving the fresh corpse, she moved to her bag and unzipped it, revealing a smaller briefcase inside, along with a blonde wig and a heavy coat. She then eyed the maid's clothes, but the sound of people in the hall outside the room told her she had no time. Putting on the coat and zipping up her bag, she threw it over her shoulder and went to the balcony; she then opened the sliding door, eyeing the tree branches not far from the ledge. In the distance she saw the movements in the strip mall across from the other side of the hotel and knew she didn't have much time as she leaped into the tree, grabbing the branches to break her fall as she tumbled to the ground.

Knowing the Tahoe was on the other side of the building and seeing an entrance, she hurried back inside the hotel and caught her breath and took off the red wig, dumping it in a garbage can and exchanging it for the blonde one as she slowly moved in the direction of the laundry room. There she had seen a door leading to where she knew the Tahoe was parked.

Upstairs, as the smoke was clearing when the agents rushed into the hotel room from the hall, they found four of their comrades had been shot; one was dead. The body of the assassin, Hermann Stangl, had fallen into a bullet-ridden table, split in two by his weight, his head partially blown away and his brains oozing out. The agents were aghast at seeing their dead friend but stayed on point and searched the spacious two-room suite.

"All clear," was called out over the radio, and they knew the room was free of danger. The outside agents stormed the building, leaving the parking lot unattended and giving Mingyu the moment she was waiting for.

Seeing her chance, she ran from the hotel in the blonde wig and heavy coat; she pulled the keys from her pants pocket and opened the Tahoe. Throwing the bag over her shoulder to the back seat she started the engine, shifted the vehicle into reverse, and backed out from the parking space.

The couple that had the room the maid was cleaning heard the commotion and ran to their room to hide. And when they saw the dead maid, the woman screamed, and the man called the front desk on his cell, not wanting to touch anything in the room.

"Woman down! Casualty," came the second announcement over the radio. "Downstairs, back side of building, room three twenty-two, looks like a hotel maid." The radio alerted the agents inside that the woman they were after was on the move.

Agents saw the SUV move, and as she turned from the lot, her tires squealed when they hit ice on the road, causing the Tahoe to fishtail. Regaining traction, she fastened her seat belt as she sped away from the hotel.

A swarm of men ran to their cars to pursue the Tahoe, and Mingyu knew she didn't have much time. Driving recklessly, a glare caught her vision in her rearview mirror, and as she looked to see what it was, the Tahoe hit another patch of black ice as it was nearing a curve. The giant SUV swerved, and Mingyu felt the steering wheel jerk in her hands as she looked back to the road. The vehicle was starting to slide, with the back wheels moving to the passenger side, and she jerked the wheel to the right to correct the slide, but in her panic she overcompensated, and the SUV hit a pothole, sending it toward the side of the road.

Seeing the wheel spin, she grabbed at it, trying to control it, but when she looked to the windshield, it was too late. The Tahoe hit the small inclined embankment on the passenger side and bounced back onto the road, crossing the lanes to the ravine on the other side. It smashed against a tree as it went over spinning, sending it down to land on its passenger side in a shallow stream below.

The glass exploded from all the windows, including the sun-roof—a violent sparkling shower that attacked her from all directions. The seat belt kept Mingyu alive and strapped in her seat, and when the movements stopped and she realized she wasn't hurt too badly, she looked to the back seat. The briefcase that'd been inside the bag had fallen out and was lodged against the passenger door, partly submerged in the water.

"No," she screamed as she unfastened her seat belt and fell into the seat next to her, feeling her shoulder and side get wet from the stream. She could hear the sound of sirens and knew she didn't have much time to finish her job. Moving in the broken glass and debris from the stream, she got up and climbed to the back seat and pulled the briefcase from the water. Pulling down one of the armrests and stuffing her bag under it, she made a makeshift level surface and placed the briefcase on top. She then put her ear to it and listened, opening it slowly.

Inside was a laptop attached to a heavy metal housing unit, and everything seemed intact. She lifted up the screen and tried entering the code; it sparked, burning her fingers. Trying it again, the keyboard panel popped up from the concealed lower section of the device, and the screen above flickered to life.

"It's down here," came a voice from above.

Mingyu looked up through the broken driver's side windows and could see movement in the wooded area above her. Quickly she read the second access code in the concealed compartment of the device and entered it, watching the screen change to a map of the East Coast on the right, and on the left, radar spun above the coordinates that were brought up below. She then clicked on the radar giving her the current location of the target.

She knew it was too soon, but she didn't have much time as she tried to figure out the new coordinates to send the warhead before the men arrived around the Tahoe.

Typing as fast as she could, her heart stopped when she heard the unmistakable sound of a gun clip. Looking up, Mingyu saw the gunman had his weapon pointed right at her. She slowly moved her left hand up from the keyboard and grinned, giving him the universal hand signal to fuck off.

"What the…" the gunman said as her right hand tapped in a code on the concealed keyboard, detonating the bomb held within the computer casing.

The explosion blew the vehicle from the water and into the trees, killing Mingyu and the men around and near the SUV. The men arriving at the top of the road were blown back against their cars in the blast.

Getting up, they looked down to see the fiery remains of the burning dead men and the SUV engulfed in flames.

CHAPTER 99

T he signal Mingyu sent from the briefcase made it to its destination on board a fishing boat up the coast anchored offshore in a bank of fog. The computers in the main area lit up with the signal, and the sound of hydraulics could be heard within the boat. A timer flashed and then began its countdown as the top of the bow opened, and a torpedo launcher was raised into the white, ghostly sky.

The countdown reached its end, and the torpedo was fired from the deck. It hit the water a few yards from the bow and was gone, leaving a small wake in its path. And as it made its way out to sea, a second timer started on the fishing boat, and in a matter of moments, it was blown from the water.

The vessel sank quickly, following its anchor to the bottom of the ocean.

CHAPTER 100

The top-of-the-line disguised military speedboat Ed Savage had boarded with fellow agents Wes Thrasher and Robert Forrester was decked out with a bank of computers running along the interior, like the president's *Marine One*. And when he saw the thermal imaging on a computer screen of his nieces on board one of those rusted relics, he saw red. Imagining his beautiful nieces locked in squalor and fearing the danger all around them, he wanted two things: his nieces' safety and those two assholes who had taken them dead.

"What's the game plan?" Ed barked. "Is the drop happening now?"

"Confirmed, sir," a uniformed man said, moving down from the bridge toward them. "Captain Redman," he said, extending his hand.

Ed shook it. "Ed Savage. Is one of them on the ferry?"

"If he is, we haven't found him yet," Captain Redman said. "However, the other one is near a payphone not far from the tugs."

"They're alone?" Ed shot back.

"As far as we can tell. We have a decoy there monitoring, and no other movements have been reported on or near the tug."

"Have you had visual contact?"

"Yes, sir, movement behind the portholes combined with the thermal imaging. They're in there, sir."

"What am I missing?" Ed said, looking from the captain to Wes and Robert. "This is *too* easy! What's wrong here?"

"You're overthinking it, Ed," Robert advised him. "They're idiots who managed to do a pretty damn good job. Now let's go in there and get them out."

Ed heard the engines roar, and the boat moved away from the shore; his phone vibrated with a text. But when he answered it, the phone's service cut out as the boat moved farther away from the dock. He saw only the first message Maura sent: *Any news on the girls?* Ed felt the speed of the boat as he put his phone away, and a few minutes later they were nearing the decoy eyeing the tugboats.

Warning sounds filled the room, and the computers all flashed and went dark.

"What's happening?" Ed shouted over the noise.

"Code crimson, sir! We have incoming!" the second lieutenant shouted, holding up a printout.

"Bring it up now, Lieutenant!" the captain yelled as he stared at the black computer screens.

The second lieutenant's fingers were working his keyboard as fast as he could. "Got it, sir!"

Everyone on board watched the computers screens flicker and come alive, focusing on the map of Block Island off the shores of New Shoreham, Rhode Island. The torpedo was brazenly close to the US Coast Guard Academy in New London, Connecticut, a fact everyone thought the minute they saw it.

"What's the heading?" the captain shouted.

"North-northeast, sir, toward Martha's Vineyard and Nantucket," the lieutenant's voice cracked as the shock of what they were seeing played out.

"Can you ID it?" Forrester yelled, moving to a computer.

"Satellite imagery coming up, sir," the first lieutenant shouted as she zeroed in on the 3-D imagery she transferred to the screens of the ship.

"Bloody hell," Thrasher yelled, seeing the older warhead design, knowing it was from the *Manchester*.

"She's been modified!" Forrester yelled even louder than before, and as his fingers hit the keys in front of him, the imagery of the original torpedoes from the *Manchester* came up on an adjacent screen.

Two long, domed casings were now on the sides of the torpedo, indicating that electrical modifications had been made to the ancient weapon of war.

"A modified tracking system's been added," he said in a calmer voice, focused on finding a way to disable it.

"He's coming back to the tugs." Ed turned to the owner of the voice and saw the officer holding his headset listening intently. "Surveillance has him moving away from the payphone."

"I've got to go now," Ed barked. "Thrasher, you're with me! Forrester, hack that damn thing, and get it stopped!"

"On it," Forrester shouted, pulling up the coordinates of the torpedo. Grabbing a headset, he punched in a code. "Navy sixteen twenty-seven, navy sixteen twenty-seven, come in," Forrester yelled into the mouthpiece.

"Sixteen twenty-seven, code please," Forrester heard in his headset as he switched it to speaker.

"Forrester six, structural integrity has been compromised."

"Hold for relay, sir," came the voice over the radio.

Hearing that, Ed motioned Thrasher to follow, and they went to the back of the vessel as their boat slowed to a stop. The crew was quickly getting the smaller speedboat into the water for the men to board. The driver was waiting for them, and the men jumped on, opened the bags waiting for them, and saw the weapons they'd need once they got there. Putting on his shoulder strap, Ed grabbed the gun inside his bag and checked it to make sure it was loaded. He then holstered it under his arm and strapped a knife to his leg, noticing the crossbow secured in a large gun casing next to them as he put on his earpiece.

The small speedboat moved away from the chaos, and Ed picked up the binoculars and eyed the broken-down tugboat his nieces were on.

Out at sea, the navy ship responding to Agent Forrester was turning hard portside in order to turn toward the direction the torpedo was traveling. Their men were on high alert, and technicians were busy trying to intercept the torpedo's radio signal.

Forrester wasn't getting anywhere. Everything he was trying was failing. "What's its location?" he heard the captain yell behind him.

"Just passed Martha's Vineyard. Nantucket's in its sight."

The sweat was pouring off Forrester's head as he hammered on the keyboard, trying to come up with a way to stop the cursed thing.

The tugboat the girls were trapped in was sandwiched between two older ones and tied off and anchored just offshore. The problem was there was no direct way to enter the tugboat straight on; they had to board one of the outer vessels and make their way to the center one from there.

Ed motioned to the driver to go to the farthest one away from shore, thinking if the kidnappers were to come back, they'd arrive at the closest one.

"Navy sixteen twenty-seven, are you getting anywhere?" Forrester shouted.

"Negative. Initializing SSTD system."

"We're too bloody close!" Forrester almost screamed over the radio. Frantically he tried everything he could think of. The thought of the navy using its Surface Ship Torpedo Defense System to locate, track, and intercept the torpedo so close to US soil sent shock waves through his body. The magnitude of an underwater explosion would be a disaster for the East Coast, and he wiped the sweat from his brow with his forearm and continued to search for a way to stop it.

CHAPTER 101

Sam Savage held Raquel's hand as they walked the beautiful beach of Nantucket. Their time together had been a blessing for not only him but for her too. Their torn-apart lives and the hurt that had come with it seemed to be fading as the healing began. The breeze coming in off the ocean picked up, and Raquel brushed up against the man who'd not only entered her life but saved it as well.

Moving to their beach setting, Sam picked up her large cardigan and wrapped it around her, along with his large arms as he pulled her close to warm her.

"I don't want today to end," she said, looking up into his eyes.

Sam loved her sexy Colombian accent and lifted her chin, kissing her passionately as the wind picked up, blowing the sand all around them.

"Come on, Ms. Delgado, time for me to take you home and cook you a Savage special."

"Ay, there's only one Savage *special* I want," she said, moving her hand down his muscular chest to his groin.

Sam blushed as he pulled her tighter and kissed her once more. "Babe, you're gonna love everything I've got for you."

"Tell me."

"Nope, it's a surprise," he said, reaching down and picking up the bottle of chardonnay and glasses, tossing them in the basket they'd brought along. Picking it up with the big towel for two, he put his other arm around her. "I don't want today to end either," he said as they started back toward the Savage home on Nantucket Island.

CHAPTER 102

T he early luncheon Marlo Savage and the cast of *Tycoon Wives* had been held hostage at was nothing but a snobby awards gala for the shrew who demanded it be filmed for the next season, even though the filming for all the Cinema Shake-Up sequences hadn't been completed yet.

The sequence was from *The Golden Girls*, and Marlo was in awe of how Marilyn Hart had been able to convince the network to re-create an *exact* replica of the living room set at the Pier Production Studio, which was actually an old warehouse situated on a pier in Martha's Vineyard. The cost alone must have been huge to ship and build everything to please the queen bee of the show. Marlo also thought Anthony Caspian probably had his hand in this, like everything else in Marilyn's life.

Being ushered into hair and makeup, Marlo looked at the nicely framed photo of the character Dorothy she was assigned to play, a character she could easily pull off. But the character of Blanche was the one she wanted, and that part had gone to Marilyn.

Sitting in front of the mirror as her assistants hovered around her, she picked up her phone and cringed at the text message she'd sent Ed and was pissed off that he hadn't contacted her. She turned off her phone and tossed it on the counter; picking up her script, she wanted to push the ugly thoughts of her husband's cheating from her mind. She didn't know for sure whether the thoughts were true, but something in her heart was telling her they were.

When she was called to the set, she was ready; her heart was racing a bit, and she was going to outperform Marilyn Hart if it killed her. In the time that passed, until the last few minutes of the scene, everything changed for the *entire* cast of *Tycoon Wives.*

CHAPTER 103

By the time Ed Savage boarded the farthest tugboat from shore, Lou Sabello was easily spotted on the Staten Island Ferry, dressed like he was in school with the rest of the senior class. Wearing the high school jersey, a baseball hat, jeans, and even the school's letterman jacket, he was spotted shoving a slice of peperoni pizza in his mouth from a vendor on board the ferry.

Photographs were taken from all directions of the man in his forties trying to pass himself off as a teenager, and, laughing, the agents waited for him to pick up the drop. The Staten Island Ferry was nearing its port, and a message was radioed to Ed, letting him know.

Ed peered from behind a rusted door seeing the middle tug his nieces were being held on when his earpiece buzzed with the information; he then signaled Thrasher down the corridor that the coast was clear. Getting on the main deck of the tug, they moved to the railing, which was slightly lower than the tug in the middle, and they climbed up and over the rusted railings and landed quietly on the next tug's deck.

Ed quickly looked around, noticing a fire ax behind the thin breakable glass still intact on the broken-down vessel, just as that uneasy feeling came back to him. The feeling hit him like a hammer: it reminded him of that last assignment he'd been on when he was double-crossed and the women were killed in that tragic explosion all those years ago, blown up in the getaway boat. And when Thrasher moved up next to him, pointing to a side entrance, Ed's mind flashed to the lying eyes of Agent Miller from that night, and he paused.

"You got something you want to tell me?" Ed said, questioning his longtime friend, his mind confused between him and that treacherous traitor who'd tried to kill him on assignment all those years ago. The odd feeling returned from the moment in the limousine when he had suddenly known Thrasher had been keeping something from him.

The immediate sadness in Thrasher's eyes was something Ed did not expect, and Thrasher pushed by him to go inside the tugboat. "Not now, Ed. That shit can wait," Thrasher said, moving deeper inside the rusted remains of the corridor.

Getting to the stairs, they raced down to the lower level, and Ed was horrified to see some of Kate and Lana's belongings on a metal drum near a closed door with a chain on it. Both men froze, seeing how close they were, and Ed moved up to the door and spoke in a calm voice.

"Lana? Kate? It's Ed."

"Uncle Ed!" came both their voices from behind the closed door.

"Get us out of here before they come back," Lana pleaded.

"Are you both all right?" Ed said, with a heavy sigh of relief.

"Yes, we're fine. Just get us out of here!" Kate cried out, almost in tears.

Ed reached for the door and pulled on it hard, seeing the rust break apart around the lock, but the chain was newer than the old tugboat, and he knew he needed something to break it with. The C-4 explosives they'd brought with them would have the door blown away in seconds, but given the condition of the rusted boat, it was a risk he didn't want to take. And with the recent image of those two women dying, blown from the water, haunting his thoughts, he had to find another way. Remembering the ax upstairs, he ran back to the upper deck, broke the glass with his elbow, and grabbed it, returning in less than a minute.

"Go for it," Thrasher said, nodding as he was looking out a porthole for the kidnappers' return.

"Stand back from the door," Ed yelled.

"We're ready!" the girls yelled back, and Ed swung the ax.

The blade hit the door near the handle, and Ed pulled it back out, bringing a partial section of rusted iron with it. He swung the ax again, this time hitting the chain. The door handle dented with the blow, but Ed saw the edge of it pull away from the door.

Anger filled him, and he swung the ax again, hitting the door handle at its base, separating it from the door. He then used the ax as a battering ram and punched a hole through the rusted steel. Turning the ax, he pulled it back out, busting the lock completely and sending the chain to the floor, allowing the door to swing open.

Inside he saw Lana and Kate against the far wall; they were huddled next to each other, and when they saw their uncle, they ran into his arms. The strength the girls had within them melted as their emotions got the better of them.

"Ed, we have to go," Thrasher said, entering the room.

"Uncle Ed, he's right! They killed that girl!" Lana said, almost crying.

"What girl?"

"Emily Waters! That kidnapped girl last year," Kate said.

"Look, we found this!" Lana said, holding up the medical bracelet.

Ed took it and looked at the woman's name printed on it when the sound of an approaching boat could be heard coming closer.

CHAPTER 104

"**N**antucket is clear," the second lieutenant practically shouted over the busy command center on board the military speed-boat. "The speed just increased."

"Where's it headed?" the captain shouted back, looking to the live monitor of the torpedo heading out to sea.

"Checking sonar, sir!"

The blip on the panel he was looking at was huge. His eyes wid-ened when he read the code flashing on the panel near the signal, and he punched it into his computer. His jaw dropped when he real-ized the torpedo's target was the biggest ocean liner in the world.

"Sir! Target identified: HMS *Queen Anne II.*"

Silence hit the room in an instant. Everyone was trying to grasp the fact that four thousand souls were the target, sailing far too close to US soil, and every crew member flew into action. Emergency dis-tress calls were immediately sent to warn the doomed liner, along with the president, navy, air force, FBI, and CIA.

"How fast is she going, Lieutenant?" the captain barked.

"She's at full speed, sir!"

"Forrester, any luck intercepting it?"

"Working on it," Forrester said; his computer's many open win-dows were tracking as he entered the countless codes to break into the torpedo's guiding signal. Entering the command to dip the tor-pedo down to the bottom of the ocean, the torpedo bobbed a bit on screen and changed direction slightly and began its descent into deeper water.

"It's changing course!" the captain shouted, looking at the large monitor.

"Where the hell do I send it?" Forrester frantically yelled as he continued his work.

"Sir, what about the southern arm of the Greenland Trench?" the first lieutenant suggested, looking up from her computer.

The captain knew the southern Puerto Rico Trench was the deepest place in the Atlantic, but it was also too far and too unstable. The North American and Caribbean tectonic plates slid past each other there, and the area was prone to violent earthquakes and tsunamis. The southern arm of the Greenland Trench, however, was too new of a discovery, and no scientific information had been collected to show if any fault lines ran beneath it.

When NASA's Operation IceBridge report regarding the massive mega-canyon discovered beneath the Greenland ice sheet became public information five years ago, the NASA press release gave a shocking report that a behemoth trench larger than the Grand Canyon had been found, and the southern arm, as it was called, descending from the land under the ice to carve a deathly abyss along the Atlantic ocean floor ran for hundreds of miles with a trajectory aimed right at the United States. While no signs of volcanic or seismic activity had been reported, it was simply an uncharted abyss.

With the warhead hot and loaded, he had no choice but to make the call. "Lieutenant, find the deepest point of the Greenland Trench's southern arm, and patch the coordinates over to Forrester."

Within seconds the coordinates flashed on Forrester's screen, and he went to work entering the numbers, saying a prayer that he could keep the torpedo on course.

CHAPTER 105

Menard International Shipping was not only edging out Federal Express and UPS as a leader in the world of package delivery over land, air, and sea, but the company's stocks were held privately, and over the years, the owners had always refused to go public. The company was flush with cash and kept investors away in droves as the tightly held family company ran their empire as they saw fit.

The company grew and later entered the ship-building business and soon planned not only on building the biggest cruise ship in the world, but they'd had it christened by Her Majesty The Queen, with the cost of naming it the HMS *Queen Anne II* in the millions. The first-class accommodations were unparalleled, with the size of the staterooms larger than most luxury suites, and when it first sailed, tickets had sold out months in advance due to the ship's design of yesteryear, including suites within the two repurposed and reimagined black-and-red smokestacks on the vessel.

The money rolled in, and soon they announced an even bigger ship, and construction even started ahead of schedule. Then came the news the company was going public, and the stocks soared as the date loomed for the public to buy. It seemed everything the company did turned to gold, but just before going public, one of their planes crashed.

The company endured the smears of the talking heads yammering on about a sign the stocks would plummet, and the numbers had done just that, but by the next day, they'd jumped almost back to where they'd been prior to the crash.

The investigation continued, and when the second plane went down nine days later, stocks fell and the company was in deep trouble. Investigations into the crashes found pilot error had been the cause in both disasters, and when the credentials of the pilots were looked into, it was found they'd been fired from different airlines for many infractions, including being under the influence. The FAA suspended all their flights as an investigation into their hiring process went underway, and the cash-flow problem that followed ballooned to a breaking point.

With the news covering every detail of the disaster Menard International Shipping was facing, people came out from under every rock. Smelling blood, they all wanted their fair share—except one, who wanted it all.

The consortium had a way of finding people at their weakest and riding to the rescue for the sole reason of getting their fingers into businesses in order to take them over. The majority of companies they *helped* either became theirs over time or became insolvent and collapsed under their own mismanagement, and only a few had escaped them completely by paying off their high-interest loans on time. Some of them after doing so even stayed in business with them, like Nathan Savage had with Savage Construction.

Menard International, however, was not one of them, and when they defaulted on their loans, the consortium's draconian punishment was swift. The ugly do-or-die situation Menard International Shipping was faced with translated to losing the company completely, and when they threatened to not only sue but to bring in the royal family of England to shine a light on the consortium, a lesson had to be taught.

CHAPTER 106

T he two US Air Force jets blasted over the *Queen Anne II* at such low altitude that everyone aboard the liner was at first scared, and they jumped at the loud sounds of the engines swooping overhead. Then, as the crowds of passengers mobbed the decks, they became excited and cheered at seeing the amazing aircrafts turn in the sky and circle back toward them.

Her Royal Majesty's *Queen Anne II* was at full speed ahead and a day ahead of schedule on her seven-night cruise to New York. The captain had been encouraged to test the engines of the giant ship but had planned on slowing the ship soon so the passengers got their full seven days at sea, when the radio call came in.

"Radio contact from the US Air Force, sir!" the navigation officer, holding his headset to his ear, said to the captain.

Captain John Romero lowered his binoculars with a stone-cold face, and instead of allowing the call to be placed on speaker, he picked up another headset, nodding to the navigation officer, who clicked off his feed and lowered his headset to the console.

"This is Captain John Romero, HMS *Queen Anne II*. Go ahead."

The crew was dead silent as they studied every move the captain made, and Captain John Romero knew they were watching as he listened intently.

"Something on sonar, sir!" the navigation officer said, looking up from his screen.

With Her Royal Majesty's *Queen Anne II* at full speed ahead, the captain was notified of the clear and present danger headed her way. She needed to abort her course and make a complete turn, but with her speed and size, it would take over twenty miles of ocean for her to complete the task. The last thing the captain heard was the pilot informing him they'd sent out a distress call, and help was on the way.

"Hard starboard!" the captain called out to his crew on the bridge.

"Hard starboard!" the second-in-command staff captain repeated back as the underwater explosion directly in front of them far off on the horizon interfered with the ships antennae to her satellites, wiping out their computers, and the bridge monitors went dark.

"Close water-tight doors," the captain barked.

"Water-tight doors nonresponsive, sir," his second-in-command barked back frantically, grabbing a phone on the wall to the engine room.

Seeing his staff captain barking orders into the phone, the captain moved to the ship's alarm and inserted his key, lifting up the protective cover, and hit the ship's alarm himself.

The sound of the alarm ringing throughout the ship frightened the passengers and crew alike, and some thought they saw some kind of explosion in the distance off the bow, and when word spread, panic ripped through the mobs on deck, including to the four Savage teenagers who were at the ship's pool at the time.

Seeing the panicked passengers around them, they heard the blast of the emergency flares being shot into the sky, and watched them rise higher and higher, knowing something was terribly wrong.

CHAPTER 107

A gent Forrester's hacking of the torpedo had it headed to the bottom of the southern arm of the Greenland Trench. He'd mapped out an underwater cavern and had hoped he could get the torpedo to detonate under the ocean floor, minimizing the danger being so close to US soil. Unsure of its location and going by coordinates he prayed were correct, the notification of a subsea earthquake coming up on a screen told him it had detonated near the bottom of the ocean.

The underwater fireball reverberated back against the trench, and the ocean floor above it lifted the sediment like a volcano was erupting beneath. The Greenland Trench cracked open further when a sinkhole on the ocean floor appeared farther out along the seafloor, causing the ocean above to swell. A massive pressure of water shot back out from within the cavern and up the southern arm of the Greenland Trench, causing an avalanche within it. An earthquake measuring 7.1 on the Richter scale shook the area, and the initial velocity of upward-moving water broke the ocean floor at an angle heading out to sea directly at the approaching *Queen Anne II*, rushing to the surface in a terrifying explosion.

The column of water rose up from the sea in a giant plume like a spray dome lifting high up from the water. On the bridge of the *Queen Anne II*, some of her computers started coming back online, flickering; navigation spotted the explosion from her telescope feed and patched it through to the ships' bridge computers. The crew saw what looked like a faint crack of light within the spray dome for a split second as the screens flickered, and the giant swell of water that formed headed their way.

Passengers on the decks screamed in terror, not knowing what was happening, and chaos quickly spread while the incessant alarms added to the nightmare.

Leaving their towels, the teenage Savage girls, Nicky and Roni, grabbed their tunics and held on to their brothers' hands as they raced to their staterooms.

With the detonation happening in the cavern, the avalanche helped shield the United States, bringing a smaller wave headed to her shores; the larger portion was sent out to sea, and the ship continued its turn away from the danger.

"Belay hard starboard! Manual override if you have to, but get her back on course!" the captain ordered.

"Yes, sir!" the staff captain called back.

The crew barked orders into emergency radios to the men manning the engine room as the rest of her computers flickered back to life on the bridge. The captain could see the ship veering away from the shock wave as the order was canceled. "Come on! Come on! Get back on course," he shouted.

Down in the ship's casino, Charlotte Savage was with Audra and Roxie Savage as panic swept through the ship. The three women were alone, and the thought of their family spread out on the ship added to their fright as they ran from the blackjack table to the grand staircase of the liner. As the ship switched course from its hard starboard turn to port to face the shock wave headed its way, the ship violently rolled portside, and the women were thrown to the ground and slid about twenty feet, coming to rest at the base of the glass elevators filled with frightened passengers.

Rhett, Nicky, Shep, and Roni Savage were slammed into the wall outside their stateroom when the ship changed course. Getting one of the staterooms open, they raced inside.

Chase and Landon Savage were headed to the casino when the ship leaned portside, and they were thrown against a railing in the grand lobby. Seeing their wives and their mother, they ran to them as the ship rolled starboard, catching them as they started to tumble toward them. They pushed them back and held on to the railing until the sliding finally came to a stop.

"The kids? Where are the kids?" Roxie screamed, scared out of her mind.

"They went swimming but knew to meet us here soon, so if they're not here, they should be in our rooms," Chance said.

The passengers around them were beyond scared, and as the ship seemed to level out, the Savages made their way to the grand staircase to go to their staterooms, where they hoped their children were safely tucked inside.

The giant ship bounced on the heavy seas as it accelerated on a direct course at the surge of water headed its way. From the bridge, navigation reported a water surge of seventy-eight feet headed in its direction.

CHAPTER 108

Trent York was tired from his late night flight to Hyannis, Massachusetts. Booking the last-minute trip was costly, and knowing she tutored kids at her home, he knew he'd catch her there in the late afternoon. He also booked a hotel for the night. He needed to find out the truth, and the one person who could tell him *owed* him too.

He felt guilty for the text message he'd sent Ed since he'd already left Port Roberts, and knew he had to cancel his meeting the family with his dad. But when Trent got something in his mind, he was like a dog with a bone. He checked out from the small hotel and got in his rental car and headed out to a place he knew like the back of his hand. All those years of growing up with his aunt Marta in Chatham, Massachusetts, had been a blast, living so close to the ocean. Now it was time to pay a visit and get some solid answers.

Pulling into the driveway of the waterfront home, he remembered his life with Marta and how guilty she'd felt when the truth had finally come out. The surprise visit he planned was exactly what he needed to put an end to all of his questions, he thought. He still had his key, but standing at the door, he knocked, and moments later he saw the shadow behind the curtain, and the door swung open.

"Trent! I had no idea you were coming," Marta said, moving away to let him in. "Did you forget your key?"

"Surprise! Hello, Marta," Trent said, avoiding the question and using her first name like she wanted after the truth had come out. "You don't have coffee on by chance, do you?"

"Yes. Of course I do," Marta said, giving him hug. "Come on." Marta led him to the kitchen. Getting a mug, she poured him a cup and turned with a happy smile. "I'm so glad to see you. How are you?"

"I'm good," Trent said, sitting at the kitchen table and wearing a broad smile. "I'm not interrupting any classes, am I?"

"Oh no, my last student just left. What's got you in such a great mood?"

"I met him. I met my father, Ed Savage."

Marta's smile turned to a questioning look, and Trent put her at ease.

"It's okay. Mom told me everything." Trent smiled and looked around in the kitchen. "God, it feels good to be here."

"It does?"

"Of course. You know I have to tell you—this whole mystery about my dad means nothing to me anymore. He's awesome! We had a great time, and we met by accident at the park near the gallery. I took one look at the guy and instantly knew. I'm surprised I'd never figured it out before."

"So you had a nice visit?"

"Marta, yes, we did. It was a little awkward at times, but I like the guy. And I'll tell you something too; Mom told me about the whole Parkwood Plaza incident that instigated their divorce, and when I talked to Ed about it, I mean my dad, he told me pretty much the same thing and that since it was so long ago—and now we were meeting—he wanted to start fresh."

"Ed Savage just brushed it aside like it was nothing?" Marta said, looking a little shocked.

"Pretty much. He told me so much had happened with his family, our family—boy, I'm really having a time with that. But with the headlines and everything that's recently happened, all he was grateful for was finally meeting me and starting now—that he'll always be in my life. I couldn't have asked for a better afternoon."

"Well, I'll be damned," Marta said. "I always knew Mr. Ed magnanimous Savage was a keeper."

Trent knew he had her; he just had to keep the conversation going. "Did you know Mom still watches his shows? Oh, when Jeremy isn't home, of course."

"Oh, I know she does, and I'm proud of you, Trent. You've really grown up to be a smart and understanding man," Marta said, taking a sip of her coffee.

"Marta, if there's one thing I've learned after pretty much a lifetime of wondering, it's that nothing is easy; we're all human, and sometimes things happen in life that you may not like or understand, but in the end, things work out for the better, if you want them too. I mean, look at you. I remember moving into this house after you remarried—and how you were always glowing. I'm so happy for you, Marta."

"You remember all that?"

"Marta, why do you think I was so protective of my stepsisters? I hated that their father put his hands on you like he did."

Marta recoiled at his words. "You know about that?" she said, looking hurt.

"Marta—I'm so sorry," Trent said. "I didn't mean to bring that up, and yes, Mom and I had a long talk after the truth of my dad came out. She told me everything—I guess as a way to clear her conscience. But the important thing *now* is we've all grown and can now be free of all the secrets. Me? I'm just happy to have my whole family. That's you too, my other mom," Trent said and gave her a smile.

"Oh, Trent," Marta said with tears forming at her eyes. "You have grown into a beautiful man, and I'll say it again. I'm so proud of you."

"Thank you, Marta. But while we're talking, I need to ask you about Jeremy. A while back I'd walked in on him and Mom during an intense argument, and I was worried about Mom. You don't think Jeremy would ever hit her, do you?"

"Hit Jillian? Oh God, no," Marta said and actually laughed. "Jeremy can be an asshole, I'll give you that, but the first and *only* time a man ever *attempted* to raise a hand at my sister was when we were in college. They had argued, and he pushed her back, and she tripped. She not only kicked him in the balls, but she had him arrested and then sued the hell out of him. No—I pity the fool to ever raise a hand to her. And Jeremy Bigelow isn't that type of man anyway."

"He sure likes to yell. Especially when he's mad."

"Yeah, that he does. He's certainly not like your father. Oh, Trent, I'm so glad all the questions are behind you and you've connected with him."

"What do you mean by saying Jeremy's not like my dad? Certainly he's yelled a few times."

"Oh, I'm sure, but not like Jeremy. Honey, I'm going to let you in on a little secret about your father. Your grandfather Nathan Savage was like my ex-husband, only worse, and even over all the times I'd seen some pretty crazy arguments, Ed would *never* lay his hands on anyone—especially after what his dad did to his brothers growing up. He put Roman and Logan in the hospital after a beating once."

There it is, Trent thought. He had the suspicion his mother was lying to him about the past, and now he knew. Part of him wanted to blurt out the fact he'd just tricked her into telling him what he needed to know, but he actually loved his aunt Marta and didn't want to hurt her—or *anyone,* for that matter. "Oh, I almost forgot," Trent said, reaching into his coat pocket and pulling out an envelope and handing it to her. "Here, this is for you."

Tearing the seal, Marta pulled out the invitation to the opening of Trent's gallery exhibit and smiled brightly at the hand-delivered invitation. "Trent! You didn't have to come all this way just for this," Marta said, standing to hug him.

Standing to greet her in a warm hug, Trent sighed in her arms. "Marta, you're my family no matter what, and I'd love for you and everyone to come if they can. It would mean a lot to me."

CHAPTER 109

The reports coming in to Agent Forrester confirmed the detonation had indeed occurred in the underwater cavern, decreasing the magnitude of the shock wave headed to US soil. Not knowing the damage as of yet or how bad the repercussions could become, he notified Ed at once.

"Ed? Ed! You've got to get out of there now!" Forrester radioed.

"Forrester," Ed whispered into his radio, "Negative. Target approaching, and I'm not risking getting the girls hurt."

"Ed, you don't understand. It detonated, and there's a surge of water headed in all directions."

"Roger that," Ed said. "We're moving."

Hearing the radio transmission disconnect, Ed moved to a porthole and saw the small speedboat nearing the tugs until it disappeared from his sight.

"Come on. Stay close, and follow me," Ed said, pulling his gun from his holster.

Retracing their steps to the staircase, they climbed back up, and Ed gave them a hand signal to wait on the stairs; he then moved ahead and peeked over the railing near the broken glass from where he'd attained the ax.

The bullets that came from the speedboat not only surprised Ed but nearly hit him as he felt the wind of one of them mere inches from his head. Ducking down and moving back to the stairs, he saw the frightened looks on his girls' faces when they rushed to get below.

"Take cover!" he yelled, and everyone scattered into the bowels of the nasty, rusted tugboat as Ed thought more danger was headed their way.

CHAPTER 110

y the time the surge of water from the shock wave headed out to sea and was in front of the ship, the height had increased to just over eighty feet. To make matters worse, a second sinkhole opened up in the ocean floor, causing another swell behind the death wave, increasing the height on the terrifying wave's backside. Still, at around the height of an eight-story building, the ship hit it dead on, not knowing how bad the other side would be.

The pilots of the two US Air Force jets could do nothing but watch, each saying a prayer for the trapped souls onboard, and watching the aerial reconnaissance being recorded on their monitors.

As the bow of the ship met the wave, water sprayed on its decks, and the ship rose higher, climbing the giant wave at full speed. And as the bow lifted, everyone not holding tight to something went with it.

Rushing through the crowded main hallway, Chance and Landon led the ladies closer to their staterooms when the ship hit the wave. Grabbing on to the women, the men held the handrails tight as the room-service carts and trays in the halls came toward them, and the giant ship rose up. Higher the mighty ship climbed, and as some of them lost their grips and grabbed on to each other for support, one of their stateroom doors opened, and they saw their kids hanging on for dear life.

"Don't move! You stay there and hold on!" Chance yelled from two cabins away.

The giant vessel crested the wave and rolled, tossing the teenagers into the hall and they were all thrown forward with the mighty ship when it came crashing down on the other side, losing a few life boats and anything left out on its decks.

The captain and crew watched as the bow went underwater, and giant sprays of water lifted up on both sides of the doomed ship. The bow then lifted, and the giant ship rocked like a toy, shifting violently port and then starboard several times, sending people from one side to the other before leveling out on the open sea.

"We made it, sir!" came the gleeful cry from his staff captain.

"All stop!" the captain barked. "Assess damage."

"All stop!" was repeated as the mighty ship drifted closer to land, and water poured from its decks when the alarm finally went silent.

CHAPTER 111

The sound of the approaching wave roared behind Sam and Raquel as they neared the beach path to the Savage home on Nantucket, causing them both to look back in utter fear.

"No!" Raquel screamed, seeing the giant wave hit the beach behind them.

"Come on," Sam yelled, grabbing her hand and dropping the picnic basket as he led her up the sand dune to the house.

With the house in sight, the water hit them before Sam could get them safely inside. The wave picked them up and smashed them against his home, and they were washed off the porch into the railing, which snapped when Sam hit it with his bad shoulder, letting go of Raquel and sending them into the yard.

"Help me! I can't swim!" Raquel screamed. Sam saw her go under, her arms thrashing about, and witnessed the look of pure terror on her face as she came up gasping for air.

Sam tried swimming toward her as more water pushed them against the separate guesthouse, and they bounced back in the flow. Sam grabbed on to the roll bar of their Jeep Wrangler as the wave lifted it and saw Raquel screaming as the monstrous wave sent her back out to sea.

No, not this time! Sam thought. "Raquel, grab on to anything! I'm coming for you!" Sam yelled over the sounds of destruction. Taking a deep breath, and feeling the pain in his shoulder, he let go and swam with all his might in the direction of the kindest woman he'd ever met since Cara.

The wave sent Raquel into a lifeguard sign posted on the beach near Sam's home, and it snapped with the force of the water. Nearly passing out from the blow of the wood sign, Raquel managed to grab on to it to keep afloat. Blood poured from her head, and the water washed over her face, the salt burning the cuts and slashes on her flesh. When she opened her eyes, she saw the sky above her, calm and beautiful, and she raised her hands to God and cried out Mia's name before passing out and slipping from the safety of the sign and sliding under the water.

Motionless, the waves moved her body over the beach back toward the open sea when Sam's hand reached her arm and he grabbed her, pulling her up above the waterline.

"I got you, baby. I got you. Wake up! Please, God, let her wake up!" Sam yelled as he swam with her in his arms to find anything he could hold on to.

CHAPTER 112

A isha Thomas got out from the taxi and climbed the single set of stairs to the dock when she arrived at Pier Productions where the segment of the Cinema Shake-Up was being filmed; how she wished she'd declined the assignment to cover the event. Entering the building she saw the On Air sign was illuminated, and an assistant raised her finger to her lips telling her she needed to be quiet as the filming was progressing inside.

She was led to a monitor, and beyond was a window to the set where she could see the cast filming the last few moments of the segment.

The cheesecake was sitting on the familiar kitchen table, and a slice was on a plate waiting for the ladies to move from the living area to the table for the final scene.

Picking up the plate and delivering a brilliant zinger, Marilyn Caspian Hart's character, Blanche Devereaux, took a giant bite of cheesecake, and the director yelled, "Cut!" The crew applauded.

The laughter quickly changed to whispers of confusion as the sound of the emergency sirens on the island blasted, alerting everyone in the area that some sort of danger was on the way when the lights went out in the building.

"What's going on?" Marilyn screamed in the darkness as emergency lights flickered.

Watching all this play out in front of her, Aisha turned and looked back to the entrance and heard the scariest sound she'd ever heard in her life—and it was crashing toward them.

The wave hit the dock and lifted a portion of the building with it, and it came down in a loud, splintering crash. The cast ran with their assistants and crew to the exits, and in the bedlam, one new assistant kept his eye focused on Marilyn Hart.

As the wave continued on shore, the waterline rose and flooded the warehouse, causing the glass entryway to come crashing toward everyone trying to escape. The lights in the building came on for a brief moment as the water smashed everything inside the building, hitting Aisha and an assistant as it made its way to the set. The emergency power supplied by the exposed electrical cords sparked when the water hit them, and a curtain caught fire. The flames quickly raced up to the rafters of the old warehouse, and the fire spread out above them as the water careened inside.

Marlo Savage screamed and Madeline Roberts tried holding her up, worried for her condition as the water slammed them down to the floor. Pulling Marlo up, Madeline tried keeping her above water as they were pushed to the living room set and knocked against a false wall, clinging to it for life when it separated and they lost each others grip in a scene no one had prepared for. Marlo was pushed against scaffolding with heavy wood boards across it and when she tried coming up for air she hit her head and panicked feeling like she was running out of air. Grabbing the metal pole of the scaffolding, she pulled herself from under it and came up for air and clung to it for dear life as the water rose around her. She could see the others from the light of the fire above, and the smoke that descended like a death cloud frightened her, and she screamed for help.

"Let go!" Aisha screamed at her, grabbing her by the arm holding the scaffolding in order to escape the building with her help.

Marlo turned to her and saw the one woman she hated with all her being. In that moment everything in her mind froze as part of the ceiling came crashing down nearby. Marlo screamed and in her panic let go and felt Aisha pulling her through the water to a side emergency door. Getting to the door, they both frantically pressed against the push handle, and it swung open to the back side of the pier, and the pressure from the water inside the building pushed them out against the wood railing and down the pier toward the shore.

Madeline Roberts was next to follow them out, along with the rest of the cast, Shamori Hanson, Cassidy Meyer, Tonya Lipschitz, and Carmen Reynolds, with the exception of Marilyn Caspian Hart.

Pushing and shoving her way to the front when the disaster hit the pier, she was pummeled with water and broken glass when the wave hit. When a cameraman pulled her to safety, she saw the others leaving from the far side of the building and made her way for it, leaving the cameraman, who was helping others, behind.

As the water was rising in the battered building, an assistant she didn't know called out her name and swam to her. As she reached for the kind man risking his life to save her, he pulled her toward him. Looking over Hart's shoulder, making sure no one was looking, the supposed hero turned villain and dunked her under the water. Panic ripped through her as her thoughts of safety turned to murder, and she tried in vain to fight the man holding her under the water until the last breath of life left her lungs.

The man then dove under the water with her and pushed her to the floor, lifting a heavy camera stand that had tilted over and covered her with it before coming up for air and escaping the building behind the other cast members.

CHAPTER 113

E d Savage instantly knew the so-called idiots who had kidnapped their daughters had firepower they'd known nothing about.

"Ed," Thrasher whispered.

Ed looked over to see Thrasher stepping back in from a side galley where he was pointing up to another way out. Ed then moved over and looked out the doorway.

"I'll go and cause a diversion," Thrasher said. "Get the girls out and to the boat."

"No," Ed said, looking at his friend. "I'll do this, and you take them to the boat. I owe you, and you know I do."

"Ed! You didn't know Fred was still alive that day they found him on the other side of the door," Thrasher said, believing Ed had figured out the truth. "You need to be with the girls!"

The facts were there, out in the open at the worst possible time, and anger rose up within Ed as the shots from a semiautomatic blasted the far side of the tugboat where Ed had just been standing moments before. Bullets demolished the rusted-out tugboat, and the girls started screaming.

Ed holstered his gun and then grabbed Thrasher's shoulders and shoved him in the direction of the girls, then he ran up the galley way to the far steps that led topside. Thrasher got up and could hear the small speedboat circle back the way it had come, and he dashed to the porthole and saw the movement of the strap to the semiautomatic blowing against the bastard who shot at them, and he opened fire.

A spray of bullets hit the speedboat, and Ed rushed to the rusted, broken railing of the tugboat and looked down to see the driver looking in the direction Thrasher had fired as he turned the speedboat against the tugboat for cover. Hitting the larger craft and bouncing away, the rusted edge crumbled under Ed's feet and he jumped from above, landing on him in his boat, knocking the semiautomatic from his hands onto a life vest on the back bench seat, and attacked the bastard firing at his family.

CHAPTER 114

As the water pushed the women of *Tycoon Wives* down the pier, some of them went over the side, including Marlo Savage and Tonya Lipschitz. Through it all Aisha had lost her grip on Marlo and ended up across the street from the pier, hanging on for dear life to a streetlight until the water level lowered. When Marlo went over, she hit a piling and doubled around it, desperately trying to hang on, but when the sharp pains started in her stomach, she knew she was in trouble and slipped under the water. Tonya Lipschitz, the bought-and-paid-for bitch whom Randall arranged to make Marilyn Hart's life miserable, screamed as she was washed out to sea when the monstrous wave receded.

When the water moved away almost as quickly as it'd come, Marlo's body was lying on the beach under the pier against a piling. She was unmoving, and it wasn't until Madeline Roberts lifted herself from the sand and sat up, pulling her long black hair away from her eyes, did she see her from her position down the beach. Madeline screamed out Marlo's name and got up, running to her, tripping in the sand, and landing face first as she hurried to the fallen woman. When she got to Marlo, she rolled her over and screamed for help. When she looked back down, Marlo spit up water and started coughing, gasping for air. The laughter came through Madeline's tears, and she reached down and pulled Marlo up into her arms and saw Shamori Hanson in the distance and screamed to her for help.

Marlo opened her eyes and saw the two women holding her. Her head was pounding from a blow she'd received in the water, and she heard Cassidy Meyer in the distance screaming for Tonya. And when she looked in Cassidy's direction, Aisha Thomas moved to her side just as the pains in her stomach increased, and she blacked out.

CHAPTER 115

Sam carried Raquel's lifeless body up the beach until he was in shallow enough water to lay her down and give her CPR. Breathing into her mouth twice, he then began chest compressions on the beautiful woman who somehow had saved him from the mounting depression he was so desperately trying to escape.

"Come on! Breathe!" he shouted to the heavens as he went back to giving her two breaths, and then he started the chest compressions for the second time, when she suddenly coughed up the seawater and began choking for air.

Tears shot from Sam's eyes as he propped her up to help her expel the water from her lungs. He was crying and laughing at the same time when she opened her eyes; her facial features were locked in a terrified expression. She screamed out and started crying. He held her in his mighty arms, and she clung to him as he rocked her and kissed the top of her head. And as he looked to the sky, he saw the moon in the still-daylight hours, its crescent smiling down at him like Cara had once mentioned she thought it did when they'd been on that same beach last year.

CHAPTER 116

The time with Marta had been bittersweet for Trent, and his mind was full with the family history he'd just learned. He was angry with his mother, and he had a right to be, but he also had the feeling there was something *more* that was missing. He knew his mother had problems with Jeremy and wondered if that had something to do with the lies she told him. He wanted to go straight to her and lash out at her for all of it, like he was feeling with Marta earlier. But when he thought how happy he was meeting his father, he thought nothing good would come out from it. He needed time away from his mother to sort things out, and he started his car and sighed, hearing the radio he'd left on.

Putting down the window to take a last look at the house, he remembered how his thoughts of wondering who is father was seemed to be all he could think about—now it was something new, another layer to figure out. He put the gearshift in drive, and that was when he heard it—the strange rumbling sound getting closer and *louder*.

Turning off the radio, he looked back out the window and shut off the car. Opening the door, he knew. He'd not only heard that sound before photographing the shots that *National Geographic* had asked to use, but he had seen some dangerous waves and knew trouble was on its way.

Running to the house, he heard Marta scream from somewhere within it, and then the sound of splintering wood and breaking windows met his ears. As he got to the door, the wave smashed into the back of the home, and water came over the top of the house and all around it. Utter fear gripped his heart, unlike when he'd been running toward disasters to get photos in the past—this time it was different. He'd always been far enough away, but this time he was actually *in* it. He pushed open the door and looked back as he tried to close it to watch his rental car fill with water and get pushed out onto the street.

Water was filling the affluent home, and he saw Marta get thrown against the staircase and hit her head on the wall. He yelled to her, and she opened her eyes and screamed.

"Climb up!" Trent yelled over the destruction.

More water filled the home, and he saw Marta go under. Then she raised her hand for the railing and lifted herself up and began to climb the stairs. Fighting the water and the debris of furniture inside, Trent made his way to the railing and grabbed on to it, pulling himself over and landing on the stairs.

Upstairs, Marta panicked; she ran to the master bedroom as the water lifted the home from its foundation, causing it to warp in a freakish sort of way like a building moved in an earthquake. Frightened, she screamed and ran to the far wall to hide next to a tall dresser.

Trent made it up the stairs, and the warping house splintered along the hallway walls. He heard Marta screaming and raced to the bedroom just as a loud cracking sound ripped through the floor down the center and up the walls, splitting the room in half and shattering the windows and sliding glass door to the balcony, like half the home was ripping away from itself. The home tilted, and the dresser pinned her against the corner she was hiding in as more water from the pressure of the mighty wave filled the room. Marta screamed for help, unable to move in the rising water.

Trent York saw the terrified look on Marta's face as she pushed on the dresser to escape, and he made his way to her in the raising water. Pulling the heavy piece of furniture away, he grabbed her, and together they moved through the water to the edge of the sliding glass door when the home turned in the wave and lodged back onto the ground in a loud, splintering crash. The sudden force destroyed the floor beneath them, and they were washed into the home's backyard through the shattered sliding glass door and across the broken balcony, getting separated again with the receding water.

CHAPTER 117

The speedboat hit the side of the tugboats as the two men fought, and Ed's gun came loose from his holster and fell to the floorboards of the boat. The anger flowing through Ed's veins pumped his adrenaline, and he felt like Superman. Grabbing the prick, he punched his face several times, when the guy threw his fist into Ed's stomach and pushed him back into the steering wheel, turning the boat around in a fishtail that nearly flipped the boat—knocking the semiautomatic weapon tangled with the life vest overboard. Seeing Ed's gun on the floorboards in the back of the boat, the kidnapper turned to grab it.

The fishtailing of the vessel caused the shooter to lose his balance, and Ed thrust the boat into high speed, knocking the man to the back of the boat. Ed advanced, tackling him back down as he tried to get up in the moving boat. When the man raised the gun, Ed hit his arm as it fired innocently into the empty sky above and fell back inside the boat. The man then grabbed Ed's arm with his other hand and punched him in the face, knocking him backward, and grabbed Ed's knife that was strapped to his leg.

Both men got up, and the bastard swung the knife exactly like agent Miller had all those years ago on his last mission with Agency One. When Ed arched his back, the speedboat hit a partially submerged piece of rusted tugboat at its high speed and became airborne, twisting from the angle it hit.

The boat overturned midair, and the shooter grabbed the steering wheel and swung the knife again as both men were thrown into the water.

Thrasher and the girls were on the top deck of the tugboat, and he froze with his gun pointed, waiting to see who would come up for air first. When Ed finally appeared, he scanned the water for the other man and then quickly followed the girls to board the rescue boat to pull Ed from the water. Seeing this, Ed turned in the water to see their smaller speedboat move around the tugs to where Thrasher and the girls could safely board the craft.

Ed could see the girls waving at him, and he looked around and saw the boat he'd been on bobbing upside down in the water. Smoke was coming from its engine, and soon it would be under the water with the rest of the dead fleet of New York's finest tugboats in their ocean graveyard.

Hearing the rescue boat's motor, he turned while treading water and saw his nieces on the bow coming toward him. Knowing they were safe gave him ease, but he hated that he had to tell Lana that her mother was dead, and he looked away in thought. Deciding to wait until they were safe at home, he looked to the boat as it got closer and saw the girls' faces turn to sheer terror as they began to scream.

Turning in the water, Ed saw the man moving near a piling with a warning sign posted to it like he was supported on something submerged under the water. The strap of the gun was tangled with the life vest, and he aimed the semiautomatic directly at him. Ed knew he was trapped, and as he was about to dive under the water, the spear from the crossbow he'd seen on board the boat fired over his head, hitting the man in the throat, pinning him to the piling just above the waterline.

When he looked back, the rescue boat was right behind him, and the girls were reaching down to help pull him aboard. Rolling over the side of the speedboat to the floor, he looked up and saw Thrasher holding the crossbow, and the two men looked at each other, knowing that even though their past was muddied, they were looking at a fellow comrade that they could trust forever.

"Get us out of here," Thrasher ordered as he placed the cross-bow down on the floor near the metal casing, lifted up a bench seat, and pulled out a blanket and threw it to Ed.

Kate picked it up and wrapped it around her uncle, and both girls were at his side trying to warm him. The group could see the man struggle in the water under the warning sign until his life was gone, and the growing blood slick surrounded him when they heard the cries of gulls overhead. Looking up, they watched one dive down and land in the water near the man and began to peck at him, signaling others to join in the free meal.

When the speedboat arrived at the larger military vessel, the crew was standing by to assist as quickly as possible. And when the girls were safely aboard, Ed rushed to Forrester and looked at the computer screens.

"How bad is it?" he said in a low voice, watching the computer screens near the girls shut down for security purposes.

"Reports are just now coming in. Nantucket was hit bad, followed by Martha's Vineyard. Massachusetts is ground zero for where the worst is headed. We should be okay down here, outside of a more aggressive tide," Forrester said, smiling at his friend and comrade in arms.

"What about Lou Sabello? I heard they spotted him on the ferry."

"Apprehended. They cornered him after he picked up the phony drop. He then jumped overboard and tried to swim for it, but when he came up for air, he was surrounded by thirty men with guns aimed right at him."

Ed smiled and shrugged at the silly images of his attempted escape in his head. "The guy may be an idiot, but there's evidence of Emily Waters on the tugboat. You may not be familiar with the case, but she was kidnapped last year, and her body was found on Staten Island. Alert the police on this new evidence, and maybe we can bring some closure to another family."

Forrester immediately began entering the girl's name in his computer when a lieutenant came up to Ed with dry clothing. It was military fatigues, but he was glad to get out of his wet clothes. Taking them, he reached for his phone and discovered it was gone. *Probably lost it when the boat turned over,* he thought, remembering he had no coverage at sea. "Hey, can I borrow your satellite phone to call my brothers?"

"Sure," Forrester said, handing it to him.

"Get us back to the helicopter. I need to get the girls home."

"Roger that."

Ed looked back at the girls, who were being handed blankets to warm themselves, and then moved away to talk privately as he punched in Roman's number; the call was answered on the first ring.

"Hello?" He heard Roman's broken and frantic voice.

"Roman! It's me, Ed. They're safe, brother!"

"Oh, thank God...are they hurt?"

"No, a little cold but they're fine. We'll be dropped off at Savage Tower, and I'll drive them home."

"Ed...the news is terrible. I can't believe everything that's happening."

"I know. I just want to get the girls home to you. I haven't said anything about Gabby yet—I just don't know how right now."

Roman choked up, and Ed could hear his brother fight back the tears. "Ed, there's more."

Ed leaned against the bulkhead and braced himself. "What now?"

"Zolie's missing. Logan and Maura found that she'd gone to Vreeland Hills with Stevie Galloway yesterday, and they think she's still there."

Ed thought back to the text he'd received from Maura and now wished like hell he had his phone. "Roman, I received a text from Maura, but all she asked about was the girls. Have you heard from them?"

"No, and I've called several times."

"Okay. Hang tight, and we'll be there as soon as we can."

Ed hung up and called his office; his secretary answered promptly. "Ed Savage's office."

"Paula, Ed here. I need a new cell phone in my office with my phone number assigned to it and charged fully when I get there in a few hours. Call my carrier now, and go downstairs to one of the stores in the lobby mall, and get me a new phone. My passcode is forty-three forty-three."

"Yes, sir, forty-three forty-three. And the girls…sir?"

"Thank you for asking, Paula; they're safe." Ed hung up the phone. He then called Sam, and the call went straight to voice mail, and he hung up. When he handed the phone back to Forrester, he looked over his shoulder and watched the smaller speedboat being lifted to its hold. Moving to his girls, he hugged them tightly. At least one nightmare was over.

The sediment along the southern arm of the Greenland Trench was finally clearing in the murky water, revealing the shifting of the ocean floor crumbling down the trench's abyss as the movements were finally slowing to a stop. However, down the coast under the ocean's floor, a second earthquake struck, registering 6.9 on the Richter scale, and it was centered directly off the shores of New York.

CHAPTER 118

Moving back around the destroyed home, Trent was in shock. He'd been knocked against a neighbor's home and was able to hang on until the wave receded. The debris was everywhere and when he looked to the section where they'd been separated, he saw her. She was caught up in the cross legs of an overturned picnic table lodged within the destroyed balcony of the home. "Marta!" he yelled as he ran to her, the mom who raised him since birth, climbing up the broken walls of the homes first floor to get to her, and when he did, he felt her cold skin. She was unresponsive, and he was terrified she was dead. Yelling for help, the panic took him as he tried waking the poor woman in his arms.

CHAPTER 119

The Oktoberfest celebration at the harbor always drew a large crowd, and with the military boat nearing the busy docks on Staten Island, and the crew knowing of the aftershock, it was imperative to get everyone on shore as quickly as possible. The crew's impatience was wearing thin as they waited for the other boats to clear for the large vessel to dock. And when it finally did, Ed noticed the movements of the other boats being bumped into each other as the tide started to withdraw from the shores.

The siren that sounded next alerted everyone that danger had suddenly arrived and threw everyone into a panic. The chaos spread over every yacht in the harbor, and a stampede of frightened people clogged the several rows of docks and walkways to escape the unknown danger coming their way.

Yelling for everyone to hurry, Ed grabbed Lana's hand and helped her down from the craft, turning to help Kate. They heard the sound of barking dogs trapped on a boat that had been knocked free further down the dock toward shore. When Ed got Kate down, they saw Lana running down the dock and turning on the portion that was a dead end, right near the boat with the dogs.

"Lana, no!" Ed yelled as they watched her run down the walkway to the end and jump from the dock and land on the boat moving away in the tide. Thrasher and Forrester joined Ed, and he grabbed Forrester and shoved Kate against him. "Get her out of here!" Ed yelled.

"The limo should be in the parking structure, top floor," Forrester yelled back.

"No, Uncle Ed!" Kate screamed back over the chaos.

But it was too late; Forrester had a good hold on her and got her moving down the dock, past where Lana had turned to save the dogs.

Grabbing Thrasher, Ed ran to the edge to see Lana start the engine and gun it, steering back toward the dock in a panic. The dogs were barking, sensing the danger, and when the men saw she was going to hit another boat that had drifted in her way, they realized the crash was unavoidable.

Behind them on the next dock over, a yacht backed into the dock they were on at full force, severing it and splintering the side smaller walkways that ran from it. The vibration from the impact caused the men to lose their balance just as Lana's boat turned from the hit, and with the pulling tide, it tipped against the smaller walkway, knocking Thrasher into the water and Ed to the walkway. The dogs being up in the bow of the boat, jumped free and ran down the splintering floating dock, and Lana was thrown into the water. Thrasher saw her and swam to her, grabbing her, and together in the moving tide, they managed to grab on to a line from a boat on the next section of dock near the military vessel.

Panicked, Ed got up and ran back against the crowds of people fleeing the docks. Keeping his eyes on his family, he turned on the section that jutted out to another dead end and ran to the boat where they were trying to climb back onboard. Getting to them, he reached down, and Thrasher helped lift Lana into his arms, and Ed pulled her up from the water. They then helped Thrasher up when the sound of the wave was on them, and the people were screaming all around them.

The wave hit the harbor, and everything that had been pulled out to sea was now coming back like a very vindictive Neptune himself was waging a fierce battle on the people of Staten Island.

Ed and Thrasher got Lana between them and ran as fast as they could to the main dock and turned toward shore. Running as fast as they could, they could see Kate and Forrester running up the steep planks in a mob of people to the main building where a restaurant was overlooking the harbor, when Kate stopped and turned, looking back in absolute horror when the wave hit them, knocking them down along the dock and pulling them under the water.

At the restaurant, Kate pulled away from Forrester and screamed, seeing the wave engulf her family, when a man slammed into her, knocking her against the railing. She fell to the ground hard, and Forrester pushed through the crowd to keep her from being trampled when the wave hit them, slamming them into the restaurant and pushing them along the walls to the edge, where they slipped around the building and disappeared under the water.

When Lana came up for air, she was in Ed's arms, locked in an uncle's death grip, and he turned her to face him and saw she was okay. He smiled, thanking God she was all right, and hugged her tight against his body in the freezing water. He then saw an overturned sailboat. Its massive sail was floating in the water, and the sailboat itself was lodged against the debris of the docks. Swimming and grabbing on to the fabric of the sail, they climbed to the mast and made their way along it to the side of the sailboat to climb from the water.

"Ed!" came Thrasher's loud voice, and together they saw him hanging on the decorative heavy netting around the restaurant. He was waving his arm, and Ed knew at least he was safe.

"You okay to move?" Ed asked.

Lana nodded, and together they moved along the side of the sailboat to where it was lifted up onto the damaged part of the dock.

Climbing up to the balcony of the restaurant, Thrasher saw Ed and Lana moving over the obstacles and could see they were trapped with no way to shore. Eyeing a small rowboat lodged on top of a larger boat, he made his way to it, pushed it over the side, and jumped down into it to help his friends.

Across the street, Kate had been washed into a courtyard of a building that housed a clothing store a few steps down from the street level with a bar upstairs on its second floor. With the water receding, Kate felt the heaviness of a wet rack of clothes behind and on top of her, like the tentacles of a sea monster grabbing its prey to kill it. Unable to move from the floor, she sat up above the waterline and clawed at the wet clothing and flung it away from her, she then tried to stand, realizing a display stand was trapping her legs in the cold and flooded building. Pushing on it with everything she had, she realized it was no use—she was trapped. Frightened, she cried out for Forrester. She was alone, and she could see people running outside of the courtyard on the street, sloshing in the ankle-deep water, when a pipe burst from the bar upstairs and water began pouring down behind her. The panic grabbed her by the throat when she realized she could drown, and she began to scream for help.

Forrester was frantic; he'd been hit with God knew what while underwater, and the sudden blast of pain that shot down from his hip had caused him to let go of Kate, and he was scared for her life. Searching for the lost and innocent girl, he saw a woman with long dark hair stumble ahead of him, and he rushed, limping from the pain in his hip, to grab her. Seeing the frightened look on the stranger's face, he let go, telling her he was sorry, and he watched her run off as the feeling of dread was all around him.

Moving down the block, he started to cross the water-filled street to the harbor when he heard her. Her cries for help were lifted over the panic all around him, and he turned to see the entrance to the courtyard and moved as best he could to save her.

"Kate! Kate! Where are you?" Forrester yelled, moving into the courtyard, and splashing up the water as he moved down the steps into the deeper water. The pain he was feeling would have to wait.

"Here! Over here!" Kate yelled back, grabbing a wet T-shirt from the store and waving it over her head.

Forrester turned his head and saw her. Her head was above the waterline and water was pouring down from a pipe behind her, she was terrified and he knew he didn't have much time. Not realizing the store was a few *more* steps lower than the ground he was on, he tripped on the steps and fell hard, landing against the brick entrance to the store. His body spun, and he landed on his back creating a giant splash.

"Forrester!" Kate screamed, seeing him stir in the water and roll over and get to his knees, shaking the pain from his body.

"I'm all right," the man responded, taking deep breaths to gain his balance. Getting up, he moved to her and saw her trapped under the heavy display case.

"I can't move it," she said, her hands under the water pushing and tugging back and forth on the edge of it.

"Are you hurt? Anything feel broken?"

"No. But I should be asking you that."

"I'm fine," Forrester lied, moving to grab the edge of the display. "Now, when I lift, pull your legs out." He watched her nod and reached down into the water and lifted with all his might. Lifting it up slightly, she pulled herself free, and he dropped the fucking thing, feeling the pain in his lower back shift to his hip and sting like boiling hot water was running through the joint space, and he fell to the ground.

Kate crawled to his side and pulled the kind stranger she'd only met such a short time ago and lifted his head to her chest. She pushed away his wet hair, and he opened his eyes. "Forrester! Are you all right?"

"We need to get to the parking garage across the street from the harbor. Ed knows to go there," he said, shifting his weight to sit up next to her.

"Can you move?"

"I'm not out of the game yet."

"Come on," Kate said, helping the man up, and together they made their way to the street. They could see the parking structure in the near distance. Helping the man as he limped along the messy, water-filled street, Kate prayed her family was safe as they moved along amid the many lost souls, each in a state of shock over what they'd all been through.

Realizing they were trapped once seeing the other end of the wrecked sailboat, Ed looked back to where he'd seen Thrasher to see he was now gone.

"What do we do now? Swim for it?" Lana said, shivering from the cold.

Ed was exhausted, and he too started to shake from the cold. All he could do was put his arm around her to try to warm the poor girl when he heard his name carry over the destruction behind them. Turning, they saw Thrasher rowing toward them in the small boat, and they moved to where they could jump from the stricken sailboat safely into the rowboat once it got there.

Watching his friend move the boat to them, Ed couldn't believe how their lives had come back together like bookends of a horror movie—from the disastrous fire that had killed his friend's partner to the murders in the mountains and everything that had happened since then and now. He was at a loss for words as he looked at the man he owed his and his family's lives to. "Damn, I'm gonna owe you big time," Ed said as they settled in the front of the boat.

"Wait until you get my bill," Thrasher shot back, the innocent grin turning to a smile on his face.

"Have you seen Kate or Forrester?" Ed quickly said, standing in the boat and looking ahead toward the restaurant.

"Not since I saw them running up to the building when the wave hit us."

"Come on—we need to find them," Ed said as he reached over the water to push a wayward boat from their way that was floating in front of them.

The moments seemed to last forever until they were near the rocks of the shore where they could finally touch land. Climbing out and standing on top of the rocks, they saw the damage, and amid the chaos, Ed spotted the parking garage across the street standing tall. Its rooftop was intact, and he knew Forrester would do everything in his power to get Kate safely to the top floor.

At the parking structure's base, Forrester and Kate noticed the entrance ramp went down a couple of feet from the street level for its first level of parking. Water was rushing down from the upper floors, and Forrester pointed to the up ramp that rose above the waterline that was too dangerous to climb. They were both cold, and he prayed the limousine was there and that someone would be there to help them. Seeing people sliding down with the water rushing down the ramp coming from above, he gestured to the stairs, and they sloshed through the water, pulling open the door, they grabbed on to the handrail and climbed up to the dry floors above. Getting to the top floor, Forrester pushed open the stairwell door, and, as if the top floor had been privately reserved, the lone limousine sat parked, backed to a wall where the driver could watch the entire rooftop from his position.

Smiling and waving his arm, they moved toward the limousine, hearing the car's engine start and the driver's door open. Then the driver stepped out and opened the back doors as Forrester and Kate passed the down ramp, noticing the closure signs posted blocking off the roof's parking area.

"Get the heat on now!" Forrester ordered as he helped Kate climb into the back seat. "Any word on Savage and Thrasher?"

"Nothing yet," the driver responded, getting back in the car and cranking up the heat.

Kate watched Forrester hobble to the building's edge and look over the wall to scan for her family, and when she saw him waving his arms, she knew. Getting back out from the car, she ran to the edge, getting to Forrester's side, and together they saw Ed, Lana, and Thrasher. They were coming from the far end where the rocks were forming a barrier along the shore, and she waved her arms with the man who'd saved her. Seeing them wave back, she smiled, feeling Forrester's arms come down around her to warm her.

"Come on," she said, moving back to the limousine. "You need to get off that hip."

Inside the warming back area of the car, Kate pulled a bottle of whiskey and poured a healthy shot for the man next to her. "Here," she said, handing it to him. "You deserve this." Watching him down what she poured and seeing his reaction cross his face, she poured him another shot and grabbed a glass for herself, happy for finally feeling like the worst was behind them.

A short time later, they saw the rooftop door open, and Ed, Lana, and Thrasher stepped onto the roof. The driver got out from the car and waited until they were near to open the warm back compartment of the vehicle.

Ed held the door, and Lana climbed in, and when Ed looked in and saw Kate was drinking with Forrester, the look he shot him was priceless. "If I didn't know you better, I'd shoot you right now with your own gun!" Ed laughed, climbing in behind Lana and moving over for Thrasher. "You'd better have saved me some of that."

Kate blushed, pouring him some in her glass and handing it to him.

"Thanks, sweetie. You two all right?" Ed asked.

"Yeah, we're fine," Forrester said.

"No, we're not," Kate said. "He's hurt. I think his hip is broken."

Everyone looked to Forrester, and the concern was obvious in Thrasher. "Robert, what happened?"

"I don't know. Something hit me underwater, and it hurts. I don't think it's broken, but it needs to be looked at."

"And you, Kate?" Ed said point blank.

"I'm fine. Uncle Ed, he saved me. I was trapped, and he hurt himself further trying to save me. I owe him my life," Kate said, smiling at the new hero in her life.

Ed looked from Forrester to Thrasher and realized the two men were like his brothers. "We need to get you to a hospital. Can we get a chopper to land here?"

"Maybe, but I don't think this is a good place," Lana said, pointing to the small mob of people that moved up the ramp of the parking structure and were congregating to look over the edge of the building at the mess around them.

At that moment, Forrester picked up the phone and told the driver to take them back to the helicopter, and the car started moving to the ramp when an agent saw them from his parked car on the level below and got out and moved the closure signs for them to pass. Forrester then put down the partition window to ask for the drivers cell phone and sent a text to the pilot, alerting them they were on the way and a second helicopter was needed.

Moving down the last ramp to the flooded first level, the limousine splashed up the water as the driver floored it to the exit ramp that rose back up to the street. With a smile on the drivers face, he turned the vehicle away from the parking structure, and the car wound its way away from the harbor and back to where Ed and Thrasher had landed to meet Robert, a time that seemed like a lifetime ago to Ed after everything that had happened. And when everyone got out and moved to board the helicopter, Ed looked back and saw that Thrasher was standing next to the car watching them go.

"Hang on a minute," Ed said to everyone as the girls boarded the helicopter.

Running back to the limousine, Ed ignored the pain in his knee and held up his hand. "Wes! Robert, what are you doing? Come back with us; we're not done, my friends."

"You're going to Savage Tower. I'm waiting for the next one to get looked at," Forrester said, pointing to the sky from the limousine at the approaching helicopter waiting to land.

"We'll get this sorted out another time, Ed. Hell, too many years have gone by so what's another few days? Now go on and be with your family," Thrasher added.

"Are you sure?" Ed said, looking at the man and seeing him in a new light.

"We're good, Ed—I mean that. Now go on, or I'll shoot you for pinning me with your cane against the mail truck when we first saw each other in that warehouse near Black Ridge," Thrasher said with a laugh. "Remember that one, buddy?"

"Oh, yeah, sorry about that," Ed said, recalling the day Lisa had been saved. "Okay, but we need to talk soon. I insist, Thrasher!"

Wes watched Ed move back to the helicopter and board, and when the doors closed and the helicopter took off, he climbed into the limousine with Agent Forrester.

Forrester poured another drink and offered it to his friend.

Thrasher took it, downing the entire shot, and leaned against his friend and sighed. "It's been a hell of a day, Robert."

"One hell of a day, Wes," Robert repeated. Turning to his long-time friend, the two men looked in each other's eyes and kissed passionately.

From up in the sky, Ed Savage looked down and saw the second helicopter land. He thought of the pain Thrasher had gone through all those years ago and had kept it to himself because he didn't want to hurt him. From their training in London, he knew keeping personal issues quiet was crucial in their line of work, and yet he also knew he'd broke that rule on the tugboats because he wasn't thinking clearly, and it could have cost them their lives. He'd been away from Agency One for too long, and now he had a new respect for the man who had saved not only his wife's life but his own and his nieces too, and he was going to pay him back someday—he just didn't know how.

CHAPTER 120

When Hailey and Sandy Storm returned to Wendy's townhouse, they knew they'd left the place a mess after they'd come back to take another look for clues as to who this mysterious S. was who'd paid for Sandy's medical expenses. The only positive thing was they'd left the heat on, so the place wouldn't be as cold as it had been yesterday, and they still had the basement to search.

Not finding anything in the basement and with the day draining away, they went back upstairs, going over the places they'd already searched, looking in her office again, every drawer in the place, pockets in every garment. Still not coming up with anything, they were feeling hopeless. Coming in to the living area with a shoe box filled with mail, Sandy sat on the sofa and dropped it on the coffee table to go through it.

"I already went through that one," Hailey said, coming in from the kitchen with a fresh vodka on the rocks she'd just poured for herself.

Frustrated, Sandy dropped the mail and looked at her drink. "Well? We've looked everywhere. I don't think there's anything to find here," she said, getting up and going to the kitchen and spotting the bottle of vodka on the counter.

Following her, Hailey leaned against the doorframe. "Maybe we're going about this the wrong way."

Sandy had grabbed a glass and opened the freezer for ice when she turned to her sister. "What do you mean?"

"Well, if the Savages said they didn't pay it, then we need to find a way into the hospital's accounting area and dig there."

"How are we going to do that?" Sandy said, filling her glass with ice.

"Tomorrow morning I say we go to the hospital and barge in Storm-style and find what we need."

Sandy laughed as she poured the last of the vodka, barely filling her glass. "Hey, thanks for leaving me some, lush."

"There's another bottle in the cupboard." Hailey rolled her eyes and pointed.

Opening the cupboard and seeing the booze, Sandy reached for the vodka in the back of the cupboard, moving a few others to get at it. "That's strange," Sandy almost whispered as she pulled out a bottle of expensive-looking tequila.

"Tequila? Oh girl, you're in a mood," Hailey said with a laugh.

"That's not it," Sandy said. "Wendy hated tequila, and I don't know of anyone she was seeing lately whom she'd want to have it in the house for."

"Let me see that." Hailey reached for the bottle.

Sandy handed it to her, dug out the vodka, and finished pouring her drink. "It was my hospital bill after all; maybe we can get some answers there."

"Wait a minute; I saw a receipt somewhere with this on it," Hailey said, putting the bottle and her drink down to open a kitchen drawer.

Inside, among some coupons and other papers, she pulled out the receipt and scanned it. "Yep, I thought I saw this, and she spent a fortune on it, too! Over three hundred dollars!"

Sandy nearly dropped her drink. "She spent that much?"

"Maybe it was one of the Savage men and their expensive tastes," Hailey said, placing the receipt next to the bottle on the table. "It wouldn't be the first time Wendy slept with someone else's man."

Sandy shot her a look and dismissed it, not wanting to dredge up the past. "Let me see that." Picking up the ornate bottle, she looked at its unique metal leaf design wrapped around the glass and then looked away in thought. She knew she'd seen this exact bottle before. But where? "Wait a minute; where's the stuff we found on Patty Galloway?"

"Patty Galloway? She doesn't have a dime. Neither does her sister, that Stevie woman."

"That's not what I mean," Sandy said, heading to Wendy's office. There she found the file, and as she was going through it, Hailey came in and looked over her shoulder.

"What are you looking for?"

"It's not here."

"What's not here?"

The sudden realization lit up her face. "It's not here because it didn't exist until *after* she was dead." Sandy turned on Wendy's computer.

"What is *it*?" Hailey said, watching her search for Patty Galloway's name. In seconds a list of articles appeared on the screen in front of them.

"Here it is," Sandy said, clicking on the link and reading, "Patty Galloway Heads To Raven House."

Opening the article, it showed the historic, monstrous hospital and the list of doctors who worked there. "Where is it?" Sandy said, scrolling down the page to see the shaded link at the bottom that Wendy had clicked on before. "Here it is," she said, clicking the link.

The new page opened, and there was a photo of Dr. Stanley Sinardi standing in front of a massive desk in his home, and on the shelf behind him was that exact bottle of tequila. "There it is! See it? I knew I'd seen that bottle before."

Hailey reached to the computer and enlarged the image. "Yep, that's it, all right. Good work, girl. Not to mention this Stanley Sinardi could be our mysterious S."

"But I don't understand the connection," Sandy said. "We'd been working on the Savage case together, and she never mentioned a word about this guy."

At that moment an e-mail notification popped up on her computer: "Your Deposit Statement Is Ready—Port Roberts Savings."

"She didn't bank there," Sandy said, watching the notification bubble disappear moments after it came through to her sister's computer.

Opening her mailbox, Sandy saw it and clicked on it. The two sisters looked at each other and clicked on the link to her account. A new window popped up asking for a login name and a password.

"Any idea?" Hailey said.

"Yeah, I've got Wendy's death certificate in my bag, and if we hurry, we can make it to the bank before it closes."

CHAPTER 121

"She has *how much* in this account?" Sandy said to the bank representative.

Looking up from her computer, she hit the print button. "One hundred and twenty thousand dollars. I'm printing the statements now," the woman said.

Watching the woman get up from her desk to retrieve the printout, Sandy turned to Hailey. "I knew nothing of this!"

"Wendy did like to keep her secrets."

Sandy looked at her sister, and they both knew Wendy's mistake of sleeping with Hailey's boyfriend years ago, fracturing the relationship forever. "What do we do now?" Sandy asked.

"Keep cool," Hailey said as the woman came back with the papers. Smiling sweetly, she reached for them and spread them out in front of them. "Tell us what we're looking at here."

"Deposits. All cash deposits of under ten thousand dollars each to avoid authorities," the representative said in a distasteful voice. "She also took out an ATM card, and here are the locations where she used it."

Sandy read the addresses and pointed to a bank branch near Vreeland Hills Sanatorium. "This one doesn't make any sense. Why would she have driven all the way out there long before Patty Galloway was even sent to the sanatorium?" she said, looking at her sister.

The look on Hailey's face told her to shut up, and she looked to the representative and smiled. "Oh, wait a minute," Sandy said, lying through her teeth. "We interviewed one of the responding officers from an armed robbery who lived out there for a story we were working on."

"Thank you for your help," Hailey said, gathering up the documents. "We'll be in touch when we're ready to deal with closing the account," she said, putting the statements in her bag.

"Yes, thank you," Sandy said, following her sister's lead. "Oh, look—it's closing time. Don't want to keep you."

Outside in the parking lot, Sandy caught up with her sister. "Sorry. I wasn't thinking."

"Girl, you need to learn to shut your mouth."

"I know. What if Sinardi asked questions at the bank?"

"You're jumping way ahead here. Come on—we need to go back to Wendy's to figure out our next move."

"Our next move is to go to Raven House and question this asshole," Sandy said, getting in the car.

Closing her door, Hailey looked at Sandy. "How's this instead? Say Wendy's been working for Sinardi. Look, I know your report from Black Ridge was full of venom and spite, but I also know you didn't know the Savage family until the RV accident. So where did all the anger come from in the reporting? Wendy seemed to be the one leading it back then."

Sandy seemed to recollect the past for a moment. "Wendy did seem to be keeping things from me. Like when I photographed Marlo's chart in the hospital she was in up there, she had that image but didn't use it when I gave it to her."

"That's not enough, but it's a start. Okay, here's what we're doing. We're going back to Wendy's and pulling everything we can find on Patty Galloway and the hospital. And I'm taking another look at her regular bank records."

"That bitch double-crossed me," Sandy growled as Hailey pulled the car from the bank's parking lot. "And I'm going to find out *everything* about Stanley Sinardi!"

CHAPTER 122

The frantic call arrived at Jillian's penthouse just as she got home from a long day of shopping. Trent was in shock, telling her of the disaster at Marta's home and that she had been seriously injured and taken to Chatham Hospital.

"Injured? How? I don't understand this at all," Jillian said, feeling shocked at the news. She'd been so busy spending Jeremy's money that she didn't even know of the earthquake and the waves generated from the disaster hitting all around Port Roberts, Upstate New York.

"Mom, they're running tests on her now. We were nearly killed when the house was destroyed."

"Destroyed? Oh my God! What happened? What's wrong with my sister?"

"Mom, turn on the TV—it's everywhere. There was an earthquake somewhere off the coast, and it triggered a tsunami. But we got separated, and when I found her, she was knocked out. She hasn't woken up yet."

"Woken up yet! Oh my God!" Jillian cried. "Trent, you were only here yesterday. What on earth are you doing there?"

"Well, I came to invite her to the gallery. It was a supposed to be a surprise," he said, keeping the real reason quiet.

"Are you all right?"

"Mom, I'm fine," came the words too easily. Trent wasn't all right, and he knew it. The shock of what happened was building inside him, and he didn't realize how bad it was going to get. He was holding it together as well as he could, and he didn't really know how to handle it, and he realized it as soon as the words came out of his mouth.

"What about the family? Are they safe?

"Yes, thank God. They weren't home when it happened."

"Trent, I'll be there as soon as I can," Jillian said, hanging up the phone and looking at the pile of shopping bags thrown in her living room. Running to her bedroom to pack a bag, she called Jeremy and told him of the news.

CHAPTER 123

ort Roberts was beautifully lit on the cold early evening when they were approaching Savage Tower. Ed had radioed to have his helicopter do a lap around the city so they could land him in the military helicopter on his building's roof. Once down, Ed's teeth were chattering from the cold water he'd been submerged in. They were all freezing, and Ed needed to get them home.

Exiting the helicopter, they moved toward the stairway, and when the military bird took off, the wind hit them hard. Stepping off the elevator to his office floor, they saw half the lights had been shut off, and the quiet emptiness unnerved them. The cold had chilled Ed to the bone, and once inside his private office, he moved to his bedroom in the adjoining room to the closet and grabbed a couple of sweatshirts and pants he wore at the building's gym and tossed them to the girls, who were glad to put them on. He then pulled out his long black cashmere coat and wrapped it around himself, trying to stop the chill running through his body.

Moving to his desk, he picked up his landline and saw the new cell phone charging near it with a note from Paula telling him his car had been returned from West Point and the valet had the keys. He grabbed everything without thinking with his other hand, putting it all in his pocket. Punching in a number, he ordered his car to be waiting for them downstairs with the heat set on high, and when they got to the warm Range Rover, they were glad he had.

"I just want to take a long, hot bath when I get home," Lana said, leaning back in the front seat.

"That makes three of us, I bet," Kate said from the back seat. "Uncle Ed, I know you like showers, but I really think a bath will be better for you to warm up in."

"You're probably right, Kate," Ed said, hoping Roman had heard from Logan and he'd have the time.

CHAPTER 124

O pening the front door of Zolie Vanderran's home, Ed looked at the clock and thought the kids would be home by now. And when Roman moved from around the corner and saw his daughter was safe, he sighed in relief and opened his arms.

"Daddy!" Lana ran into his arms. "Don't let me go, Dad," Lana whispered.

"I never want to," Roman said, squeezing her harder.

Kate was right with her, and Roman hugged both the girls, not wanting to let them go. "Uncle Roman, it was awful," Kate said. "But you should have seen Uncle Ed! He was so brave."

"You're wet!" Roman said, pulling back and feeling the dampness from the sweats they were wearing. "What happened since we spoke, Ed?"

"We got caught in the wave at the harbor," Lana said.

Roman looked from Ed back to the girls. "Are you all right?"

"We're good, Dad," Lana said. "Ed here has some spectacular friends."

"Where is everyone?" Ed asked, knowing they'd kept the kidnapping away from the other kids.

"Lisa's upstairs sleeping. The rest went out for dinner to be with Tucker and Chet; they've been gone all day and should be home soon," Roman said, looking hard at Ed. "Oh, and I'm not sure where Amanda is."

"Dinner?" Ed said, looking at Roman, who shook his head. He shot a look back that told Ed they didn't know about Gabby yet.

"Where's Mom?" Lana asked.

"Yeah, where are Mom and Dad?" Kate followed.

The television in the next room Roman was watching was reporting the news of the volcanic explosion and subsea earthquake and aftershock that had caused the damage in the first place. Ed immediately knew the government was covering it up and wondered when and if the truth would ever get out. He then looked over to Roman and knew the time had come to tell the girls of Gabby's death.

Pulling away from her father, Lana heard the television and looked toward it.

"Let me shut that off," Roman said as they moved into the room. Reaching for the remote, the news went to Martha's Vineyard, where Aisha Thomas was reporting from the destroyed Pier Production Warehouse, and he paused.

"Hang on—don't shut that off," Ed said.

The four gathered near the television, and Roman turned up the volume.

"The reality TV show *Tycoon Wives* was caught in the destructive wave that hit the island during a filming event," Aisha said, holding the microphone with a blanket wrapped around her. "I arrived on location moments before tragedy struck. Marilyn Caspian Hart, an original cast member with the show, was killed in the panic to escape the doomed building behind me targeted by the wave. The other cast members are shaken up with minor cuts and bruises with the exception of two: one was airlifted to the mainland in Boston, and one is still missing. Calls to the family have gone unreturned, and until I hear otherwise, I'm not releasing the names of the injured or missing cast members. This is Aisha Thomas signing off for now. I will be heading to Boston to follow up on this story."

Ed looked at the woman on the television, and his heart dropped. Reaching for his phone, he hit the home button, and the main screen asked for a first-time user password. Ed entered his passcode, forty-three forty-three, and waited as the screen advanced. He saw it hadn't completely charged, and the screen went black.

"Damn it!" Ed barked. "I told her to charge the damn thing."

"My phone's charging right there, Ed; plug yours in," Roman said.

Moving and exchanging the phones, Ed hit the home button, and the phone lit up. Waiting for it to go through its reboot process seemed like forever. On the television they watched the report showing the destroyed pier and the surrounding area.

The phone's screen finally showed the password bubble, and Ed entered the code, watching his main screen come up. With the power cord charging the phone, it started vibrating, signaling there were text messages, mail, and voice mail waiting for him.

Seeing the numerous messages from Aisha Thomas, the group knew the news was bad, and Ed called her immediately. "Aisha!" Ed barked into the phone. "I'm home, and I just saw you on the news. My phone's been out. My God, tell me what happened to Marlo."

The others listened and watched Ed get the news, and as he did, they saw him shiver.

"Boston General Hospital? Do you have her room number?" Ed paused. "Thanks, Aisha," Ed finally said, hanging up. "They found her unconscious below the pier after the wave hit."

"Oh my God," Lana said.

"She was complaining of cramps and stomach pain when they airlifted her," Ed said, hitting a button on his phone.

"Oh, Uncle Ed, I'm so sorry," Kate said.

"Boston General Hospital," Ed said to the phone's computerized voice asking for information.

"This just doesn't end. Where's Mom?" Lana asked again, looking to her father and hearing Ed's phone repeat the hospital information it had found.

Ed looked to his brother and saw the damage in his eyes.

"Go on, Ed. I'll take care of this," Roman said.

"I'm so sorry." Ed unplugged his phone and quickly ran up the stairs to his suite. As he got to the top, he heard his nieces break down in tears, and he grasped his phone to his heart as shivers shook his body and tears formed in his eyes.

Knowing that Roman must do this on his own, Ed got to his room and plugged his phone in with his charger cord and turned on the shower. He then went back and punched in the phone number for the Boston hospital. As his calls were transferred around, he remembered the last text Marlo had sent him about Aisha's baby being his, and he cringed, waiting in absolute silence.

"Hello," came her weak voice.

"Marlo! It's me. My God, I just found out. Are you all right?"

Marlo burst out crying, and he listened to her take in several breaths until she finally said the news he feared most. "Ed...I've lost our baby."

Ed's world came crumbling down around him that very moment. "Marlo, I'm so sorry. Honey...I'm so sorry," he repeated.

"It hurts, Ed. I just can't right now. Where...where are you?" Marlo said over her sobs.

"I'm at home. The girls are safe," Ed said. "I just brought them home."

"What? What are you talking about? What girls are safe? Did something happen to Ava and Lisa?"

Ed realized that with everything that had happened, no one had called Marlo after she'd left for New York to tell her of Lana and Kate's kidnapping. "No, Marlo, nothing happened to Ava or Lisa; they're fine. I don't know how this happened with no one telling you, but Kate and Lana were kidnapped."

"What? When did this happen?"

"After you left for New York. It was when they were riding to West Point that they were taken. I just now brought them home," Ed told her quickly, not really wanting to tell her of Gabby's murder. "I'm sorry, honey, but with everything happening, I simply forgot to call you."

"What else are you sorry for, Ed? What else haven't you told me?"

Knowing the secret of sleeping with Aisha was no longer a secret, Ed wanted nothing more than to talk to his wife about the situation face to face. Taking a deep breath, he continued, "Marlo, so much has happened, and the family is...breaking down. There's something you need to know right now. My God, I don't want to tell you this, but Roman's downstairs telling Lana and Kate that Gabby is…Gabby is dead, honey."

"What?"

"All I know is it's tied to Parnell's murder, and it's killing me," Ed said, knowing he had to keep his other life secret.

Marlo burst out crying, and Ed wished he could be there to comfort her. "Ed, my God! Ed, how can this be happening again?" Marlo sobbed. "It's more secrets again, isn't it?" Marlo said, hearing only his breathing on the other end of the line, which told her what she needed to know. "You slept with her, didn't you?"

"Marlo, not now, please. Let me get there to take you home."

"Answer the question! Did you sleep with Aisha Thomas?"

"Yes." The heavy emotion in his heart was clear as he continued, "Marlo…you'd served me with divorce papers. I know it was wrong. Please forgive me," Ed cried into the phone.

Marlo must have dropped the phone because her cries seemed farther away. But as he pressed his ear to the phone, he could hear her sobbing as she repeated the same words over and over again: "Secrets and lies…secrets and lies."

"Marlo? Marlo? I'm so sorry. I'll make it up to you, and I'll be there soon."

"No."

"No?"

"No…I need time."

"Marlo, we can get through this," Ed said, when he heard the call disconnect. She'd hung up on him, and he stared at his phone, softly placing it down on the dresser. He was in shock; his heart hurt, his head was full. So much had happened and was *still* happening, and the call had only added to the coldness in his body, heart, and soul. Looking toward the steaming shower, he moved to it, taking off his clothes.

He adjusted the water temperature and hung his head under the intense heat, attempting to shake the chill within him. Heavy tears came over the loss of his baby and the loss of Gabby and, most likely, the loss of his own wife. He'd also forgotten to mention Zolie, Maura, and Logan, and it was gnawing at him that he didn't have a moment to tell her...

God, please let my marriage survive.

CHAPTER 125

E d Savage didn't want to turn off the water. The hot water was almost lifesaving, and he'd kept increasing the heat to awaken his freezing limbs. When he finally did turn off the water, his skin was red, and he was sweating when he stepped out onto the bath mat. Grabbing a towel and drying off, he wrapped it around himself and grabbed another towel and dried his hair, dabbing the sweat that continued to pour from his now-overheated flesh.

Moving to the cooler air of the bedroom, he grabbed his robe and put it on and then picked up his phone and looked at his messages. There he saw the last texts from Maura: *Any news on the girls? At Vreeland Hills Sanatorium with Logan. Did you know Zolie was here with Stevie Galloway? Call me.*

Just as he was about to try to return her call, there was a slight knock at his door.

"Dad?" Tucker said, opening the door a bit.

"Tucker, come in," Ed said, noticing his son's wet eyes as he put down his phone.

"Dad, I just heard about Mom and Gabby. Is Mom okay?"

"No, she's not. She lost the baby."

"Dad, I'm so sorry," Tucker said, standing a few feet from him until Ed reached out his arm and pulled him into a hug.

"Me too, Son," Ed said, patting his back. Hearing the vibration of his phone, he let go and moved to pick it up, seeing a message from Sandy Storm.

"Dad, everyone's home and crying downstairs. What do I do?"

Ed read Sandy's message: *I have proof I didn't leak that last interview from my sister. She was working with someone you know.*

"Dad? Is that from Mom?"

Ed looked from his phone to see the hurt in his son's eyes, and his heart broke. "Tuc, go downstairs and tell everyone I'll be down in a short while. Let me get dressed. I need a few minutes," Ed said, avoiding his question.

"Yes, sir." Tucker moved toward the door and closed it behind him.

Ed then called Logan, Maura, and Zolie; each of their phones went straight to voice mail. He then hung up and texted them a group message: *Get in touch with me ASAP!* He then looked at Sandy Storm's message and called her.

"Ed?"

"Sandy, what's with the message?"

"I'm putting you on speakerphone. My sister, Hailey, is with me, and we've found something."

Ed knew he'd heard her name before but thought it was Halle and remembered he'd told his friend Ellie Collins at Titan Studios about the sister breaking some "Sorority Murder" story in Connecticut.

"Ed Savage? This is Hailey Storm. We haven't met, but I've been working with my sister, and we've discovered something and would like to work with you on it."

"What is it?"

"Well, we'd like to make a deal first."

"Spit it out now, or I'm hanging up."

"Tell him," he heard Sandy say in the background.

"Mr. Savage, Wendy was working with someone you know, and we don't know why, but we have an idea. His name is Stanley Sinardi—*Dr.* Stanley Sinardi," Hailey said.

"Sinardi?" Ed felt the nasty déjà vu from his past like it was yesterday.

"Yes. Dr. Stanley Sinardi—and he's taking care of Patty Galloway at Vreeland Hills Sanatorium."

Ed's mind went in a million directions at once, and he couldn't think straight. "What exactly did you find?"

"Give us the exclusive, Ed. We want to make things right," Sandy Storm said.

"Tell me what you've got. Now! I'm not promising a damn thing."

"Fuck you, Ed Savage," Hailey shot back. "We'll get this damn story on our own."

"You listen to me, lady," Ed said, hearing the disconnected tone for the second time tonight. "Damn it!" Ed shouted in his room. He could feel his blood boiling, and he punched in another number.

"I was about to call you," Tallulah said. "I'm so sorry, but when I saw the news, I did some digging. How's the baby?"

"Tallulah, she lost it."

"Jesus, I am so sorry."

"Thank you, but that's not why I'm calling. That dead reporter's sister Sandy just called me. She's working with her other sister, a woman named Halle or Hailey Storm. They just told me they've discovered Wendy was working with Stan Sinardi, and he's Patty Galloway's doctor now!"

"Sinardi? He's the guy from that show I hated…ghost something."

"*Phantom Finders*, and if she was working with him and she's dead now, that means she was working with him during *or before* all the hell that went on at Black Ridge!"

"Oh God! All right, I'll pull everything I can to see if there's a connection and get back to you. But, Ed, you were there; didn't you meet her doctors?"

"Yes, some younger guy named Hollerman I met with Logan. I never heard or saw Sinardi's name, and there's more. Zolie went to Vreeland Hills yesterday, and she hasn't returned. Now Maura and Logan have gone after her, and we haven't heard from them either."

"Do you want me to send a team there now?"

"I'm headed there now. Can you get Thrasher to meet me? I think Forrester's been too hurt and may need surgery. He saved Kate's life."

"Forrester's been cleared—no fractures. I'm looking at the report now. He's in some pain, and I know he wanted to get back to London. Let me look into it, and I'll call you back as soon as I can. Oh, and Ed—Thrasher, Forrester, and you have always made one hell of a team."

"They're great guys, Tallulah. Thanks," Ed said, placing the phone back down; he then went to the bedroom door, opened it, and listened. He could hear the family all the way from downstairs, and it was sad. Closing the door, he went back to the bathroom and took off his sweat-soaked robe.

After he got dressed, he looked at his bed where his coat, wallet, and keys were laid out. He then moved to his closet and pulled down an already packed bag that had a heavy weight to it. Grabbing his stuff from the bed, he unplugged his phone and went down the stairs, placing his things on a table near the front door, and then headed into the family room, where everyone was gathered.

Seeing his daughters, Lisa ran to him, and he picked her up and kissed her, giving her a big hug.

"I want Mommy," Lisa said.

"She'll be home in a few days." Ed reached around Ava as she came to hug him. "I love you, Ava."

"I love you too."

It was hard to leave; all the Savage children were there, and their hearts were broken. He looked to his own: Tucker, Ava, and Lisa; then to his brother Sam's, Chet and Heather; then to Roman's, Lana, Danni, and Chase; and finally to Logan's, Kate, Macy, and Ty, wishing he could do or say something that would help and wishing Trent was with them. The only one not there was Amanda, and he wondered where she was.

Knowing he had no choice but to leave, he told a small white lie about going to Marlo right away, and he eyed Roman to walk him out.

Stepping outside in the cold night air, Ed opened the back passenger door of the Range Rover and tossed his bag inside.

"What time's your flight to Boston?" Roman said.

"I don't know yet. I am going there—eventually. But for now I'm going to the sanatorium to bring home Logan, Maura, and Zolie."

"You want me to go with you?" Roman said.

"Could you after what happened? No, it's better that I handle this."

"I appreciate it, Ed. My mind keeps going in a circle along with my emotions."

"Don't worry; I've got this. By the way, where's Sam? I haven't seen him."

"You're not going to believe this."

Ed looked to him and swallowed. "Don't, Roman, just don't. What is it?"

"He's fine. But he called while you were upstairs. Did you know he'd gone to the Nantucket house?"

Ed remembered hearing Forrester tell him Nantucket and Martha's Vineyard were hit with Massachusetts being ground zero. "The wave—my God, him too? What happened?"

"He's there with Raquel Delgado. The wave hit them pretty bad, and they're at the hospital on the island getting checked out. He said they'd be home as soon as they can."

Ed leaned against the SUV. "Roman, I don't know why this is still happening, but it *has* to stop. Keep everyone here. No one leaves until I get back. Can we do that?"

"I'll take care of it. Watch your back over there."

Ed nodded as Amanda's car pulled near them and parked.

"Uncle Ed, I just saw the news about *Tycoon Wives*. Is Marlo all right?"

The look on his face told her everything. "No, honey, she lost the baby. Now I need to get going."

"Oh God, this family has suffered too much! I'm so sorry," she said, giving Ed a hug. "I've been trying to call Mother, and she's not returning my calls. Dad called from London, and he's worried too."

"Come on inside," Roman said, reaching up and putting his arm around her. He then looked back. "Ed, take care and call us with *any* news you get."

"Will do." Ed got into the Range Rover and started the engine; he then looked over and saw Roman open the door, turn back, and wave. Ed waved back and pulled away from the house.

Vreeland Hills Sanatorium was just over an hour away without traffic, and it wasn't long before Ed was locked in bumper-to-bumper traffic. He completely forgot about the freeway shutting down for construction and knew he would be getting there sometime before midnight. *Oh, great,* he thought, shivering at the memory of that horrible-looking place, and to add to the endless night of misery, it began to rain.

CHAPTER 126

T he rain was coming down hard at Vreeland Hills Sanatorium, and Dr. Todd entered Stevie Galloway's room with a file. Flipping on the main lights, he moved to her bed, tossing the file on the counter and reaching for her restraints.

"I bet you'd like to go home now," he said with a car salesman's smile as he released her left wrist.

"Who are you, and why am I here? I've done nothing to deserve this."

"So many questions." Dr. Todd laughed. "You'll have your answers very soon, but first I need to take you to your sister. It'd be better that way and even a little fun."

"What are you talking about?" Stevie said, feeling frightened at the man's strange comments as he released her other wrist.

"Come on. I'll show you," he said in a giddy tone, picking up the file and waving it in front of her. "The sooner we get this over with, the sooner you can go home." He truly was enjoying his show.

Getting up from the bed, Stevie followed the man back to Patty's room located not too far from hers. She saw the open room she thought was Zolie's and paused. "Where's Zolie Vanderran? She was here with me, and I heard her in that room."

"The English lady left hours ago," Dr. Todd continued, wanting his masquerade to lead her to think she'd been ignored all this time. "Here we are," he said, unlocking Patty's room. "After you."

Stevie watched the door creak open and stared into the dimly lit room to see her sister lying in the bed, just as she had left her.

"Stevie!" Patty said, seeing her.

"Go on—take a seat." The doctor motioned to the chair next to the bed.

Stevie rushed to the chair and took her sister's hand. "Are you all right?"

"She's fine," the doctor said, opening the file and turning on the overhead lights in the room. "It's time for all of us to have a little talk."

Both women looked to the man in silence.

"Very good. You're listening," he said, pulling out a large photo from the file. "I'm going to show you something you didn't know anything about. But before I do, I want you to remember the last time you saw your mother."

"You bastard!" Patty yelled, thinking of the horrendous accident that'd killed her.

Stevie recalled waving good-bye with her twin brothers, Melvin and Leroy, on that ugly day and stayed silent, wondering what was about to happen.

"No, the bastard was my father, Dr. Victor Vreeland," Todd said in a strange, calm tone. "And this is why," he said, turning over the photo and holding it in front of them.

Patty's and Stevie's eyes widened as they looked at the photo of their mother. At first they didn't know *exactly* what they were looking at until the second photo was shown to them.

It was again of their mother, but this one was of her sitting on the floor near a strangely shaped radiator. It looked like she was trying to stay warm, and when Patty looked to the radiator in her room, she realized the photo had been taken right here.

"What is this? Some sort of trick?" Patty said, nudging Stevie. "Look over at the radiator. It's the same as the one in the picture."

Stevie got up from the chair and moved to the radiator. She then reached for the photograph, and Dr. Todd handed it to her. She held it up and saw the same bent portion of the radiator that was exactly like the one in the room. "What are you doing? I don't understand this. Our mom was never here," Stevie said.

"Stevie, Patty, it's time you knew the truth," Dr. Todd said, pulling more of the photos from the file and tossing them on the bed.

The sisters began looking through them.

"Your mother actually survived the accident, ladies, and it was my bastard father who brought her here."

"You're lying! These photos are fakes," Patty yelled. "Momma was dead at the scene. I watched them put her and Pa into those black bags and zip them up."

"Yes, her death was called at the scene. But she'd been in shock—most likely from the accident, the pregnancy, and all the lies she'd been keeping. She was revived at the morgue in front of my father, the great Victor Vreeland, and back then he called the shots. He had her brought here for study."

"That's a lie." Stevie finally spoke. "We buried her."

"No, you buried the patient my father *set on fire* as a replacement for your mother's body so no questions would be asked." Dr. Todd paused, letting that one horrible fact simmer as he enjoyed the torment on the women's faces. "I even remember my father dragging me down to the basement to watch that patient burn in the hotbox as a punishment. I had nightmares for a long time after it was over," he continued, as he watched their tears come. Feeling his pulse racing, he was excited to deliver the most monumental blow of them all: "By the way, the twins she was carrying survived."

Like fathers, like sons—he's slipping—trust him now, and be free. Do it now, Patty—do it now, came the message from the grave to Patty's mind in a voice she did *not* recognize.

The crying came to a complete stop, and both sisters looked up as Dr. Todd dropped a few more photos on the bed. There, in the last batch, were photos of their mother holding twin infants while sitting in the same room they now occupied. The room had changed slightly since the pictures were taken, but the barred window and the radiator were unmistakable.

Rose Galloway sat at an angle in the pictures with one baby cradled in each arm. Her long hair was over her shoulder, and she had slightly turned toward the camera, showing one baby completely while the other was partly hidden by her hair. But the most noticeable things Patty saw in the photo were the many scars that decorated her mother's face, received when the glass had exploded from the windshield in the accident. She remembered crawling to her mother and seeing the shards of glass in her flesh as she was crying, trapped in the burning car.

Patty picked up one of the photos; her voice was soft, filled with love, as her tears wet her face. "Why? Why was she kept from us? I needed my mother. Those horrible Cullens did unspeakable things to me. Why didn't you let Momma take care of me?" She cried, remembering all the pain that'd destroyed her soul.

"Unspeakable things?" Dr. Todd's voice changed from his deadly calm to an innocent youthfulness, from before hatred had touched his heart. "You don't even know the meaning of unspeakable."

He's like you. But he's not, came two separate voices that filled Patty's ears, and she looked toward the bathroom and then turned her head to look toward the mirror over the counter. It was like there were *others* in the room. *He's not like those other assholes in the white coats. This time!* Patty looked back to her mother's voice coming from the bathroom, as if answering the other voice in the mirror.

"It wasn't me that took her from you. It was my father," Dr. Todd repeated, remembering his own hell and seeing Patty looking at the photo of her mother with the twins. Then the memory of setting the fire nearly blinded his mind because it was *him* who had murdered their mother all those years *after* his father had imprisoned her, and an internal battle waged in his head over the *things* he'd done.

But *now* he was different, so that made everything just *fine*, he told himself. "You see, I'm just like you—cheated by my father. He stole the life I should've had—the way he cheated you from having yours," the doctor said, compartmentalizing his tragic choices into that space in his head he put the things he didn't like—*things* he decided he didn't do and suddenly feeling the tenderness for the first time of a *connection* to someone who shared his pain—pain received from the same monster. Happy with his coping mechanism he'd developed by pretending he'd never done the horrible things he knew he did *helped* him, because when *he* felt good, then *he* could be the best doctor ever. Seeing her vulnerable state suddenly softened his heart, and he felt like himself again when his life had been happy in South America. "Medical records state the twins are hers, but there were many infant deaths in this hospital. I'm sorry for that," Dr. Todd said, thinking of the basement sacrifices his father performed and not wanting to mention that part of his horrendous past. He honestly didn't know if the twins had lived or why his father had chosen to do some of the horrible things he'd done—things he had *taught* Todd to do as well. And he wondered just how long his father would have allowed those children to live if he hadn't believed that by sacrificing them he would gain the powers he said the mother owned.

"What is it that you want?" Stevie asked.

The evil touching Todd's soul seemed to evaporate as he thought of his life in South America; he felt the strength of his old life coming back to him, seeing the betrayed lives of the women in front of him. But like blinking his eyes, the vileness drowning his heart that seemed to fade away came back stronger as he looked away from the women in the ugly building they were in. His mind was a battlefield set afire over the atrocities he'd done in his life, and they seemed to be flashing through his mind—one evil act after another. He thought of the young Kayla Bennet he'd met downstairs who reminded him of his own daughter, and he pushed the ugliness of everything else from his mind, focusing on the women in front of him and the happy life he knew he could have again.

"To help you, of course. To help you both reclaim the lost lives my father took from you." Dr. Todd moved forward to release Patty from her restraints. "Things will change for you. For both of you, I promise," he said, releasing her right wrist from the long chains bound to the floor. He then reached across and released her other wrist as his thoughts changed on the women in front of him.

Feeling freedom for the first time without a nurse walking her for exercise since she'd been placed there, Patty rubbed her sore wrists as she climbed from the nasty bed and stood next to her sister. The women instinctively hugged each other, and Dr. Todd saw the love flow between them. With everything that had happened, they had been able to stay together, unlike him and his brothers, which angered him.

"How are you going to help us?" Patty asked from her sister's arms.

"Your mother came back to life, and in a way I'd like my life back now too. My brother Blake is gone, and I miss him so. There's no bringing him back, but my brother Eric is still out there, and I desperately want my last family member back in my life."

He thinks he's telling the truth, came Rose Galloway's voice, this time heard by both her daughters.

"Mother!" Stevie and Patty yelled as they looked toward the bathroom entrance.

"You heard her too?" Patty said.

Stevie nodded, and Dr. Todd looked to the spot where he'd read their mother had died in the fire long ago. There was no way the women in front of him could have known that. He'd even read every report on Rose Galloway and the special powers his father thought she possessed, like telepathy and telekinesis. Unless Sinardi had mentioned something, there was no way these women would know. He'd spoken with Sinardi about what had happened to Patty—her adventure in the mountains and some ocean hotel where'd she tried to kill as many as she could, all aimed at a well-known family she hated.

He didn't hear what the sisters had just *thought* they heard, but he smiled. He had a good feeling. "Stevie? You heard your mother just now?"

"Yes, like I did last night."

"She called to me when I arrived," Patty added.

"Patty, had Dr. Sinardi mentioned anything about your mother?"

"No, nothing at all."

Not wanting to draw attention from the authorities who lived in the outside world past the hospital doors, he knew Patty could never leave. He thought of the rooms downstairs, how beautiful they were, and he *wanted* to help this woman.

"Patty, your crimes that brought you here will *keep* you here. There is nothing that can be done about that now. Those were your bad choices. But I can make being here better than you can imagine." Dr. Todd stared at the far corner of the room, where he knew the camera was set.

"Damn Savages," Patty muttered.

"What was that?"

"Nathan Savage destroyed my mother."

"Savage?"

"That's the family she went after," Stevie said.

Dr. Todd wondered where else he'd heard that name before, outside of Patty's chart, and he knew the drugs he'd put in the drinks Stevie and Zolie took were only to knock them out. "Patty, the drugs Sinardi has you on can cause hallucinations. But you, Stevie, that doesn't explain you hearing her too."

"Let us go now," Stevie said.

"I can't release Patty, but I can prepare a better room than this. Besides, the drugs are still running though you," he said, looking back to Patty. "Let me make the arrangements."

"Thank you," Patty said, mostly believing her mother's voice was real and starting to actually trust the man in front of her.

Dr. Todd now wanted to know more from Sinardi about what had brought this woman to his hospital; he wanted to see her chart again. When he'd first read it, part of the history had been missing; Sinardi had told him it had been misplaced.

The sisters watched him move to the counter. Opening the drawer, he lifted the old camera recovered from the accident that started this nightmare for the Galloways, and placed it on top of the counter next to a hairbrush, which was also found at the scene. Then he opened a cupboard and pulled down the small wooden toy piano. He turned the small crank on the bottom and placed it next to the hairbrush. The tune was "London Bridge," and the Galloway sisters knew it well. "She used to brush her hair while humming a children's song, she loved that tune," he said remembering listening from the hall in his youth. He again looked to the far corner of the room, where the camera was, before collecting all the photos and stuffing them into the file and leaving, locking the door behind him.

Moving down the hall, the name Savage crossed his mind, and he recalled the poster behind Sinardi's door. Sinardi had been keeping things from him, he thought, and it angered him. Many thoughts had been angering him lately, like what his life could have been, and the women behind the door helped him see that.

He wanted to take another look at that poster and see if there was anything else he could find about Patty Galloway's history and how her world had been destroyed—like his life when he was forced to leave his hospital. He also remembered the last time he'd spoken to Nurse Pam, who'd stayed at the hospital after he'd fled.

The phone call he'd placed weeks after he'd left filled him with more threats than he'd bargained for. Nurse Pam Porter told him his brother Eric had heard the rumors of him murdering Blake and sworn he'd kill him the minute he laid eyes on him. He'd extended his stay there before going back to Germany in hopes of catching his nefarious little brother to murder him "Vreeland-style." Pam had told him Eric didn't believe his brother ever went to Canada, and lastly Pam had mentioned Eric had offered her a job in Germany, and she was going to take him up on it.

Yes, he got the feeling Sinardi was hiding things from him, and with the Galloway woman on his side, for the first time in years, Dr. Todd thought his own redemption was at hand.

It was too bad, really, considering what was coming.

CHAPTER 127

rriving in the room not far from Patty's, Dr. Sinardi caught the last of the recording on the monitor and listened to what the so-called great Dr. Todd Vreeland was saying to *his* patient—his patient whom he needed for his plan to take revenge against Ed Savage. Infuriated, he left the back way from the room and hurried to the basement, passing Dr. Hollerman on the way.

"Oh, Doctor, she's ready…in *the room*."

"Thanks, Doctor," Hollerman replied with an eager smile.

"Personally, I think she likes us at the same time."

"I was thinking that myself," Hollerman said and winked back.

"Meet me back up here when you're finished. Oh, and stay out of the basement tonight."

"Will do, boss."

Getting downstairs and moving along the cells, he hit the main lights, and the entire corridor lit up in the dreary basement. "Wake up, my children; I have an offer for you," Sinardi shouted as he came to the Brockmans' cells, stopping at the oldest, Belinda.

She was standing near the glass, quietly looking at the man filled with excitement standing on the other side. Her hair was still neatly brushed, and her gown had been changed to a clean one.

"You're looking fresh today," Dr. Sinardi said. "How'd you like to return to the fifth-floor rooms you once called your own?"

"And leave all *this* behind?" Belinda growled back.

"Listen to him!" came her sister's voice from her cell. "Yes, we accept. I want all my beautiful clothes back," Belynn said from down the corridor.

"Murder is what he wants," Belinda said, reading his mind and raising her voice so her sister could hear.

"Yes, I want you to murder that man I brought down here earlier. Dr. Todd Vreeland must die!" Sinardi said with his voice full of scorn. "Now, when I release you two, you will be free to kill him when he comes down here."

"You'll release our brother, too," Belinda said, her voice filled with conviction.

"Why? He's useless," Sinardi barked.

"Prices will be paid, just like the price you paid for banging that girl on the meat rack in the butchering plant," Belinda cooed behind the glass.

"Fine, he'll have his old room next to yours upstairs," Sinardi said, thinking that was a small concession. Grinning like an idiot and full of glee, he left the corridor, moving to a safe place locked away from the main area of the basement, and hit the magnetic door release to the cells. He then rushed from the room, hearing the sounds of the doors opening, and raced up a back stairway to the main floor of the hospital, thinking of a way to get that traitorous prick, Dr. Todd, to the basement.

Leaving in such a joyous rush, he didn't notice that he'd accidentally released the magnetic doors on the fifth floor as well.

CHAPTER 128

ogan Savage had been searching for a hidden release when he heard the magnetic door click within the doorframe. Pulling on the door that had locked them in their prison for the last several hours, it now easily swung open.

"It opened," Logan said to the women.

"Don't let it close again," Maura said, getting up from a chair in the room.

Zolie got up from the bed, and she rushed to Logan, still dressed in the clothes she'd worn yesterday and damned if she was about to wear anything hanging in that closet.

The three stepped out into the beautifully lit hall and saw no one was there.

"Stay close. We're getting out of here," Logan said, leading the way.

Getting near the grand staircase, they saw the clock on the foyer of each level and saw it was near midnight, and Zolie moved toward the elevator, not seeing any construction signs like she did on the sixth floor.

"No," Logan whispered. "We can't risk it in case it opens on a floor where someone is waiting for it. We're taking the stairs."

"Besides, they weren't working on some the floors," Maura whispered to her sister.

Grabbing Zolie's hand, he led them past the elevators to the stairs, and as they made their way down the first few steps, they heard people talking below; they turned and ran back and continued down the hall into a part of the building they had not explored.

"Where does this lead?" Maura whispered in the dimly lit hall.

"I don't know," Zolie said.

"There's got to be another stairway down in this old building—a fire escape, an employee area, anything besides the grand staircase we came up. Come on. I'll get you out. Just stay close and keep quiet," Logan said as the sound of the thunder outside seemed to shake the old building, causing the lights inside to flicker as he led the women down the long, dimly lit, lonely hall.

CHAPTER 129

Stevie Galloway moved to the door and tried to open it, feeling the same impenetrable door she'd banged on trying to get out when they'd first arrived. Giving up, she turned to see Patty lifting up the hairbrush she'd used to brush their mother's hair that day of the car accident, remembering how she'd told her over and over along the many years since reconnecting after she'd run away. Stevie watched as the anger filled her sister's face, and when she looked up, Stevie actually took a step back frightened from the look on her face.

"I wondered what happened to this." Patty said nudging the camera. "All I got from the police was the film inside," she shook her head at their ugly past. "Now you listen to me," Patty continued. "Just play along with this simpleton in the white coat, and we'll be out of here soon."

"We'd better be," Stevie shot back. Her earlier attitude was back, and she was over the whole situation. "Everything's gone, Patty: the gas station, the store and café…even your run-down cabin is gone. I lost the lease on my rental when the headlines ruined my life, and we have nothing. We may have nowhere to go, but I definitely want to get the hell out of this place!"

"Not everything's gone," Patty said as she started to brush her own hair with the relic in her hand. "Marcus Bowers may have tricked me out of my holdings—but one of his followers stole money from him, and it's in a secret safe deposit box in Black Creek Savings."

"Safe deposit box? How will you get the money if someone else has it?"

"There's enough to get us out from here, and we can start a whole new life anywhere we want. We just need to escape this place, and our new lives await," Patty said, putting down the brush. "Oh, and I killed the bitch who stole his money—I have the key hidden where no one will ever find it, and I was waiting to surprise Marcus with it after the revenge at the hotel."

Stevie felt the hatred from the lies destroying her family and her life—thinking of when she'd run away after the accident, only to be beaten in an abusive relationship. Wanting it all to end, she agreed with playing along with whatever this Dr. Todd wanted, and she planned on doing anything she could so the two of them could escape.

CHAPTER 130

r. Todd stood at the poster and read Ed Savage's name next to Sinardi's. He then went to the desk and saw Patty Galloway's chart next to an expensive Birkin bag and a Rolls-Royce keychain. Placing down the Rose Galloway file with the photos, he turned on the desk lamp, opened the chart, and flipped to the history and saw it was still missing. He could feel his frustration rising and opened the lower drawer where he'd found his father's notes regarding Rose Galloway, and he looked there for the missing history from Patty's chart. Pulling out the papers and only seeing his father's notes, he stuffed them back in haphazardly with some sticking up beyond the drawer and then grabbed Patty's chart and threw it in, slamming the drawer shut.

Angry, he exited *his* office in such a hurry he didn't notice the door hadn't shut all the way, and he raced to the sky bridge.

Moments after he left, Stacey Porter arrived and let herself in the open office. She was carrying some files, and she eyed the beautiful Birkin bag on the desk. Moving to it, she dropped the files and picked up the bag to admire it. Hearing a noise from down the hall, she dropped the bag and grabbed the files, picking up the Rose Galloway file with them, and hurried out from the office, leaving the door ajar like she'd found it, with plans to come back to steal the beautiful bag.

As Dr. Todd took those first few steps on the third floor, he heard something in one of the laboratories down a darkened hall. Quietly, he moved toward it, when he heard the sound of a woman crying. Looking inside the darkened lab, he saw a back office door close with the distinct blueish light from a television flickering through the frosted glass. He quietly moved to the other side of the door and listened. Slowly opening it, he saw Kayla Bennet; she had grabbed a blanket and was crying on a sofa in the office.

"Working graveyard?" came his voice from the darkened lab.

Kayla jumped with fright nearly dropping the remote turning to him.

"Sorry, I didn't mean to scare you," Dr. Todd said, noticing her tears. "What's the matter, Kayla? Why are you crying?"

Kayla immediately wiped her face with the blanket. "Nothing— it's nothing, sir," she said, holding the blanket tightly over her shoulders.

Worrying and wondering about this particular girl, Dr. Todd moved and sat next to her. He gently took the remote from her hands and muted the television, and as he looked at her, he felt something strong for the girl. "Kayla, I want you to trust me here. Tell me what happened."

Kayla lowered the blanket, and he could see her scrubs were torn, and she had scratch marks on her neck.

"Who did this to you?"

"It's nothing. I should be used to it by now," the young girl said, looking up at the man she hardly knew. "I didn't tell you this earlier, but my mom was a patient here."

Dr. Todd listened to her voice, and it reminded him so much of his mother; the thought occurred to him that this young woman could be either his or one of his brothers' daughters.

"I was lucky enough to be raised here, so I owe my life to the hospital," Kayla said, pulling the blanket back over her torn scrubs.

"I was looking for Dr. Hollerman and Dr. Sinardi when I heard you in here. Have you seen them?" Dr. Todd asked, seeing her flinch at hearing their names and hiding his sudden desire to protect this young woman. "Did either of them do this to you?"

Seeing her nod in shame as she looked away, his anger flared. "Kayla, are you telling me they both attacked you?"

"They have the room they lock me in at times, and I have to stay there until they have their way with me."

"Sinardi and Hollerman?"

"Yes, Sinardi was first a while ago, and then Hollerman came in. At least it wasn't at the same time like they usually do," she said, hiding her face in the blanket. "Hollerman just let me out a short while ago. He was pretty quick this time."

"Where is he?" Vreeland barked, ironically feeling empathy for a victim after years of inflicting the same torment on numerous women himself.

"I don't know. He told me he was going to meet with him and to not go near the basement at all tonight."

"I'll take care of this, Kayla. You can believe that will happen!" Dr. Todd said.

"Please don't get me in trouble. I have no place to go," she pleaded, getting up.

"I won't say a word," Dr. Todd said, actually feeling like a father for the second time in his miserable life. And the feeling of the torment touching his soul seemed to abate, it was like his evil twin living within him was in battle, losing to the strength of the good son he once was.

"Thanks for talking to me. I come here to hide, and now I'm feeling better. I'm going back to my room to go to bed," Kayla said.

"Don't worry, my dear. I'll fix everything," Dr. Todd said, watching her move past him. "By the way, do you know anything about that poster on the wall behind the door in Sinardi's office?"

"He hates that other guy. It's his fault he's here...or something. I don't like being around when he goes off on his tantrums over missing out in Hollywood, 'cause he makes the sex hurt harder," Kayla said, lowering her head as she left the room.

Dr. Todd walked her back to her room, and on the way there he had her point out that other room where the men took advantage of her. Seeing the old examination room he imagined them playing doctor on this innocent girl, and his anger rose. Once she was inside her own room, he went looking for Dr. Sinardi.

Getting to the grand staircase, he took them to the main floor of the west building, knowing the massive torture basement was connected under the grounds between the two towers. Quietly moving down the stairs to the basement to the long-forgotten corridors of the mostly unused portion under the West Tower, he paused when he heard laughing. Silently he moved to see the lit room, where it sounded like two people were having sex. There, he found Nurse Pam riding his brother Blake and having a good old time doing it.

"What the fuck is this?" Todd said in absolute shock. He watched Pam turn her head and smile at him, and he could see his brother Blake grinning at him beyond her shoulder as he pushed her off from him.

"Well, this isn't how we planned it, but I love a good twist in a story! Huh, Todd?" Blake said, standing at full attention, naked in front of him.

Todd stood before his *bigger* brother and watched him catch the pants Pam threw to him and then looked at his face and saw the scar on his cheek from the fight they'd had when Blake threw him into the elevator shaft.

"No, this is some trick." Todd blinked and took a step back as his brother put his pants on. "I destroyed you that night…with her," he said, pointing to the two-faced snickering whore who seemed to have betrayed him.

"Look at me, Brother. Is my face burned with acid?" Blake laughed, seeing the thoughts race through his brother's mind as he grabbed his shirt from the bed. "Do I have a scar across my forehead? On my body?" He pointed to his head and waved at his unscarred, muscled body, where Todd had cut and sewn on those foul fat sacks.

Todd remembered seeing his brother on the table; his face had been swollen and covered in bandages. And his mind flashed to lifting up the bandages when Pam had come to his side and shot more liquid cocaine into his mouth. "Who was that on the table?" Todd barked, realizing the truth.

"Come on, you remember that night. Who else was there?" Blake said brushing his fingers over his scarred face.

Todd's mind raced over the years of killing and saw Bob, the annoying X-ray tech he'd enjoyed killing, and Lorena, whom he'd strangled during sex in the midst of a blackout he later had visions of doing, and *then* he remembered. "Marvin!" Marvin Newman was there that first night they'd fought, but when he had needed him the most, he had taken a few days off, or so he was tricked into believing. "Marvin never came back to the hospital, and you told me he quit, Pam," Todd said, pointing like a snot-nosed brat tattling on a sibling.

"You told me he quit, Pam!" Pam mocked the man she'd learned to hate as she laughed at him.

Todd's skin turned red with anger, and that's when Blake pulled a gun from his lab coat hanging on a peg on the wall near the bed. "I can't believe how stupid you are—not knowing that was Marvin and not me? Yeah, we're similar in size and hair color, but I'm your brother, and now I feel insulted. Should I just end his poor life now, Pam?"

"Sure," Pam said, really not caring. "Shoot him in the dick first," she said with a smirk.

"Fuck you, Pam!" Dr. Todd yelled in his coldest voice, actually scaring her and making her flinch. Seeing his brother look in her direction, Todd bolted from the room, running back the way he'd come.

"Serve me!" Blake yelled down the corridor in the same voice he'd used when he called up the elevator shaft. "That was too funny!" He laughed, and Pam joined in as their laughter carried down the corridor.

Hearing his brother and realizing he'd been tricked all these years angered him like never before; when he heard the sound of a gunshot, he hid behind a corner. Quietly he listened. He didn't hear their footsteps coming near; all he could hear was the laughter of two true demons coming from the dimly lit corridor.

His mind was too full—it felt like his head would burst; he'd thought for a split second that he'd found some sort of redemption with the similarities with Patty and meeting Kayla, but now it was one dirty trick, a giant dirty trick that his bastard brother and that dirty bitch had played on *him*, and he'd lost so many years of his life because of it: running from country to county in South America, finally finding love and trusting it for once, only to have it taken away from him so tragically. There was nothing left, he thought. Turning and running up the stairs, he was furious. If it was the last thing he ever did, Todd was going to even the score and make things right, and it was going to *hurt*.

Getting to the sixth floor, his head spinning, he went back to Patty's room and unlocked the door, stepping in to see them standing at the counter. "Has anyone been up here since I left?"

"No," both women said, shaking their heads.

Seeing what his father had done to this woman's childhood, what Sinardi was doing to Kayla (a young girl who could quite possibly be his own daughter), and his own destroyed life, his mind became clear as he saw the countless faces of those he'd murdered and realized he'd become the thing he hated most—his father! The evil things he had done that he had to live with were there, but now, learning of Blake and Pam's vile trick, he was done. The evil touching his heart grew, and they all were going to pay!

The Galloway sisters watched him move away from the door, leaving it partly open, to the far corner of the room, where he reached up and broke something up on the wall where a small red light had been illuminated.

Moving near them, he threw the object in the garbage container, when the sound of someone coming could be heard from the hall. "Keep our conversations quiet," he said, purposely leaving the door unlocked and barely shutting it completely. He saw Dr. Hollerman coming toward him.

"Dr. Hollerman," he said with a smile, knowing the time to murder J-Hole was present, and he moved toward him, keeping him away from Patty's room. Meeting him a room away from Patty's, he extended his hand. "Hey there. You sure handled yourself like a regular actor earlier. Join me for a tequila?" he said, patting the man on the back and leading him to the sixth-floor operating room.

"Yeah, I could use a stiff one," Hollerman said with a grin.

Like the stiff one you gave Kayla? Dr. Todd thought. "I didn't know you guys were such tequila drinkers."

"It's mostly Sinardi, but hey, I'm not refusing the expensive shit." Hollerman laughed.

"Here we are," Todd said, leading him into the old viewing room that was now an office.

"What happened in here?" Dr. Hollerman said, seeing the knocked over mop bucket, the moved shelves, and the wall destroyed behind it in the operating room before following him in.

"Yeah, I saw that a few minutes ago myself. Looks like someone was fucking around in here. Anyway, Dr. Sinardi told me he had a bottle or two in here, and I wanted to check it out. Well? What do you say? Share a tequila with me?" Dr. Todd said, smiling and reaching for a new expensive bottle of Don Julio Real and two glasses. "Now that's a fancy bottle," he said, holding it up and showing him the metal leaves on the sides of the bottle as he cracked the seal.

"Well, maybe just a couple," Hollerman said, adding a stupid laugh as he watched Vreeland pour the drinks.

"Say, have you seen Dr. Sinardi recently?"

"I passed him a short while ago; he was headed down the east stairs."

"I want to thank him for telling me about the bottles he kept up here. I just love tequila." Handing him a glass, Dr. Todd grinned. "What shall we drink to?"

"I like you, Dr. Vreeland. You sure had me going earlier with the women. For a moment I thought you were really mad at me. Here's to a long career together. I get the feeling you're going to teach me a thing or two," he finished with a wink.

"Here's to learning," Dr. Todd said, grinning as he raised his glass to his next victim.

They clinked their glasses, and Dr. Hollerman took a tiny sip of tequila as both men kept their eyes on one another. Then Dr. Todd grinned and downed the entire glass he'd poured for himself and looked at Hollerman with a challenging stare.

"All right then," Hollerman said, downing the glass and leaning forward, coughing. He tried to catch his breath when the bottle of Don Julio came flying up in Dr. Todd's hand and cracked J-Hole in his cheek, smashing his nose and breaking it.

Flying back in a spin and losing his balance, J-Hole turned and hit his eye socket on the corner of the huge wood desk. His head bounced back, and Todd swung the bottle again, hitting him in his face watching the blood spurt from his nose as he hit the floor. Rolling over in a daze from the sucker punch, he felt Dr. Todd on top of him and at this throat.

"You like hurting young girls during sex, asshole?" he screamed into his bleeding face.

Choking for air, the younger man reached up, grabbing Todd's collar with one hand and clawing at his throat with the other. Pulling Todd down on his outstretched arm, choking him in return, Todd bit his tongue and lost his balance. Hollerman rolled over and was quickly up on his feet. Seeing he had a chance, he kicked Todd in the face when he saw him turn to face him and nearly fell over, grabbing the desk for support.

Turning away to run, Hollerman saw the IV pole through the bloody veil coating his eye. Grabbing it, he lifted it up and smashed it down on Todd's face, pushing with all his weight until the metal cross stand scraped across Dr. Todd's flesh, slicing his cheek and bottom lip. As the stand hit the polished floor, it slipped out from under Hollerman, and he nearly fell but gained his balance as Dr. Todd got to his feet and grabbed his lab coat from behind and yanked back, pulling the man back to him. He then grabbed his throat and pushed him back against the bookshelves, knocking things to the floor and punching him hard in the face, watching him fall back to the floor.

Dr. Todd spit blood, eyeing a large pair of scissors on a medical tray, and grabbed them as Dr. Hollerman sat up and rubbed the blood from his eyes. But the timing was too slow because when he could finally focus, Dr. Todd had already grabbed him from behind and pulled his head back with one hand, while holding the scissors high above his head with the other.

"Compare notes with Bob when you get to hell, jackass!" Dr. Todd screamed as he plunged the large scissors down into the asshole's damaged eye, letting him fall back to the floor, screaming. He then grabbed the handles and opened the scissors inside Hollerman's head, twisting them as he pulled them out.

Dr. Hollerman put the palms of his hands over his torn-out eye as blood poured down his cheeks, screaming like he never had in his life.

Holding the scissors, Dr. Todd eyed the bottle of tequila, grabbed it, and got on top of Hollerman and sat on his chest. "Time for another shot, Doctor!" Todd yelled, dropping the scissors and jamming the bottle into Hollerman's mouth.

Hollerman turned his head, and Dr. Todd raised the bottle and squeezed his head between his knees, smashing the bottle down and breaking teeth as he crammed it further into the man's mouth. Tequila poured down his throat, over his face, and into his eyes. It burned with the blood, and Hollerman could barely breathe.

"Be glad I'm murdering you with the good stuff, you little fucker!" Dr. Todd raged, as he pushed down on the bottom of the bottle deeper into the man's throat.

Hollerman's body started bucking underneath the weight of his murderer as he tried to breathe, and that was when Dr. Todd had had enough. He then grabbed the scissors by his side and raised them high, bringing the weapon down into J-Hole's other eye and ending the grand performance.

Realizing J-Hole probably hadn't seen it coming made Dr. Todd sad, and he'd warned both Hollerman and Sinardi when he'd berated them in front of Zolie about that. Watching his victim take his last breaths angered him so he ripped the bottle from his mouth flinging it toward the elevator, and bitch slapped the hell out of him to bring him back in order to kill him again. And when Hollerman started moaning and flinching, Dr. Todd realized his chance for a second act was at hand.

Grabbing the scissors, he pushed down with all his strength and pulled them as far open as he could for the second time, hearing the cartilage cracking and breaking within Hollerman's skull until the bridge of his nose burst open and the blades snapped. He watched his chest rise for the last time, choking on broken teeth and chipped glass as he uttered his final breath. That was the only satisfaction Dr. Todd got.

Leaning back, Todd laughed, extending his legs to stand as he eyed the pit he'd throw him down, and as he started dragging J-Hole over to the pit, he slipped in the water he'd kicked over from the mop bucket. Todd fell, hitting the back of his head, *and it hurt*. Getting up in a rage, grabbing the IV pole Hollerman had used, he lifted it up and turned it over as he plunged it into the dead man's stomach.

Tequila and blood burst from his extended abdomen, and Dr. Todd pushed down, skewering him like a bloody kabob. He then used the IV pole to push him like a mop into the elevator shaft and shoved him inside. As Hollerman fell into the darkness, the IV pole caught in his intestines, and Dr. Todd let go of it, sending it down with him.

"What a waste of good tequila," Dr. Todd said, kicking the bottle down the elevator shaft on top of his victim.

Down the hall from the operating room, Patty picked up the camera she'd used that fateful day and studied it, remembering filming her family on the last day of their lives together. With the camera in one hand and the hairbrush in her other, rage consumed her and she threw the camera into the mirror shattering it to pieces. At the sound, Stevie looked to the door and saw it was open and moved to it. She then opened it looking to see if anyone heard them.

Patty then looked at the hairbrush in her hand. Seeing the past and wanting nothing to do with it any longer, she threw it on the counter, watching it bounce off the broken mirror behind it. "Come on. We're leaving," she said, moving to the door.

Stevie backed away and moved behind her watching her open the door wider, when the brush from the counter flew from its place and slid across the floor.

Both sisters looked at the haunted thing, and Patty felt Stevie's hand pushing her back.

"Go," was the only word they needed, and the two women trapped inside fled down the hall.

Inside the room, the ghost of Greta Von Staller appeared in the shattered fragments of the broken mirror and stuck her head out and looked toward the door, happy with making their acquaintance—and who was the true spirit who not only *owned* this land but was the source of Rose's telekinetic abilities when she was a patient there.

CHAPTER 131

I t was only days ago, yet it seemed like forever to Ed when Lana and Kate had ridden up that day when everything started to change again. He remembered being happy and seeing his nieces wave to him on his way to work. Now it was after midnight, and he could see the intimidating structure of the sanatorium looming in the foreboding darkness under the rain. The traffic had been worse than he'd ever seen, being so late at night, and the downpour didn't help. The construction project was longer than he thought, and it had closed most of the freeway, and the traffic had been backed up for miles on the smaller, nearly impassable roads.

Pulling up the long drive to Raven House, Ed looked at his phone and saw no messages from Tallulah about Wes Thrasher or Robert Forrester meeting him there. Dropping his phone back in the console as he drove along the driveway, he saw Logan's Cadillac Escalade and Zolie's Rolls-Royce. He parked close by against the curb.

Shutting off his engine, he got out and opened the back door, reaching for his heavy bag and opening it. He dug underneath the clothing inside and pulled out his holster and two guns.

Taking off his coat, he heard his phone vibrate in the console and saw it light up with a message. Moving to the driver's door to get it, he saw the text from Tallulah: *Caught Thrasher and Forrester before they left the hospital—they're on their way.*

Knowing the cavalry was coming, Ed felt better looking at the grisly building in front of him. Closing the front door, he felt the

wind blow and felt its cold, deathlike grip. Turning, he saw the unmistakable flashing lights of an approaching ambulance. Keeping
his eyes on the vehicle, Ed put on what he needed from his bag
and then put his coat on and stuffed the weapons in his pockets as
he scanned the area where the ambulance was headed and saw his
chance.

Closing the back door and manually locking it, he ran over
around the end of the building and hid behind the tall shrubs near
the bay doors and watched as the ambulance pulled inside and
backed into the patient-loading dock. He waited for the driver and
passenger to get out to attend to the patient in the back, when he
made his move, sneaking along the building and making his way to
the main loading dock as techs wearing scrubs came out from a side
door to help with the ambulance.

Getting up the loading dock stairs, he caught the door before it
shut and ran down the hall, trying to get away from all the commotion before being seen. As he rounded a hall corner, he saw exactly
what he needed. Next to the locker room was a laundry cart pushed
up against a wire rack of scrubs. Seeing that the doors inside had
push-button combinations, he smiled, grabbing the scrubs off the
shelves along with a white lab coat, and hurried down the hall to the
stairs.

All he knew from his time here with Logan was that Patty would
be on the sixth floor of the East Tower. They'd gone in the West
Tower entrance and had been led up to the fourth floor, where that
doctor's office was. This was the only place in the hospital where he
could look for clues, so he decided to start there.

After climbing the stairs and arriving on the fourth floor, he
made his way to the main hall and slipped into a waiting room.
Closing the door behind him, he saw more offices behind a counter
and moved behind it, placing the scrubs on the counter and turning
on the computer. When the password dialogue box popped up, he
shrugged and took off his wet coat, pulling his guns from the pockets
and stuffing the coat under the desk. He then put the large scrubs
on over his clothes, secured his firearms—one in the holster over
his scrub shirt—and grabbed the lab coat and put it on, stuffing his

other gun in the lab coat pocket as he moved back to the waiting room door. Slowly he opened it. Seeing that all was clear, he continued on his way until he came to the area he remembered.

Passing by the directory, he went right to the office Dr. Hollerman had brought them to and found the door locked. He then pulled out a small zippered case from his pants pocket under his scrubs, and as he was about to open it, he saw Dr. Hollerman's name on the placard and remembered what Sandy and Hailey Storm had said about Sinardi. He then moved back to the directory and saw Sinardi's office was located just two doors down from Hollerman's.

Passing by Hollerman's office, opting to see what Sinardi was hiding, he was surprised to see the door was slightly open. Looking for the placard, he noticed it was missing, and a small light was on in the room. Quietly he entered, seeing the desk lamp had been left on, and he shut the door behind himself. Passing the desk, he went to the windows, keeping to the shadows as he looked up at the East Tower and saw bright lights on in the rooms at one end of the fifth and sixth floors. He then looked down and saw the skyway bridge to the East Tower and knew that was his only choice of getting to the light. He was sure there'd be a way over to the other wing through the basement, too, but he didn't like the thought of searching for a passageway in the bowels of a creepy hospital in the dead of night.

Moving back to the desk, he immediately spotted Zolie's bag and the keys to her car. Putting the keys in his pocket under his scrubs, he read the notes on the calendar and searched the papers and charts beside it. Then he opened the top desk drawer and found the prescription pad of Dr. Stanley Sinardi. Just seeing that man's name caused his temperature to rise. Pulling the pad out, he held it up and tore off the top few pages and added it with Zolie's keys. Then he spotted papers sticking out from the bottom drawer. Opening it, he saw the single chart with Patty Galloway's name on it and grabbed it, along with a few of the pages underneath, placing it on the desk in front of him.

Seeing the room number, E606-F/Galloway, written on the chart, he grabbed a pen on the desk and wrote it down on a Post-it. He then looked to the window and realized Patty's room was on the sixth floor, in the sixth room, and on the sixth wing, F, of the hospital. A shiver ran down his spine as he then opened the chart and looked for the doctor's orders to see what, if any, notes Sinardi had made regarding his intentions for Patty.

The flash of lights across the window caused his eyes to dart to them, and he rose from the desk to see what was happening outside. There he saw a car pull up with its high beams on and knew he didn't have much time. And when those two idiot Storm sisters got out, trouble had most definitely arrived.

Quickly moving back to the desk, he grabbed the chart and tossed it back in the drawer, when he noticed the pages he'd pulled out with it still on the desk. Grabbing them to stuff them back in the drawer, he saw Rose Galloway's name on them and paused to read them.

He couldn't believe what he was reading; the room number was the same one they now had Patty in: 666…he didn't even want to think what that meant, and if these papers were indeed true, Rose had lived past the date of that horrible accident his uncle Niles Savage had caused. Pulling the chart back from the drawer, he gathered the rest of the papers and stuffed them in Zolie's bag, catching the Post-it with them. He then grabbed the bag and moved back to the hall; seeing that it was clear, Ed made his way to the main grand staircase he'd seen with Logan.

At the third floor, he saw the direction to the skyway and started to move; he held up Zolie's bag and looked for a place to hide it. Not really seeing anything that could serve as a good hiding place, he remembered the plants on the first and second floors he'd seen when he was there with Logan. Running down the stairs, he was surprised when he got to the landing and saw the plants had been torn up from the planters, and when he looked to the first floor, he saw the dead plants lying on the tarps. Using the terra-cotta planters, he placed the purse inside one and turned it over, pushing it back behind the others to conceal it. He then made his way back up to the skyway.

CHAPTER 132

Outside, at the main doors to the hospital, Hailey and Sandy Storm saw the posted sign telling them the building was closed for the night. Trying the door and finding it locked, Sandy shrugged. "Now what?"

"I don't know. We saw Ed's Range Rover, so we know he couldn't have gotten here much sooner than we did with that traffic. And if *he* got in, we will too," Hailey said, marching away from the entrance.

"Wait for me," Sandy said, following her and pulling up her hood to keep the rain away.

As they hurried through the wet grass, the smell of cigarette smoke drifted close by, and they jumped when they saw the shadow of someone emerge from under an awning and run out to the parking lot. The woman had a newspaper over her head, and they saw her car lights flash as she unlocked the door. They hid against the building as they watched her open her car and lean inside. She appeared to be searching for something in her console.

"Come on," Hailey said, pulling Sandy by the hand toward the East Tower.

They came to an area with a side door under an awning with a bench and a cement ashtray, possibly for staff breaks. There in the ashtray was the glowing red ash from the partly snuffed-out cigarette; the side door was propped open with a heavy-duty rubber door wedge.

Looking back, they saw the woman close her car door and heard her car alarm reengage as she started running back toward them in the rain. Opening the door, Hailey pulled her sister inside and pushed the door back to where it'd been.

"This way," Sandy said.

Looking for a place to hide, they ran through a small break room and out into a main hall and ran down it until they came to an intersection. It was either right or left, and they chose left, which led them to a staircase leading down to the basement.

"No, I don't want to go down there," Sandy whispered, turning back to hear footsteps announcing that someone was coming straight at them.

"They probably won't be going down here, so we have no choice," Hailey whispered, reaching for her and pulling her down the stairs beside her.

At the bottom they came to a large landing area with double doors leading to the basement. There they saw old, broken medical equipment left to die on dusty shelves, and when Hailey opened one of the basement's double doors, Sandy grabbed a discarded suction canister and lodged it between the doors.

"Why are you doing that?" Hailey said, watching her.

"Because I've lived through a hotel massacre and seen enough horror movies to know better," Sandy said, gently closing the door, making sure it wouldn't lock them in the scary basement. Turning to face her sister, she looked into the dimly lit corridor and took a step back. "Now where?"

"We'll find another stairway up and go search Sinardi's office," Hailey said.

"But which tower?" Sandy pointed to the map on the wall behind her.

The basement connected both massive buildings together, and they could see the area was huge on the diagram, with arrows pointing to the West Tower.

"I don't know; we'll figure it out," Hailey said.

"Oh, I forgot," Sandy whispered, fishing out the small device in her pocket that'd recorded their sister's death at the hotel.

"What?" Hailey whispered back.

"I'm not missing a thing," Sandy said, holding it up to Hailey as she pressed record and placed it back in her pocket, leaving the top exposed so that everything they were about to deal with would be caught on tape.

CHAPTER 133

ogan, Maura, and Zolie had tried so many doors along the hallway and found them all either locked, a patient's room, or leading them to a dead end, that when they heard the sound of people moving toward them, they hid in an exam room until they were gone. The waiting seemed endless, and when they finally got near the end of the hall, their hopes lifted when they saw the sign leading them to the stairs.

"Thank God," Maura said, rushing ahead and pushing open the fifth-floor door. Hurrying, she was shocked to find Patty Galloway on the stairs when the door shut behind her.

"You!" Patty screamed. Seeing Cara's face on the woman's twin who had killed her brother Leroy before she'd pushed the meddlesome bitch over the falls at Black Ridge fed her anger to a boiling point. Caught with that insane woman between her and the door where Logan and Zolie were, Maura screamed, and Patty ran down the stairs after her. As she got to the next floor, Stevie was coming up to see what was happening when Maura saw her and opened the fourth-floor door. Running down the hallway, Patty was right on her heels. Seeing her sister run from the stairs, Stevie followed her as Logan opened the fifth-floor door above and yelled for Maura. The quietness greeted them, and Logan looked into Zolie's frightened eyes.

"Maura!" Zolie yelled.

Seeing a light turn on behind them down the long hall they'd just walked, they had no choice and rushed into the stairway, and Logan quietly closed the door, hearing a noise above them.

"Maura?" Zolie whispered, looking up the foul stairway.

The noise above greeted them again, and they rushed up the stairs to see the entry to the sixth-floor skyway. The doors had been chained shut, and the bricks around the doorframe were cracked, letting in the cold night air like a warning of the dangerous passage ahead. A small metal-and-glass door to a fire extinguisher was open, and the wind from the foreboding skyway's damaged doorframe was blowing it against the wall, making the noise.

As Logan looked down the long sixth-floor hallway, frightened for her sister, Zolie turned away from the sky bridge to hell and ran back down the stairs as fast as she could. Not stopping at the fourth floor, Zolie kept going to the third, where it oddly ended, and the door was ajar. Pulling it open with Logan now a floor above her, Zolie ran into the dimly lit hallway, scraping her shoulder on the metal shelves shoved against the wall and illuminated only by the green exit sign and a few nightlights in the distance. When the door behind her closed, it made a clicking sound as it shut. Moments later Logan pulled on the door, and it wouldn't budge. The door was locked, and he pounded on it.

"Zolie! Zolie! The door's locked."

Hearing his muffled cries, Zolie ran back and tried pushing the door open, but it wouldn't budge. "Logan, it won't open!" Zolie cried, fearing being alone again in the terrifying place.

"Keep trying," Logan pleaded, hearing her push on the handle and feeling the vibration as she did.

"It's no use," Zolie screamed, stepping back and bumping against the overfilled shelves packed with medical supplies.

Adjusting her eyes in the faint green light of the exit sign, Zolie saw something flash in front of her.

"Mrrrooowww," the cat moaned as it opened its yellow eyes and hissed at her. It jumped in her face, knocking her against the far wall. Zolie screamed, and the cat started clawing at her. Its claws pulled her long hair and scratched her face and head. Zolie was waving her arms trying to get the angry feline off her when she stumbled back into the shelves and fell to the ground, bringing the shelves down on top of her.

"Help me," Zolie screamed. She could hear Logan pounding and pulling on the locked door only feet from her. Knocking a box between her and the cat, she freed herself, stumbling on the supplies scattered all over the floor as she tried to stand. The cat leaped at her again. Landing on her chest and began clawing at her throat. Zolie grabbed the rabid animal and ripped it from her body, tearing her clothing and flinging the beast into the edge of the fallen shelves. She screamed once more and the animal attacked again. Putting her hands out, she batted the animal, striking it against the wall, where it fell to the floor and ran down the hall away from her.

Zolie collapsed. She could feel blood coming down from the top of her head under her hair where the cat had scratched her, and under her jawline. Then she crawled to the door and pushed on the handle, crying for Logan's help.

"Zolie! Are you all right?" Logan yelled through the door.

Stopping her tears and wiping away the blood, she put her back to the door and turned her head against it. "I'm fine!" Zolie yelled back. "A bloody cat just had a go at me!"

"Zolie! Get to the main stairs, and wait for me there. I'm going after Maura, and I'll meet you there. Do you hear me?" Logan yelled.

"Third-floor stairs—got it. I'll meet you there!" Zolie yelled back, looking down the dimly lit hall in front of her, wondering where that nasty demonic cat from hell was hiding. Quietly moving down the hall, she feared a door would open at any moment and a monster would jump out, like she imagined they were trying to do one flight above her.

Maura ran down the hall and heard Patty screaming behind her, and when she turned her head, she stepped on a towel that had been left in the corridor and tripped against an old display case. It moved away from the wall as she grabbed the end of it and tipped it over behind her, continuing her escape when the noise of the falling cabinet woke the patients, and they started banging on the windows of their locked doors, scaring the hell out of her.

Passing a wall table with giant vases on it, she stopped and swung it out into the hall. She heard Patty slam into the broken display case and scream. "You bitch! I'll make sure you're dead this time!"

Maura then saw an emergency staircase and took it.

Logan opened the fourth-floor door of the stairway and heard the sound of people ahead of him moving in the dimly lit hall.

"Find her, Stevie!" came the voice that he knew belonged to Patty, and he quietly moved deeper down the corridor, when a patient behind a door right beside him spotted him through the glass and screamed as loud as she could, causing all the other patients to join in her frightening chorus.

Logan jumped and hit the wall with a loud thump, losing his footing and falling to the floor. Seeing he was safe with them secured behind locked doors, he got up and ran down the hall, passing an exam room before coming to the fallen display case in the middle of the hall. Pausing for a moment, he heard a sound coming from the room behind him. When he turned, Patty swung the heavy medical award that had come down with the display case straight at his head. Hitting him hard, she knocked him out.

CHAPTER 134

D r. Todd wiped the blood from his lip as he took the stairs to the fifth floor, seeing Dr. Sinardi moving toward the room Zolie Vanderran was being held in. Thinking Sinardi was in on Blake's dirty little trick and wanting to burn him in the hotbox, he needed to get him downstairs, and the only way to do that was to play along. "Dr. Sinardi!" Todd yelled. "Help me," he said, falling against a wheelchair to the floor.

Sinardi turned around and was surprised to see Todd's condition. Rushing to him, he helped him up and saw his bloodied clothes and bruised face. "My God, Todd, what happened?"

"Downstairs in the basement!" Todd lied. "I was attacked."

"By who? Who attacked you?" Sinardi demanded.

"You're not going to believe this, but my brother...he's alive! And that bitch Nurse Pam is with him!"

"That's nonsense," Sinardi said, realizing the murderous *Exorcist* siblings were doing the job he'd given them, and he smiled on the inside but showed deep concern for the good doctor. He wanted Todd back in the basement so they could finish him off.

"No, I'm telling you—my asshole brother is alive!" Todd said.

"You're overworked and imagining things," Sinardi said, smelling the tequila on Todd's breath. "Have you been drinking tonight, Todd?"

"What? Yes! I had a drink upstairs after I tried cleaning myself up after they tried to kill me," Todd barked in Sinardi's face.

"Your brother hasn't been seen in years, Todd! No one knows where he is."

"I'm telling you he's here!"

"Then show me. Come on and follow me. Together we'll put an end to this," Sinardi barked back.

Seeing Sinardi move to the only working elevator, Todd's eyes filled with hatred, and he followed him, thinking that diverting him away from Zolie's room was a bonus. What he wanted was to hear him scream in the hotbox. Once the scum was dead, he would then deal with Blake.

Getting in the elevator, Sinardi pushed the basement button and looked to Dr. Todd. "Now, tell me again: what did you see in the basement?"

"I'm not going to be psychoanalyzed by you, asshole. I know what I saw."

"Do you? Do you know what you saw? You saw the sorcery of the Brockman siblings. I know you did; I could tell by your reactions. How do you know it wasn't another one of their tricks?"

"Because you need to allow the telepaths a clear vision into your thoughts—they weren't even on that side of the hospital's basement!"

"They're locked up on the east side. Are you telling me you were on the west side? How can that be? Maybe their powers have grown stronger?"

"Bullshit," Todd barked when the elevator stopped at the basement floor.

When the doors opened, both Dr. Sinardi and Dr. Todd were surprised to find two women standing outside the car.

"Who are you?" Sinardi snapped, surprised at seeing the intruders inside the hospital.

Recognizing him from his picture online, Hailey Storm tried pushing her way inside the car, wanting to leave the basement. "Dr. Sinardi, Hailey Storm. I know about your affair with my sister Wendy. I just have a few questions."

Keeping her from entering the elevator, Sinardi looked at the African American woman next to Sandy Storm, a person he *did* know.

"I don't know how you two got in here, but you're leaving now!" He pushed her back, swinging her against the wall next to the elevator.

Sandy moved around them and saw Dr. Todd put both his hands up, blocking her escape. "I don't think so," Todd said, reaching back in and pulling the elevator's red stop button.

Sinardi then grabbed Sandy's wrist and shoved her next to her sister. "Now I want answers," Sinardi fumed. "How did you get in here?"

"I'm asking the questions," Hailey shot back, causing Dr. Todd to grin at the pushy little bitch. "You paid our sister. I want to know why!"

"You paid my hospital bill, too, didn't you?" Sandy added.

"What the fuck is this bullshit all about?" Dr. Todd yelled, hating these women for being here and keeping him from the enjoyment of killing this fucker.

Dr. Sinardi laughed. "Wendy was far more superior than you two dumb bitches," he said, wanting to brag about his brilliant design before the Brockman siblings killed them all. "I hated holding that part of your interview for so long before I leaked it to the world. But what a pay off!"

"This has to do with Ed Savage and that show you did with him all those years ago, doesn't it?" Hailey spat.

"Maybe you're not as dumb as you look," Sinardi said with a grin. "Yes, it's all true. I hired Wendy after I saw her first broadcast, and she couldn't wait to put the screws to Ed Savage."

Hailey was pissed off, and she couldn't wait to *put the screws* to this asshole. "That can't be all of it! You paid her big money for helping you—money you don't make. I checked you out, and my source at the city told me your salary. So who is *really* in charge? Is it you?" She glared at Dr. Todd.

Sinardi could hear one of the Brockmans coming and played along. "Oh, Hailey, dear, sweet, stupid Hailey, I've been bilking the insurance companies and the state for years. More than half my claim patients are dead, and you'll wish you were too when you see your so-called dead sister! Come with me," he said, moving toward the cells he'd left open.

"No, I saw her die," Sandy said, shocked at what she was hearing.

"Did you? Then who's around the corner?" Sinardi said, hearing the footsteps moving closer. Turning around, he saw the figure of a woman in the dark corridor, and as she moved into the light, both Storm sisters witnessed the return of their dead sister moving toward them in a slow, limping gait.

"Wendy? Oh my God…it *is* you," Hailey said, moving toward her.

"No, this can't be," Sandy added, too scared to move.

Sinardi marveled at the strength the telepath had in warping the minds of two people at once. Seeing the middle sister, Belynn Brockman, he then glanced at Todd as she reached out to the women. "See, Dr. Vreeland. You didn't see your brother Blake at all."

"Who let them out?" Dr. Todd yelled, sensing a trap.

"Who let them out?" came the snotty little mocking sound of Pam's voice from behind them as she came skipping down the corridor in the shadows like a frolicking little whore.

Todd whipped around and saw the two-faced slut come to a stop and hide at some crates stacked up near an electrical box.

"Tee-hee," Pam laughed in a girly way he'd never heard from her before.

"You can cut the act, Pam," Blake's raspy voice boomed in the blackness of the corridor as he fired the gun.

Todd jumped at hearing his brother's voice and felt the bullet brush right by him and the unmistakable sound of Sinardi as he screamed out, taking the bullet in the side. Looking back, he saw Sinardi spin and fall to the ground, the side of his white lab coat turning red with his blood.

"There are no guns down here," Sinardi said in shock as he cowered on the ground.

The women screamed and looked back at Wendy to see her face change into that of a stranger, and as Hailey focused, Belynn Brockman's face changed once more from her normal self to a rage-filled Wendy, who lunged at her, grabbing her and pulling her to the ground.

"Help!" Hailey screamed, and Sandy ran, grabbing the insane woman on top of her sister from behind and pulling her off, flinging her against the wall. She then helped Hailey up, and the two ran screaming down the corridor.

Todd started to move toward Pam, when Blake stepped into the light, holding the gun. "Do it. I'd love to finally end your miserable life right now."

Todd stopped in his tracks; the fear of looking into his dead brother's eyes turned his blood to ice.

"Blake, please...this has to end. I want us to be us again," Todd begged.

Sinardi looked up from the ground and could see Todd's back and could hear his fear in his words as he *thought* he was talking to his brother. The pain from the bullet caused him to close his eyes, hearing that the young Blake Brockman did, in fact, have the same special powers as his sisters. Crawling around Todd to see the young Brockman, Sinardi's smile faded when the *real* Blake Brockman appeared *behind* Blake Vreeland as his normal self, wearing a smug smile.

No, this can't be, Sinardi thought, looking back to the crates. "Belinda? That is you...isn't it?"

"Who the fuck is Belinda?" Pam said stepping into the light, laughing as she pulled the electrical lever, killing the lights, and moved along the wall to Blake.

Far away in the bowels of the sanatorium, Belinda Brockman moved as gracefully as an angel toward the door Sandy Storm had left open.

CHAPTER 135

E d Savage arrived at the skyway and opened the doors. It was cold in the long corridor high over the courtyard due to the cold wind and rain coming through the broken windows. Hearing the heavy rain above him pelt the ceiling, he ran to the other side and pushed open the door. Not seeing a directory he paused, and looked in both directions. Choosing to go down in the same direction that he'd traveled in the opposite building, thinking it would be safer to find that identical back staircase like the one near the ambulance bay so no one would see him, he hurried down the hall, but when he'd gone a ways and hadn't found it, he realized the buildings were slightly different.

Far behind him Zolie moved from her hiding place. She had been waiting by the grand staircase in the rear section of the third floor lobby for Logan but heard Patty on the floor above and ran down the hall and hid in a supply room. When she thought it was safe, she moved back to the hall and heard something behind her. Running, she looked back and tripped on a hallway bench and screamed as she fell. Getting up, she hurried along, returning to the stairs, and looked up, waiting for Logan near the giant stained glass windows.

The scream Ed heard behind him caused him to jump, and he turned and started moving back toward it.

Zolie could hear the heavy rain outside, and when the lightning flashed and struck across the sky, causing what was left of the lights to flicker out, she panicked. The flashing of the sky outside seemed to cause a multitude of shadows to move inside the hospital, as if her mind was playing even more tricks on her. She saw the statue of Victor Vreeland near a grandfather clock cast its shadow up the wall, reaching to the heights of the ceiling, and it seemed to be watching her as she moved to look down the staircase.

With the lights out and rushing down the hall, Ed tripped into the corner wall where the corridor turned and tumbled to the floor. It was pitch black now, with the safety lights and exit lights completely gone. He reached in his pocket for his flashlight.

"Mrroooowww," came the distinct sound of a demon cat in the darkness, the cat that had been stalking her, and when Zolie turned, it leaped from the old grandfather clock, knocking her back she batted the beast over the railing, and went tumbling down the stairs into the shadows at the bottom. Zolie stirred, trying to get up, but when she raised herself an inch from the ground, the dizziness overtook her, and she fainted in a dark corner of the second-floor landing.

Moments later, the beam of Ed's flashlight made its way up the corridor to the third floors lobby at the grand staircase. Looking for where the scream had come from, the lightning flashed again, and he heard the sound of equipment crashing down on the floor above. Moving up the stairs, he got to the fourth floor and looked both ways into the dark corridors.

Patty Galloway saw his flashlight and froze, watching him move away from her down the corridor. When he was far enough away, she turned her head and spotted the back emergency staircase; moving quietly, she went to it and closed the door behind her.

CHAPTER 136

When Maura passed the third-floor door on the fire escape, she knew she could either take the skyway or risk trying to find a way out from the East Tower. Scared, thinking of what her sister Cara had gone through in the mountains and not wanting to go back to that awful skyway, she continued down the stairs and screamed when she came face to face with her dead sister, Cara Vanderran Savage, coming up from the first floor. Allowing the shock to dissipate, the twin looked down at the woman now in front of her. "You're not my sister!" she screamed just as Patty came around the railing above her and stood just one flight away.

Whipping her head back, Maura saw Patty and gasped—she was trapped. She rushed to the second-floor door and pushed it open and ran down the corridor just as Belinda Brockman moved to the top of the stairs and faced Patty Galloway.

"Mother!" Patty's voice was filled with emotion as she rushed to the woman she loved.

"*You're being tricked.*" The distinct voice hit Patty's ears as she reached the woman who looked exactly like her mother. "*Lies, lies, lies,*" continued the loud voice in Patty's mind, and she blinked hard. When she reopened her eyes, she saw the woman's face transform from her mother to an absolute stranger.

"Trick me, will you!" Patty hissed and reached up, grabbing the woman by the throat and swinging her to her side and pushing her back through the second floor door.

Hearing this, Maura looked back and saw the two women in battle and panicked. She had to get out of there, and it had to be now, she thought, as she rushed through the building filled with its locked doors and endless hallways. Coming to what looked like a classroom of sorts, Maura rushed in eyeing the exit door she thought was to an outside fire escape. Closing the door behind her, she rushed to the door to find it locked. Trapped and hearing Patty down the hall, she then pushed the large desk up against the closed door. Seeing the windows, with the lower part being the narrow rectangular ones adorned with handles, she ran to them and looked out to see the ground illuminate with a flash of lightning. In that moment she saw that the second floor was actually higher than she'd realized due to the grand first floor's thirty-foot ceilings below her as she tried opening the windows against the storm outside.

Back in the hall, Belinda rolled on top of Patty and slapped at her face with her clawed hands. She screamed, ripping her nails across Patty's cheek, and laughed as she rose up and ran to the fireplace at the sitting area near the grand staircase.

Patty sat up, feeling the sting of the scratches, and witnessed the bitch escape. Getting up, she ran to the sideboard near the stained glass window, where a heavy vase was sitting. Grabbing it, she turned to see Belinda running at her with the fireplace poker. She was screaming, and when she got close, she swung her weapon, hitting Patty on the shoulder and knocking the vase from her hands. Her laugh was now a vicious cackle that only a true witch could own, and she laughed when Patty fell to the floor.

The flash from the bolt of lightning was too bright in the dark building, and in that moment of blindness, Patty jumped up and pushed her to the floor, seeing the fireplace poker fly from her hands. Feeling for the vase she'd dropped, Patty grabbed it and smashed it against the back of Belinda's head, knocking her back down as she tried to stand. Patty was the one laughing now as she spotted the poker.

Lunging to it, she grabbed it and turned back, flinching when she once again saw her mother's face on the evil demon. Patty watched her as she ran to the sideboard for a bronze statue that was sitting there. As she turned around, her mass of wild hair flew around her head as the lightning flashed behind her, illuminating the stained glass window.

"Come to Mother, my slut daughter!" the witch said, taunting her.

Patty watched her raise the heavy bronze statue, and she charged straight at her; she threw the poker at the thing before she could deliver a strike, pushing her over the sideboard with the statue in hand and smashing the stained glass above, shattering it to pieces. Belinda Brockman flew out into the wind and rain, where she landed, impaling herself on an obelisk next to a statue of Cornelius Vreeland in the courtyard below.

CHAPTER 137

Logan Savage shook the pain from his head and stood in the hall. The screaming patients had quieted down, and he made his way down the hall as fast as he could. His eyes had gotten used to the darkness, and way down the hall, he could see the green light of an exit sign flicker to life, which had him thinking the emergency generators were *finally* coming online.

Far ahead of him, Stevie Galloway moved up the hall, searching for Patty, and saw the flashlight beam from a doctor in a lab coat. She reached for a metal bedpan from a supply area off the hall; spotting a tray of surgical instruments, she grabbed them as well and hid in an alcove. Waiting for the man to pass, she stepped from her hiding place and flung the surgical instruments to the floor, causing a loud, echoing racket.

Ed Savage heard the sounds behind him and turned as the bedpan hit him squarely on the side of the head. Seeing him fall to the floor, Stevie ran, hearing someone coming up behind her. Moving quickly, Logan saw the lights coming back on in the building just as he arrived to see his brother Ed dressed as a doctor stirring on the floor.

"Ed, Ed!" Logan shouted, pulling his brother up in his arms.

"What the hell was that?" Ed said, trying to stop the ringing in his head.

"I heard it too. Something metal hit you," Logan said, seeing the bedpan on the floor.

"Where is everyone?"

"Maura and I found Zolie and were trying to escape on the far stairs. But something happened, and Zolie got locked on the third floor. Maura's got to be on this floor."

"That was Maura who hit me?"

"I don't think so because I got whacked upside the head too."

"If it wasn't Maura, then…who?"

"The psycho sisters: I heard Patty call out to Stevie to *find her.*"

"Not them again."

"Ed, Dr. Sinardi and Dr. Hollerman locked Zolie in here, and they trapped us in Zolie's room. She's scared out of her mind."

Getting up off the floor, Ed kicked the bedpan and shut off his flashlight, putting it in his pocket. "Let's find them and get the hell out of here."

CHAPTER 138

D r. Todd managed to find his way to the electrical panel for the basement section and lifted the lever, turning on the lights. He blinked the blackness away and saw the elevator door close and the dripping blood on the button. "Sinardi!" he yelled, moving toward the elevator, trying to stop it.

Feeling his brother's hands on his shoulders yanking him back, Todd turned his head and met Blake's fist. The punch slammed him back against the elevator, and Blake grabbed him, pounding his head against the elevator door. Blood spilled from his nose, and he lost his footing, falling to the ground.

The next thing Todd felt was the needle in his neck; he opened his eyes wide to see Blake hovering over him, pushing the plunger deep into his flesh, delivering the drug.

"No, you don't understand. The Galloway women are here!" Todd cried.

Hearing this, Blake stopped. Seeing that the drug had only been partially expelled from the syringe, he ripped the needle from his neck, scratching it across his brother's flesh. "What are you talking about?"

Todd felt the drug try to take him down, but he fought it. "Her daughters, Blake—Patty and Stevie Galloway are here! Surely Sinardi told you."

"Who's this Sinardi?"

"The man you shot. You're not working with him?"

"I've only been working with Pam—*just* Pam."

"Where've you been then?"

"Germany, with Eric, of course," Blake said with a laugh.

"Eric's known all along?"

"You're such a joke. We've all known. We've just been waiting for you to come out of hiding to pay you back. It was Marvin Newman you killed that night, you stupid fuck! That man used to have your back more times than I can count, and you mutilated him. Know that, you bastard!"

"Pam, that liar—I'll kill her!"

"It was mostly her idea," Blake said, laughing at his brother. "She's the one who threw the acid in his face."

"But that patient who was shot that you blamed for doing it. I saw his body on the news."

"What a loser. We told the fool he could leave, and when he did, security was under the impression he'd escaped after killing another patient—a patient who I personally murdered—and they shot him. Now, where are the Galloway women?"

The anger spiked in Todd, thinking of that duplicitous witch Pam, and he knew, given the chance, he was going to make her scream with pain. But with his broken dream of trying to make things right over too many years of hatred, he knew things would *never* be right between them again, *even* if Blake believed the truth. "I left them in her room, Rose's old room on the top floor."

"Right down the hall from where you thought you'd left me to die—is that where you're talking about, little brother?"

Todd's head was pounding, and he could feel the drug in his system leaving him weak. "Please...it's time we come together. I beg you, Blake. It was our father who killed our mother! Just like I told you before."

"Lies!" Blake screamed and punched his brother in the face again. "Pam! Pam, I need your help here!" Blake yelled, looking around as he dragged Todd away from the elevator by his feet, toward the cells.

"I'll help you if you help me," came the voice of a young man behind them. Todd twisted his body and looked back to see the young Brockman sibling moving toward them from the shadows.

Blake flinched at seeing the young man who looked so much like him. "Who are you?" he said, dropping Todd's legs to the ground as he inspected the younger man.

"Blake Brockman—I'm a prisoner here. If I help you, all I ask is that you help me in return."

"He's a telepath, just like his sisters," Todd said, attempting to move away inch by inch across the floor.

"No, my sisters are, but I am not. Oh, and, sir, he's trying to get away," the young Brockman said, pointing to Todd.

Blake turned around and advanced on his brother so fast Todd couldn't help but be overtaken. Weak from the drug and the horrible ringing in his head from the beating he'd sustained, Todd swung at his brother but missed. Blake kicked him in the stomach and emptied the syringe into his brother's neck.

"I need a cell," Blake barked at the young version of himself.

"Use mine! My old one is upstairs; Sinardi promised," Brockman said, moving to Todd and grabbing his arms. "Grab his feet, and I'll lead the way."

Blake Vreeland liked the young man and thought this could be the perfect younger brother to replace the bastard he was going to keep locked away forever. Grabbing Todd's feet, he lifted him up. "Lead the way, then," he said, grinning.

Seeing the young Blake Brockman's cell, Blake Vreeland shook his head. "This won't do."

"It's quite miserable, sir."

Vreeland laughed. "No, it's not that. What I need for *this* patient is a more private cell, and I know just where to find it." Taking over, Blake led the young Brockman farther away from his cell to a corridor that led to a dead end.

"Oh, you mean Sinardi's private cells," the young man said when he recognized where they were going.

Blake Vreeland stopped at a support beam along the wall and looked at him as he dropped Todd's legs to the ground. "You know about these cells?"

"Yes, sir, Dr. Sinardi has one ready for that man he hates so much. It's located right behind that wall," he said, dropping Todd's arms and pointing to where Vreeland was standing.

"Who is this man he hates?"

"I don't know. But he says he's a real savage, and he's going to let Patty take care of him. Maybe you can get Kayla to take care of your brother? He's partial to that one."

"Kayla? Who's that?"

"She's a nurse he fancies. My sisters were laughing about how he liked her," Brockman said. "They told me his mind was growing stronger, and he wasn't to be trusted. They're scared of him," he added. Knowing Kayla was a weak spot for him, he fed that particular bit of information to Blake—knowing *he'd* be the perfect choice to tell.

"Hmm," Blake Vreeland muttered as a wicked thought crossed his mind. *Maybe this guy in front of me would be a better choice to watch over Todd, seeing as he looks so much like me. Too bad he has to die tonight, though,* he thought.

"Well, let's go take a look at the cell, shall we?" Blake Vreeland said as he pushed on the back side of a support beam, and part of the wall moved, leading to the hidden cells.

Moving down the dark, damp corridor, Blake came to the cell and dropped Todd's legs, nodding for Brockman to do the same, and turned on the main lights. There, the cell had posters on one wall of a show called *Phantom Finders,* and one person's face on the poster was crossed out with bright-red spray paint.

"This will work fine," he said, moving back to Todd and grabbing his legs. "Come on—let's have some fun."

Brockman lifted his arms, and together they dragged him in the cell door. It was on a slightly higher elevation with a slope leading into the cell. A hose hung on the wall that was used for water torture on the trapped souls, and it burst forth with either icy cold or extremely hot water, depending on how the torturer felt that day. The slope dipped down a few feet to keep the stagnant water in, keeping the smell and the mildewed floors for as long as possible in order to sicken the patient trapped inside. Slime and dirt would collect on the thick glass windows below facing the viewing corridor.

"Great! Now lift and swing, and on the count of three, throw him down the slope into his new home," Blake Vreeland said, laughing. "One, two, three!"

Together they watched Todd tumble down the slick, slimy slope and crash against a gnarly-looking table, knocking it over and scraping his side when his shirt lifted up.

Blake clapped his hands and patted the younger man on the shoulder. "Thank you for helping me out! I promise I'll repay you very soon," he said reconsidering the man's fate. "By the way, do you mind if I call you something besides Blake? Don't get me wrong; Blake's a great name," he said and winked, "but this could get confusing."

"I don't care. What did you have in mind?"

"What's your full name?"

"Blakely Kenneth Brockman."

"Well, then, it's either Little Blake or Ken."

Blake Brockman laughed. "Well, sir, I did see you with that nurse in the basement, and you're definitely the bigger Blake, but not by far."

Blake Vreeland actually turned a shade of red and laughed it off. "And here I was thinking that you'd take it offensively if I called you Little Blake."

"Take your pick; nothing bothers me."

Blake Vreeland looked at the younger man, who looked eerily similar, and saw the confidence of a strong man who'd kept his strength even though trapped in the hell of this hospital. "Okay, Little Blake, like I just promised, I'm going to make your life here better than you've ever thought possible, but for now I'd like a few minutes alone here, if you don't mind."

"Thank you, sir, and I completely understand," Little Blake said, feeling like his life was really about to improve. He then looked down at Todd Vreeland in the cell before returning his gaze to his new benefactor. "And I promise, sir, I'll never disappoint you like he did."

Blake Vreeland watched Little Blake turn and disappear down the corridor into the darkness. He didn't want *anyone* to know he was there yet, and he planned on murdering the young look-alike before the night was over, but something in his mind was telling him this particular prisoner would come in handy, and he looked to his brother with contempt, thinking how easy this exchange of brothers could be.

CHAPTER 139

The dark storm clouds continued to sit over the hospital, as if casting an impenetrable blanket of darkness over the horror show playing out inside its walls, yet in the cemetery, a darker shadow moved from the grave of Victor Vreeland.

The lightning flashed, and the rain poured down on the quaint little cemetery behind the sanatorium, and a figure moved from the mud forming at the base of the tombstones. It seemed to be looking for *something* particular as it traveled up and down, scrambling through the stone monuments to the dead as if it were a maze. Moving away from the boneyard, it stopped at the massive building and disappeared; the shadow literally sank back into the earth as the sky rained down from the heavens. Reemerging in front of the ornate statue of Dr. Cornelius Vreeland, it moved up the obelisk near it and into the impaled woman.

Belinda Brockman gasped. Her eyes shot open, and they were as black as the night as she reached up the obelisk, past the gashing hole in her chest, and pulled herself up and away, letting her body fall to the wet ground. Standing in the mud, her old hospital gown now soaked with both filth and blood, her wet hair wild as the wind whipped into a fright, she looked like a soul driven mad, wearing the expression of the damned.

Turning back to the building, she went to the door. With a flip of her hand, the doors swung open, and the wind and rain blew into the building as the creature once again entered hell. Moving to the main stairs, she paused, looking up from the first floor. She sniffed the air, smelling Zolie's perfume somewhere above her. In her mind she saw her lying on the landing between the second and third floors. Ignoring her for now, she moved across the foyer and descended the stairs to the basement, where the doors blew open, announcing her arrival. She heard screaming as she entered the area, and seeing a large surgical knife on a cart, she picked it up and followed the screams.

Hailey and Sandy Storm had run off in the darkness to escape the gunshot, yet they thought they could hear someone behind them, and when they turned a corner and saw a lighted area, their fear grew as they finally felt trapped in the horrible place they were in. Looking for a way out, they came to the broken elevator shaft and saw the body; the young man was caught up in the rusted cables, the back of his head had been cracked open and as his weight shifted, a second body of a doctor fell from above—his stomach had been ripped open, and his intestines had been pulled and seemed to be snagged on something caught from above, and both women screamed. Belinda heard them and moved closer.

"This is all your fault! We never should have come here!" Sandy screamed, backing away from the body.

Pam Porter heard the sisters arguing and hid behind a column nearby to watch the fun. But she wasn't the only one; Blake Brockman was behind the Storm sisters, watching them from afar.

"Look out!" Hailey screamed, seeing the other Brockman sister appear out of nowhere and move out from the shadows behind her with a brick in her hand.

Sandy turned, and Belynn swung the brick, connecting with Sandy's head with a loud crack and knocking her to the ground.

Hailey then saw the bitch turn toward her and raise the brick. "Oh, hell no!" Hailey said as she turned and ran, running right into Pam who shoved her back into the fiend knocking the brick away just as her sister Belinda came around the corner holding up the knife. Hailey panicked as she turned to stare directly into the eyes of the dead, she screamed as Belinda Brockman stabbed her in the chest. The blade sliced her lung, and she gasped for air, falling to the ground, hearing the evil laughter in her ears.

"Belinda? You're stronger," Belynn said, rushing to her sister in crime.

"It's a beautiful thing, sister," Belinda said, her soul now blackened by death. "You'll love it too." Raising the knife, she pulled her sister to her and stabbed her in the back, pulling the blade out so that she could watch the new Brockman blood drip from the blade.

Pam watched in horror as a shadow of fog suddenly emerged from within Belinda, her eyes blinked and it reached out and engulfed her sister. Belinda laughed, watching the terror cross her sister's face.

"No," Belynn cried, barely speaking the word and seeing the betrayal as her life started to fade.

"Now we'll always be together," Belinda said, stabbing her once more in the chest.

Belynn released a guttural moan, and Pam watched Belinda fall in an instant, along with her sister. As her head lolled to one side, the dark shadow left Belinda behind as it sank into the floor.

Pam was shocked at what she'd just witnessed and slowly moved toward the bodies. Looking at Belinda's black, lifeless eyes caused her to take a step back. She then looked down at the peaceful face of Belynn, when her eyes shot open.

It was as if a film of black oil filled her eyes like a demon, as her body moved slightly, and she smiled up at Pam. "Thought you'd seen it all, didn't you, bitch? Ha-ha, ha-ha, ha," Belynn laughed.

"The whore has no soul," Belinda screamed, rising from death. Her muddy gown was covered in their blood, and Pam watched her get to her feet. The thing tilted her head, and the wild, mud-caked hair seemed to dance back and forth as the witch stepped toward her, and Belynn rose from the ground to join her.

"It really is beautiful, eavesdropper," Belynn said, wearing a spinster's grin.

"Get her!" Belinda screamed, throwing the bloody knife directly at her. It sliced Pam's forearm as she raised her hands in defense.

"Fuck this!" Pam said and turned, grabbing her forearm as it bled.

"No, it's fuck you, Pam!" the twisted sisters screamed back at her and laughed.

Pam ran, taking a quick look back to see their silhouettes in front of the light, laughing at her from the depths of hell. She turned and kept running away from the damned and demented sisters, when she heard them scream out as if they could not breathe. Stopping to look back, she saw the shadow swirl around them like a tornado and move to the floor, letting the women fall to the ground, as the shadow seemed to focus on *her.* She screamed. Running away to find the doors open that led out of the basement, she ran up the stairs, holding her arm as she bled.

CHAPTER 140

lake Vreeland left the basement and was happy with the turn of events. He couldn't wait to tell their other brother Eric the good news of finally enslaving Todd to teach that bastard a lesson he'd never forget. It had been too long since he'd been home in their family hospital, and he hated the fact the state of New York was running it. Too many years had gone by, and tonight he was finally getting back what was rightfully his birthright. The more he thought about it, the angrier he got. He passed an employee dining room and went to get something to drink. Pulling a cold bottle of water from a refrigerated display, he turned to see the young woman looking at him. She was eating a bowl of cereal. He moved to her with a kind smile. "Skip dinner last night?"

"You could say that," the young woman said, suddenly recognizing the man in front of her from the many portraits in the sanatorium. "You're Mr. Vreeland! I had no idea you were all back."

Blake smiled, already thinking he was allowing one person too many to know he was back. "We were *all* back? Who else have you met?"

"I met Dr. Todd Vreeland. He's great. I'm going to like having him work here."

"You met my brother Todd. I'm Blake. Very nice to meet you."

"I'm Kayla," the young woman replied as she extended her hand to him.

Blake grinned, thinking of what Little Blake had told him of Todd liking this girl and was glad he'd reconsidered murdering him as he reached for her hand, and when he grabbed it, he pulled her over the table so fast she felt her feet lift off the floor. Pulling her into his muscled chest, he turned her around and covered her mouth with his large hand, smothering her against his chest until she passed out.

CHAPTER 141

Maura Vanderran heard Patty Galloway calling her twin sister's name in the outer hall, and she knew she was trapped. Unable to open the windows, she looked around the classroom for something to break them with. She saw a lab area with tall wooden stools and ran to them, holding one up to test the weight. Feeling the lightness of them, the panic entered her heart when she heard Patty at the door turning the knob. Ducking down, she saw Patty's face look into the room through the small, narrow window and held her breath, hoping she wasn't seen.

Looking back, Patty was gone from the window, and Maura eyed the heavy teacher's chair she'd pushed away when she'd shoved the desk against the door as a blockade. Quickly, seeing it was all clear, she grabbed the chair and wheeled it over to the windows and then took another look back to spot Patty's face once again staring in the window of the door.

"I see you, Cara, and I'm coming to kill you, bitch!" Patty screamed.

Scared out of her mind, Maura grabbed the heavy chair, barely able to lift it as she swung it at the windows. The chair bounced off the glass as if made of nothing more than rubber and fell to the floor, breaking one of the armrests off. Laughing, Patty continued to slam her body against the door, pushing it a bit, getting it to budge. She managed to get it open enough to reach her arm in and try to push the heavy desk away. Screaming in defeat, Maura looked back to see Patty's grinning face. "I'm gonna kill you! I'm gonna kill *you,* and then I'm going to kill your children!" Patty raged behind the door, her fingers scratching the inside of the door as she pulled her arm back.

The emotion all women felt when their babies were in danger magnified the strength within Maura as she grabbed the chair, lifted it up, and charged, smashing the glass with the heavy steel wheels of the chair. The wind blew the last of the rain into the room, and she let go, watching the chair fall from the second floor and smash to pieces on the cement sidewalk below just as Patty pushed the door open enough for her to climb over the desk.

Seeing her jump down from the desk, Maura didn't have time to get out, but she picked up a student desk and swung it as Patty got her footing. The desk smashed against Patty, breaking in half, and Patty fell into the other desks and chairs as Maura made her move.

Climbing out and onto the wet ledge, Maura looked up to the sky to see the clouds part and the full moon shine down as the sky sent bolts of lightning in all directions, lighting up the wet grounds below her. Thankful the rain had stopped, she looked down from the second floor and spotted to her right a brick column that she simply couldn't get around without falling. Her only way was to pass over the unbroken portion of the windows to where a rainspout was running down the building. Moving with her back to the glass, she heard Patty scream and toss the furniture as she got to her feet.

The wind hit her, and the ledge was slick, and she saw Patty appear at the broken area of the glass and smile at her. "You're about to die!" Patty screamed into the wind, her hair flying behind her, and Maura nearly slipped, crying and clinging to the windowpanes with her fingers.

She then looked again, and Patty was gone. She had a about a meter to go when she heard Patty in the classroom rage behind the glass.

The explosive pressure from behind her and the glass breaking all around her body made Maura jump forward from the ledge, trying to leap far enough away so as not to hit the sidewalk. The smaller desk Patty had used to break the glass flew with her, and Maura's aim worked, and she landed in the wet grass below.

Unfortunately, she felt freedom for mere seconds before the sudden shock of hitting her head on the ground knocking her out cold. Her body rolled down the incline, away from the building, landing in a small pond facedown, her head under the water.

The lightning flashed, and Patty looked down to see the wretched woman under the water and smiled. Moving away from the window, she shoved the desk away from the door and swung it open, searching for her sister, Stevie.

Maura inhaled the cold water and came to, coughing up the nasty pond scum, and attempted to lift herself up. Thankful that the cold water had revived her so quickly, she climbed out, slipping in the wet grass and sliding feet first back into the pond. Her head spun in circles, and she once again passed out, but this time well above the waterline.

CHAPTER 142

"If Maura isn't on this floor, maybe she went to the third and is with Zolie," Ed said to Logan as they passed an examining room on the fourth floor.

The lightning flashed outside, and Logan flipped on the lights, watching the fluorescent bulbs flicker in the ugly room. The table was covered in dried blood, and he moved to the window, seeing the grounds illuminated when the lightning released another flare.

"What the hell?" Logan pressed his hand to the glass. "Ed, it's Maura!"

Ed rushed to the window, and when the lightning struck a moment later, he saw her lying near a pond.

Below them on the landing between the second and third floors, Zolie Vanderran woke from her fall. Her eyes blurred, and she noticed the lights had returned. Crawling to the railing of the grand staircase, she pulled herself up and heard the sound of the vicious cat echo below. Staring down, she heard the movement from the animal and witnessed the yellow eyes peek around the stair landing and look up at her.

"Mrroowwww." The cat warned, and Zolie turned and grabbed at the railing, moving away as fast as she could. Getting to the third floor, Zolie turned and grabbed a chair next to the stairs and threw it down behind her at the cat as she looked for another weapon.

Above her, Ed and Logan looked away from the window in complete shock, and both men moved toward the door. Running down the hall, they finally got to the main staircase and sprinted down the steps.

Seeing a picture on the wall, Zolie ran to it to try and rip it down for protection, and when it wouldn't budge, she ran down the corridor with the cat close behind.

Just as the men hit the third floor, the cat leaped at Zolie, and she screamed, feeling its claws at her back. She fell forward, screaming in agony, hitting her head against the wall and causing the scratches on her head to bleed again, and the men saw what was happening and ran toward her.

Logan got to her first and grabbed the cat and threw it back at Ed, who kicked the damn thing against the wall with his foot, feeling his bad knee whip side to side. When he came down, the pain shot through him, and he fell to the floor. Forcing the pain away, he saw Logan help Zolie up and make their way toward him. "I've got this," he said, getting up and looking into his brother's eyes. "Go. Get to Maura."

Logan nodded and raced down the stairs.

"Ed? Ed?" Zolie said, leaning into him, wiping the blood from her eyes.

"I got you, Zolie. I got you," Ed said, comforting her as the cat crept up behind them and leaped into the air, scratching Ed on the side of his head and neck where Sam had shot him. "Aaahhh!" Ed yelled in surprise, and Zolie grabbed the cat from behind and tore it off Ed's body, sending it flying as Ed pulled his gun and fired, hitting it in the back paw and hearing it expel a loud hissing sound as it ran down the hall.

Ed felt the stinging burns of the scratches and saw the blood drip down from the side of his head as he reached for Zolie. Moving slowly down the hall, Ed spotted the lab and the bandages and supplies on the tables inside. "In here," Ed said, leading her to a table near the center of the lab. Tearing open the bandages, he saw their blood splatter to the floor.

Zolie leaned against it and swooned, catching the table's edge as she watched the blood drip down onto her blouse.

CHAPTER 143

ogan arrived on the first floor and was surprised the doors were wide open. The wind was blowing in, and he ran out into it toward the pond, where he saw his wife lying partly in the water.

"Maura!" Logan shouted as he slid down the wet grass into the pond and pulled her completely free. Laying her on her back, he patted her cheeks. "Maura! Come back to me!" Logan cried, hovering over her when she opened her eyes and reached for her head.

"Oh my God, Maura!" Logan cried, lifting her into his arms and feeling her cold skin. Panicked, he picked her up and began moving toward his Escalade.

Back inside the elevator, as the doors opened on the first floor, Stevie stepped out just as Pam came around the corner. The two women stared at each other, and Stevie saw blood running down Pam's arm and onto her scrubs.

Stevie's mind flashed to the night in the Mystic Theater with that blonde British woman, and she panicked.

Reading the woman across from her, Pam saw the strange look in her eyes and pulled a switchblade from her pocket. "Bitch, you don't have shit," Pam spat as she advanced on the blonde woman.

Stevie was trapped—her anger had been silently building since learning her mother had lived and her miserable life since she'd run away had all been for nothing. With the money her sister told her about, she realized she was more like Patty than she'd realized, and seeing the switchblade coming at her, she raged with anger and wanted this woman dead.

Pam screamed, and with the switchblade in front of her, she swung it at the woman's face. All Stevie could do was dodge the blade and reach out to grab her hand holding the knife before the bleeding bitch killed her with it. Struggling for the weapon, Stevie reached with her other hand and bent her wrist back, causing the knife to fall onto the floor.

Pam punched her in the stomach, and as Stevie recoiled, she kicked the knife across the room. Pam turned toward it, and Stevie pushed her hard to the ground, watching Pam start to crawl toward the weapon. Stevie grabbed her legs and pulled her away from it and then jumped on her back. Grabbing her hair, she pulled her backward, trying to snap her spine.

Pam screamed as a bolt of lightning struck the building, and the lights went out. It was like the storm overhead was angry it was dissipating and wanted to continue playing its part in the horror movie playing out below.

At the Escalade Logan started the engine and turned on the heat, hitting the button to warm the seat she was in. "Come on, Ed!" he said, looking up to the open doors of the hospital.

Upstairs in the lab, Ed Savage heard the footsteps behind them in the darkened building and turned as the sound of gunfire filled the air. He felt the blast of the gun hit him squarely in the chest, knocking him backward against the medical supplies, and he pushed Zolie Vanderran down and away from himself for cover. He heard Zolie's scream, and the sound of smashing medical equipment pierced his ears as he saw them both hit the floor. Zolie's cries for help faded in his mind as he slipped into his own darkness.

Zolie hit the side of her head on the edge of a counter and could feel more blood coming down from her temple. She could hear the killer at the entrance and crawled into the darkness to get as far away as she could. The lab was big for the old, crumbling hospital, but from the moonlight, she could just make out an exit door in the back wall.

When the man found Ed Savage lying on the ground, he laughed. Ed was motionless on the floor, and the man raised his gun just as Zolie stumbled against a cart, pushing it and breaking the glass vials on its top as she ran for the door. The man looked to her at once and aimed his gun, firing, missing her by a fraction of an inch.

Zolie screamed as she slammed into the door; when it opened, she took off down a back hallway. The storm outside was not letting up. The rain had stopped, but the wind was fierce, and she could hear the wind and the branches of the unkempt landscape scratch against the small square windowpanes, like claws of a monster digging at them, trying to get her.

"Damn it!" the man with the gun yelled as he followed in pursuit, slamming into a counter and pausing for a moment as he swooned. Blood dripped from his wound onto the countertop. He looked down and wiped it away, knocking over more lab equipment as he continued the chase.

Zolie heard him as she got to the stairs and ran down the three flights as fast as she could. Getting to the main level, she pushed open the emergency doors and ran out into the wind, staying close to the building for cover. She could see her car parked near the garden, and in the distance was Ed's Range Rover. Seeing and feeling that freedom was finally within reach, she used all her remaining strength to run as fast as she could to hide.

As she got to her car, the sound of several rounds of gunfire filled the night, and she screamed when the glass shattered from her Rolls-Royce. She tripped on the curb to the garden and fell to the ground, rolling down the small embankment to join Ed in the strange darkness fleeing the terror and death, her memory flashing to the beautiful evening of that first dinner at her home after the madness at Black Ridge had finally ended. Or so it had seemed.

Stanley Sinardi laughed seeing the stupid woman fall, thinking he'd killed her. Moving back inside, letting the doors swing open in the wind, he went back up the stairs to finish off Ed Savage with the drugs he had prepared. He was giddy with his plan and couldn't wait to watch the movie he planned on filming of Ed waking up in the prison he'd prepared for the bastard who had ruined his career—giving him a nice nasty place where he could think about it for the rest of his life. And having Patty to torment him was an added bonus, he thought, since he couldn't rape and kill Zolie in front of him after he'd trapped him.

Hearing the gunfire, Logan looked over the blowing leaves of the courtyard to see a woman fall in the distance near Zolie's Rolls-Royce. He saw a man reenter the hospital and left his SUV, running after Zolie and finding her lying at the bottom of a lower garden. Rushing down the slope, he saw Zolie move; she turned her head and screamed, obviously thinking that a killer was about to finish the game.

"Zolie! No, it's me Logan!" he yelled over the thunder.

Opening her eyes, she burst into tears, and he picked her up and carried her from the garden.

"I'm fine; I can walk," Zolie said, feeling Logan let her go slowly from his arms as she balanced herself on the wet grass. Holding her close, they moved to the Escalade, and he placed her in the vehicle with her sister.

Back inside, Pam screamed, "No!" She turned over and knocked Stevie off her back. The pain shot through her, and she grabbed her knife, and as she turned toward Stevie, she swung the blade, aiming for Stevie's throat she lost her balance and sliced her above her breasts. And as she tried to swing the knife again, a hand grabbed her other arm from behind, pulling her back with such force it pulled it right from its socket, and she dropped her weapon.

Nurse Pam looked into the rabid eyes of Stevie Galloway's sister and screamed. Patty laughed and then grabbed Pam's switchblade and a handful of her hair, but as she went to slit her throat, Stevie stopped her.

"No, this bitch is mine!" Stevie said, holding her hand to her chest to stop the thin line of blood that was dripping down her chest. Rage filled her, and she grabbed the knife from Patty and looked Pam right in the eyes as she slit Pam's throat. The thin line of blood appeared across Pam's neck like an evil red necklace, matching the jewelry she'd just given her, and Pam's eyes rolled back in her head. Patty shoved her face first to the floor. Stevie then looked to her younger sister, and they embraced, feeling the cold wind blow in through the open doors. Moving away toward a small café in the lobby, Patty saw the knives and smiled.

Ed Savage rolled over and shook off the hit he'd just taken. His vision blurred, and his ears were ringing when he pulled down his collar to adjust the bulletproof vest he'd put on when he'd seen the lights of the ambulance when he'd first arrived. Getting to his feet, he stumbled out into the hall and moved toward the stairs when he heard the sound of the cat. Taking off his lab coat and stuffing his other gun in his scrub pocket, he moved down the hall and saw the yellow eyes stalking him. "Mrroowwww," the cat warned as he got closer. Swinging the lab coat out in front of him, he then heard the sounds behind him.

Stomping in after kicking open the back door to the lab, Sinardi laughed, shoving lab furniture out from his way as he moved over to where he'd shot Ed Savage. His own pain received from the gunshot he'd taken in the basement was almost invisible, replaced by the elation he was feeling right now that was currently feeding his adrenaline rush. Then the lightning flashed, and he saw the blood splatter on the floor and that Ed Savage was gone.

Turning around in the darkened lab, he screamed, "Savage!" Madness filled his mind, and he grabbed on to the table nearby and flipped it over, destroying everything in his way as he lumbered toward the door. Moving down the hall, Sinardi got near the stairs, when he heard *that* horrible voice.

"Hey, shithead," Ed whispered from somewhere behind him.

Sinardi swung around, and Ed threw the cat he'd caught in his lab coat in Sinardi's face. Ed had been holding the cat in a death grip, and the feline was pissed to high hell when he struck.

"Meeeoooooooooooooowww," the cat screamed out and hissed when it landed, claws extended, on Sinardi's face. It bit down on his forehead, drawing blood, and continued to scratch him, ripping at his eyes. Sinardi tripped backward and fell against the giant windows of the third floor. Reaching up, he fired the gun, scaring the cat, which jumped for cover and ran back down the hall.

"Savage! I'll fucking kill everyone you love," Sinardi screamed, blood dripping from his bleeding eyes and swinging the gun in Ed's direction, firing at random while wiping at his eyes.

"Fuck you," Ed said, raising both guns and firing into the bastard and shattering the glass behind him. Sinardi was hit several times; firing back, he hit Ed in the left shoulder as he fell back through the broken window. Falling to his death, Sinardi hit the glass atrium below and then crashed through it and landed headfirst on the curb, the force snapping his neck and ripping his head partly from his body as he connected with the cement entryway. A pool of blood emerged beneath him, and his open eyes stared into it. From above, the gargoyles seemed to be looking down at their prey through the shattered atrium, or perhaps they were simply staring at the dark shadow that appeared to be feeding on the blood around him.

Ed Savage pulled off his scrub shirt and ripped open his shirt underneath; he wanted to take the vest off his body. Dropping it on the floor, he checked his bleeding shoulder. He then picked up his stuff and made his way down the stairs to see Logan moving through the open doors.

"Ed, you're shot!"

"Yep." Ed leaned against his brother as they made their way out of the building to the running Escalade.

Freeing themselves from Raven House, Ed and Logan saw the heavy dark clouds above them lighten just a bit as the sun began to rise somewhere over the Atlantic. Stepping a few feet from the entryway, Ed's phone vibrated for the first time since he'd been in the thick-walled building. Pulling it from his pocket, he saw more messages than he cared for at the moment. And when he looked up, he saw the limousine pulling onto the grounds. When it stopped, Thrasher and Forrester jumped out, guns ready.

"You're a little late," Ed said.

Lowering their weapons, Thrasher called up to the men and glanced at Logan. "It's a long story," Thrasher said with a smile that turned to fright.

Screaming like twin banshees, Patty and Stevie came running out from the building with knives raised over their heads.

"Get down now!" both Thrasher and Forrester yelled.

Logan shoved Ed to the ground as the agents opened fire on the Galloway sisters, shooting them dead in a barrage of bullets. Looking up and seeing them fall; Ed saw the ending had finally come. Their screams fading to silence once and for all with the fresh smell of gunfire marking the ending of hell the Galloways had for the Savages.

From up above in the East Tower, a faint shadow of a woman with long hair moved closer to the glass window, and the ghost of Rose Galloway appeared and looked down at her fallen children. A tear came down her cheek, and anger crossed her face as she faded from the window back into the world she was trapped in—within the walls of the nasty sanatorium.

Between the storm and the thick, impenetrable walls of the hospital, the skeleton crew working said they didn't hear the previous gunshots until the barrage had been fired at the Galloway sisters. The truth was, the few who were there were under Sinardi's strict orders and had been told not to leave their rooms at night since Zolie had been taken captive, knowing Ed Savage would soon be there to save her, and he could spring his trap.

Police were then called, and after Logan helped Ed into the back of the Escalade with Zolie, more agents arrived behind the limousine.

"Go on; get out of here," Thrasher said to Ed and Logan. "We'll handle the police."

Pulling away from the hospital, Logan got to the main road and pulled onto the freeway, hoping the closures were now passable, when they head the sirens and saw the cars speeding toward the sanatorium on the other side.

Sitting in the back seat with Zolie, Ed Savage looked up front to see Logan and Maura sitting quietly. He noticed the body language and could feel the emotion—the weight of a profound love that neither of them could find anymore. They were all in shock, and Maura was hurt the worst from her fall, yet he could sense the dissolution of their marriage before his eyes. He knew his brother loved her, and he also knew he was hurting with the fact she was leaving him, and he hated it.

Closing his eyes, Ed's thoughts went to his other brother Roman and the day Gabby had died. How distraught he had been and still was over her loss. How he hated that day, and how his family was falling apart before his own eyes, which brought the image of his closest brother, Sam, into his mind.

Ed hated seeing his only confidant in the family suffer, seeing Sam's slow-moving demise like an unstoppable passenger train headed for a decimated bridge over a chasm after losing his wife, Cara, such a short time ago; her death had left him an empty shell.

Ed then opened his eyes and glanced at Zolie, who was staring out her window. Ed knew that losing her sister Cara was still haunting her.

He then turned his thoughts to his own life and the disastrous turn it had taken. Marlo had lost the baby, and the mess with Aisha Thomas that he'd created made him hate himself all the more. This was a complete demise of the Savages. His own life and his entire family had been decimated, and there was nothing he could do to fix it.

He looked out his window at the world passing by and prayed his family would somehow survive.

CHAPTER 144

lake Vreeland looked out the window of the West Tower and smiled. It was clearly time for him to take back *his* hospital, but before he put that plan into action, he needed to clean up a few things. Knowing he didn't have much time with the authorities on the grounds, he rushed to the basement, and as he got near the problems that needed to be taken care of, he heard the whispering voice of a sad young man. Quietly, he moved toward him and listened to what Little Blake was saying while sitting on the floor next to his dead sisters.

"You killed our parents. Now, in your own way, you've killed yourselves with your gifts. What a waste it has all been. Now I'm trapped in your hell and alone forever."

Blake's heart broke for the young man. He truly didn't know if he was guilty of the crimes that had brought him here, but with the pain of his own family, he wanted nothing more than to help the lost man, and he felt he could *trust* him.

Seeing the blacked-out section of the basement the lightning had caused in several places in the hospital, he looked over and saw the circuit breakers and reset them, watching the lights come back on. He then looked back to the poor young man. "You're not alone, Blake."

Little Blake smiled and raised his head, turning to see the man who'd now be his captor...or his friend. "Please don't put me back in my cell. I hate it down here."

"You'll have a better room and then some; you just need to trust me and wait a short while. I'll see to it personally, but I need your help. All this…needs to be attended to," he said, waving his hand and looking at the boy's sisters. "Also those other two back there." He motioned behind him. "Can you help me with that?"

"Yes, sir. What would you like done?"

Blake smiled and held up his hand, signaling him to follow. "I'll show you," he said, turning and moving to the hotbox. Getting to the vile murdering machine, he turned it on and heard the gas ignite, and it roared with life. He then turned to the young man. "Think you're able to do this?"

"They would have wanted this, sir," the young man replied.

Blake Vreeland smiled and gave him an approving nod. "Be quick about it; we don't have much time." He then went to visit Todd in the private cell he'd specifically chosen for him. Rushing down the corridors, he passed the Storm sisters and saw something catch his eye near Sandy. Seeing the small device, he grabbed some gloves from a supply cart around the corner and came back, picking up the recorder.

"Hmm," he thought as he rewound the device and pressed play. Hearing Dr. Sinardi's confession was just what he needed until he heard his brother's voice, and knew *his* voice would be on it too. He then found the exact spot where Sinardi had finished bragging of his crimes and pressed record. Leaving it on to tape over the recordings of what really happened. He then looked at the spot where Sinardi had been shot. There was a pool of blood that was drying at its edges and a violent crimson smear leading to the elevator, where more blood decorated the panel of buttons.

Seeing the ease of this *present*, he pushed the call button for the elevator and went to the drying pool of blood and dropped the recording device into it and turned it over. He then picked it up in his gloved hand and stood next to the elevator. Seeing the empty elevator arrive, he saw the blood splatter inside and tossed the recording device into one of the corners of the car and then let the door close.

Realizing there wasn't enough time, he dragged the reporters over to the hotbox, took off his gloves, and saw the young man having a last moment with his sisters. Feeling the heat of the monstrous machine warming the ground it sat on, he opened the giant door and tossed in his gloves, watching them immediately start to melt in the increasing heat.

"We need to get this going now," Blake Vreeland said to Little Blake.

Offering an almost reverent nod, the young man lifted one of his sister's arms and started dragging her toward the hotbox. Getting a move on himself, Blake hurried away, passing the young Brockman's old cell to the dead end in the corridor. Looking back, he pushed on the back side of a support beam, and a wall moved, leading to the hidden corridor. Rats ran from the opening, and Blake entered, closing it behind him.

The cells along the viewing corridor were nasty. It was cold, and the blankets inside the cells had fleas crawling all over them; in one cell a corpse was decaying right by the glass window, as if the poor soul had died while saying good-bye to the outside world that he could no longer see. That cell was directly across from his brother's. *What a perfect view for Todd,* he thought.

Turning, he saw that his brother hadn't moved since being thrown into his cell. Blake could see the blood on his side from scraping it on the table he'd knocked over, and he was lying in an awkward position. Everything in the cell was arranged with purpose, to make staying in there as miserable as possible, and the drugs he was currently on to keep him passed out would later seem like a blessing after he woke up to this new home.

Blake looked at the *Phantom Finders* posters in the room and saw the men's names on them, Sinardi and Savage, and wondered why Sinardi had wanted Patty Galloway to watch over this particular prisoner, and his thoughts went back to what his brother had said about Rose Galloway's daughters being in the hospital.

Could he have been telling me the truth? he thought. "What do I do with you?" Blake Vreeland finally said to himself, looking at the fair-haired little brother whom at one time he'd loved. "Sad," he said, shaking his head when he saw his brother begin to stir. The wide smile returned to Blake's face, and he rushed down the hall out of view near the secret passageway and waited in the darkness.

The sound of Todd moving was music to his ears, and the terrified screaming that followed was even better than Christmas morning.

Prisoner Todd Vreeland woke shivering cold. The dampness in the cell chilled him awake, and when he saw his surroundings and the corpse across from his cell, he screamed out and raced to the doors of the cell and tried in vain to open them, "Blake! It was our father who started all this! Please believe me! Blake! You deplorable bastard! I'll get you for this!" Todd yelled.

Blake couldn't help but laugh, and he reached up to the rope secured to a spike in the wall for the finishing touch. Untying it, he pulled violently and could hear her struggle from above as he dragged her from the rafters in the ceiling. Then with one mighty tug of the rope, he heard the scream of the young Kayla as she was pulled from above, to drop in front of Todd's cell. Screaming as she fell, Todd turned to see the young woman's neck snap and her body swinging like a pendulum in front of his cell—Kayla Bennet was dead.

Todd was shocked. His mind flashed to seeing his daughter swinging on the tire swing of the tree she used to love to climb over-looking their beautiful city in Concepción. He ran to the glass walls and slammed his fists against it, crying as the madness set in.

"Fucker!" was the last drawn-out word Blake heard from his pathetic little brother as the secret wall closed behind him, muffling the sounds of the damned as he laughed happily at what he'd done.

Making his way back to the basement and passing the dead Dr. Hollerman in the elevator shaft, Blake looked in and saw a second corpse and hurried along to see the young Brockman standing by the hotbox. The flames inside were roaring, and the ashes would soon be blown to the winds.

"Forget the old elevator shaft," Blake said. "When the police ask, tell them you heard the Galloway women laughing about killing the two back there."

Looking at the man in charge, the young man smiled. "I'll take care of it."

"You better get back in your cell; they'll be here any minute."

Blake Vreeland then made his way to the Death Tunnel that led to the chapel on the grounds, that was used to take the many bodies out in the dead of night. There he got in his car and drove away, passing their great-grandfather's old home on the edge of the grounds and planning his triumphant return in a few short days.

Little Blake Brockman watched the hotbox turn the women to ash, and seeing a few ashes rise in the diabolical contraption, a coldness came over him, and an angry look crossed his face. He looked into the hotbox and grinned as the blackness that had *always* dwelled within him turned his eyes black to match his soul. He was happy—happy with his plan to let Blake Vreeland hear him talking with his dead sisters. But he was most pleased with himself for sending his shadow soul to the Storm sisters to keep them dormant so he could have the pleasure of watching them burn alive in the hotbox, allowing them to awaken fully in order to understand *exactly* where they were before he slammed the nasty machine's door closed on their pathetic lives, watching them panic as the heat increased before sending the shadow back in to awaken his sisters so they too could see that their usefulness to him was concluded. Allowing them all to see him watch them as they caught fire and burned, screaming in flames as they finally were snuffed out once and for all.

He thought back to that first day he'd arrived at Vreeland Hills Sanatorium. At that young age, he was just beginning to understand the *gift* he had of feeding his soul on the torment of the damned. And he thought of how the immediate heightened elation came when it grew to manipulate the weak and battered-minded and abused individuals into doing things they'd never do. Meeting Dr. Victor Vreeland and seeing the evil that lived within in him had been another gift; his sons, however, were stronger, except one. Taking advantage of his poor son Todd had been easy. Feeding off the conflicted and tormented pain the boy had endured from everyone was like a buffet, and manipulating his mind with the horrifying thoughts and dreams he'd introduce to *help* better see the road to madness had felt like a picnic, seeing as the young man had psychopathic thoughts already running through his head. Todd's betrayed mind was an easy target until he left—and the remaining Brockman couldn't send his shadow to those who were too far away from him.

Blake, on the other hand, was inherently sadistic like his father Victor Vreeland. At least when he was younger, he'd never walk away from punching someone in the face for sport. However, with age and time away from the sanatorium, he'd seemed to grow out of it—maybe even soften a bit—but that mean streak was always there, running through him. It could come out like sudden lightning with a sharpshooter's aim—and he seemed to like the lone Brockman, and that was Little Blake's plan. Even with his highly educated skill, Little Blake had a harder time influencing Blake's mind with the ugly thoughts he'd plant for him, like he had easily done with his stupid brother Todd—but he managed to do it all the same. Little Blake laughed knowing the fun and games were far from over.

CHAPTER 145

Their time at the Berman Medical Center wasn't as bad as it could have been, and when the police showed up to take their statements, Ed heard Zolie mention her bag was missing and must still be at the sanatorium. He reached his hand down to his pants and could feel her keys in his pocket with the prescription-pad sheets of Dr. Sinardi, and he remembered the notes he'd stuffed in her bag about Patty's mother living past the accident. He pulled the sheets he'd taken from his pocket and looked at them; he could see the trace of what Sinardi had written along with his signature from the previous prescription, along with his name and identification numbers. Wanting to save this for Tallulah, he stuffed it back in his pocket when they came to take him for tests. Being wheeled away, he saw Logan being interviewed and knew he'd take Zolie home, but he kept her keys quiet for now.

Maura had suffered a broken ankle and knee pain. She had a massive headache from the fall, but it could have been a lot worse, and she'd be staying in the hospital with him.

Zolie was prescribed antibiotics for the serious cat scratches she sustained, and with some of them being on the top of her head, it made it difficult to treat them without cutting her long hair. She had a black-and-blue bruise on her temple and several others from tumbling down the stairs in that wretched place. And she couldn't wait to get home so she could make arrangements to return to London, where all her dogs awaited her. If she never saw a cat again, it'd be too soon.

The bullet that hit Ed's left shoulder grazed his right acromion, sending a small fragment off that was feared to have traveled down into the joint space of his shoulder, due to the discomfort and pain Ed was telling them he had. Surgery was needed, and he sadly agreed to be admitted.

Confined to a hospital bed, he was wheeled to a large, comfortable room, where he tried again to call Marlo. He hadn't spoken to her since she'd hung up on him, and that damn text message she'd sent him haunted his thoughts. He knew everything that had happened, and the frantic voice message from Aisha after leaving the sanatorium told him how Marlo had tricked her into telling her everything. It was the worst possible time with her losing the baby, and he knew she was hurt, and he desperately needed to make things right. Most of all, he was scared.

The long, hot bath was exactly what Marlo needed once she finally got home. She was tired, hurt, and angry with all of it. The press had been an absolute nightmare with their nonstop questions involving not only the disastrous wave that hit the studio warehouse but also the death of Marilyn Caspian Hart. There weren't too many questions about the still-missing Tonya Lipschitz, though. Most of the fans hated her, and the few who didn't kept quiet. But when it was reported Marlo had lost her baby in the catastrophe; it was those questions that hurt her the most. Filming was put on hold, but the story was hot and Randall Bishop was pushing for more, and now she felt like she was right back where she'd started after that damn trip into the mountains. Worse, with everything that had happened and everything she now knew, the contract she'd signed for having *Tycoon Wives* film at Zolie's estate was looming.

Hearing her phone ring and seeing it was her husband, she ignored it, turning her head to look out the upper-floor window at the beautiful trees on Zolie's estate. Her cold, blank stare blurred as she thought back to when Aisha Thomas had arrived in Boston to "help" her in her delicate condition. She remembered how she'd lied to her, telling her Ed had confessed to the whole affair and how she knew the baby she was carrying was Ed's. She started to cry, remembering the sudden stabbing pain to her heart when Aisha had nodded and confirmed the thoughts, turning fiction into fact. She could still remember the entire ugly conversation.

"I'm so sorry for all of it!"

"I need you to tell me everything, and I'm only giving you one chance," Marlo demanded.

"It was just that one time, that one time I called him and he met me for a drink. He was a mess; he was hurting. You were divorcing him."

"Don't you put this on me!" Marlo could still hear the venom in her words echo in her mind.

"We got hammered, the both of us, and we went to my place for the night. But you have to know: I don't know if it's his…or Danny's."

"Well, aren't you the busy one. You need to tell me about the next time you two were together, because Ed certainly did," Marlo said, overplaying her hand, but by then she really didn't care.

"Bitch! You lying bitch!"

"You're calling *me* the bitch! You knew *exactly* how he was feeling, and you made your move, you home wrecker!"

"Look, I'm sorry for everything that's happened. God knows I am. But you…you need to take some responsibility, too!"

Coming back from the conversation, Marlo mumbled as she refocused on the trees outside. "*My* responsibility?" She turned to the phone that was now ringing again. "No, Ed Savage, last time was the rehearsal—this time is the final act!"

CHAPTER 146

hatham Hospital was hectic with the overflow of patients, and when Jillian entered the intensive care unit, she saw a nurse at her sister's side. The sound of the machines and the bruises on her sister frightened her, and she started to cry.

Leaving the cafeteria, Trent made his way back to the ICU, and when he got there, he saw the nurse leaving his mom's side, and he stopped at the door. Seeing her wet face as she sat next to her only sibling, his heart broke. "They say she's doing better," he said in almost a whisper.

Turning to her son, Jillian stood, and they embraced. She pulled away and put her hands on his shoulders, "Let me look at you." Jillian almost cried seeing his bruises. "Oh my God—I don't know what I would have done had something happened to you."

"Mom, I'm okay—I'm just glad I was there," Trent said, remembering Ed holding him the same way when he'd first met him.

"Oh, Trent. Promise me I won't lose you. I know you love those storms you chase, but I want that to stop. Please. You're all I've got," she said, pulling him into a hug.

Trent could feel his heart race, and he wanted to tell her how scared he had been, how he wasn't prepared for what had happened—but the lies he *now* knew she had told him of his father striking her were bigger than all the years of wondering about who his true father really was, and he kept it bottled up. He looked up at her and smiled. "Mom, I'm glad you're here, and you don't have to worry about me. I'm fine," he lied.

Marta stirred in the bed, and they looked to her. "Nurse! Nurse, can you come back in here?" Jillian said in a concerned voice to the nurses' station across from the small ICU room.

"See, she is doing better," Trent said, smiling at his mother.

CHAPTER 147

The sneak preview of the early filming of *Tycoon Wives* was explosive. Never in the history of the show had footage aired so early. But with the death of Marilyn Caspian Hart and the missing Tonya Lipschitz, along with the disastrous footage caught at Pier Productions in Martha's Vineyard, all eyes were on *Tycoon Wives*, including those of Marilyn's ex-husband, Anthony Caspian.

The *Tycoon Wives* king, Randall Bishop, was riding the high wave from the ratings; the hot water around him had cooled completely, and even the ladies who heard about the rumors of the CEO's daughter started coming around again after the spike in ratings. Randall Bishop was being interviewed all over town, and he loved the attention. He was finally free of that prima donna who threatened his job on a weekly basis, and he was blissful over the fact he'd never have to deal with the likes of her or her ex-husband again.

The problem, outside of paying that idiot off to murder Marilyn, was that the idiot was still alive, and *that* was a constant worry, like the constant worry of Anthony Caspian releasing the recording of his insider knowledge of the doomed film he'd invested so heavily in. No, he was done with all of it and was now in charge of his own destiny; he wasn't playing second fiddle to anyone's song and dance anymore.

He was especially well versed in the happenings of the Savage clan. But after reading the recent events in Upstate New York, with the family yet again in that cursed city of Port Roberts, Randall thought he'd tear a few more pages out of the Savage playbook and put them to use.

Planning on the trip upstate with a film crew to visit Marlo, he called his friend who'd helped him out with the Marilyn problem and told him he had a room booked at the Vander Place Hotel, where the crew would be staying, and he wanted to pay him a bonus.

Yes, this time Randall would be taking care of things *his* way, and after the next couple of days, he'd be in the clear. Thinking everything was finally going to work out, he called his friend Bentley Fencer to meet for drinks at their favorite pub.

CHAPTER 148

The over-the-top raid at the hotel for the assassin Hermann Stangl was a hard one to explain to the public. The government agencies involved in his capture, along with the explosion and fireball of Mingyu's Tahoe, sent the Internet conspiracy theory trolls into overdrive—especially with the other story of the volcano's sudden eruption under the Atlantic that no one knew ever existed and caused so much destruction on the Eastern Seaboard.

Satellite imagery of the location in the Atlantic was suddenly gone from all sources on the Internet, and the cover-up was well underway *before* the public was told of the reason for the earthquake that caused the tsunami. The fact was that if the American public knew those missing warheads had been so close to American soil for all those years since they'd gone missing—and that some were *still out there*—would be a public-relations nightmare that no agency wanted to deal with.

The good news they were keeping under wraps was the discovery of the other torpedo, which had been buried in the sediment near the casing they'd found. Of the eight warheads that had gone missing when the *Manchester* submarine disappeared in 1955, they had three, and the one meant for the HMS *Queen Anne II* brought the number to four. Now the missing *Manchester* was only *half* as dangerous, a few military men joked, knowing that four warheads were still out there somewhere.

The bad news they were still investigating was who exactly it was that sold the warhead to the consortium in the first place. All remaining leads were destroyed in the SUV and hotel.

The only news they could release, however, was the fact that one of the guns found in Hermann Stangl's room was an exact match for the gun used in the murder of Parnell F. Bancroft, and when *that* story made the papers, it made one person very angry.

CHAPTER 149

The stolen police report Jeremy Bigelow had acquired showing the ballistic data regarding the type of gun used to kill Parnell F. Bancroft was in Jeremy's briefcase when *his plan* was supposed to go into effect. That got fucked up when his associate, a hired thug, called him and told him Ed Savage's Range Rover had been found at a crime scene at some lunatic asylum.

The plan was simple, he thought: have his associate plant the gun under the seat of his SUV like the report said Ed did up in the mountains, and tip off the police. Even drilling the barrel of the gun to fuck it up so they couldn't fire it to test it would be a pain in the ass for Ed Savage to sort out. He used to laugh, thinking how fun it would be to then leak the story to the press so Savage Construction would suffer and Bigelow could reap some of the glory since losing Donert Tower. It wouldn't repay him for the millions lost over the Donert deal, but it was a start.

Pissed off that the police now having Ed's SUV meant he would have to plant the gun at a later time. He told his associate to hold off until further notice. Angry over the fact this would take away some of the heat his little time bomb of sorts would have, since Ed was again being splashed in the news with the new Wendy Storm allegations. Hanging up the phone in his office, he turned in his chair and got up, looking out the windows toward Savage Tower, when his secretary knocked on the door; opening it, she peeked in.

"Sir, turn on your television. They found out who killed Parnell!"

Jeremy turned his head to see his perky, smiling secretary looking at him from the door, but when she saw his reaction, she immediately closed it. Picking up the remote from a sitting area in his office, he turned on the set and flipped a few channels, finding the right news station reporting the story. The breaking-news banner across the bottom of the set infuriated him. "Parnell F. Bancroft Murder Solved," it stated in giant letters, and he blew his top. "Damn it!" he growled, looking at the television as the story went on to say the man responsible was also being investigated in several *other* unsolved murders and that they weren't identifying him until such matters were thoroughly investigated, but they had solid proof he was Parnell's murderer.

Another waste of money, Jeremy thought, in what he'd paid for the stolen police report and the gun, let alone the thug who now had his secrets.

CHAPTER 150

The three blocks of prime downtown land Berman Park was located on was not only owned but also leased to the city for one dollar a year by one of the wealthiest families in Port Roberts, New York. Berman Medical Center was located directly at the east end of Berman Park near the water, and the family had their eye on that land where the Grennings' old apartment buildings sat. Over the years they had submitted offers to buy the land and had been promptly refused without so much as even the time taken to read the proposals.

Beau Berman, the head of the family and lead surgeon and CEO of the family-owned medical center, knew the Grennings and understood the family had owned the land since the Bermans had first built the hospital. He understood and respected the business aspect of Grenning Lumber—but when he saw the sign in front of the buildings and learned they were slated to be demolished, he wanted that land.

The real estate in Port Roberts was expensive, and with Beau Berman's heart for his patients, he now wanted to build another facility on the opposite end of the park that could be seen from his family's hospital. The problem standing in his way was that annoying Wall Street rich guy Tasker Grenning, with his vision of building a row of glass condominium towers facing the park, that man was the only obstacle in need of a wrecking ball.

High up in his office on the top floor of the hospital, Beau cast his eyes over the park, past Gallery 26, to that row of abandoned apartments destined to come down, and he wondered if his family's power in the city could bring about eminent domain.

CHAPTER 151

When Sam Savage arrived at his brother's side in the hospital, it was a complete reversal from when Ed had visited Sam. The circumstances were different, but they now had shoulder injuries to compare war stories with. Worse, Ed feared Marlo was gearing up for a confrontation, and he'd lose her, like Logan was losing Maura. He still hadn't heard from her, and they were coming to take him to surgery soon. Sam told him he and Raquel had left the hospital on Martha's Vineyard, and that he'd paid a private citizen to take them to the mainland on their boat, so they could get home.

"You and Raquel Delgado, huh?" Ed said with a warm smile for his brother who had lost too much. "I'm glad you're both all right, but more importantly I'm happy you found her. She's hot!" Ed laughed.

"Yeah, I don't know where, if anywhere, this is going, but what I can tell you is she helped save my life well before that damn wave."

Ed wanted to tell his confidant the whole story, but there were even some things *he* had to keep secret, and the remaining missing warheads was information too dangerous for anyone to have. But Patty Galloway was another story.

"Hey, I need you to keep this between us," Ed said in a tone Sam knew well.

"What's going on?"

"Hand me my pants over there," Ed said, pointing to the shelf they were on.

"You need me to hold your wallet during surgery?" Sam questioned his serious tone, tossing them to him.

"Ah, that's a good idea too, but no, I need you to do me a favor," he said, pulling out Zolie's keys and holding them up for him to see.

"What are you doing with those? Oh God, do I want to know?" Sam said.

Ed flashed his signature grin.

"Oh, I don't like where this is going." Sam laughed. "All right, spill it."

"It's easy. Zolie's missing bag is under a terra-cotta planter on the stairs between the first and second floors of the sanatorium, and I need you to go and get it, and when you do, you can drop these in it for me," Ed said. "See—easy."

"And Zolie put one of her oversized expensive bags under a giant terra-cotta planter for safekeeping and forgot it, right?" Sam said with his own devilish grin.

"Don't even try stealing my shtick," Ed shot out as the pain in his arm shifted, and he let out a holler.

"I'm Ed Savage, and this is another *Savage Mystery*," Sam said, mocking his brother's serious voice used on his show. "See? I can do you easy. And I'm younger and hotter than you, too!"

"Uh-huh," Ed said. "Seriously though, I did find her keys next to her bag on Sinardi's desk, and I was going to leave it there until I found the papers on Patty Galloway's mother in a drawer."

The fun left the room like it had been shot from a cannon, and Sam turned serious. "Papers?"

"Sam, all I had a chance to garner was the fact that Patty's mother was alive *after* the accident, and she was taken to Vreeland Hills Sanatorium. She was even in the exact room they had Patty in."

"That is messed up!" Sam said, letting the gravity of the news sink in. "My God, all Patty would go on about was the loss of her parents. And now you're telling me one of them survived, and she didn't know?"

Ed nodded.

"Jesus, you mean all this could have been different had Patty known her mother was alive, and none of this shit the family's gone through would have ever happened?"

"You and I are the only two who know this, and it needs to be kept quiet until we get those papers and know everything. Oh, those building look the same—remember go to the West Tower."

"Got it. West Tower. Give me the keys," Sam said, holding out his hand.

Ed tossed them to him right as the door opened and his nurse came in to take him to surgery.

"I'll see you when you come out, and I'll take care of that errand first thing in the morning," Sam said, moving out of the way.

"You don't have to wait here. To be honest, I need some sleep, and after surgery I'm planning on catching up until they release me."

"All right, then. I'll see you tomorrow," Sam said.

CHAPTER 152

R andall Bishop wasn't the only person booked into the Vander Place Hotel for the event; Marlo had moved out from Zolie's estate and taken a suite there while she waited to drop the bomb on Ed, ending their marriage once and for all. Deciding on where and when played out in her mind when she met Randall in the lobby.

"Marlo, so good to see you. I'm so sorry about the baby. How are you?" Randall said, thinking of the ratings boost her personal catastrophe would bring to the show.

"I'm doing better. Thank you for meeting me here," she said, leading him to a private table in an exclusive restaurant that wasn't open for dinner yet.

"Of course. Not a problem. We're still set to film at Zolie's estate, right? Get a peek into where you're living as a starting point for the show?"

"There's a slight problem with that."

Randall braced himself, wanting nothing more than to get Zolie or Maura on camera. "Oh?"

"Well, I did have my lawyers go over the contract you sent me, and you're right: I did sign to have you film at the location where I'm living." She paused a moment, looking away, rethinking her decision to release the information this particular way, when her mind kept seeing Aisha Thomas and listening to her say: "Bitch! You lying bitch!" The anger in her flared, and she turned back to Randall, ready to tell him about her divorce. "There have been some developments in my living situation, like where *exactly* I'm living."

The anger was now burning within him, and he made a mental note for the lawyers to address this loophole Marlo had found immediately. The smile left his face. "What did Zolie do? Kick you out?"

"No, it's nothing like that at all, but I'm now living here at the hotel."

"So you moved out for a short time so we couldn't film? That's a little sleazy coming from you," Randall said in a sharp tone, misreading her words and thinking this woman was like the dozens before her who had weaseled themselves onto his shows just to end up being total disappointments. With Marilyn gone, his power-hungry manner boiled to the surface. "Let me make something clear: I don't like games, and I'm not playing by your rules. I've seen them all, and I control the filming and the editing, and I can turn these crazy bitches on you in an instant. I'm disappointed. You fooled me completely. I had expected more from you, Marlo."

Realizing he'd misread her and not liking his tone *or* his threats, Marlo's kind demeanor changed in a snap at seeing his true colors. "Let me make this clear to *you*, Randall. I honestly felt bad for this and wanted to honor the contract, and what's this bullshit of turning these crazy bitches on me? What are they? Fembots? You know, on second thought, maybe I'll be a one-season wonder and quit when this year's over."

"Ah, this is how you want to play it?" Randall snapped back. "You know, we *never* really wanted you anyway, darling. It was Zolie all along. Getting Cara was the way in, and since both Zolie and Maura declined, you were all that was left. Oh, and with having you under contract, it will be fun to turn you into the most hated *Tycoon Wife* on earth."

"*Darling?*" Marlo mocked, seeing this asshole for what he truly was. "Oh no, you're the darling whose rules we're playing by now. Oh, oh, oh." Marlo laughed. "You think you know the rules of Hollywood? Baby, I've been married to it longer than you've been around. We're now playing by your rules, and you're just too stupid to know it!" Marlo spat back, angry with herself as she got up from the table, thinking she'd been about to tell this reptile of her divorce with Ed. "And to think I thought Marilyn was a hard one! Better watch yourself, pal, because I could follow her playbook and eviscerate you every chance I get and enjoy it, like that bitch Marilyn Hart did for years with her backhanded compliments. And furthermore, the terms have now changed, Randall Bishop, and you can pack your shit up and get the hell out of my family's hotel because there isn't going to be *any* filming."

Watching her leave, Randall leaned back in his chair. "It's going to be fun suing you for all the money Ed inherited, you stupid bitch!"

Marlo's shoulders went up hearing him behind her, and she turned with a deadly smile. "That comment is going to cost you in ways you'll never see coming."

The cold look she shot him added to the heartless, cruel smile was something different than the scared look he'd expected, and he actually felt nervous she was hiding something from him as he watched her leave the restaurant. Anger flashed through his body, and he banged his fists on the table before getting up and heading to the open bar across from the restaurant.

Marlo stopped at the front desk and ordered security to make sure Randall Bishop's reservation was canceled and demanded he not be allowed access to the private floors of the hotel. She then pointed him out as she saw him moving to the bar.

Filled with rage, she retreated to her room and remembered her homework she'd done on *all* the cast members and meeting that lovely man Anthony Caspian years ago at a function with Ed. She knew his divorce from Marilyn had been arranged because he was going to jail and that he'd still loved her when they'd separated, and she remembered the cryptic conversations she'd heard over the years during the scandal.

With the elevator door closed, she looked in the mirrors and saw Randall's anger in herself. And she remembered her anger to Ed and Ava and how ugly she'd been to them before she remembered the rape. No, she wasn't going to do that to her family.

CHAPTER 153

The autopsy of Marilyn Caspian Hart ruled her death an accident, and when Anthony Caspian had the report delivered to his jail for millionaires, he made a few phone calls. The man had connections all over Hollywood, and the last call he made hit pay dirt.

Pier Productions kept cameras running both inside the buildings and outside. The footage of the wave proved to be of great value, and they took advantage of it. However, the cameras inside had caught a few things too. The power source for the cameras came from two separate locations from outside the building in case one went down during shooting. This way they wouldn't lose money on downtime because they could always depend on the other power source backing them up.

He wanted and got the footage from that horrible day Marilyn had taken her last breath, and when he saw her struggling to get to an unidentified man with the water rising around her, he wanted to know just who exactly that man was, especially because that was close to where Marilyn's body had been found. The rest of the footage was of no use; it showed a spray of water hitting near her, and when the spray dissipated, she was gone. The man on the footage, however, gave a clear shot, and Anthony ordered that man be found.

CHAPTER 154

Sam Savage arrived at the sanatorium and took one look at the place and was glad he'd only had a tsunami to deal with. The place gave him the creeps, and he couldn't wait to be on his way. Ed's Range Rover was being pulled up on a tow truck, and Zolie's Rolls-Royce with the broken windshield was parked near it. It looked like the investigation was winding down, and he grabbed his backpack to put Zolie's bag in and threw it over his shoulder as he looked for someone in charge. He saw some men over at the East Tower where Ed had told him the Galloway sisters were killed, and a few others were gathered at the tow truck when he stepped inside the West Tower.

"We're closed for visitors," came the stern woman's voice from behind.

Turning in her direction near the elevators, he immediately noticed her demeanor change from a menacing guard dog set to attack to a slutty horned-up sex kitten once he noticed her eyes go right to his crotch after getting a good look at him. Figuring he'd try his charm, he flirted with her and smiled. "Hi there, um...Stacey," he said, leaning in close to read her name badge. "I'm not a visitor. I'm investigating last night's events, and I need to speak with the detective in charge. Can you help me with that?" He flashed his own devilish grin.

"Ah, yeah, I can help you with that," Stacey said, pushing out her chest. "Hang on a minute. I think they're over at the East Tower."

Sam watched her leave and rushed past the reception area down the lobby to the rear of the building where the stairs were. He saw the plants on the tarps, and grabbing the railing, he swung around and lifted the yellow construction tape to go under, and headed up to the landing between the floors where Ed said he'd left Zolie's bag. Getting to the landing, he saw the planters clustered together, and one of them had been turned upside down. Moving to it, he quickly turned it over to find…nothing.

Standing up, he looked around the area and saw the dirt near the pot had been disturbed, like it had been scraped across the floor, and when he searched the area, he found a Post-it with a room number scrawled on it. Picking it up, he heard people coming up the stairs below him. Putting his hands in his pockets, he moved to the next flight, staring up at the higher floors, as if he was exploring.

"What can I help you with?" a uniformed detective said.

"Wow, this is some place," Sam said. "I'd hate to be sent here."

"Sir, I'm going to have to ask you to come down here."

"Oh, sure," Sam said, moving down the stairs.

"Mind taking your hands out of your pockets?"

Looking over the detective's shoulder, he saw Stacey looking at him with suspicion. "I think you're looking for these," Sam said, pulling out Zolie's keys dangling from the Rolls-Royce key chain. "Go ahead and take them. You fuck up that car without the key, and you'll be paying for damages and then some."

The detective held out his hand, and Sam dropped them into his palm.

"A private word, please," Sam said, moving past him and winking at Stacey as he led the detective back down the stairs, outside and away from the listening ears of the place. "Do you have a card? I'm going to need that to tell my sister-in-law who I just gave her keys to. I'm Sam Savage."

"Sir, I'm sorry for all this. Just following protocol."

"No problem," Sam said, looking at the busted glass in the windshield of the Rolls and wanting to hammer in the point. "That's sure gonna cost a fortune to get fixed."

"I bet," the detective said, handing him his card. "Name's Vince Berry."

Sam glanced at the card and put it in his pocket with the Post-it. "Thanks, Vince. So, Zolie told me she dropped her things on the stairs, and I found her keys there. But what I didn't find was her purse. Know anything about that?"

Sam watched Vince's eyes look to his backpack, and he took it down and opened it in order to prove that only his wallet, phone, and gym clothes were inside. "Didn't want to leave this in the truck," Sam said, pulling out his wallet, grabbing one of his cards and stuffing the wallet in his back pocket. "So did you find her purse?" he said handing him his card.

"No, sir, nothing like a personal bag has been found that I'm aware of."

"Can you ask around? I'll wait a bit."

"Sure thing, Mr. Savage," Vince said glancing at his card.

Sam watched the detective move back in the building and took another look around the creepy place. Shaking his head, he went to his truck to wait.

CHAPTER 155

Anthony Caspian's eyes and ears were everywhere even though he was locked away at Sing Sing for the rich, and he had people who were still loyal to him. At the bar in the Vander Place Hotel, Randall Bishop was enjoying his whiskey ginger when his friend sat down near him. The two looked at each other and did not say a word, and at that moment a photo was taken from the lobby by a cell phone and quickly tucked away.

The friend ordered a drink and when it arrived he paid for it in cash. It wasn't long after Randall got up and left that his friend got up and followed him outside.

Seeing him on the steps to the skeet-shooting area, he followed along. The water's breeze was on the cold side, and he hurried to see Randall walking along the edge toward the lighthouse in the distance. The tall grass had grown, and the land sloped a bit, and when he saw Randall disappear down a slope, he quickened his step even more.

Getting to the slope and not seeing him, he stopped and called out his name. That was when Randall made his move.

From his crouched position in the grass, he rushed toward the man and pushed hard. But the man was strong and felt something was off and was prepared. Turning just as Randall hit him, he pushed back, knocking Randall to the ground. He then jumped on him and punched him in the face five times until his fist was bleeding.

Randall was crying for him to stop, and the man looked at him in disgust.

"Dumb sissy!" his hired thug said. "I was content with what you already paid me. This could have been all over. Now it's just beginning, you stupid fuck. I want ten times what you paid me, and I'll call you tomorrow to collect it."

"Wait a minute," Randall said, spitting blood.

"Don't even try to tap-dance your way out of this shit TV boy. You *will* pay me." He then pulled out his phone and took a photo of the bloodied Randall Bishop lying in the grass like a bawling baby. "And this will be my insurance, asshole."

He then wiped his bloody fist off on Randall's shirt and looked up. Seeing no one around, he crouched back down on top of Randall. "You'll pay me ten times what you did, or you'll wish you threw me over this cliff." He then spit in his face, got up, walked slowly back to his car at the hotel, and left.

More photos were taken of the man leaving, including the license plate of his car. Then as Randall made his way back to the hotel, his camera crew was outside still taking establishing shots of the hotel and got him on film as he tripped down the stairs from the skeet area, covered in blood.

CHAPTER 156

The following day at Berman Medical Center, Ed was waiting for the wheelchair discharge service and thinking of what Sam had told him of not finding Zolie's bag and what had happened while he was at the sanatorium. He looked at his phone, wanting to hear back from Tallulah since filling her in on what he'd found out when Sam got back to his room.

"I can't understand where the bag went to," Ed said, wanting those papers on the Galloway woman.

"The dirt around the pots looked like the pot had been moved, but it was still upside down."

"What was the name of that detective again? I want to give him a call."

"Vince...something. I still have his card," Sam said, reaching in his pocket. He pulled out the card and the Post-it was stuck to it. Ed recognized it at once.

"That's Galloway's room number," Ed said.

"How do you know? I forgot to tell you I found it near the planter."

"Because that's my handwriting on it, and it must have gotten shoved in the bag when I stuffed the papers in it."

"Do you remember anything you read from the papers?"

"I told you. Rose Galloway's name was on it, and I remember looking at Patty's chart, which had the same room number on it. I remember thinking Patty's mother had lived and all the ramifications of that, but I needed to get out of there and find Logan and the women, so I had no time left to read. That's it."

The door opened, and the nurse was back with the wheelchair.

"Perfect timing. I need to get out of here," Ed said.

"I'll go get the car." Sam hurried along ahead of them.

Outside Ed saw Sam's truck pull up, and he rose from the chair, thanked the nurse, and was on his way. "Get me home, Sam. I still haven't heard from Marlo."

CHAPTER 157

When the recording of Randall Bishop's involvement with the insider-trading scandal hit the news outlets, it seemed like the tidal wave from hell, and it felt more destructive than the recent tsunami for the poor beleaguered producer. Anthony Caspian made a deal for a lighter sentence in exchange for bringing down Bishop since he didn't have to make nice for the woman he loved, and the arrest was blown all over the news. There was Randall being handcuffed and taken out from his high-rise office building; his face was bruised purple and black, and it showed him being placed inside a police car.

Then the footage of him tripping down the stairs with the bloody face was leaked and splashed all over the Internet with the tagline, "Ding Dong the Tycoon Witch Is Dead." The networks picked it up to add to the pile on what was happening in poor Randall Bishop's life, and the person who leaked it after years of abuse kept it secret and went out to a bar, where most of the *Tycoon Wives* crew was out celebrating.

And to make matters worse, Tonya Lipschitz's body washed up on shore in Massachusetts. A shark had bitten off her head, and the tattoo above her hoo-ha that said *Feed Me* identified her to the masses. When her head was found a few miles away, the Internet jokes began that even the shark that'd attacked her hated her too. And when *that* was added to the Randall Bishop mess, it spoke volumes of the trashy life he had been leading behind closed doors because it was no secret they had slept together after she was on the show. Then, as a possible add-on story, an assistant who had survived the Pier Productions disaster was now reported missing, and the entertainment gossip shows went on and on, bashing Randall Bishop over all of it.

Marlo saw the news at the hotel and didn't know what to think. She had known something was up and hadn't had a chance to talk to Ed because of the mess their marriage was in. She hadn't reached out to anyone about what she thought, and now her suspicions were true. She watched as the news anchor said since he'd lied under oath in the trial, more charges were coming, and Marlo thought Randall Bishop's life in Hollywood was over.

The parent company of *Tycoon Wives* put out an immediate statement that Bentley Fencer would be taking over the show and that all filming on all current projects would halt until things could be finalized.

Bastard had it coming and then some, judging by the black eye, she thought as her cell phone started ringing. Seeing it was a New York number similar to the executive offices at *Tycoon Wives*, she answered immediately. "Hello."

"Hello. Marlo Savage?"

"Yes."

"Marlo, this is Bentley Fencer. I'm sorry to be calling you so late, but it has been a hell of a day."

"I bet it has."

"Marlo, I've been disassociated with the show pretty much since I created it. But they're bringing me back to run it until we figure out if I want to keep doing it. But that's not the reason for my call. I understand there was a misunderstanding between you and Randall."

"He called it a misunderstanding? That's rich, seeing what's on the news."

"Yes, it's quite the story. Anyway, I'm calling to tell you Randall called me before his arrest, and come to think of it, he was probably talking to me with his messed-up face at the time."

Marlo laughed at the thought, and while never having met Bentley Fencer, she thought his wit was worth getting to know better.

"Marlo, he told me what happened, and if you don't want to film any certain places, I'll personally amend your contract for the current year. I want to help you, and I'm so sorry for the way he treated you."

"Bentley, thank you for saying that. And it was a misunderstanding on Randall's part. See, you're going to hear about this soon enough anyway so I may as well tell you. I was about to tell him that Ed and I are divorcing, and I left the estate because I just can't be around him now. I felt horrible because he talked about how much the viewer would love to see where I lived, and then when he said those horrible things to me, I gave him both barrels."

Bentley laughed. "You certainly did. And I'm sorry for your divorce. I tell you what: some of the film crew is still up in Port Roberts getting establishing shots; can they come to the hotel and get your exclusive?"

Marlo paused on the line.

"Marlo, are you still there?"

"I'm here. I'm just thinking it over."

"I'll throw in one hundred thousand dollars in your sister's name to any charity you'd like. I give you my word, and I'll e-mail a signed contract to you to show good faith," Bentley said, knowing the network needed the good press after the Randall Bishop fiasco.

Marlo remembered Maggie being shot at the Vander Place Hotel before it opened and thought it was a nice gesture on his part. "Okay, I'll do it."

"Thank you, Marlo. They'll be in touch with you soon."

"It was a pleasure, Bentley."

Hanging up, Marlo poured herself a drink. It'd been months since she had enjoyed one, and that call was definitely worth celebrating.

CHAPTER 158

When Ed got home and saw Marlo had moved out, he knew it was over, and he blamed himself for not telling her right away. He really didn't want his marriage to end, and maybe if he told her that, she'd give him another chance. Maybe if she listened, really listened to him explain his reasons for waiting to tell her, she would understand. And as much as his mind wanted him to believe that, his heart told him otherwise. Standing alone in his massive suite, he looked toward her partly emptied walk-in closet and sighed. Hearing his phone ring his heart filled with hope, but when he saw it was Tallulah, he just nodded to himself, thinking this was all on him, and he answered.

"Hello?" he said, hearing the defeat in his own voice.

"Ed? You sound awful. Are you in pain?"

"You could say that. What do you have, Tallulah?"

"I have the reports from Vreeland Hills, and I wanted to let you know what we found."

"Go ahead; I can use the distraction."

"Sandy Storm's recording device was found in the elevator with Sinardi's blood on it. It looks like he took it from her after he killed her. She'd been recording everything since they entered the basement, except her own death, like her sister Wendy did at the Vander Place Hotel. Her blood was found on a brick collected near some strange cremation device in the basement."

"Oh God…those stupid women," Ed said.

"Yes, well it appears it was Wendy who had been working with Sinardi. The Storm sisters got his confession on tape bragging about hiring her to smear you, and not only that, but he cheated the government out of hundreds of thousands of dollars in bogus insurance claims."

"Damn, they did good."

"Yes, they did. There's even an unidentified man's voice on the recording we believe is Dr. Jack Hollerman's. He was working with Sinardi and we have a witness that overheard Patty and her sister talking about killing him. His body was found in an elevator shaft."

"What a mess. Did you find her sister? Halle Storm?"

"Halle's a byline name she uses; her birth name is Hailey Storm, and Ed, we believe they were cremated in that basement, and there's not much left to go on, except that more than two bodies were burned in that basement."

"Oh, God...he killed them both?"

"Seems so. What we don't know yet is how Sinardi got shot *before* he tried to kill you. The bullet shot in his side certainly wasn't from your gun, Ed."

"And the gun wasn't found?"

"Nothing, and judging by the looks of that place, I doubt we'll find it."

"At this point I kind of don't care if it's found at all. I'm just glad this whole thing is over with."

"The state is doing a thorough investigation, but on the bright side, they told me Drs. Blake and Eric Vreeland had contacted them from Germany and told them they were coming back since the lease to the state was coming up, and they wanted to take back their hospital."

"After the goings-on in that place, I don't blame them," Ed said. "Tallulah, how impossible would it be to get in there and search for the Galloway woman's records?"

"Unless the records are stored on a computer or in a single file, then we'll start looking right way; otherwise, it'll take months! That place is endless, and who knows what would be found in there? That's one place I really want to stay away from."

"I know the feeling. So, can you swing it?"

"We can start, but if these Vreeland brothers get here, all bets are off. By the way, what do you expect to find anyway? The Galloway family is dead. There's no one left."

"I know. I just want to know about this woman now that I know she was alive."

"It's like your mystery shows, Ed. Maybe the Vreelands will let you do a show out there one day."

"There's a thought. It even sounds like one of the *Savage Past* specials we shot. Oh, were you able to lift Sinardi's signature off the prescription pad I sent over or find anything else out?"

"Yes, we're running it against the state of New York to see what prescriptions he'd been writing and if he has anything out there with his name attached to it, but who knows where that will all lead, if anywhere. But one thing we do know for certain is that the note Sandy Storm showed you about paying her insurance was in fact Stanley Sinardi's handwriting."

"Well I'll be damned. I figured it was a long shot like what happened with that Black Ridge pharmacy with Lisa, but I never thought for a moment it would lead to the note. If something comes up on the Galloway woman, I want to know it. Thanks for the update."

"It was like old times, Savage Nine."

"You never give up, do you?"

"Where's the fun in that? Good-bye."

"Good-bye, Tallulah," Ed said. Hanging up the phone, he looked in the mirror across from where he stood and actually saw a smile on his face. He then looked to Marlo's empty closet and knew the time was now. Leaving his bedroom, he left the home and went to his favorite car, his Challenger, and started it up. Yes, he was going to see Marlo, but first he wanted a drink in a place where he could just be alone.

CHAPTER 159

Driving his classic Challenger convertible, Ed felt liberated wearing a new baseball cap on the cold but sunny day. His shoulder was hurting him, and he didn't care. He stopped taking the pain meds because he didn't like the altered feeling he experienced when he was on them. The shoulder scope surgery was a success, finding the small fragment and washing out the joint space. He was sore, but didn't need or *want* the pain medication. Slipping on his sunglasses as he turned into the brilliant sunshine, he made his way to a speakeasy he knew where he loved the music. Getting out from his car, he opened the trunk and tossed in his cane, feeling like he just didn't need it anymore, even after kicking that damn cat! Something was happening within him, and he could feel it but didn't *see* it; he already had too much on his mind.

By the time he ordered his second whiskey, the news was reporting that the body of a man had been found drowned in an open sewage line that had been under repair. The man had been missing from his last assignment at Pier Productions, and he was both a cameraman and an assistant that worked for the same network where the big story of the day was happening, with Randall Bishop and his *Tycoon Wives* reality show.

Ed listened to the news, wanting to see if there was anything more about the cast, silently hoping he'd see his wife in happier times, and when it was announced that two-time Academy Award–winning actress Tatum DeLorca was in talks to replace Marilyn Hart on the show, a move the producers had decided to do outside of their regular casting process, Ed looked at the woman on the television and smiled. He hadn't worked with her in years, but he noticed she was still as beautiful as ever—and it was no secret her marriage to one of Hollywood's biggest directors was over because her nasty divorce was splashed all over the trashy rags along with Ed Savage's headlines. Finally, when the coming attractions ran across the screen, they nearly knocked him off his barstool with the teaser: "Tycoon Wife Really Headed for a Divorce This Time."

Ed looked around the bar, and the minutes waiting for those damn commercials seemed endless. He looked at his watch, and it was a few minutes before the hour, so he knew the story was a sound bite. Picking up his glass, he took a healthy drink, and the news came back on.

There he saw it: the statement put out by the production company's new front man, Bentley Fencer. "You're hearing it here first. Marlo Savage just alerted *Tycoon Wives* that she is divorcing her husband, Ed Savage, and in this difficult time, we wish her the best. And, Marlo, I want you to know your family at *Tycoon Wives* is by your side should you need anything."

Finishing his drink, Ed threw money on the bar and left without a word to anyone. He was going to the Vander Place Hotel, and this was going to get ugly.

Unlocking his car, his phone rang, and he saw it was Trent; in that moment, everything stopped in his mind, and he answered the phone.

"Trent, how are you?"

"Dad, are you all right? I just saw it."

"I did too. It's not a good day, Son," he said, holding back the emotion when thinking that Trent was the first among his family members to call him right away.

"I need to see you. I…well, want to see you." The nervousness in his voice was audible.

"Is something wrong? You sound upset! Are you okay?"

"I'm fine. But Marta—she's…she's been hurt."

For the second time, Ed immediately thought of Massachusetts being ground zero in the path of the wave Robert Forrester had told him about, "Oh my God, Trent. What happened?" He couldn't believe he didn't think to call her with everything that was happening.

"She's in intensive care. When I found her, she wouldn't wake up."

"When *you* found her? Trent, are you telling me you were there? Was that behind the text you sent me? My God, Trent—what happened? Now, tell me the truth. Are you all right?" Ed barked as his father's worry swelled up from the ground he was standing on and covered him.

"Dad, I'm fine," Trent said, knowing his dad was dealing with more heartache than he deserved, and he was sorry he called because he suddenly thought he was adding to it. Taking a breath, he continued, and the nervousness in his voice increased. "I've seen this stuff before but never of this magnitude. And I'm sorry, but yes, sir, that was behind the text. I had to figure some stuff out on my own. I didn't mean to lie! I was leaving when it hit, and thank God I was there too, because I don't think Marta would have gotten out from the home. Dad." Trent's voice continued to shake. "Dad—Marta's house was *destroyed*."

Ed could hear the emotion coming from the boy over what he'd just gone through, and the scared tone along with the thoughts of losing his other mom who raised him since birth were coming loud and clear over the line. "Where are you, Trent? I'll come and get you now," Ed said, putting everything else out of his mind.

"I'm at the gallery. But Dad, it's not necessary. I'm okay. I left Mom with Marta, and you're dealing with too much right now. Dad, I'm sorry for calling and adding—"

"Trent, stop." Ed interrupted his son's trembling voice. "Don't you leave the gallery—I mean it. I'm on my way."

"But, Dad!"

"I'll be there in twenty minutes," Ed said, hanging up.

CHAPTER 160

The powerful engine of the classic Challenger roared in Ed's ears as he drove over to the gallery, and he arrived earlier than the twenty minutes he thought it'd take him to get there. Pulling into the alley and parking in the back, Ed hurried as he rushed from his car to the back door of the gallery. Seeing the door ajar, he pushed it open and entered, hearing the loud music as he moved up from the back area and saw the refrigerator door open with a new six-pack of beer sitting on the shelf with one bottle missing. He shut the refrigerator door, and when he came out from the back, the first thing he saw was the image of Trent on the life-size cardboard cutout. When he rounded the counter, he saw his son fumbling with a floor easel, and watching the easel come apart and break to the floor. "Trent!" Ed called out over the loud music in a voice filled with a father's worry.

"Damn it!" Trent yelled out as he stepped away from the mess and turned to see his father standing a few feet away.

Ed saw his bruises and realized his son was more hurt than he'd led on. He moved to him seeing the hard look on his son's face as he reached out and pulled him into a hug. "Trent. What is it? What's wrong?" Ed said, holding his son.

Trent sighed and felt his father's love as he pulled away and moved over to shut off the radio. His mind had been stuck at that moment he opened Marta's front door, and the sheer terror that was waiting for him on the other side had greeted him—grabbing him by the throat—and he truly wasn't prepared for it. It had scared him bad, and he had no one to turn to because all he could think of was to save Marta at the time. The shock he'd felt that'd been bottled up inside him was finally coming out—all of it was coming out—and he felt like a baby. His mind was torn over being given away at birth and lied to, and now he felt the embarrassment of being in his father's presence at his weakest after so much had happened in *his* father's life. He knew it had been too much, and the last thing he wanted to do was add to his father's worry. "Dad, I thought we were…I thought we were going to die," Trent finally said, choked up and finally letting it all out. He wanted to cry, and as he let out a heavy sigh, he was reminded of seeing his mother crying as she sat on the bed next to Marta.

Ed looked at the young man in front of him and was reminded of the narrow escapes he'd survived in his own life that had spooked him. That raw emotion that had come from nowhere that tormented him was now tormenting his son—the son who had grown up to be exactly like his old man without any influence whatsoever in his growing years. Ed knew that feeling because he'd felt it before and tried humor to get him to shake it off. "You did it, Trent. You did what every man goes through, and you came out on top. It's okay to feel this, and trust me, it's the same every time," Ed said with a proud smile at the man his son had grown up to be.

Trent managed to laugh over the choked-up emotions running thorough him and even smiled, but he withdrew with the lies running through his head that his mother had told him and blurted out the malignant poison to purge it from his soul. "She lied! She lied about all of it, Dad!"

Ed took a step back, seeing the hurt coming from his son, and he realized immediately Jillian was at the center of it. "Trent. Look at me," Ed said, putting his hands on his boy's shoulders. "Whatever it is, we can work through it, and remember I told you I'll never lie to you."

"Mom told me about the Parkwood Plaza Hotel and how you'd accused her of having an affair with Jeremy and that you hit her." Trent saw the shocked look cross his father's face and continued before Ed could say a single word. "But I know that can't be true. I knew it. I knew it when I went to Marta's and tricked her when I told her I was worried Jeremy might hit Mom because I'd seen them fighting. Marta told me that'd never happen, then she told me about your dad and what he did to Roman and Logan and that you'd never do that. I've lived with the lies my whole life, and I just wanted answers, Dad. Answers so I'd not have to ask you about it because I didn't want to ruin meeting you, and now I have."

Ed saw the wickedness from the woman he'd married all those years ago play out in front of him and he was truly concerned for his son. "Trent, you didn't ruin anything. And you didn't lie either when you sent the text. Trent, you did nothing wrong here." Ed's heart broke hearing the abusive destruction Jillian had put their son through.

"Dad—look, I know we don't know each other, and I know you're hurting right now too, and I'm sorry you're seeing me like this. It's just that I've hurt my whole life not knowing the truth, and it sucks, and when I got here, I heard the news on the radio and looked it up online, and I saw the *Tycoon Wives* stuff myself, and I just wanted to help you if I could."

And there it is, Ed thought. The truth of her lies hurting the most innocent, the one she should have been thinking of instead of herself, all at a time when he needed her most. Ed saw the selfishness in her and was reminded of how ugly that woman could be, and his anger flared over his ex-wife—and his current wife, Marlo, for allowing that damn interview in the first place. Now knowing his son could have been killed and the hurt Jillian had caused him all these years infuriated him, and he was going to make it right. "Trent. You're going to be fine now, and we'll fix this. We'll fix all of this. I promise."

"Dad, I'm such an idiot," Trent said. "I didn't know what to do. I didn't know what to do, and I was scared, and if I had, maybe Marta wouldn't be hurt."

"Trent. You never know what you're going to do in a situation like that. You fly by the seat of your pants—every time! And it never gets easier, and it's always different. I've been there, and I can help you with this. Now, you're coming home with me, and that's final,"

Ed barked in a father's tone, knowing the boy was hurting worse than he'd imagined. "You need to trust me on this, okay?"

"I'd like that, Dad."

"Come on—you're riding with me."

"Dad, I need to get my stuff. It's at the hotel, and I think you were on your way to see Marlo. I wasn't thinking when I called you, and I should have waited. So go to her, and I'll get my stuff. Then just text me, and I'll come over when you're there."

"You're okay with that? You're going to be all right?"

"Yeah, Dad. I just needed somebody—somebody I could talk to that I believe in. I'm fine. I just want you to be okay, and I'm so sorry you're going through this."

"I love you even more for saying that, Trent; thank you."

"God, we're a mess," Trent said, coming out of the harsh mind trip he'd been on.

Ed laughed. "We'll work through it, Son. Proud of you, and I do need to sort some stuff out. Come on—lock this place up, and let's get this day over with."

"I couldn't agree more, Dad."

Together they moved to the back of the gallery, and Trent hit the lights, shutting down the front area. Once outside, he closed the back door and locked it.

Thanks again, Dad," Trent said. "I love you."

"I love you too, Son."

Trent got in his car and started the engine, and Ed waved to him as he got in the Challenger watching him back out and drive down the alley. Ed took a deep breath and started the powerful engine, turned on the radio, and pulled out, heading straight for the Vander Place Hotel.

CHAPTER 161

S hortly after the HMS *Queen Anne II* emerged from the wave, a navy cruiser that had been in the area met the ship at sea, and men boarded the luxury liner. Under orders from the British Intelligence Agency and the United States of America, they seized control of the ship and confiscated all computer intelligence recorded from the explosion and brought the ship to port. She was escorted to New York City, where the *Queen Anne II* was then docked, and all further cruises were canceled.

The company was under an investigation and also ordered the ship to port. The government had been watching the consortium and had known about the bombing of the building in Venezuela, and now, with the attack on the *Queen Anne II* so close to US soil, it was taking a harder look, trying to bring more of them to justice. The internal investigation of Mingyu Min's (her actual last name) and Hermann Stangl's bank accounts provided direct leads to top officials within the consortium, and arrests were being made. With both Hermann Stangl and Mingyu Min dead, finding out who had sold them the warheads was going to be hard. The computer that'd been shot several times in the raid was in a lab, but it was painstaking and almost impossible to gather any further information from the destroyed device. The wire transfer of the twenty million led to an empty bank account in the Cayman Islands, and the information on the account's owner was proving to be false. Agency One then added the mystery of who had sold the warheads to the consortium to the long list surrounding the *Manchester*, which only added to the head-ache of finally solving the case.

Finally, back in Port Roberts, Charlotte Savage and her family quietly went to their homes in the Savage-Vanderran housing devel-opment next to the Vander Place Hotel, and once there they stayed away from reporters, with the new Wendy Storm story making the rounds.

The goings-on at Vreeland Hills Sanatorium then made the news when it was reported that Patty and Stevie Galloway had been shot in an attempted escape. The twisted facts of the true story were re-leased courtesy of Wes Thrasher to the police, and the cover-up be-gan regarding Rose Galloway.

Of course, the kidnapping of Kate and Lana Savage also made the news, and they were excused from West Point while a thorough investigation was taking place. And with the girls being sent home, it gave Lana time to grieve the loss of her mother and be at her father's side.

Watching these stories appear one after the other after getting home, Charlotte Savage had a meeting with her sons and asked them if they'd sell their shares to Ed and his brothers and move to Miami with her. Chance and Landon both vehemently disagreed with her, and the arguments that followed seemed endless.

Then, when Chase and Landon privately visited with their cousin Roman Savage, they learned everything that wasn't reported on the news, and they were glad their mother didn't know all the circum-stances. On the bright side, the only relief was the fact that the en-tirety of the Galloway family was now gone. Knowing there was no one left to fear didn't erase the ugly pain the family was now feeling, but finally the end was in sight.

The will of their father, Niles Savage, left his 15 percent of Savage Construction stock split between his sons, with his oldest son, Chance, receiving 8 percent and Landon receiving 7 percent. They had worked within the company, mostly on outside ventures and were never a problem, and they looked forward to getting more involved with the company in the near future.

CHAPTER 162

When Marlo opened the door to her room, she was in tears—serious tears, like Ed had seen from her throughout their entire marriage. Her eyes were bloodshot, and her skin was red and wet from crying.

"Oh God, Ed, I'm so sorry," she said, running into his arms. "I made a terrible mistake; that wasn't supposed to air this soon."

Ed pushed his way into her room so he could close the door. "What are you talking about? I just saw my life explode on a TV in a bar—a bar where I've been sitting, attempting to get the courage to come over here to try to talk to you," Ed said, keeping the rest private.

"I screwed up. I screwed up big! Things have been horrible for me, and I've been alone just like last time and I...I'm sorry! Ed, our baby," she said, and more tears came.

Seeing her break down, he moved to her, his mind was racing between the ugly truth of Jillian hurting his son and that damn interview he just saw, but he also loved her. "Let it out," Ed said, holding her and rubbing her back.

Taking a deep breath, she pulled away from him and tried to hold back her emotion. "We've been through a lot, you and me."

Ed didn't expect this comment, and he waited for what was coming.

"I need a drink. How about you? You know I hadn't had a drink until today," Marlo said.

"How many have you had?"

"Just one over an hour ago. I'm not drunk. I'm just seeing everything clearly, and I'm happy. And I'm sad, Ed."

He had not seen this side to her before and was confused. "Marlo, you're not making any sense. Say what you need to say," Ed said, watching her pick up his favorite bottle of Jim Beam's Devil's Cut bourbon whiskey from the bar in her room and pour two glasses, neat, just the way he liked it. She didn't even bother icing hers like she preferred.

"Here," she said, handing him his glass and moving over to the large window in her room overlooking the water. She took a healthy drink from her glass, followed by a deep breath. "You're right; this is good without the ice," she said and smiled as her eyes welled up with tears.

"Marlo, what's going on?"

"We're fine, Ed; we're just done is all, and it's incredibly sad because I do love you. But too much has happened, and I just can't get past this latest…" She paused, not even wanting to say it. "Seeing you with her breaks me down too much, and I just can't. I know where we were back then and how horrible I was and how horrible everything was, but I never left *your side* while being in a right state of mind after being raped by those two men. It really was always *our* baby, Ed."

The anger in Ed turned to raw emotion, and he lost it. Tears came down his face, and he reached out for the woman he loved and took her hand. He pulled her to him and hugged her, and when he looked in her eyes, he kissed her passionately, and she kissed him back. But deep down he knew she was right, yet somehow she was able to show her love to him at the worst time in their lives.

"Come on—sit with me. I need to explain a few things," Marlo said, leading him to a sofa and grabbing the bottle of whiskey from the bar and setting it on the table.

A guest towel was on the arm of the sofa, and she dried her eyes with it and looked to Ed, handing it to him. "No one's looking but me, baby, so go ahead."

Ed smiled over the hurt and dried his eyes.

"Ed, Randall Bishop came at me, scaring me like I've never been scared by a man in my life. Well…with the exception of all the bullshit we went through in the mountains, but you know what I mean."

"What did he do?"

"He was here. He ripped into me for not filming at Zolie's, and you know me—when my buttons get pushed…well, let's just say I ripped back, and the words were ugly. Anyway, I told him to go, and he threatened to sue me and do ugly things to me and my character. Then I saw what happened to him on the news." Marlo stopped and looked at the blank screen of the television, downing the rest of her drink. Reaching for the bottle, Ed grabbed it.

"Here, I got this," he said, pouring more in her glass.

"Another producer then called me, Bentley Fencer, telling me Randall had told him everything, and he wanted to make it right. He offered me a one-hundred-thousand-dollar donation in my sister's name to any charity I chose, and he was sorry for what Randall had said to me."

Ed finished his glass and poured another.

"Ed, I'd already told him the real reason I moved out from Zolie's."

"Oh, Marlo, he's deflecting the story from Randall to our divorce."

The quietness in the room that followed was deafening when they both realized they'd just heard the words come out of his mouth naturally.

"See, Ed. You see it too, don't you?"

Ed looked into her beautiful face and was afraid to say anything as his emotion filled his throat.

"Come on—it's okay," Marlo said, and the smile he saw on her face was the smile he'd seen when he'd first met her.

He nodded, and the words just came. "Yeah, I see it too." Ed took a deep breath and expelled all the pent-up ugliness within him as he looked back to his wife. "You're the most amazing woman I've ever had the pleasure of knowing, Mrs. Marlo Savage."

"No kidding." Marlo smiled at the man she'd spent most of her life with. "Ed, there's more, and it's not as bad as you're going to think it is, but hear me out." He nodded, and she continued, "Bentley Fencer sent a film crew over here earlier, and I made a more detailed announcement. That hasn't aired yet. But judging by what he rushed to get out there, I have a feeling it's coming soon."

"Is it bad?"

"Actually, no, I don't think so. I think I carried myself like I am now. It was like I was above myself, watching me speak for those few minutes I allowed them to be here. I have a copy, but I can't play it."

"Where?"

"There," she said, pointing to the fireplace mantle. "It's one of those weird tapes, and I don't have a machine to play it on, but I know you do."

Ed got up, went over, and picked it up. It was from a camera, and he did have the ability to watch this at their home, and he really didn't want to go back to where Ellie Collins had been murdered—but he knew he eventually would.

"Take it. I know what's on it, and I want you to see it before it airs."

Ed brought it with him and placed it on the table; he picked up the bottle, taking a drink directly from it. "Are you telling me we're about to have the most amicable divorce in Hollywood history?" He looked down at her and watched the smile cross her face.

"Mr. Savage, don't take this the wrong way because I want the best for you and the children, but I'm game if you are," she said, reaching up and unbuttoning the first button of his pants under his belt.

"I don't know who you are, Mrs. Savage, but I'm game," Ed said, placing the bottle on the table and reaching down and pushing her back onto the sofa.

Pushing him off of her, she unbuttoned his shirt and rubbed her hands over the hairy chest that drove her wild. "I'm glad it's growing back. I hated that you had to wax it for that shaving cream commercial Rachel wanted you to re-create for that ad you did."

Ed smiled, and when he tried to take her blouse off, she took control and pushed his hands away. Then she slowly unbuttoned her own blouse and stood up; he stood with her and reached around to unfasten her bra.

Letting their shirts fall from their bodies, she pulled on his belt, unfastening it and pulling it free. Then she finished unbuttoning his jeans and let them fall to the ground, grabbing his big dick with one hand, and with her other she lightly let her long nails rub slowly over his chest, sending chills up his spine. She then lowered herself to the floor and took him entirely, just the way he loved it.

Ed's head rolled back, and he could feel himself hard as a rock, and he allowed himself to enjoy it before reaching down and bringing her up off her knees to join him. Unzipping her skirt and letting it fall to the floor, he kicked off his shoes, and stepping out from his jeans, he picked her up and took her to the bedroom, placing her gently down on top of the bed.

Her breasts were beautiful, and he caressed them as he licked and kissed her flesh, making his way south until she was moaning, a sound he always loved to hear, and when he got her where she loved the most, that's when he moved on top of her. Looking at the woman he loved, he slid inside her. She moaned with the feeling that took her to heaven, and the lovemaking lasted longer than they both could remember. It was intense, and in the hours that passed, they each said good-bye in the gentlest way two humans could possibly do. It was tender; her body was accepting, and she gave herself to him in a moment that would dwell in their memories forever.

CHAPTER 163

Back at Zolie's compound in the days after she brought Maura home from the hospital, Zolie's husband, Tom Kenowith, flew back to take care of his wife. His business was going well, and when he learned Zolie wanted to return to London, he was glad to be bringing her home and away from the States and the mess that seemed to never end there.

But before he whisked her away, he took all the adults living with Zolie on her estate out to a dinner, and they finally had an enjoyable evening after the nightmare they'd been through. And when the subject came up about staying at her compound, Zolie told them they could stay as long as they wanted, but the Savage men knew it was time to move on. They told her when their new homes were completed in the Savage-Vanderran housing development next to the Vander Place Hotel, they'd be moving there, and everyone seemed to be on the same page, agreeing that was a good idea.

When Sam asked Zolie and Maura if they'd be filing charges against the sanatorium, they both looked to each other and shook their heads. With Sinardi, Hollerman, and Patty dead, and the state of New York's health system cash-strapped, they really saw no need. Zolie did question if she should file charges against Dr. Todd Vreeland, but after thinking of the time with the man he really never harmed her *that she knew of.* Looking to the future, Zolie wanted nothing more than to leave for London and put this all behind her.

One of the conversations at the dinner Ed zeroed in on was when Zolie mentioned that Stevie Galloway told her she'd put all her things in storage. Ed had excused himself from the table and made a call. The next day Tallulah had the address for the storage facility. With no next of kin and the death certificate in hand, agents swarmed the storage facility, and Ed had everything moved to a Savage warehouse, where he personally could go through everything the woman owned in his own time. The sad part was there really wasn't much there of this poor woman's life and nothing that showed Stevie knew her mother had lived past the accident. It was another dead end, but at least he knew, as far as he could tell, that there were no VCR tapes showing the accident Patty had made and was talking over like a narrator—like she had sent to Marlo at Pine Crest hospital in Black Ridge.

The investigation at Vreeland Hills Sanatorium on what happened to Rose Galloway came to a grinding halt when Blake and Eric Vreeland returned and put a stop to it. They held a press conference stating they were taking the hospital back from the state of New York and would be running it as a family business once again. The transition date was quickly approaching, but patient care would not falter during the change of hands.

Once the meddlesome reporters were off the property, the brothers breathed a sigh of relief. Blake couldn't wait to show Eric the *surprise* in the hidden cells, and he was delighted when Eric grabbed the fire hose and aimed it a Todd, yelling at him over the death of their mother and the sinister surgery he'd performed on who he *thought* was his brother.

"Eric! Don't!" Todd held up his hand.

The spray hit Todd right in the face, knocking him over. He slid with the harsh force of the ice water when Eric turned the evil torture device off. Seeing his younger brother choke on the water, he remembered the day he'd seen him at the bottom of the stairs, wet from the fish tank, and the saddened look of defeat on his face, the same look he was now seeing, and he remembered being struck by their father.

"Fuck this," Eric said, dropping the hose and moving away from the cells with Blake following him, laughing over the whole thing.

The betrayal ran hot in Todd's veins as he listened to Blake laugh at him. Learning they'd been conspiring against him this whole time, he swore he'd get his revenge.

And, as promised, Blake Vreeland gave Little Blake his choice of rooms on the fifth floor and told him after he looked into his case, if they could come up with the right fit, maybe they could also come up with a job for him. And depending how things worked out, Blake Vreeland thought he'd take him under his wing like the little brother he *should* have had.

As for his actual brother locked up and hungry in the hidden cells, he decided he'd have Little Blake be his guard and food server, so every day Todd Vreeland would see a stranger being treated better than he'd ever been treated. This was just that added insult for Todd to think about during the long, lonely days to come.

Zolie Vanderran's missing Birkin bag, of course, was now the property of Stacey Porter, the charge nurse who couldn't believe her luck in finding the bag after she'd gone back to Sinardi's office to steal it, only to find it gone. She'd later found it when she was given the task of cleaning up after Patty's and Stevie's bodies had been taken away. Though she had wanted to stay on the scene in the East Tower to snoop and flirt with the men in uniforms, they sent her to the West Tower to do busywork. Being given the orders pissed her off, and when she was told to sweep the dirt on the stairs, she moved the pot and saw the strap under the inverted terra-cotta planter. Finding the exquisite bag, she ran to her locker in the nurses' lounge and hid it, and when she came back to finish her job, she stepped off the elevators to see some hot guy wander in who just happened to be looking for it. She couldn't believe how lucky she was for the second time.

Taking the papers on Rose Galloway she found in the bag to Blake and Eric Vreeland had been a proud moment for her; she also had a file with photos of the woman, and she didn't remember where she had found it. She walked in on them going through the things found in Stevie's car that they'd brought up to the hospital from the

Holiday Inn when they took her keys while they had her locked up. Stacey was told she'd get a raise when Blake took his father's papers and the Rose Galloway file back from her, and when she left the room, Eric pulled the VCR tape they had found in Stevie's trunk under the carpet next to the spare tire and went to one of their old private offices and studied up on their father's favorite patient. When they turned on the television to play the tape, an entertainment gossip show was on, and Marlo Savage was giving an interview.

Ed Savage had watched the interview well before it aired and was so proud of Marlo for the kind and respectable way she announced their separation. She had tears of nothing but love in her eyes, and she promised to God she was going to be there for Ed and their children for anything and everything they needed. But the sad truth was, Marlo stated, it was time for them to part ways.

She never mentioned Aisha Thomas because, as she told Ed, she wanted to protect the family more than any spite-filled rhetoric was worth. She also told Ed that when Randall had turned on her and she saw the ugliness within that vile human being, something inside her realized she never wanted to be like that to the man she had loved most of her life. She told Ed that too much damage had been done, and the new chapter in their lives would still be beautiful. Of course, when he wondered if there would be benefits, she shook her head and smiled.

Aisha Thomas finally received her test results from that day she'd seen Marlo at the doctor's office, and when she found out her ex-fiancé was in fact the father; she called Ed and told him the news. The conversation had been entirely different than when they'd first spoken, and Ed saw that his son Tucker had heard part of that conversation. Aisha was happy with the news and really wanted to give her ex Danny another shot. Ed congratulated her and to be honest was relieved, given the recent loss of his child with Marlo and all they were going through.

There were only two difficult things about the beautiful separation between Ed and Marlo Savage. First was the fact that Logan and Maura's divorce wasn't as amicable. Sure, Ed was hurting over his loss, yet he understood, and as unfortunate as the whole thing was, he was making the best of it. Logan had told him what had happened when Lucy had flashed him her chest after the yacht crash, and in a fit of rage during a fight with Maura, it'd come out, which only added to the ugly mess he was facing. Logan told him the difference between their divorces added to his confusion of seeing them acting as if nothing was happening outside of living apart, which was the complete opposite for Logan because he was so hurt over Maura falling out of love with him. For Maura, it was completely different. She was saddened by the fact she'd fallen out of love with the much younger man, and she truly didn't want to hurt him, but she couldn't go on in the relationship feeling the way she did. Maybe she thought seeing the younger girls throwing themselves at her buff and handsome husband played a part of it, and hearing her fears confirmed with that little schoolgirl tramp made it all the more clear. But no matter what happened or what was said, the more he complained and compared their separations, the nastier their divorce became by the minute.

The second difficult thing was the press. They were dumbstruck at seeing Ed and Marlo act like they always had when things had been going great. Ed especially liked his wife's remark when she said, "Why be an asshole about getting a divorce?" That line wouldn't die, and it appeared on tabloids everywhere after the interview was printed.

Jillian York Savage Bigelow, of course, saw the interview and didn't quite know what to make of it. She had all but given up on having anything with Ed, but now maybe things might turn out differently. Her scheming thoughts quickly turned against her when a nurse stepped to the intensive care unit's door and told her Trent had called to get an update on Marta and that she'd told him Marta was doing better and moving from intensive care to a regular room and that Trent didn't have time to talk to his own mother when she'd asked him if he wanted to.

Jillian was surprised with the news and dismissed the nurse and was left with the empty coldness of the lies she'd told him. She then received a text from her son: *I'm home—think I'll move in with Dad for a while.*

Jillian looked up and saw the look on the nurse's face as she glanced over the counter of the nurses' station, a look that said she felt her pity her. She knew deep down Trent wanted to connect with his father and was happy for him that he was doing that. It was just her being scared she'd lose him forever that she'd told him those stupid lies—and now she feared the price she'd pay would be her worst nightmare.

Later, when Ed called in about the Emily Waters case, he learned Lou Sabello had been incarcerated at Rikers Island during her kidnapping and murder. Further, when questioned about the Savage kidnapping, Lou sang like a canary, telling authorities Lenny had told him stories of making big bucks in his crimes in the past, but he had never mentioned Emily Waters. Also, with his friend dead, he put the blame on Lenny for coming up with the idea, when it had been his with regard to the Savage women to try to get a lesser sentence. Not that it mattered, though; he'd broken his probation and was looking at a lot of years back at Rikers.

CHAPTER 164

Eric Vreeland ejected the VCR tape and shut down the television, shaking his head in confusion. "I just don't get any of this. Dad was obsessed with Rose Galloway; that we can agree on. And trust me when I say I was glad to leave for Germany to get away from his stories about her. But this Patty woman! Good God, Blake, I don't know about you, but I'm glad it's over."

"If there's one thing I've learned from dear old Dad, it's that it's *never* over," Blake said, opening a file cabinet and pulling out a large key ring. "The storage rooms on the seventh floor roof had been locked up and off limits to the state. I wonder if everything's still up there."

"I hate those rooms. But I've decided to open the seventh floor in one of the towers to connect the grand staircase right under the skylight in the remodel I told you about. Why it was never done that way in the beginning is beyond me. We just need to decide which tower we want to call our new main entrance," Eric said, moving to the window and looking at the opposite tower. Turning, he saw his brother holding the keys.

"I've always wondered why the grand staircases stopped at the sixth floors. I want that sixth-floor skyway fixed too," Blake said.

"It's all in the budget. We'll get this place looking better than brand new when we're done. You want the East or West?" Eric said, putting down the VCR tape and putting on his lab coat, remembering how their father had turned those two top seventh-floor rooms into storage dumps and how after his death they'd never bothered to go up there.

"I'll take the East Tower and call you if I find anything," Blake said, looking out the window at the wind blowing the trees and putting his own lab coat on. He looked back in the file cabinet and grabbed the West-labeled key ring and handed it to Eric and watched him leave the room, noticing he'd left the VCR tape. Picking it up and putting it in his pocket, he made his way to the small stairway leading to the roof. The elevator had been turned off to the seventh floor since the state wasn't supposed to have access anyway, and it was one more thing to attend to of the many things piling up on their lists.

Opening the door and stepping out on the roof, Blake scared the ravens nearby, and they took off in a startled fright. The wind hit him, and he hurried to the double doors of the seventh-floor room, fumbling through the keys before finding the one he needed, and he opened one of the doors. The place was a mess. Slamming the door shut against the bone-chilling wind, he looked around the dust-covered boxes stacked in rows along the walls and up to the windows. More boxes of medical records and God knew what were stacked in rows, making a narrow path in the old and forgotten room, and he knew this wasn't going to be an easy task. He moved deeper into the room to the far end where a desk his father used to sit at for hours on end sat across from a fireplace under a glass skylight. He remembered how his dad had told him he'd unwind here with his charts and plan his course of action with his patients. Moving to the chair, he picked up the sheet covering it and tossed it aside. Watching a dust cloud emanate from the old fabric as he moved the old leather chair from the desk.

Hearing the ravens outside landing on the skylight above him, their claws scratching the glass as they made themselves comfortable, Blake looked up and remembering being frightened of the gargoyles when he was younger—and tying Todd up in the middle of the night up there to leave him alone to be scared until their father found him the next morning, which gave his little brother nightmares growing up. He laughed. It was good to finally be home, and he sat down at his father's old desk, and a feeling of déjà vu came over him. He remembered his mother telling him that when he felt that, it was life telling him he was where he was supposed to be.

Eric opened the West Tower roof door and felt the same cold wind hit him as he rushed to the smaller rooftop floor and quickly let himself in. When the building was first opened, both seventh floors were meant to be recreation rooms for the severely sick so they could have an outdoor area to themselves on the building's rooftop for therapy.

But over the years, when tuberculosis was eradicated and they started housing the criminally insane, they used the top floors for the most dangerous patients who couldn't be trusted on the ground-floor recreations areas with the less-violent patients. The rooftops at the time had tall electric fences around them, so if the prisoners had attempted to climb them, they'd be shocked and knocked to the rooftop. That plan had been quickly terminated when a riot broke out, and six men were killed in the West Tower's recreation room, and all outdoor activities had ceased for all the patients in the building.

Around that time, Victor's father, Corbin Vreeland, had gone completely mad, and this was when the hospital turned darker and more violent. Corbin Vreeland was a Satanist and had taken over the West Tower's seventh floor as his own, and being able to see the moon through the skylight had made *that* room a place you'd not want to be in during his rituals on his special nights. After Corbin had died, Victor took one look at the room and knew he'd have to do something; after lying cheap linoleum tiles on the floor and painting everything in a color that could only be described as "old institutional tuberculosis sanatorium green," he locked up the room and walked away from it.

The patients who had been assigned in the work crew, however, were treated to a wonderful cyanide dinner so their stories of what had been in that room before the cleaning would *never* be told. In later years, Victor had taken the East Tower's seventh floor as his and left the West Tower and its bloodstained secrets closed off—and from his identical room on the top of the East Tower, he could keep an eye on it, like a sentinel of sorts with the raven gargoyles.

Eric stood looking at the peeling paint and was faced with his own treasure trove of boxes to sort through.

Blake pulled the VCR tape from his pocket and tossed it on top of the desk; he then searched the drawers, and after finding nothing, he slammed the last drawer closed and sat back in the chair. To his left was a stack of old wooden boxes with hinges; picking up the smaller one, he opened it and saw it had old and yellowed papers stacked loosely and a leather bound journal inside. Someone had made Xerox copies from a strange-looking book with symbols on its cover. The pages inside were written in Latin, and he knew the language well. Sorting through them, he smiled when he read the words *Cantus Mortuus*. "Spells of the Dead," he said with a wide smile and sat back in his father's old chair and began thumbing through the pages—until he saw it.

There he saw the handwritten diagram of the sanatorium and the *graves*. The number of dead around the building was in the thousands and the plots each had 666 souls assigned to them. He remembered hearing about this growing up, but when he'd asked about it he was advised it wasn't his time to *know*. Picking up the journal, he saw his grandfather's name, Corbin Vreeland, engraved on the cover and he thumbed through it. *What was it I was in line to learn from you Corbin?* he thought as he read the dark passages inside.

Scanning the pages as he turned them he spotted it, the hand drawn tower, but it really wasn't a building but more like a watchtower of tormented *humans*. Like a beacon or sorts with rays coming from it like it was a powerful conduit used as a booster to reaching the most evil of all. Reading the scribbled notes below, he was shocked at learning what his grandfather believed. Here, his grandfather thought he'd deciphered a particular 'Spell of the Dead' where by surrounding a sacred place with an army of murdered—they could not have died naturally—in six plots of six hundred and sixty-six, it was said to amplify the powers of the blessed one—the so-called blessed one that would follow Satan's path and become truly powerful. And according to the strange book he'd had the copies of its pages from—six sections of six hundred and sixty-six souls were needed to summon Satan himself to anoint the blood of the 3,996 damned on his disciple to be his chosen one.

"Damn it!" Eric yelled when the stacked boxes near him fell over in a crash to the floor. Files and old X-ray films scattered from the open boxes, and he stood looking at the useless junk. Moving to assess the mess he'd now have to clean up, he noticed the bottom box was rotted, and rats had gotten to it. Seeing the next stack of boxes near it start to tilt, he grabbed a stronger box to shore up the tall stack and kicked the rotted one away. Getting the boxes stable, he noticed the worn-out linoleum tiles had been broken up and chipped away, and when he moved another box, he saw that underneath the tiles, something was painted on the floor. It was a point of some sort with a strange raven's-head symbol painted within it. Having never seen this before, he started moving the next taller stack of boxes to see what was underneath.

"Fucking insane!" Blake said out loud, and stuck the copied pages he'd found in the journal marking the page, he then placed everything back in the smaller box and tossed in the VCR tape with them. A chill ran through his body at the thought, he looked out the windows and could see the West Tower and he stood, looking at the menacing woods surrounding the place. Imagining the countless dead out there waiting for their final job, like his grandfather must have once thought, and standing in this very spot in his father's office scared him. *Jesus! What a legacy*, he thought. He then sat back down and placed the box on the desk and opened the medium-sized wooden box that was beneath the smaller one. Inside was a photo album, and he pulled it out and saw the pictures of his entire family: their beautiful mother he'd missed so much, all because Todd had told their innocent mother to meet him at the sanatorium after he had gotten in trouble at school—and had left that door open, and the patient had killed their mother. Blake wiped the wet from his eyes as he looked at his mother and flipped the pages of his past, seeing one beautiful picture after another taken at a time when he had loved his brother Todd—until he came to the last page.

There he saw the loose stack of instamatic photos from the camera his dad loved of his mother, only she was naked, and they were shot in their parent's bedroom. Blake pulled them out and quickly sorted through them, and being embarrassed, he threw them back in the photo album and shut with a loud snap. *Was Todd telling me the truth?* he thought. He then looked to the third larger wooden box under the middle one, and it seemed to dare him to open it.

Eric cleared more boxes from the broken tiles and saw the paint markings on the floor. He saw that someone had tried scraping the linoleum tiles away and realized the missing pieces were in some of the boxes in the room. Standing at his discovery, he saw the second point of a star emerge from the large bloodstained wooden floor it was painted on. He looked to the ceiling to see the same glass skylight above and saw the raven gargoyle looking down from the rooftop, like it was about to swoop down and snatch up the doomed soul trapped in the room and eat him alive. Remembering how that damn thing had scared them as children, he then noticed the ceiling around the skylight, which had more faces of the gargoyles looking down at him through the ugly peeling green paint.

The memories of his youth came back in an instant: one after another they flashed in his mind, and one particular event chilled his blood. It was when a nanny had been watching the boys one evening before their mother had died. She'd been angry with them and told them a ghost story to scare them before putting them to bed as payback. It was about their great-grandmother Cassandra and how she was a witch and had put a spell on Cornelius to murder his wife, Greta. Then, once having taken over as mistress of the manor, she'd performed séances on the top floor and murdered those she hated as sacrifices in the middle of a pentagram she'd kept hidden under a grand carpet so as not to frighten the staff who served her up there during the daylight hours. He remembered how they had gone up there to try to find the pentagram under a carpet later, but there was nothing there—only the linoleum-tiled floor and all that horrible green paint. Now he knew it was true. The fierce wind hit the building, and the smaller rooftop room seemed to shake like the devil's hands had it within its grasp and was cherishing it, and he was taken from his thoughts and backed out of the room.

Blake moved the middle box to the floor and opened the larger wooden box. The top swung back and smacked the backside of it with a loud crack against the dry wood. There amid some packing papers was his father's diary. Pulling it out, he opened it and saw it filled with his father's handwriting. Paging through the dates, he came to the date their mother had died, and there he saw it. The truth Todd had been telling him of his entire life. The many passages he read were different ways to murder his wife, Claire, and the last one, with the words "naked photos," was circled.

The shock set in at once. "All this time," Blake said in the empty room. The turmoil within him caused him to shake, and nausea built in his stomach. He couldn't believe all the years of hatred of his brother had all been for nothing. He didn't know what to do or think. Too many years had gone by, and when he rubbed his eyes, he felt the scar on his cheek, courtesy of his victimized little brother, and he remembered the vile surgery Todd had performed on Marvin Newman thinking it was him—and his anger returned.

That entire setup had been a fiasco. And the murders—Todd had killed so many that ugly night of the fire. He had murdered Lorena, that stupid scrub tech who always fucked up his neurological cases, and Bob, that idiot X-ray tech who had constantly bumped the patient's table when bringing in the C-arm. But the guy had always been there for his cases, and as incompetent as he was, Blake knew he could count on him. "Oh, Slobert (the nickname he'd bestowed the imbecilic fuck-up), you did not deserve what you got," he said out loud, lost in the thoughts of his mind. Then there was the fire to consider, and the patients who lost their lives that night— Todd needed to be taught a lesson, he thought. *No*, he needed time. He needed time to think, and he threw the diary back into the box with the packing papers and discovered there was something buried in the bottom of the box. Digging down in the box, he felt it—the smaller jeweled box he'd bought for his girlfriend Natalie. He felt the smile cross his face as he opened it to see the letters and photos inside. Pulling them out, he saw one that was sealed. He turned it over and saw his name across it and tore it open. The smaller photo fell out, and he picked it up and saw her holding a little girl. He knew it was his daughter, and the smile widened across his face as he picked up the letter and unfolded it.

The letter was beautiful and sad—beautiful over the memories they'd shared but sad when later long after he'd left, she'd become hysterical over him leaving and became a patient at the sanatorium. Feeling the sadness of it all, he got to the last part of her telling him how she had found out she was pregnant after he'd disappeared and that she'd named his daughter Kayla Bennet, using her maiden name to protect her from the horrible rumors that plagued the hospital after his supposed murder. Realizing he'd killed his own daughter as a cruel vice to punish his brother Todd, Blake yelled out at the top of his lungs and began crying, pounding his hands on the desk in a rage that would not leave his soul. He jumped up from the desk and pushed over a stack of boxes, turned and reached into another and grabbed a thick stack of medical charts and flung them across the room, hitting a large portrait covered with another dusty sheet, knocking it over. "Why?" he screamed, noticing the portrait—the same portrait that had hung in their home when he'd pushed Todd down the stairs. Lumbering to it in his wrath, he picked it up ever so gently and stood it up, lifting the filthy sheet away to see the smiling faces of his family before everything had changed. He looked into the eyes of Todd staring out with a happy smile. Their mother was standing behind him with her hands on his shoulders; she was beautiful and smiling, and his eyes became wet. "I'm so sorry, little brother."

Eric had shut the doors to the West Tower's seventh floor and heard his brother's screaming carry over from the other building. Shocked, he ran to the rooftop door and made his way to the third-floor skyway. Running across it, he took the elevator to the sixth floor and took the same smaller set of stairs to the roof. Rushing into the East Tower's seventh floor, he saw Blake moving away from the desk. An old, dusty sheet had been thrown over the chair and what looked to be wooden boxes at its side. "Blake! What is it?" Eric yelled, seeing the harsh look on his brother's face and the thrown files across the room.

"I can't find anything! This place is a mess!" Blake snapped back, harnessing the maddening rage that was like a toxic surge he had to dam up to keep from spewing forth. "I'll deal with this later."

Knowing his brother had a temper, he blew it off as just that, "Well, we have all the time in the world now that we're back," Eric said. "Besides, you're going to love what I found, especially because we used to look for it when we were kids."

"What are you talking about?"

"The pentagram. It's there—I found it painted on the floor in the other tower. Come on—I'll show you."

Blake smiled and followed him out, locking the door behind him. "You're right, Eric. We have all the time in the world," Blake said, following him across the rooftop. As his mind filled with misery, his rage inside wanted to grab the first patient he saw and throw them over the building. He glanced back to the smaller seventh-floor windows and saw the boxes inside. He then looked over the building to the dark woods surrounding them and a chill ran up his spine over the countless dead out there, lying in their graves like they were waiting for their master to call upon them for some twisted version of burning-man Vreeland Style—and he knew the answers to the endless thoughts popping up in his head just might be found in that storage room. *Satanism* he thought. He knew his grandfather Corbin had been mad with it, and he remembered his father, Victor, having his private meetings with him and sometimes hearing about it. He thought of his father's diary and knew he'd have to come back alone to study it. Besides, there were more pressing things to con-sider; he knew he'd felt bad when he thought he'd killed Todd when he threw him down the elevator shaft, but when he'd seen him alive that day after the surgery, his anger had spiked. He had his own guilt to deal with, and he needed time. He needed time to find out these things from his family's legacy, and now that Eric was back, he'd have the time to do just that—and he decided to let Todd sit in his cell until he'd been punished good and long enough for trying to kill him. *Then I'll say I just found out the truth,* he thought. *But for now, that cell will do him just fine.*

The setup he and Pam had planned had gone way too far; it was meant to test his little brother, to see exactly what he'd do if given the chance to do as he pleased. It was all part of a medical study he'd been working on to prove to the medical world that under the right circumstances, one of his brilliant lobotomies could turn a raging madman into a complete gentleman—and by using his own brother to do it, he would garner stardom in the medical community forever. However, when it had gone too far with the fire—a fire he knew Todd had set—and the police asking too many questions, he had known it was time to disappear.

Following Eric away from the seventh floor down the stairs to the sixth floor, they got in an elevator, and Blake suggested he'd rather pay a visit to their father in the cemetery. They'd all finally come home, he thought, and it was time to return the sanatorium back to the Vreelands.

As the elevator passed the fifth floor, Little Blake Brockman sat in his old room with the nice view of the graveyard. Things were about to change around this place, and he couldn't have been happier. He was pleased with himself for planting the seed of Kayla Bennet in Blake's mind knowing he was her father, and he felt his strength grow. His shadow seemed to be darker as it ebbed and flowed from his soul within the room. The guilt he knew Blake Vreeland was feeling of murdering her would be nothing but pure joy Little Blake would relish as things were changing for the better. *Yes*, he thought, the Vreeland legacy of evil that had poisoned the grounds for over a century made the place feel all the more like home.

As he looked at the cold gray skies once again since being released from the basement, a sense of tranquility surrounded the young man—until the muffled moan from the ceiling above him broke his happy state. Looking to the ceiling, Little Blake grinned and turned back to the window. Yes, things were getting better when he realized he wasn't *alone.*

Above him, in that closed-off and windowless room with the many mirrors on the wall, the stained figure on the floor rose up and crawled to a corner and disappeared within the many cracks of the old walls of the building.

CHAPTER 165

When the evening of Trent's gallery opening finally arrived, it was truly a Savage event. Every member of Trent's new family was there to show support. Marta had sent the most amazing flowers as a thank-you for saving her life, and with her condition on the mend, she was sorry she couldn't attend.

The highlight of the evening was when Trent had thanked his new family in his speech for welcoming him and unveiled the new signage of changing his name from Trent York to Trent Savage, of which Ed couldn't have been more proud. The to-do list he'd had his assistant attend to was to change all the signage, and as Trent was making his speech, his assistant moved about the gallery swapping out the cards under each piece with Trent Savage's name on it.

The animosity between Ed and Jillian was colder than the waters rusting the *Andrea Doria* at the bottom of the Atlantic—especially after talking with Trent, and hearing of her lies of a miscarriage—but Ed was cordial and was planning on handling *that* problem in his own "Savage style." He'd pieced together the timeline, and when he talked to Marta when he'd checked up on her, she'd told him Jillian wished they were still together, thinking that maybe there was a chance with his divorce from Marlo. Ed zeroed in on the date the inheritance had hit the papers, and it *all* made sense. He'd heard the rumors of trouble in Jillian's marriage and realized she was still vying for a life with his money, no matter who she hurt. After the event, of course, Jillian and Jeremy quietly left without so much as a word.

That evening of the event, Marlo had seen something in the young man that touched her heart and wanted to do something special for him by overseeing a party to welcome him to the family. She planned it for the following week and did it for Ed, knowing he'd appreciate it, and the added bonus of it pissing off Jillian made it simply all the better.

Trent was still nervous meeting everyone, but as the days passed, it was getting less and less foreign, and he started feeling like he belonged in a family that was his, and the night of Marlo's welcoming party was better than he could have ever thought. But after seeing Marlo's kindness in the midst of divorcing his father, one thing Trent did know was that Ed Savage was a man he wanted to know more about, and he knew he was a kind and honest man, unlike the lies he'd been fed his whole life by his mother.

Ed's son Tucker and his cousin Chet got an extension from the military and were happy to have the time with their family, and they realized they had a lot in common with Trent, including playing polo like their dads did. But when Trent mentioned his Harley-Davidson that he loved riding, they became fast friends. Trent was another voice that could join Chet when teasing the girls that the Harleys were better *man's* machines than the Indian motorcycles they had replaced.

That was the perfect time for Lana and Kate to surprise both Tuc and Chet with their test scores. They had beat them, winning the bet, and the family shared a good laugh over it.

CHAPTER 166

T he board meeting at Savage Construction continued, with Ed, Sam, Roman, and Logan announcing the addition of Chance and Landon Savage to the company. Together, the six Savage men sat down to figure out their plans going forward. Chance and Landon knew more about the hotel business and were running the Vander Place Hotel and the housing development next to it where they all had homes. *And* when Landon mentioned Marlo had been talking with his wife Roxie, and Audra about her restaurant goals for Savages; he told them she wanted the area between the Mystic Theater and the lighthouse at the far end of the bluff for a custom built restaurant with unobstructed ocean views. That was when Chance opened a file and passed out the rendered designs he and his wife Audra had worked on.

Hearing this Ed grinned. He knew all about Marlo's plans because she'd talked to him about them extensively—and he was keeping her biggest ambition quiet and waiting for *her* to make the announcement to the family—that the top floor of Savage Two would house a restaurant Port Roberts had never experienced before, and the coming topping off ceremony that was ahead of schedule was when she was planning on letting everyone know.

Flipping the rendered Savages restaurant deigns in front of him, Logan remembered where he'd seen Mingyu before. She'd been in his office in London in talks with an associate over the purchase of a hotel, and he quietly made a note to talk to Ed about it privately and

investigate it later. After the meeting Ed felt good about his cousins coming aboard in a more official manner, and when he got to his office, he found the new script for *Precinct Wars* had been delivered from Trask Studios. He opened it, glad for the diversion.

When his phone rang, Paula announced the caller was Tasker Grenning, and Ed leaned back in his chair and smiled. He could still hear his father refer to them as *Savage and Task,* over their many business projects that started after he'd moved home from London to begin work at Savage Tower. Tasker Grenning was a few years younger then Ed, but their friendship began at the get-go, when Tasker interviewed Savage Construction for his very first venture. A complete gut and remodel of an old modest office tower in Port Roberts. Tasker was living in New York City at the time, and after making a ton of money on Wall Street he bought his first building—a building in the town his family had several holdings. Ed remembered seeing the building signs for Grenning's new high-rise project near Trent's gallery exhibit and reached for his phone.

"Tasker Grenning, long time. How are you?"

"I'm doing fine, my friend. How are you?"

"Better now," Ed said, remembering the good times with his old friend. "It's been a hell of a week."

"So I've been hearing. Anyway, it's been too long, and I wanted to meet you for a drink."

"Sure, name the place."

"There's an old speakeasy called the Hush-Hush. Do you know it?"

"I haven't heard of that one. Where is it?"

"It's on the waterfront near the south end. Can you meet me there around six?"

"Yeah, that sounds good."

"I'll look forward to it."

"See you then," Ed said, hanging up the phone. He then did an Internet search and saw photos of the place; it looked nice, and he wondered why he'd never heard of it.

Clicking a local news site, he saw a short story on the Dutchman, the story he'd done on *Archive Raiders* all those years ago and how it had risen up in the midst of his investigation of the *Manchester* in the Catskills, just like Tallulah had reminded him of his past working assignments when working at Agency One. He was surprised when the double-eagle coins were in fact traced back to the 1930s prohibition gangster, Dutch Shultz, and how it sparked a "gold rush" in the Catskills with treasure hunters searching for more of the lost fortune.

Later that evening, Ed arrived and saw Tasker sitting at the bar. "Of all the speakeasies…I thought I'd seen them all," Ed said, walking up to his old friend Task.

Getting off his barstool, Task gave his old friend a handshake. "Ed, goddamn it, you get better looking as time moves on. No wonder you got into show business and I got buried in the numbers game. What can I get you?"

Ed looked at Tasker's beer in the frosted glass, and his mouth watered. "I'll take an IPA in one of those," he said, pointing.

"Make it two. And can you bring it over to that table?" Tasker said to the bartender, pointing to one at the far wall.

"Sure thing," the bartender smiled.

Leaving a ten-dollar tip on the bar for his first beer, Tasker grabbed his drink and briefcase, and led Ed to a table and sat down.

"You know I've been meaning to call you," Ed said.

"Yeah? Then I'm glad we're here."

"My agent called me and told me about a certain dating show."

"Oh, damn," Tasker said, laughing. "What did *she* want?"

"Well, it's no secret Marlo and I are divorcing, and she told me they were doing one focused on the available men of New York, and she mentioned your name."

"Oh boy, yeah, well, they're recruiting now, and…yes, I signed on to do it."

The bartender came over and dropped off the drinks. "Anything else?"

"No, I'm good—thank you," Ed said.

"Yeah, thanks. You can put his on my tab," Tasker said, nodding.

"So how come you've never married? You're worth millions; I think they would be lining up in droves to get to you."

"Ed, I wish I knew the answer. I've come close twice, and as you know, I have two kids from those two times, but it always gets fucked up. What's your secret? I mean, hell, your divorce is all over, and it's the happiest divorce anyone's ever seen! What's up with that?"

"Oh, that's easy. All you need is some psycho family to try to kill everyone you love. Has a way of bringing you real tight," Ed said, flashing a grin and taking a drink of his beer. "Ah, that's good."

Tasker smiled. "It's been too long and I forgot your fucked-up wit. But I'll pass on all that."

"Yeah, not fun."

"So, Ed, I have a problem, and I was hoping you could help me."

"Sure, what is it?"

"You know I've got a lot of real estate all over the city."

"Right," Ed said. "Actually I saw your sign on a property near Berman Park."

"Hmm." Tasker smiled and raised his eyebrows. "If I didn't know better, I'd say you've been checking up on me."

"Wish I had that kind of time. What's happening with the property?"

"It's that asshole over at Berman Medical Center. He's after my land again."

"Beau? He's one of the nicest guys I've met."

"Really? Mr. Nice Guy just petitioned the city for eminent domain to take my family's land, and I'll be damned if I let that bastard take it."

"Oh, you do have a problem."

"You think?"

Ed shook his head. "What's your game?"

"Presser Pharmaceuticals."

"What are you doing? Planning on screwing with everyone in the city?"

"Seriously, I know what you're saying. Steve Presser is impossible to see, but *you* can get to him."

"And do what?"

"A land swap."

"Go on."

"Ed, I'm not giving up my land, and those glass towers are being built, and I'd like to formally commence negotiations with Savage Construction on building them. Now, I have land near the hospital that's even closer to the water, which is more expensive, only the lot is smaller than the entire end of the block the apartments are on."

"And Beau wants the larger land to build something bigger?"

"Beau wants to look out from his top-floor office over the park and see another of his buildings. That's all that fucker wants."

"And how does Presser become involved?"

"He has a building that needs to seriously come down next to one of mine. It's old, it's ugly, and the city sued them for not making the repairs fast enough after the eighteenth-floor fire."

"I know that building. And you're right: it's an eyesore."

"And I need you to get Presser to sell it to me," Tasker said, taking a drink.

"Is that all? How do you know he'll even sell it to you?"

"Because I've sent him several offers, and I haven't heard back once. He knows I'm interested, but he's fucking around, *and* I just got this from the city," Tasker said, opening his briefcase, pulling out a manila envelope, and sliding it to Ed.

Ed flipped it over and saw the familiar city envelopes he'd opened several times in his career in the construction business.

"It's a copy of his eminent domain bullshit. I'd like you to take it with you and read it over for me. Will you do that?"

"I can't promise anything, Task. We've got a lot of things moving around right now, bringing my cousins Chance and Landon into the fold. But I'll take a look at it and show the guys. I'm sure between the six of us we'll figure something out, and then I'll get back to you."

"That's all a man can ask. Cheers!" He held up his glass in salute.

Ed picked up his glass and toasted the friend he hadn't seen in too long a time, and it felt good to be moving on to other business in his life where things felt normal, because it'd been too damn long.

"You should do the show with me. It's less than nine weeks of shooting, give or take, and they're flexible with the workingman's hours. You've seen the show done in other cities, right?"

"I know what you're talking about, but I don't think it's for me."

"Ed, don't do it just for you, man! Do it for your brothers, too! Hell, you should all do it, seeing how you're all single after...how long? You should seriously think about it and talk to your brothers about it. Starting over later in life is hard enough. Trust me—I know this shit."

"I came in here for a drink, and now you have me pimping my brothers out for a TV show? Of all the speakeasies in the world."

"Here's to the speakeasies," Tasker said as the two men raised their glasses. Ed smiled; he was finally feeling good.

Walking to his car later, he saw a bus go by with an advertisement for his son's gallery exhibit, and he remembered how Trent had called him the day everything had changed in his life. Getting in his car, he drove by the building Presser Pharmaceuticals owned and got out, really taking a look at the eyesore. He was aware the city had their eye on the building and the controversy surrounding the lengthy time it was taking for Presser to renovate and repair the property. He had never met Steve Presser but remembered his father losing Presser Pharmaceuticals contracts to Bigelow Construction many years ago, and he wasn't sure if he'd be able to help out Tasker after he thought more about it.

City headaches, he thought, going back to his car. Stopping to take one last look at the building, he was happy that the problems he was now facing were normal problems that could be worked out. For right now, things were finally looking good for Ed Savage.

The End
    Or so he thought...

Ed Savage And The Decimated Savage Demise

THE SAVAGE SAGA: A HOLLYWOOD HORROR SOAP OPERA

VOLUME 2

Bryan Roberts

Dear Reader,

I hope you enjoyed my second story in *The Savage Saga*, and I want you to know that more is coming.

By now, after reading my first two novels, you know Ed Savage has a past filled with many stories of his *other* life of working with Agency One. A goal of mine all along was to take my character in a myriad of directions while moving forward—and with that, I can't wait to start volume 3.

The continuation of this saga is truly my passion, and I want to thank you for the amazing and wonderful comments you've left in your reviews on Amazon. They are a true gift.

—Bryan Roberts

www.ingramcontent.com/pod-product-compliance
Lightning Source LLC
Chambersburg PA
CBHW032251020726
47495CB00001B/65